TIGERHEART

HEIDE GOODY

IAIN GRANT

1

Greencock Farm was the last marker of human civilisation on the gated Marsh House Road, before the tarmac gave way to a stretch of compacted hardcore, then petered out into the scrubby dunes and salt marshes around Gibraltar Point. The road was narrow, bordered by deep dykes on both sides. Sam Applewhite drove towards the farm, softly humming a tune with no beginning and no end.

Sam's work vehicle, a tiny three-wheeled Italian Piaggio Ape van, didn't look like the ideal vehicle for any situation, but in her few years of employment with DefCon4, she had come to appreciate its minor charms.

Early morning on a Saturday there was very little traffic on the road. Sam had met almost nothing on the three mile drive from her dad's house in Skegness to the farm. The rising sun was low on the horizon, an unlovely pale torchlight behind the clouds; appearing to hang mere feet above the sea as Sam turned off the road and into the yard of Greencock Farm. The farmer himself was standing in the yard, bearing the look of a man who had been up since dawn. Possibly since the dawn of time. The farmhouse stood to one side of the yard, with sheds and a long greenhouse marking the other boundaries. In the centre of the yard was an area of grass, a sort of village green for the surrounding buildings, and on the green stood a large and elaborate children's climbing frame, complete with slide, monkey bars and fireman's pole.

The solidly built man had the hollow metal uprights of a ladder straddling a greasy tarp on the grass, ready to be cleaned or perhaps put back. He raised a hand in greeting as Sam pulled up.

"Is it Bruce?" she asked. "We spoke on the phone. DefCon4."

"Aye, I reckoned as much," said Bruce, nodding at the painted logo on the van's side panel. "Did it shrink in the wash?"

"Not heard that one before," she replied as she stepped out. "Come to look at your security set-up. Hope you don't mind me coming out so early."

"Early's good," said Bruce. "No point wasting daylight. Not that I'm disagreeing with Dolly."

"Dolly?"

"Working *9 to 5*. Big Dolly Parton fan."

"Can't beat a bit of country music," Sam said amiably.

"But, no, I'm up with the lark. Did you know that if you spent an extra hour in bed each day, you'd waste three years of your life in sleep? S'true. I worked it out."

Bruce Greencock didn't look to Sam like the kind of person who ever worked things out; not things like that. Then again, he didn't look like a Dolly Parton fan either. Bruce Greencock looked like a farmer. By which she meant he was a big chap, with the fatty edges trimmed off by constant labour. He carried the air of most farmers she met: a sense that he had a hundred and one things to think about, few of them fun, and none of them as frivolous as how many days a person might lose through oversleeping.

"You always start this early?" he asked.

She held out her phone, though the screen was dark and the DefCon4 app not running. "They let me make my own hours, sort of. And I've got breakfast waiting for me later."

Breakfast would be at home, prepared by her dad. The man dominated the kitchen and had a celebrity anecdote to accompany every recipe he knew. Today's breakfast was to be served with a side order of Rich Raynor, Sam's ex-boyfriend. For reasons entirely forgotten, Sam had either invited him, or he'd invited himself, to come with her to check out potential new offices for the Skegness DefCon4 team. In its entirety, the team consisted of Sam and a lightly charred cactus called Doug. Doug and Sam had been homeless since their old office had been targeted in a monstrously stupid arson attack by a monstrously (and fatally) stupid arsonist two months earlier.

"Well, we'd best crack on them," said farmer Bruce. He tilted the metal pipes he held in his hand to display the broken rusty joins at one end. "Look at that. The kids could cut themselves something wicked on that. Going to take it to my mate's and get the fixings re-brazed."

Sam nodded in agreement, assuming this was one of those situations where she was meant to nod in agreement.

He set the iron pipes down carefully and stepped back from the climbing frame. "Lola, Riley and Annabel used to love this. They've grown a bit, but I've kept it maintained for when they come back."

Sam's automatic reaction was to ask 'Back from where?', but a quicker and slyer part of her brain leapt in and stopped her. There was something about the way he'd said 'come back' that spoke of loss and darkness. Early morning or not, Sam couldn't help noticing that the farm was silent but for their two voices.

He waved for her to walk with him to the nearest sheds. "We never get thieves round here," he told her. "People only come down this way by accident."

"Some people say you can never be too careful," said Sam.

"Like the insurance companies?"

"Like the insurance companies," she agreed. "Is this just about keeping everything in line with your policy then?"

"You mean stopping them hiking up their prices for next year's cover? Aye. Something like that." He started to slide back one of the big shed doors and paused. "Why do they do that?"

"Hmmm?"

He stared at nothing. This big man with a no-nonsense face that had seen three dozen blistering summers and three dozen biting winters. This man who apparently had time to think and work things out. "Why do the insurers put your premiums up automatically if you stay with them? I don't do that. I sell cabbages mainly. If the supermarket keeps me on as a supplier I don't stick my prices up fifty percent. That's madness."

"Business," she said.

He made a disapproving, throaty sound. "People should just be more honest. If I'm going to be charging more for my cabbages, it's because I'm giving people summat special."

The idea of cabbages being special was not one that sat easily with Sam. Cabbages were surely much of a muchness, and not a particularly exciting muchness at that. Sam had no problem with healthy nutritious food, but she subscribed to what she believed was the popular opinion: that cabbages were, at best, a filler on the plate and, at worst, a deliberate punishment. As inflicted by clichéd school canteens everywhere. Cabbages were one of those vegetables which her Saxon forebears had probably eaten by the tonne, but only because they had been starving peasants and had yet to be introduced to the comparative delights of the potato or takeaway delivery apps.

"You don't think cabbages can be special, do you?" said Bruce.

Sam realised her face had given her away. "It's not a question that had crossed my mind, if I'm honest."

He made another throaty disapproving noise. "So, you've got some gizmos to keep the insurance company from bumping up my premiums."

Sam smiled. "We'll review your site security. You've already got DefCon4 motion detectors around the sheds, and alarms on the door. So, on top of that, we just need to make sure your big value and high risk items are protected." She pulled the list up on her DefCon phone app.

"High risk items," repeated Bruce.

"Especially ones that are very expensive to replace and also portable. An occupational hazard for farmers."

"I bet you have no idea how much the latest cabbage harvesting machines can cost, do you?"

Sam had dealt with farmers before, and the cost of agricultural machinery was a recurring theme. She pointed at her phone. "As a matter of fact, I do. You could easily buy a bungalow in Ingoldmells for the same sort of money."

"Yeah, but who'd want to live in Ingoldmells? It's all holidaymakers and caravans, isn't it?"

He slid back the door on the high shed and invited Sam to enter. She looked up at a trailer hooked to his tractor. At first glance, its purpose was unfathomable. Conveyor belts, wheels, chains and slicing blades. It looked like the strange agricultural offspring of a set of aeroplane steps and a dumpster.

"This one does two rows," said Bruce proudly.

"Two rows of cabbages?" asked Sam.

"Of course. The Brassicator is a two-row trailed harvester fitted with a cart elevator for harvesting of cabbage." He pointed at two huge corkscrew fittings at the front. "The intake unit lifts the cabbages onto the roller system, which removes the loose leaves and drops them with that arm into the hopper so we're left with nice round heads of cabbage."

Sam could picture it now, with cabbages moving up the conveyor.

"I've got it chained up and locked away, but apparently that's not enough," said Bruce.

"Tracking devices are what you need, according to this. I've got some here." She reached into her pocket and jiggled a bagful of small flat plastic objects. Some were the size of coins, while others were a little larger, the size of a credit card.

"They look as if they're for playing draughts. This is the future then, is it?" said Bruce.

"The present."

"Aye, the future'll be when they start tracking *us*."

She was tempted to wave her phone and point out that particular future was already here, but it was too early in the day for techno-philosophical debates.

"Surely they're not big enough to do tracking?" Bruce was saying.

"They work," she assured him. She showed him her bank card holder and the little disc stuck on it. "I put one in my dad's wallet and loaded the app on his phone. We spent an afternoon playing big scale hide and seek in Skegness."

"Really?" said Bruce, sounding as if he didn't approve of such frivolity.

"It was good exercise and, yes, it now means I can locate my elderly father whenever I need to."

"Huh," said Bruce, with something that might have almost been a laugh.

Sam pulled out one of the larger pieces, peeled off the backing sheet, and stuck it underneath the hopper of the Brassicator. She held out the backing sheet and indicated the reverse: a small printed form with neat boxes. "You write down here what you've stuck it to. What we'll do is put some of these onto a few things and you can see how they work for yourself. You install the DefCon4 tracking app on your phone, enter the details of the objects, and you'll see where they are when they're in Bluetooth range."

Bruce pulled a face. "Thieves are hardly likely to stay within Bluetooth range, are they?"

"No," admitted Sam. "There's a lot of people with the app though, and if a stolen widget comes in range of another person's app, then you'll get a location alert."

Bruce nodded. "And the insurance people like this sort of thing then?"

Sam nodded.

He glanced at the bag of widgets. "Big ones for the vehicles, and the small ones...?"

Sam fished some out of her bag. "The big ones have a longer battery life. They also have a 'scan me' message on the front, so if something gets mislaid then it might help get it returned."

"I don't mislay my tractors," said Bruce.

"No, but if you had something like a surfboard which might get swept away by the sea, you can see how that might help."

The look Bruce gave her was enough to confirm he wasn't a surfer.

"The small ones are used where there isn't room for the larger widgets. We can put one on your smartphone."

"How will I use the tracking app if they've nicked me smartphone?" asked Bruce.

"That's where I come in," said Sam. "I can access your

widgets and track them for you if needed. It's all part of the DefCon4 package."

"Let's step inside then," he said. "We'll stick one on the telly."

They went inside. It was an old house. Time hadn't so much weathered it as cemented its presence. Glazed clay tile flooring was burnished to a dull shine by the passage of a thousand feet. Painted and repainted wooden door frames looked strong enough to survive a bomb blast.

Sam put a widget on the television in a living room too well organised and tidy to be in regular use. The TV was a model that was well over ten years old; she was fairly certain nobody would ever try to steal it, and if they did, they would probably put their back out. But the security widgets were principally about the client's peace of mind. And the insurers'. A music system older than Sam got a widget, as did a polished walnut grandfather clock, and a pair of porcelain poodles on a mantlepiece crowded with oddly-angled photographs.

There was a table under the hallway stairs with an old-fashioned cream coloured telephone on top of it. Sam pointed at a grey metal cabinet beside the table.

"We should stick 'em on the shotguns?" asked Bruce.

"Definitely," said Sam.

Bruce took a key from above the fuse box on the wall and unlocked the cabinet. There was a rack containing six shotguns and one rifle.

"May I?" she asked and, at his nod, took one. Sam was always surprised by the weight of guns, and she found herself losing her balance as she picked up the heavy side-by-side double-barrelled shotgun. She nudged a loose box of shells with the stock as she lifted it out, and a handful spilled onto the floor.

"Sorry," she said, as Bruce crouched to gather the spilled red shells. He tried to insert them back in the box, but the thin side had split and he ended up stuffing most of them in his pocket to free up his hand.

Hefting the weapon, Sam slapped a tracking widget on the side of its stock.

"No, no, no," said Bruce. "That'll get in the way of aiming if you put it there."

"Sorry." Sam pried it off with her fingernails and looked at Bruce for guidance.

"Here." He plucked the shotgun from her hands and loosened the rubber butt on the end of the stock. He took the widget and slipped it in between the wooden stock and the butt before pushing it back in place. He whipped a rag from the end of the rack and polished the wood where Sam had first applied the widget, removing residue that didn't really exist. He buffed the other side of the stock for good measure and replaced the shotgun in the rack.

Sam passed him fresh widgets to apply to the other guns, and jotted down initial details on the relevant cardboard backs. The man's evident care for his guns was not surprising. Sam knew enough men to know they were capable of possessive tenderness when it came to material goods. Some men obsessively cleaned and looked after their cars. Others curated collections of vinyl LPs, or electric guitars that no one else was allowed to touch. For ex-boyfriend Rich, it might be his latest helicopter or whichever huge and impractical thing he had most recently bought. Her own dad had an amusingly intimate relationship with some of his old stage props. There was a treasure chest in the corner of their spare room that he was never going to use again but which he valued above almost all other things.

But if Bruce's care of his guns hadn't surprised her, the cleanliness of the rest of the house had done. The farmer clearly took great care of the housekeeping. There was no dust anywhere, and there was a whiff of beeswax in the air, as if the wooden furniture had been recently polished. There was an extensive collection of horse brasses on the walls of the hallway, and even they were buffed to an eye-watering gleam.

Bruce locked the gun rack, folded the polishing cloth, and hung it on a peg on the side of the cabinet. She gave him the remainder of the bag of widgets, which he put in his pocket.

"You want to show me that app?" he said. "I can stick the kettle on."

"Of course," she replied. "Not sure I can stay long. I've got breakfast waiting."

"Got my own things to do," he said, not competing but agreeing. "Pipe brazing to sort out. A visit to the bank."

In the kitchen, Sam sat at the worn but solid table as he put teabags in mugs.

"Going to sign on the dotted line for a business loan," he told her. "Farmers have to diversify if we want to survive these days."

"Oh, I know," she said. "I hear that a landowner down

Wainfleet way has turned his land into some sort of private hunting reserve."

"Elgin Jubilee," Bruce laughed harshly. "He's not a farmer though. He's a rich man playing at being a farmer."

"Probably so," said Sam. DefCon4 had sold him several kilometres of security fencing and a number of security drones. Not exactly farming supplies.

"Half his land is decommissioned RAF property. Can't put a spade in the earth round there without digging up old ordnance or a buried tank. Not proper land and not a proper farmer. Way I reckon it, any farmer worth his salt should make his living from actual farming."

He poured the teas and disappeared into what looked like a large walk-in pantry. He came out holding a massive green cabbage. He was beaming proudly – and this in a man who was not given to wasting smiles. As he gazed down at the cabbage he exuded passion and pride.

He placed it on the table, and Sam tried to summon the correct amount of interest. It was large, she had to give him that. Its crinkled veiny leaves looked fresh and firm. Too often, Sam had dealt with sad, old cabbages with yellowed leaves and a creeping stink which spoke of the extended wait between purchase and preparation. She wasn't sure it was entirely her fault, as cabbages were very often too big to fit in the fridge. This one here was a case in point. If she had to fit it in the fridge in Marvin's kitchen, she would need to remove everything else.

"Great cabbage," she said. She could come up with nothing further. There was probably a reason poets didn't write odes to cabbages.

"Good head of cabbage that, eh? This one's to show Justin," said Bruce.

"Justin?"

"Justin Johnson. At the bank. We went to school together, back in the day. Good bloke." Bruce put the cabbage into a carrier bag and placed it aside. "But shall I show you what makes it special?"

"Oh yes!" said Sam, relieved to hear she hadn't missed something obvious and would have the opportunity to show the appropriate level of enthusiasm.

From the fridge, he brought out half of another cabbage. It had been trimmed of the huge outer leaves. He placed it on the table with its cut side uppermost. There was a tangy, fresh, slightly sulphuric odour.

"What do you think about that, eh?" he asked.

It was a cabbage. Most definitely a cabbage.

"I bet you've never seen anything like this," he said.

She had. It was a cabbage. A big one; but still, definitely, a cabbage.

"It's going to make my fortune, is this," he added. "A new variety, all of my own. When I get the funding to go full tilt into commercial development, the whole world will take note."

"Right..." she said, still not getting it.

"See the stripes?" Bruce said, pointing at the inner layers. "It's the unique selling point. Biggest step forward in years."

Sam stared at the cross-section of cabbage.

"One small step for man, one giant leap for cabbagekind," she heard herself say.

"Exactly!" said Bruce. "I might use that."

Sam knew enough about cabbages to appreciate that the greenness was usually darker on the outer leaves. This cabbage definitely had that. Were there bands of darker green towards the centre? She tilted it this way and that, trying to see. "It's, um, wonderful. I'm sure Justin will be really impressed," she said eventually and handed it back. If it was indeed striped, it was a subtle effect indeed, but then, she was no cabbage connoisseur.

"It is that," said Bruce. "Glad you can appreciate it. Bank might be a bit slower on the uptake. But I've got my presentation sorted. A bit of razzamatazz. I worked it out, you see. Way I reckon it, I need to get the bank's attention."

He reached up to a high dark shelf above the cooking range, and suddenly there was a long hefty blade in his hand. He did a funny little wrist flick, and it spun and shone in his hand.

"It's a machete," he said, as if she hadn't seen it.

"Oh, that will get the bank's attention," Sam said weakly.

2

Mercedes Martin joined the other members of the Saturday morning rota in the customer area of the bank, stepping forward and then aside a little to try to help make as perfect a circle as possible. Whether it was possible to make a circle with four people was a matter for debate, but Justin was generally keen that it should be a circle. He had once said to her, completely seriously, "How can we have a proper support ring if we're not in a circle?"

She'd had no answer for that. She wasn't overly happy with him referring to the informal pre-opening staff meeting as a support ring. To Mercedes' ears, it sounded like a treatment for haemorrhoids. Certainly, as a member of staff, neither the phrase 'support ring', nor the content of the meetings, sounded particularly supportive.

"Now that we're all here..." began Justin, with a stern look at Mercedes over the top of his leather-bound tablet.

Mercedes flicked her finger at each of them, and the cups in their hands. "Literally just made you all a coffee," she said.

"I was only making a little joke," said Justin.

Mercedes glanced at the other two staff members, Tez Malik and Stevie Lingard, and saw neither of them were smiling. 'Only making a little joke' was one of Justin's classic defences – that and 'just testing you'. He could never admit to making a mistake, which was an unfortunate trait in a man who made so many.

Justin consulted his tablet. "Right, we've got the fraud prevention team coming in next week, so we all need to have our systems in order and our workspaces cleared as per policy by the end of today. That means no mugs on the counters, Stevie."

"What makes you think it's me?" asked Stevie.

"Because the last mug I found said 'Puppy Mama' on it and had a picture of one of them pugs on it."

"French bulldog," she said.

"Exactly. And nail polisher remover, too. You've got that big bottle by your workstation. I'm sure it's a fire hazard. Oh, and Mercedes—" he took an envelope from beneath his tablet and passed it to her "—we did have that chat about not having personal mail sent to the bank address."

"I do tell people," she said. She flipped the envelope over to see the words *franqueo pagado* in the top corner, and the address written in her dad's unmistakeable hand-writing. She tucked it inside her jacket.

"And we also need to do a review of the safety deposit boxes," continued Justin. "There are some dead boxes not being paid for I'm sure. Mercedes, you're on that."

As Justin ran through the list, everyone tried to kept quiet. The sooner the support ring was concluded, the sooner they could get on with tasks that actually needed doing in the town's largest high street bank. The Eastshires Bank occupied a two-storey Victorian brick building with stone window arches on the corner of Lumley Road and Rutland Road; a bank which actually looked like a bank, in a prime spot on Skegness's main shopping street. In its heyday, there would have been half a dozen cashiers behind plate glass and high wooden counters, and twice that number working in the back offices. Now, in an age when the need to go into a bank had diminished, and the need for cash had diminished even further, any day's business could be managed by a handful of people.

Justin Johnson was the branch manager and took his position of authority seriously. Mercedes was sure that ninety percent of the time, he actually believed the corporate bullshit he came out with. He wanted the support ring to motivate and energise the staff. He wanted them to process customers speedily and politely; to get the highest customer satisfaction ratings while constantly reminding said customers that whatever it was they wanted to do, they could probably do it via the bank website. Justin had attended Eastshires corporate seminars and training courses and come out with the air of a pilgrim who had received wisdom from holy lamas on distant mountaintops. He was, in short, a moron. Mercedes wasn't even sure if there was actually a real man at all under that tie and layers of corporate nonsense. Maybe just a lost little boy who couldn't bear to admit when he was wrong.

Tez Malik was notionally the branch's mortgage and business advisor, although he didn't have a problem helping out behind the counter when needed. He endured the support ring meetings with stoicism, a composed mask of a face, and a glazed look in his eyes. Tez had a full life outside work and was content enough with his lot that he didn't feel the need to share details of it with anyone. Which was a shame, because Mercedes wouldn't have minded getting to know him a little better. He was young, charming and handsome. He was perhaps a little too manscaped for her tastes – she suspected some waxing went on under that crisp shirt – but she did find him appealing enough to find herself occasionally wondering about that waxed (or not waxed) chest.

Stevie Lingard wore a similarly glazed expression. However, while Tez's blank look indicated his thoughts were elsewhere, Stevie's was just evidence there was no one at home. She might have been somewhat lacking in intelligence on the grand scale by which Mercedes found herself measuring all people, but Stevie wasn't so stupid that she couldn't work as a customer service assistant behind the counter. The hamster at the exercise wheel of her brain had just enough energy for that. Otherwise Stevie's interests seemed to amount to fruit-flavoured cider, her French bulldog Petey, and the purchase of dog beds for Petey in every shape imaginable. In her weakest, most depressive moments, Mercedes found herself thinking how lovely it must be to live such a small life with such tiny ambitions.

Mercedes herself, as a banking services consultant, filled many of the gaps left by the other staff. Greeting customers, dealing with complaints, doing loan applications and opening new accounts. She danced around, fulfilling all requirements, keeping the branch ticking over from one day to the next.

"Tez," said Justin, "check the messages on the intranet. You've got to respond to the shareholder's banquet invite."

"For sure," replied Tez.

Mercedes might have ignored that last item, could even feel her attention slipping past it, but something grabbed her. Even then, she might have let it go, but as she turned it over in her head her gaze met Tez's, and there was something peculiar in his gaze. Perhaps it was nothing. Perhaps it was a flicker of awkward embarrassment, guilt even.

"Right," continued Justin. "I've got to get ready. Farmer Greencock is coming in with a new business venture. I think he wants to show me his cabbages." He gave a goofy smile.

"Consider yourself lucky," said Tez. "I've got to tell an old man we're repossessing his house."

"And you'll handle it with aplomb, Tez," said Justin. "Support ring done. Are we good? Are we good? Are we good?" With each iteration of the question, he gestured to a different person, moving too quickly to give anyone a chance to actually respond. "Then it's lights on, curtains up and on with the show."

He spun away and headed for the back offices. Tez was moving, too. Mercedes followed him to the office door.

"Tez?"

He looked at her and then at the front door to the street. "You not opening up?"

"Are you going to the shareholder's banquet?"

"Er, yeah," he said, hesitating at the unexpectedness of the question.

"I thought we were only eligible for that if we were on pay band three."

"Yeah. It's no big deal. Just some big hotel meal. Bottles of water that cost a tenner each."

"You're on pay band three?"

He pulled an odd expression, an uncomfortable disgust. The man worked in banking, worked with money all day long, and yet he suffered from a very British distaste about discussing his own income.

"So, you *are* on band three?" she asked again.

"Is that all right with you?" he said.

She said nothing, just stepped away to open the heavy wooden double doors. Was it all right with her that Tez was on band three? Was it all right that Tez, who was considerably younger than her and been with the bank half the time she had, was on a higher pay grade than she was? Like hell it was. Eastshires Bank had a graded pay structure. Mercedes had joined the company pretty much the same time as Justin, definitely some time before Tez, and she was only now discovering that Tez was being paid more than her.

Her heels clicked on the marble floor as she walked, thinking furiously about the implications of this.

"Everything all right?" Tez called after her.

Mercedes snapped back the iron bolts that had been fitted to the original doors and then turned the key in the modern lock.

"Just working things out," she said, opening the doors to the bank's first customers of the day.

3

Across the length of her life, Sam's view of families had gone through three distinct stages. As a very young child, she had assumed hers was an ordinary family. It was a life in which her dad was absent for long periods of time or the family lived away from home, sometimes spending time in rented accommodation while he did a summer season at one of the UK's other big seaside towns. A life in which there were no siblings, but there was a parade of temporary family members: her dad's stage assistant Linda, co-stars, the occasional panto cast member. There had been a brief and confusing time in which she had believed the comics Cannon and Ball were actually her uncles.

Later, Sam had realised her itinerant and soon-to-be-fractured family was not like other people's. That it wasn't normal for people off the telly to pop round for Sunday lunch. That proper mums and dads had much more boring relationships and, it turned out, much more stable ones. Sam came to realise she was the daughter of a pair of weirdos who had eschewed normal lives and, for a brief period in her teenage years, she had hated them for it.

Later still, Sam had come to the clearer realisation that there was no such thing as a normal family. Particularly since she had started working for DefCon4 and visited any number of homes to make deliveries, perform safety checks and review security arrangements, she had met no one who really conformed to type. There were quirks and oddities which seemed perfectly ordinary from within the family unit, but were far from it when viewed from without. Households enforcing 'no shoes' policies with fascistic zeal. Families who held regular seances in the front room. Families of oddball collectors and creators. There was one memorable bunch who had insisted the absent patriarch had been abducted by big business after unlocking the secret of generating and broadcasting clean electricity from soil. They kept his laboratory room as a shrine, and warned that all of their conversations were being monitored. Sam had seen little of interest in his laboratory, apart from evidence that he liked to propagate cactus plants, but it wasn't her place to question the narrative which was the foundation for all this family held dear.

This morning's visit to Bruce Greencock, to the silent farm with the meticulously-maintained climbing frame and the cabbage-harvesting machine, was just one more example of the peculiar singularity of other people's home lives. But all that being said, Sam was still certain the life she lived with her dad was fairly atypical.

Her dad's home at the end of Albert Avenue was a vast asymmetrical bungalow named *Duncastin'*. It squatted in a veritable jungle of a garden that bordered Skegness beach (if you could hack your way through the undergrowth to get to it). It had eight bedrooms and could sleep twice that number of people, although it had been years since it had done so. Much of it was filled with the clutter of an illusionist's life lived to the full, clutter that Sam had been waging a war on for more than a year with few signs of victory.

Leaving her van on the sloping driveway, Sam went into the kitchen to find one more indication of her family's weirdness. Marvin Applewhite, silver-haired and shockingly spry for a man in his seventies, was at the hob, a skillet pan in one hand and a tea towel draped over his shoulder.

"Ah, just in time for my famous Marmite eggs benedict!" he called.

"I thought he was joking when he first said it," said Rich, who was sitting at the breakfast counter.

Rich was wearing cargo shorts below a crumpled but expensive white shirt. Spring had fully sprung, and was even turning its lazy eye towards summer, but Rich seemed oblivious to the fact that springtime in coastal Lincolnshire could still be bloody nippy round the ankles. Rich was obscenely wealthy – private helicopter and personal butler wealthy – and seemed to live as though inconvenient truths, such as the weather, were something only poor people had to deal with. Infuriatingly, this tended to work out just fine for him. Sam's ex-boyfriend lived a charmed existence which he didn't necessarily deserve.

There was a silver carry case with heavy clasps on the breakfast bar next to Rich.

"Your travelling make-up kit?" Sam suggested.

He waggled a finger, then opened the case to reveal five aerosol cannisters set into moulded packing foam.

"Travelling hair-styling kit," Sam corrected herself.

"Allow me to demonstrate," began Rich, but Marvin cut in before he could continue.

"Uh-uh. Breakfast incoming. Table settings please, Sam."

Sam went to fetch the placemats from the dresser in the corner. This would have been easier were it not for the two filing cabinets taking up temporary residence in the same corner. They had once been dark green, but rescued from the fire which had consumed her work office, now possessed a sooty aspect, with one sporting a beautiful oil-on-water patina up one side where flames had roasted its exterior.

"Attractive feature, that. Is it some of your mate Delia's upcycling?" asked Rich.

"Apparently there was nowhere else for them to go," said Sam with a sigh. "I think the fire has distorted them, though. I can't even open the drawers."

Rich hopped down from his stool and held out his hand for Marvin's spatula. "May I?"

Marvin handed over the utensil and Sam and her father watched as Rich approached the filing cabinet.

"You know, Marvin, you are not the only one capable of magic. I happen to know a couple of tricks involving filing cabinets." He pushed the spatula into the gap at the side of a drawer. There was a metallic *thunk*. He pulled the drawer open and took a bow.

Sam was simultaneously impressed and furious. She had spent a slightly drunken evening with Delia trying to pick the lock a few days earlier, until Delia had pointed out it wasn't even locked. It had never crossed her mind that whatever mechanical contrivance sat behind the lock might be so easily accessed.

"Good. Thank you," she said and brought the placemats over. They featured images of paintings from the National Gallery. Marvin got *The Haywain*, Rich *The Fighting Temeraire* and Sam gave herself Holbein's *The Ambassadors* because it had that skull on it which could only be seen from a certain angle, and had fascinated her as child. Great works of art were almost immediately hidden beneath plates of waffles, bacon, eggs and a beige creamy sauce.

"You can really smell the Marmite," said Rich in the strained tones of a man trying not to breathe.

"I served this to Sharri Lewis and Dolly Parton when we were performing together at the Kings Theatre in Glasgow," said Marvin.

"I met a fan of hers this morning—" Sam said.

"Who's Sharri Lewis?" asked Rich.

Marvin was aghast. "You must know Sharri Lewis! And Lamb Chop? Her puppet? Basically a sock with big eyelashes. Icons of the stage."

"And that's who you met this morning?"

"No. Dolly Parton," said Sam, quickly adding "A fan of hers. Bruce Greencock." She sighed. "But a celebrity anecdote does not a great breakfast make, dad." Then, eyes on Rich, she scooped a corner off her waffle with her fork and, dripping with Marmite hollandaise, put it in her mouth. "But I do like this."

"What's that noise?" asked Rich.

There was a scratching sound, from close by. As Sam turned, she was stunned to see a large brown rat climb out of the open filing cabinet drawer, twitch its whiskers and drop to the floor.

Rich gave a cry of alarm, a sort of wordless "Bay-arrrk!" and drew his feet up on his stool.

"Holy crap!" shouted Sam. She flung herself at the door between kitchen to hallway, slamming it shut to stop the creature running further into the house. "Did you see that?"

The creature skittered on the floor, turned, and vanished under the cooker.

"I think we all saw it," said Marvin drily, settling down to his breakfast.

Rich stared at the older man. "There's a rat in your kitchen."

"What am I gonna do?" replied Marvin automatically.

Sam was still looking round for the furry horror. "I'm sorry, dad. I'm sure Rich didn't mean to let a rat in the house."

"It's your filing cabinet," protested Rich.

"Which you opened."

"It must have been in there since the fire."

"You know what almost never happens...?" asked Marvin, nibbling on a waffle.

"No," said Rich.

"A single rat, on its own. You never really get that. If there's one, there are usually more."

They all turned to look at the filing cabinet. Sam shoved the drawer closed.

"If there's anything still in there, it can stay for a few more minutes while I figure out what to do," said Sam.

Rich appeared to be using the incident as a reason not to eat his Marmite eggs benedict. "You can't use some magic thing to get rid of them, Marv? Some pied piper trickery?"

"He's not an actual wizard," Sam pointed out.

"I guess I can ask Peninsula to pop round and sort it out," said Rich.

"You lend your high-class butler out to do rat catching?"

"Peninsula loves a challenge," explained Rich. "He has a cat as well, a crazy big thing. Seriously, he's always talking about enrichment activities for Motikiti."

"Motor kitty?"

"Don't be mocking Peninsula's Polynesian heritage."

"I ... wasn't."

"I'll ask him to come over."

The doorbell rang. Sam went to answer it.

"You know, I like that story. The Pied Piper of Hamelin," said Marvin.

"Who doesn't love a tale of child-abducting pest exterminators?" asked Sam, opening the door for Delia.

"It's a story about the importance of paying decent salaries and honouring contracts," said Marvin. "A subject dear to my heart. Morning, Delia."

Sam glanced around at the floor by Delia's feet, hoping to see a big rat charge outside in a bid for freedom.

Self-conscious, Delia followed Sam's eyes and waggled

her toes. "Er, homemade flip flops," she said. "Wine corks set in a flexible resin."

"Nice. It's carnage in here. Come in."

Delia was, by default, Sam's best friend and the unflappable owner of a chaotically cluttered junk shop near the seafront, so carnage was her natural environment. Although since she had entered Sam's orbit the level of chaos necessary to constitute 'carnage' had increased dramatically. She greeted Marvin and Rich with enthusiasm. Delia liked pretty much everyone, and didn't share any of Sam's low level antipathy towards Rich. Delia was of the opinion that if there was a wealthy would-be boyfriend on offer, the natural thing to do was to snap him up. This opinion might have been coloured by the fact that Delia had two energetic young kids, a house that refused to stay tidy, and a husband who worked away. Sam had no reason to suspect Delia was anything but happy and faithful, but the daydream of a carefree life of wealth and luxury had a certain pull.

"I've come to take your dad to the bank," she said.

"Ex-wives and girlfriends have already tried," shot back Marvin.

"Which is a fib," said Sam, who knew for a fact her mum had never taken anything from Marvin Applewhite, not even his name. "Going to deposit your burglar swag while you're there?" she added, gesturing to the bulging canvas bag Delia carried.

"Marbles," said Delia. She put the bag on the counter where it made a satisfyingly crunchy glass rattle. "In fact, I brought a gift." From the massive front pocket of her dungarees, she withdrew a slim cardboard box, and from that, a circular object. "Ta-da! It's a coaster made from melted marbles."

Rich picked up his mug and put it on top. "It doesn't feel all that stable, Delia. I like coasters to be a bit lower, so I'm not worried if the mug will fall off."

Delia squinted at the gap between the counter and the mug. It was about an inch high. "Yeah. They probably need to melt a bit more."

"Have you got hold of lots of marbles, by any chance?" asked Sam.

"I bought a hundred kilos of them on Etsy for a knockdown price. Do you know how many marbles there are in a hundred kilos?"

"More than you expected?"

Delia's expression was part embarrassment, part panic. "*Way* more than I expected. I'm shifting them to the workshop in batches."

"If we're doing show and tell..." said Rich, reaching for his case of aerosol cannisters.

"Ooh, please," replied Delia. "What you got?"

Rich pulled the case in front of him. "I have been delving into the fascinating world of scent marketing. Enabling customers to engage with a brand using every sense."

"Spend more money, you mean?" said Marvin. "Like the baking bread smells in the supermarket."

"Yes, that's very twentieth century, though," replied Rich. "What I want to do is to deliver an olfactory sensation that will make a visit to Doggerland imprint itself on our customers' memories. You know smell is the one sense that can whisk you straight back to a specific place and time, right? Well, I'm going to make sure that smells like this one will do exactly that."

He pressed a trigger and there was a small *tsst* sound.

"Oh..." Sam wrinkled her nose. "It's like the smell of feet."

"No," said Delia. "Not just feet. It's like the smell of the bowling alley shoe hire when a whole class of thirteen year olds have just returned their bowling shoes."

"There's a sweaty, cheesy overtone as well," said Marvin. "Or is it more like the bottom of a laundry basket if the dog's towel got put in there by accident?"

Rich looked very pleased with himself. "Great feedback, everyone! This one is supposed to evoke the smell of the Neanderthal cave. Some bodily odours, with some foody whiffs thrown in. Personally, I think a hint of woodsmoke is needed – but it's close, very close."

Rich had made his initial fortune marketing pointless tat that no one could possibly need, but which the gullible believed they wanted. He had spent the best part of the previous year apparently trying to destroy that fortune with a plan to build a zoo at the bottom of the North Sea. One populated by real life woolly mammoths and other creatures of the past. Rich planned to reclaim the pumped-out seabed and fortify it against the ocean with a wall. As far as he was concerned, the fact that the animals were extinct and the bottom of the North Sea was, well, literally at the bottom of the sea didn't seem to be a barrier.

"How are the Doggerland plans progressing?" Sam asked.

Rich shrugged. "Some parts are proving tricky. Who knew people could claim to own the seabed? I was close to getting a deal with the Candlebroke lot who supposedly own much of it, when up pop those Bonner-Sanchez energy guys with plans to build their own artificial island out by the wind farms. So, all bad news for Doggerland safari park, but we're adopting an iterative approach. The initial version will bring the key components to life with animatronics, and we'll locate it onshore until we can get a permanent site ready."

"So not an extinct animal zoo in the middle of the sea at all, then?" said Delia.

"Er, yes. Now who wants to smell the scent markings of a mature male sabre-toothed tiger?"

4

There was always a mini-rush as soon as the doors opened. The earliest customers tended to be older people, folks who'd already been up for hours and had come into town to get the shopping and the errands done. They'd be waiting outside with the universal cry of "Am I too early?" and it seemed they came as much for a chat as for any actual services. The builders and decorators and those workers who still operated cash businesses would turn up later, as would the local arcade and shop owners with their cash deposits. The mortgage and loan applicants would be spread out through the day. But first of all was the minor flood of old people, then the brief early morning lull.

During this lull, Mercedes Martin stood at the customer advice counter near the door and made some calculations on a pad. Mercedes was thirty-four years old and had joined Eastshires almost fourteen years ago. Five minutes on the advice counter terminal brought up her account and her income payments, and from that, the dates on which she'd been awarded incremental pay rises according to the company scheme.

She stepped into Justin's office. Justin adjusted a pen on his desk and looked up at her expectantly, like a boy waiting for pudding and custard. "Is he here?" he asked.

"Who?"

"Farmer Greencock."

"No. What pay grade are you on?"

Justin's brow beetled in confusion. "Pay grade?"

"Yes," she said simply. "What pay grade are you on?"

"Five."

"Five...?"

"Five b."

"Thank you."

"Why did you want to know?" he asked as she left.

"Just working something out."

Mercedes returned to the customer advice desk and her pad of calculations.

Assuming Justin had started at the same time as her and, for simplicity's sake, assuming he'd progressed through the scales at a uniform rate; and taking her own pay levels to indicate the amounts Justin would have been earning at the same level—

She went onto the bank intranet to find the current pay rates for bands 3c through to 5b and added them to her calculations. If she totted those up, she would be able to compare Justin's career earnings with her own. They had started at roughly the same time and had equal academic qualifications, and she'd applied for every promotion available to her when they'd come up...

There were some gaps in her calculations – missed inflationary adjustments and minor rounding errors – and these were magnified as her pencil and paper arithmetic progressed. But the answer towards which her calculations were heading become increasingly clear nonetheless: a mountaintop emerging from the mist. She had been underpaid almost since day one.

She refined her calculations and narrowed down the detail. She was the victim of a pay gap, of undeserved discrimination. If she intended to unleash some righteous fury over it, then she'd better have her numbers right.

On the driveway, Sam straightened the rucks in Marvin's jumper and brushed dust from his shoulder. "Get Tez at the bank to write everything down," she told him. "He knows his stuff."

"It's just a routine thing," said Marvin. "The household finances are in order. We're paying off the big debts."

"But listen to him," she urged. The household finances might be in better order than they had been for a while, but they had been brought to that point by years and years of wilful financial ignorance on Marvin's part. Sam hadn't enjoyed playing the part of an interfering daughter, but she had no choice but to force her dad to address his financial woes. Nonetheless, all it seemed she had managed was take the various fiery financial disasters of her dad's life – the credit cards, the loans, the unpaid bills – bring them out into the open, and consolidate them into one horrible monetary conflagration. "And don't make a joke about everything he says," she added, knowing full well he would.

Marvin took hold of her elbows to stop her fidgeting hands. He looked her in the eyes. "It's going to be fine, Sam. It's just a meeting. It's not my first day at school."

"And I'll be with him," added Delia from the door of her car. "I might even let him take me out for coffee and cake after."

Sam sighed, kissed him, and climbed into the front of her Piaggio Ape.

"Is this cab really designed to take two people?" asked Rich, beside her.

"You want to walk?"

He was right, though. It was a tight squeeze. But this trip to look at potential new offices was her trip, and they would do it on her terms.

"Peninsula is coming over in a bit to deal with your rat infestation," said Rich. "I told him about the enrichment opportunity for Motikiti and he's pretty excited."

"One rat does not an infestation make."

"You know there's more than one."

"And he's not to do all the ironing or feng shui the living room while he's there. I know what he's like."

They headed up to the clock tower island and out through the town.

"I don't really understand the whole enrichment for cats thing," she continued "Zoo animals need enrichment because they're in a restricted environment. Don't cats just go outside and find their own enrichment?"

"I guess normal cats would," said Rich, "but Motikiti likes

to be challenged. So what's the first candidate for DefCon4's new office space?"

"Apparently it's a single office room with a reception counter shared with another business. Parking for up to four vehicles. Which is good, because it's out of town."

They headed out towards Burgh le Marsh. Sam had mixed feelings about being out of town. It would be inconvenient, but she had to take a look.

Rich pored over his phone as she drove. His brow creased. "The sensory room is going to have a tactile mammoth exhibit."

"The sensory room at your not-really-in-the-North-Sea animatronic dinosaur safari park?"

"Yes. They're asking me if I want the mammoth to have coarse outer hair as well as the curly under layer. I think it's a yes, isn't it? I guess it's a trade-off between what feels nice and what's realistic."

Sam nodded as if she cared. "I think you'll do what's right."

They pulled onto a track which led away from the main road. It went quite a long way, but at least they weren't bouncing through potholes. Sam couldn't help wondering how the Piaggio would cope with a more rural setting as its regular base.

She stopped in the car park of a one storey structure and looked up at the reception. "Furry Frolics Doggy Daycare and Spa. I guess this is the other business on the site."

They went inside. A smiling woman wearing veterinary scrubs manned the reception desk. Or would have been manning the reception desk if she weren't mopping the floor.

"Can I help you? Just clearing up a little accident. Clyde's not housetrained, but he's such a sweetie, look at his face!"

Clyde was a Great Dane who ambled over and leaned heavily against Sam. She struggled to keep upright with the weight of the giant dog against her.

"I've come to look at the office space," said Sam.

"Oh, I see," said the woman. "Let me get the key when I've cleared this up. Oh my goodness, Clyde, you needed a number two as well! No wonder you're so twitchy. Have you seen his face?"

Sam couldn't see Clyde's face, he was now facing away from her, fully focused on relieving his bowels. She retreated to the counter and tried to ignore the smell. Rich was acting like a master perfumier, wafting a hand to catch the scent and muttering phrases like 'musky' and 'tangy, like an elk'.

Once the dog had finished his monstrous evacuation, the woman said, "Come on, Clyde. Let's show the nice people around."

Sam loved dogs as much as the next person, but she was surprised to see Clyde was joining them on the tour. Despite the woman's veterinary scrubs, it was clear this was basically a dog-sitting business. Through a gated room to one side, Sam could see an indoor space full of dog beds and feeding stations, leading to an open outside yard in which various pooches sniffed, lounged and played.

They entered a room with a desk and a row of tables along the side. There was also a large industrial sink.

"Ignore all this stuff," the woman said, waving her hands at cardboard boxes filled with used packaging and a number of stacked advertising boards. "We'll get it cleared up for you.

So what kind of a business is it? Are you a groomer? Or a vet? Please tell me you're a vet!"

"I work for DefCon4," said Sam.

"Doesn't sound like a vet."

"No, we subcontract a lot of security and public sector work. CCTV, alarms, health and safety. I get the feeling you were expecting a business relating to pets?"

"Well, yes," laughed the woman. "I mean, you couldn't run a normal business from here. Just imagine!"

As if in response to her comment, Clyde howled. It was a deafening and heartfelt reaction to some invisible stimulus. From elsewhere on the site, a great many other dogs joined him. The sound was overwhelming and slightly comical. Rich and Sam looked at each other and burst into laughter.

"Sorry!" shouted the woman. "I think they heard the binmen coming down the lane! It always sets them off! Actually, so does the postman, the window cleaner, and pretty much anything else...!"

"This is what I'm talking about," said Rich. He was stood by a tall advertising stand for dog shampoo. He brushed his hands against two square fur swatches stuck to the board: the WITH WHITMAN'S DOG SHAMPOO sample and the WITH REGULAR DOG SHAMPOO version.

"You can really tell the difference with the fibres," he said. "You get what you pay for."

6

Mercedes found herself hurrying to complete her calculations while the key components remained fresh in her mind. She had the pay grades. She had approximate times spent at each grade. She could roughly determine Justin's pay over his entire period of employment, then subtract from that her own total income for the same period of time. The resulting figure would be exactly how much more Justin had earned than her across their careers, despite their equal starts and her superior personal qualities.

A shadow fell over the Eastshires Bank customer advice counter.

The man was broad and tall with a wide brow, and an expression suggesting he had seen all life had to offer and had discovered the reality didn't live up to the pictures in the brochure. He carried a long thin package in one hand, wrapped in oily cloth. In the other he held a carrier bag, in which sat something bulbous and round.

"Bruce Greencock," he said. "I have an appointment."

She smiled, nodded and gestured at the carrier. "Cabbage?"

"My fame precedes me," he said, either seriously or with a real talent for deadpan delivery.

"Eastshires is keen to know its customers," she replied, a smooth platitude which meant nothing and came to her tongue without effort. "This way."

She was partway across the floor when Justin strode through from the back office.

"Why didn't you tell me Mr Greencock was here?" he said, with a searching look at Mercedes.

"Literally coming to you right now," she told him, not as bitterly as she might have done if there hadn't been a customer with them.

Justin gave her one of his sharp 'only joking' looks, and with a matey "Bruce!" whisked the farmer into the back rooms.

Mercedes returned to the customer advice counter, woke her computer and copied the final formulae onto the spreadsheet she had created to do the number crunching for her. She looked at the total.

Sixty-seven thousand pounds.

The actual number was not quite so conveniently round, but if anything, Mercedes had erred in the bank's favour, and yes, across the course of a career in which they had arrived equally qualified, in which he had shown no positive qualifications that she didn't possess in abundance, Mercedes Martin had been paid sixty-seven thousand quid less than Justin. She had a good head for numbers, and she knew she wasn't wrong.

And it wasn't only Justin. Tez Malik's pay progression was rising at a rate which had already eclipsed hers and looked set for a similar trajectory to the branch manager's. She could prove it. She had worked it out. She had drawn graphs.

She was perfectly aware of the gender pay gap. It was a well-documented fact. But she had bought into the assumption that it was mostly due to women taking career breaks to have children, or being more inclined to take lower-paid part-time work. But that didn't apply here. Mercedes had no children, and had absolutely no inclination of bringing another mouth into this broken and over-crowded world.

No, Mercedes had lost out on her rightful earnings in more subtle ways than crude maternity. It was not being put forward for training courses as readily as others. It was not being listened to or noticed as fairly as others. When a certain type of person spoke at Eastshires regional meetings – a tall, male, deep-voiced type of person – everyone nodded, everyone listened. When she spoke, especially if she rudely presumed to speak more than once, she was regarded with something like annoyance. An accumulation of slights, a diverging career path.

"Sixty-seven thousand pounds," she said.

"Yes, please," said the customer who had appeared before her, an older man with a cheery, lined face.

"Pardon?" asked Mercedes.

"Perhaps I'm the one millionth customer and there's some sort of prize," the man smiled.

"Ignore him," said the woman next to him. She wore blue denim dungarees and had a mass of untidy hair, kept off her face by a number of ties and hair clips. Both her manner and appearance suggested she was the much put-upon daughter of an irritating father.

"I'm here to see Tel about my mortgage," said the older man.

"Tez."

"That's the one. I'm Marvin Applewhite." There was a brief and playful eyebrow raise, as if the name should mean something to her.

"Very good. If you'd both wait here, I'll see if he's free."

"Oh, I'm not with him," said the woman, half-stepping towards the counter with a heavy canvas bag on her arm. The bag rattled noisily. "He's very much someone else's problem."

The old man, Marvin, harumphed. "That's the last time I offer you Marmite eggs benedict," he said.

"Promise?" she said. There was an ease between the two that made it hard for Mercedes to believe they weren't father and daughter. But what did she know about fathers and daughters?

Tez was standing across the lobby. Mercedes raised a hand to politely wave him over.

"And you, madam?" she asked the woman. She looked at the bulging, rattling bag. "Coins to deposit?"

"These are just my marbles," she replied.

"I lost mine years ago," added the man, Marvin, in the

manner of someone who'd been itching to say that all morning.

"Just some cheques to pay in," said the woman. "Can you believe people still actually write cheques?"

"Marvin," said Tez, coming over to greet the older man and shake him warmly by the hand. "Come through, come through."

Mercedes gestured the woman towards the customer services machines on the wall. "You should be able to automatically pay them in here."

"Ah, I did look but it seemed to be out of order."

Mercedes looked. The woman was right. Both machines were showing THIS ATM IS NOT CURRENTLY WORKING messages. Connectivity issues with head office again.

"Your machine is not working," said another woman loudly, pushing through the entrance door with armfuls of shopping and two children in tow.

"I'll be with you in a moment," said Mercedes, and addressed the scruffy-haired marble-holder. "If you take them to the counter, my colleague will be able to process your cheques."

That dealt with, she turned back to the woman with shopping and kids. The shopping seemed to be several bulging carrier bags from the M&S Food Hall up the road. Mother and children were all blonde. The mother's blonde looked like it came out of a bottle at an expensive salon. The children's blonde looked like it came straight out of an Aryan master race promotional brochure. The young boy and girl stared up at Mercedes.

"I need cash," said the woman. "I can't pay the fishmonger if I don't have cash."

Mercedes gave a small mental nod. Ewan King had a fish stall in an octagonal booth just outside the Hilldred's shopping centre across the road. In a world that had all but gone cashless, King still resisted. Mercedes reckoned a good ten percent of the cash from the Eastshires ATMs made the short journey from the cash machine to King's fish stall.

"Yes, the machines appear to be down at the moment," said Mercedes.

"But we're having monkfish Provençal for supper tonight," said the little girl, who couldn't have been more than eight.

"Mummy! How can we have monkfish Provençal if we don't have any money?" added the little boy, who must have been a similar age.

The woman glanced at the ATMs inside the bank and, seeing they were also out action, declared, "This is a disaster. Hashtag bad karma."

She raised an iPhone in her hand and snapped a picture of the non-functioning machines.

"If you need to withdraw money from your account, we provide that service at the counter," said Mercedes.

The woman glanced at the counter, where Stevie was serving a customer. "You mean, like, a person does it?"

Confusion was painted broadly across the woman's face. She was probably going to ask if the counter staff would take her card and use a 'special ATM' in the back or something. The idea that bank staff had physical access to physical money was bewildering to some modern customers.

The woman held her head up high. "We must queue if we are to eat," she announced, in a restrained, faraway voice, as if about to face the executioner's block. "But," she told Mercedes fiercely, "if my raspberry and mascarpone meringue roulade defrosts, then you will be held responsible." She moved towards the queue.

"We don't have to wait, do we, mummy?" asked the little girl, appalled.

"Edith, there are many trials a woman must face if she is to get what she deserves."

"The patriarchy makes us sad," added the boy, solemnly, but the mother was too busy swiping on her iPhone to listen.

Mercedes was not, in general, a fan of children coming into the bank. They seemed to shriek and shout far more than was ever necessary. They brought filthy toys with them, leaving toy car tracks or mucky handprints on surfaces. She'd even seen them bringing in squidgy slugs and clods of dirt, wipe snot trails on furnishings, drop messy food on the floor. Children were, by and large, worse than animals, and although they were very, very different from what she had seen of the species, this clean, well-spoken blonde pair were just as unappetising.

But, Mercedes thought, the woman was right about one thing. There were many trials one had to face to get what one deserved.

7

"Here, here," said Justin and placed a mug of coffee in front of Bruce. "It's just out of the machine but it's caffeine, and that's what we need first thing in the morning."

Bruce glanced up at the Eastshires Bank branded clock on the wall behind Justin's head. It had gone ten.

"How can I help you then, Bruce?"

The cube-like office space they were in was bland, cheap and purely functional. Aside from the clock, there was nothing to mark it out from any plain room anywhere in the world. Bruce had been in here before and decided it probably wasn't Justin's real office, just a space for customer meetings, free from distractions.

Justin clasped his thick fingers over his belly and sat back in his chair, comfortable, as if he owned the place. In a way, Bruce thought, he sort of did. Bruce had known Justin Johnson for over thirty years. They'd both been at the Earl of

Scarborough High School as teenagers, and although they hadn't really frequented the same friendship groups, it was one of the schools where everyone knew everyone else. It was odd to think how lives had diverged since then. Many had been forced to move away for work, some clung on when they should have left, and some, like Justin and Bruce, had risen and grown, princes in their own little kingdoms.

"I want to show you what I've got." Bruce sat and waited. He knew the value of timing. Farmers had a proper feel for the rhythms of the world.

"Well, that sounds fascinating, Bruce," said Justin. "I am always keen to understand our customers better, you know that."

"Oh, this isn't just about understanding me. You'll want a part of this. Everyone will."

Justin made a grand sweeping gesture. "The floor is yours, Bruce. Go ahead!" He took a noisy sip of coffee, hissed as he burned his lip, and grinned at his own buffoonishness.

Bruce stood and paced, giving himself a moment to form the words. "You know that I've been working on something special for years?"

"Right? Good."

"I have the sense that you've probably been sceptical. I don't blame you. Most people are. The dream I've been chasing sounds so much like a fantasy, I know that!"

Justin gave a small frown. "I want to make sure I capture this properly for our records, Bruce. Why don't you summarise your dream for me, in a sentence or two?" He pulled a notepad towards him and looked up, pen poised.

Bruce gave a small sigh. The idiot had forgotten

everything they'd ever spoken about. Bruce had been in this office a dozen times. Justin had probably just filed Bruce's hopes and dreams under 'cabbage stuff'.

"My dream, Justin, my passion, is to breed a vegetable that becomes a household name. Something that people ask for in the supermarkets, because it's so special."

"Like Jazz apples."

"Well, that's a fruit, Justin, but yes—"

"Cherry tomatoes."

"Technically also a fruit. Point is, I'm working on something. My legacy. You know, for my kids, see?"

"Your children have a passion for vegetables?" Justin asked.

That was a low blow. Surely Justin knew how long it had been since Bruce had seen his kids. Bruce kept his cool. "It'll provide for them financially. You'll see."

Justin nodded, but his eyes told a different story.

Bruce picked up the carrier bag, took out the climbing frame uprights which were tied together in a cloth, and put them to one side on Justin's desk.

"Ignore them. Just got to take them to get brazed later," he said. He took out the cabbage head and placed it reverently in the centre of the desk. It was an impressive sight on its own, as a beautiful fresh cabbage always was. It sat like a huge vibrant flower, its gorgeous green petals bursting with chlorophyll. "Beauty, isn't she?" he said with a smile.

Justin gave a small nod. "Very nice cabbage, Bruce. Very nice."

Bruce had expected Justin's enthusiasm to be weak at this stage, but that was about to change. If there was one thing he'd learned from watching those Dragons Den pitching shows on the telly, it was that a bit of flair was needed. A bit of drama. He reached down for his other prop. It was wrapped in cloth, but it was the work of a moment to flick that cloth away. He held the machete aloft, observing – and enjoying – the spark of alarm in Justin's face.

Bruce brought the huge knife down in a massive, two-handed blow. Yes, a bit of dramatic flair was what was needed.

8

Marvin looked round the little office. It was small and impersonal, like a consulting room at the medical centre. Visiting the bank was not unlike visiting the doctor, except here it wasn't his prostate or his liver being poked at critically by a professional.

He pointed at the small, high frosted window, which added very little natural light to the room. "Lovely view."

"Hmmm?" said Tez, who had been looking at his computer. "Oh. A bit of daylight. Nicer now summer's here."

Marvin nodded. "Nice to see a change in the weather, eh Tez? Although you must see lots of change in your line of work."

Tez looked at him.

"Change," said Marvin. "Change, as in..." He mimed pushing round coins in the palm of his hand. Either Tez didn't get it, or the young man had had a humour bypass. Marvin was finding that, as the years went by, young people were increasingly alien to him. Tez Malik struck him as very young. They had met several times before, Tez had even been out to the house, but Marvin couldn't seem to get him to meet his eye and share a joke. The lad was maybe only five years younger than his Sam, but seemed to have no cultural references that went back more than a few years. It was as if he'd just come off the production line and slipped into a tailored suit.

"I can see you have no interest in bad bank jokes," said Marvin. "Perhaps they lack currency these days."

"Marvin," said Tez, "I'm reviewing the mortgage on your house. You're aware it is an interest-only mortgage."

"You told me. Last time."

"And it has now reached the end of its term."

"This sounds like a cause for celebration!" said Marvin.

Tez looked at Marvin, his hands clasped on the desk. Finally, he was making eye contact. "Marvin, it's not a cause for celebration, I'm afraid."

"No?"

"No. According to the records I have here, you purchased an ISA at the same time as you took out the mortgage. Remember, we spoke about ISAs?"

"I do."

"You will recall that the mortgage was interest only, and the ISA was intended to accumulate enough money to pay off the outstanding debt of the mortgage."

"Yes. When I remortgaged a few years back, an interest only mortgage was suggested to me by this very bank, so I'm sure it's all tickety-boo, isn't it?"

Tez nodded gravely. "Interest only mortgages were very

popular for a time. They relied on borrowers making significant personal savings and the market providing a decent return on investments."

"Markets not doing so well?" suggested Marvin.

"Not for people trying to save or make long-term investments. There is a significant shortfall in fact." He tilted his monitor to show Marvin. There was a pink bar and a blue bar and the blue bar was not as big as the pink one. "I did mention this to you last month. I asked if you had another source of money to pay off this debt."

"I have been working again."

Tez looked at his notes. "A magic show at a retirement village and some afternoons at Putten's caravan park? Do you have any other savings I don't know about?"

Marvin shook his head as he stared at his hands, his mind numbly struggling to process what he was hearing. The one thing he'd thought would always be on his side was the house. At least the house belonged to him.

"How much do I have left owing?" he said.

Tez consulted his screen. "Four hundred and eighty thousand pounds. Thereabouts."

"You could just say half a million. It sounds cooler."

"I think four hundred and eighty thousand pounds sounds bad enough," said Tez. "I've stalled the process for as long as I realistically can, Marvin."

Marvin raised his head. "What process?"

"Repossession. You can put the house up for sale yourself, but the penalties you'll start incurring from next month will accumulate. The bank will try to get the best possible price for your house and—"

"But it's my house," said Marvin, softly.

"I know."

"It's where I live. Sam…"

Tez's arm flexed, his hand reaching out to hold Marvin's then hesitating.

"There are still some financial matters from the early two thousands that we never really got to the bottom of, but we've been over your current financial situation. Even if you were to sign the house over to your daughter, no one would grant her a mortgage to cover the debt."

"But we live there," Marvin said.

The words were coming out by themselves. His mouth, his brain, were cogs, spinning out of control. The gears were smashed, the ratchets broken. How could this happen? He was a grown man, a fully functioning member of society. This wasn't supposed to happen. It was … it was embarrassing. He had to tell Sam, but he had no idea how he could possibly tell her.

Marvin stood up, felt his legs wobble and sat back down again.

"This is a lot to digest," said Tez. "There are some legal aspects I'm obliged to cover with you. Can I, perhaps, get you a glass of water?"

"A scotch, I think," said Marvin. "I'll have it on the rocks. Like me."

Tez rose. "I'll get you that water." He went to the drinks trolley, noted a lack of water and went outside.

As the young banker left the office, Marvin's hands – God, they were trembling! – went to his phone. He had to tell her. But he had no idea what he was going to say.

9

Sam parked on South Parade outside the next office candidate. The building was one of the many seafront properties that had once been Victorian B&Bs and now housed commercial enterprises on their ground floors. This one had an arcade extending across a wide frontage. The upper storeys looked promising.

Rich got out of the Ape van, consulting his phone. "Peninsula says that Motikiti is having the time of his life."

"What does that mean?" asked Sam. She hadn't even tidied the kitchen properly, so she had quite a few reservations about Peninsula being there. As always, Rich had decided he knew best.

"He tells me that the rat body count is now five. Motikiti is a formidable hunter. Peninsula asks he might be permitted to clean your cutlery while he's there."

"We have no silver worth polishing. Tell him no."

Rich pulled a face. "In my experience, he's probably going to do it anyway."

"Tell him he can dust and organise my dad's memorabilia if he's really stuck for something to do." Sam checked the information on her DefCon4 app. "So, prospective office number two is called City Lights."

"Skegness isn't a city," said Rich.

"The office is a three room suite with a panoramic view of Skegness's bustling town centre. Apparently the best access is a fire escape at the back," continued Sam. "I guess that avoids walking through the arcade."

They found the fire escape down an alley which led to a bin storage area. Rich rattled the handrail and flakes of rusty paint drifted off.

"Fire escapes are inspected regularly," said Sam cheerfully. "I'm sure it's fine."

They climbed up the steps, which clanged and swayed in a way that made Sam's stomach tighten. She had expected they would step off at the first storey to access one of the rooms above the arcade, but there was a hand-written sign that read *City Lights* and pointed up.

"Huh." Sam pulled a nervous face at Rich and continued to climb. They emerged onto the roof of the building. There was a small fence around the edges, and a path marked out which she presumed they were meant to follow, but it was definitely the roof.

"Is that a portacabin on the roof?" asked Rich.

Sam sighed. "Portakabin or an old static caravan. Who knows? Must have used a crane to get it up here. Madness. Let's make sure this is what we're supposed to be looking at."

They walked over to the shabby metal structure. There was a key safe to the side of the door. Sam entered the code from her notes and it popped open.

Once inside Sam turned to Rich. "Well. First impressions?"

Rich rolled his eyes. "Apart from the fact that it's a portacabin on the roof, you mean? Well, number one, it's colder in here than it is out there."

Sam nodded. It was true. The cold in the portacabin had a stale, clammy quality. "I guess it's had no heating on for a bit."

"Number two," said Rich. "The smell in here is like a mildewed bin, but worse. Significantly worse. In fact, let's improve it." He pulled out one of his spray cans and gave a squirt. "Neanderthal Cave, that's better."

Sam wanted to argue that Neanderthal Cave couldn't possibly be an improvement, but after a couple of breaths she was forced to concede Rich was right. "Maybe it would air out," she said, wafting the door back and forth a little to encourage air in from outside. The words were unconvincing even to her. The hinges squeaked. The thin wooden door moved in the uneven, stumbling manner of something that would simply give up and fall off were it to suffer any abuse.

"Come on, let's explore," said Rich.

"I don't think there's much more to explore."

The room was mostly bare. There was a single desk with a coffee machine on top. The inch of ancient coffee remaining in the jug had acted as a petri dish for an extravagant bloom of orangey-brown mould which had blown up and then collapsed across the desk in a cloud of drifting, toxic spores. Sam stared hard at the coffee pot because it was a more appealing sight than the walls.

"If I'm honest," said Rich. "This doesn't look much worse than your old office."

It might have been sarcasm, but it was also arguably true. Rich approached one wall. He held out a hand but did not touch. "I don't understand. Is it poo, damp, or ectoplasm?" It glistened and oozed on the four walls and the ceiling.

Sam shook her head. She had no wish to contemplate what it might be. "At least it's not on the floor," she said, looking down and instantly regretting such a rash statement. Whatever floor covering had once been in place had been colonised by the same stuff.

"You can really feel the mould spores trying to get into your lungs," observed Rich. He walked over to the window. "Panoramic views?"

Someone had wiped a hand through the grime at some point, so it was possible to see the rooftops and mobile phone masts filling the view.

"City lights," she mused, looking at the sea. "On a clear day, you could probably see the lights of Amsterdam."

"Did you say this is a suite of three rooms?" asked Rich.

They both looked over at the two internal doors.

"I'm not sure we need to see any more," said Sam. "My mind is made up on this opportunity."

"Aren't you just a little bit curious?"

Sam sighed and opened one of the doors. It was a tiny bathroom. She knew it was a bathroom because it contained a sink and a toilet, but she wasn't able to say what colour they might be because they were covered in a layer of black mould.

"There's a sign, but I can't quite read what it says." Sam leaned in as far as she dared without touching anything. "Warning! Do not use until chemical toilet reservoir has been emptied." She closed the door slowly but firmly. "Just when I thought I couldn't hate this place anymore."

"I checked out the kitchenette so you didn't have to," said Rich, jerking a thumb at the other doorway. "There's a fridge in there that is switched off. The cheese inside has a sell by date from three years ago. I'm actually taking that with me, as a sample for the lab which is working on mammoth smells. I feel they might learn something. It's got a dark sourness to it that could be a fascinating counterplay to the more overt elephant dung tones that form the basis for their work."

10

On the desk, Bruce's Tigerheart cabbage had been sliced expertly in two. Bruce held the machete aloft in one hand and lifted a hemisphere of cabbage in the other. He had practised the movement in the mirror, the open-armed power pose that charismatic leaders always adopted. He'd read a book about it.

"What do you think of that, Justin?" he asked, his voice raised. "I guarantee you've never seen the like, eh?"

"You've gone right into the walnut finish."

Justin was leaning forward and rubbing the desk edge where Bruce's machete blow had scraped a couple of millimetres into the surface. He licked his thumb and rubbed hard, as if he might erase the nick in the polished tabletop through the diligent application of saliva.

"Aye, sorry about that," said Bruce.

"It's a Vebjörn," said Justin.

"What?"

"I picked them out myself. Came all the way from the IKEA in Peterborough. You don't mistreat a Vebjörn like that."

"Okay. I'm sorry," Bruce repeated, irritably. The man had no appreciation for showmanship. It wasn't easy to cut a cabbage cleanly in two with an overhead chop. Bruce had had to practise over and over again. He'd gone through a lot of cabbages. He held a cut half of cabbage close to Justin's face. "Breathe it in! Smells glorious, doesn't it?"

Justin's nose wrinkled in mild disgust.

"But have you spotted its USP, Justin?"

Justin looked rattled. "USP?"

"Unique selling point." God, this man was supposed to know business. "The thing that will make everyone want *this* cabbage rather than any other. No? You don't see it?"

He waited, watching Justin's frown as his eyes roved over the cabbage, searching for anything to say about it. After a moment he gave up.

"It's the stripes, Justin! The stripes! See how it's striated across its heart? Nobody else has ever created anything like it. This is my Tigerheart."

"Tigerheart?"

"Aye. Cool name, isn't it? Sounds like it should be an exotic jewel or something. And you know what? It is."

"Bruce! I'd feel very much more comfortable if you'd take your seat," said Justin. He looked like a man trying to regain his composure. He gave the cut in the desktop a final, miserable rub and leaned back.

Bruce sat down, cradling the cabbage heart and smiling down at it like an infant. This was the moment. This precious vegetable was going to secure the future his children needed. "So, what do you think?" he asked.

"What do I think? I think—"

"Apart from the minor damage to your Veburn."

"Vebjörn. Yes. I suppose it's a grand cabbage, Bruce. You've done well there."

"Yes, but you can see the potential, right? You can see how this is a vegetable destined for the best tables in the country? We're talking Fortnum and Mason food hall, I reckon. I'm offering this bank the chance to back me."

"Back you? You mean the basis for the loan you want is that you might attract the interest of a high end greengrocer?"

Bruce narrowed his eyes. "What's that supposed to mean?"

Justin steepled his hands on the desk and took a couple of calming breaths. "It's like this, Bruce. We need to look at the facts when someone applies for a business loan. The business case has to be based on economic facts, not fantasy. Certainly not a cabbage-based cabaret act." Justin had a strange, constipated look on his face, and it took Bruce a moment to realise the man was trying to look stern.

"I've put down the numbers," said Bruce. "It's all there in black and white. I need investment for seed propagation and then allowing the growth of the first crop. If the bank will lend me two hundred thousand for development then I'll be back in the black within two years, easily."

"Your numbers are wildly optimistic, Bruce. We have to consider your track record and your other financial commitments. Your debts." He looked to his computer. "It would be irresponsible for the bank to take this on, and I think you know that, don't you? You're overstretched, Bruce."

"And this is exactly the right way to fix it," countered Bruce. "Have you never heard of speculating to accumulate? This is a winner, you can see that for yourself! Look at the stripes!"

Justin made a show of peering at the cabbage. "I'm really not sure, Bruce. I haven't looked closely at many cabbages recently, but this looks pretty normal to me."

"You're joking!" Of all the things that Justin could have said, this was crushing. He could attack Bruce's business acumen, he could even attack Bruce himself, but denying the actual stripes was a step too far. A downright lie. Bruce was incensed. He flexed and unflexed his fists.

"If you genuinely believe that you have an innovative product here, have you considered other ways to fund it?" asked Justin.

"Of course I did! Tried to get one of them countryside grants, but the criteria are all wrong. Tigerheart doesn't show 'exceptional stewardship or productivity.'" He mimed the air quotes, pulling a face at the government bureaucrats who'd turned him down. "They don't care that it's special, or that everyone will want it."

"Bruce, I'm not sure what to say. If it's important to you then perhaps you might consider selling a portion of your land to provide funding? I thought those energy bods were still interested in buying you out."

Bruce shook his head. "It's farming land. Fit for only cabbages and the like." Bruce was still reeling from Justin's denial of the Tigerheart stripes. Was he trying to steal it from him? They called this gaslighting, didn't they? That thing where you pretended that things were not as they really were, and tried to convince someone else they were wrong about reality?

Justin stood and smoothed imaginary creases from his trousers. This was supposed to signal the end of the discussion. Bruce stood as well, not to show that he was ready to leave but so that he could look Justin in the eye. "This is my legacy to my children."

"You had a lovely family, Bruce."

And there it was. Bruce finally saw the brutal simplicity of his situation as it appeared to Justin. *Had.* Past tense. Has-been father. Has-been farmer.

Justin said nothing, but put his head to the side in a pose that was probably supposed to be sympathetic, but made him look like a chubby middle-aged man clumsily aping Princess Diana or Oprah.

"Tigerheart will be my mark on the world, and my lasting gift to my children. When the public see this for themselves they'll love it, you'll see."

"I'm sure they will."

"But you won't invest."

"I don't think it would be fair. Fair on you above all else."

"'Think'? So this is just your opinion?"

"I know what the bank's computers will say. It's a very refined system."

Bruce was incensed. "So you could lend me the money if you wanted to, but you won't."

Justin moved around the desk, an extended palm gently encouraging Bruce towards the door.

11

As they emerged from the horrid rooftop portacabin Rich locked the key back into its safe. Sam breathed in lungfuls of the brisk Skegness air and turned her face to the sky in appreciation of the weak but strengthening sunlight.

"I need to write a report on why that is not suitable accommodation for DefCon4," she said. "This one appeals to head office for obvious budgetary reasons. I especially don't want them to get the idea that this place would work if I cleaned it up a bit. How do I convey the true horror of what it's really like?"

Rich held up his cannister of Neanderthal Cave and his cloudy packet of ancient cheese. "Maybe a little bit of scent marketing is called for?"

She realised her phone was ringing. It was her dad. "Done at the bank already?"

There was a pause on the line. *"No. Not quite,"* said

Marvin. *"Tez has gone to get some legal stuff he needs to go through."*

"Oh. Right?" she said, making a generalised question of the word.

"Yeah. The money situation. It isn't looking good."

"Is that what Tez said? He actually said that?"

There was another pause and she could almost hear him nodding. *"Um, yes."*

Sam's dad's financial situation had not been anywhere near good for years but there was something in those pauses, in his tone, that disquieted her. She turned round. Three storeys up, she could see across much of Skegness town. She looked towards the high street and the corner building that she imagined was the bank.

"Dad. What's happened?"

"I think I made a mistake, Sam."

"Did you tell him one to many bad jokes?"

There was a creak on the line. A door opening and closing.

"Tez is back," said Marvin. *"With bottles of water."*

"Is that your daughter?" asked another voice.

12

Justin stood by the open office door. "You go and grow cabbages, Bruce. You work on paying off those other debts. I'm going to overlook the damage you've done to the Vebjörn, for old times' sake."

Old times' sake? Justin thought he was doing him a kindness because of the old days in the school yard? They'd never been friends. Bruce had hung out with the rest of the country kids. Where had Tubby Johnson been? Doing computer club with the other top set swots?

"You patronising bastard," Bruce hissed.

"Hey, come on now." Justin had the door open now.

Furious, Bruce grabbed his bundled climbing frame rods and his machete. "You have no idea how ridiculous you are! I make a loss year after year. This is my one and only chance to claw my way out of financial ruin, and you just keep looking at the clock because you have another appointment or a doughnut waiting!"

"I value our time together."

"Bollocks." Bruce stormed out into the little corridor off from the main lobby. "You could give me that money right now if you wanted to." He stepped into the customer area and waved at the counter. "You could get it for me right now. No skin off your nose."

The cashier behind the counter was staring at Bruce. As were the two women in the line at the counter.

"Er, Justin...?" said the cashier.

Bruce realised he'd been doing his pointing with the hand holding the machete. The two blonde kids standing by one of the women were staring too, wide-eyed.

"Oh," he said. "I didn't ... I just wanted my money."

"Money," said the cashier hollowly. "How...?"

"Two hundred thousand," said Bruce. "He said he could if he wanted to."

"Justin?" repeated the cashier.

A dark-haired bank woman came over from the little advice desk near the entrance, hands raised as though approaching a nervous horse. "I'm sure we can sort this out," she said

"I told him we wouldn't," said Justin.

It said MERCEDES on the dark-haired woman's name tag, which was surely the name of a car, not a person. Mercedes gestured to the cashier. "Let's see what money we have in the register. And we're going to let all these nice people go, aren't we?"

"What?" Bruce's mind flipped and spun. The woman actually thought he was robbing the place. Why didn't Justin say something? This situation wasn't what it looked like. He hurriedly tried to put the machete away. He juggled the machete and the wrapped iron pipes.

The customer at the counter, the one wearing huge dungarees, clutched her bulging bag in front of her face. "Don't shoot me," she squeaked.

"What?"

Dark-haired Mercedes was crouching away from him and moving towards the bank door.

"Don't you go anywhere!" said Bruce automatically. The woman froze, eyes on the twin barrels of iron piping wrapped in cloth.

There was silence. A huge, treacle-time silence. Mercedes crouched near the door, hands raised in the face of what she wrongly assumed to be a double-barrelled shotgun. The children clutched at their mother's hips. The other customer hid her face behind her big bag. The cashier had her hand in the till, already pulling out a thin wad of twenty pound notes. Justin stood silently behind Bruce, not saying anything, not saying anything at all. Justin knew it wasn't a gun. Why wasn't he telling them?

And the words just came to Bruce's mouth. Not sane and normal ones, but words demanded by his anger and by the tableau they had all created together, as if the world had driven them to this point and would not accept any other explanation or possibility.

"Everyone get down on the ground! This is a robbery!"

SAM HEARD the man's angry shout over the telephone.

"Did you hear that?" said Marvin, possibly to her, possibly to Tez.

"What was that?" asked Sam.

There was another shout, the unmistakeable words, *"Give me the money!"*

"Don't go out the door!" hissed Marvin's voice.

"Dad?" said Sam.

Rich was walking across the roof towards her, spray cannister in one hand, bag of mouldy cheese in the other.

"I think it's real," Tez whispered on the line.

"Do we hide?" said Marvin. *"Lock the door?"*

Sam could feel a sickening fear open up beneath her, as if the only thing holding her in place was a veil, as thin as cling film, and it was tearing beneath her feet.

"What's happening, dad?"

Rich saw the look on her face. "What's happened? Has he got lost?"

She flapped a hand at him, irritated and urgent. "Call the police!"

"What?"

"Call them. There's an armed robbery taking place at the Eastshires Bank."

"Armed? Like, with weapons?"

"That's what the word means!"

He looked like he was about to question her again, thought better of it, dropped his cheese and began dialling.

∼

THE DUMPY WOMAN behind the counter was taking money out and placing it on the counter. Twenties and tens and fives. But she was too slow, the bundles too small.

"Faster!" snapped Bruce and the woman gave a jolt of fear.

"I'm sorry," he said, realising he was still shouting even as he apologised. "I'm not usually like this."

He swung about. He pointed the lengths of pipe round at Justin who backed away in alarm, hands raised. The man was an idiot. He knew it wasn't a gun.

"Damn it, man!" Bruce swore. Justin raised his hands higher.

"That's it," said the cashier.

Bruce looked at the piles on the counter. It didn't look like a lot of money. The cashier pushed them closer together as though it might make it all look bigger.

"How much is that?" he asked. "It's not enough."

"We really don't keep much cash in branch," said the one called Mercedes. "Take it. It's what we've got."

"You got a vault in this place?"

Mercedes said "No" at the exact same moment Justin said "Yes."

Bruce shook his fake gun. "Don't lie to me!"

Dungarees woman tried to shrink down to nothing by the counter. Mercedes blinked slowly and swallowed.

"We have some money in the vault, but it will take too long to get it." She gestured at the cash on the counter with a flat hand. "Take it and you can go."

13

Take the money and run, or stay, risk it all and perhaps get your hands on whatever was in the vault? Cut your losses, or gamble it all for this week's star prize in the mystery box? Mercedes could see the dilemma as plain as anything on the bank robber's face, like a poker player holding his cards face out. The uncertainty made him look like a child. It was pathetic, almost funny. Mercedes would have laughed if she hadn't been so scared. She'd have been scared if she hadn't been so bloody angry.

And she was angry. Mercedes was surprised to find that more than anything, at this particular moment, she was furious. She was so surprised and so furious that it raised her to a point from which she could view it all with a cold objective detachment, as if she were having an out of body experience.

Mercedes Martin, thirty-four years old, who had just

worked out that she had been short-changed in the promotion and wages stakes for the past fourteen years. Mercedes Martin, who currently had a cabbage farmer's shotgun pointed at her, pointed at the letter from her dad inside her jacket that she would never read if the man's fingers slipped on the trigger. Mercedes Martin, who was very much of the opinion that she wasn't getting paid enough for this. Mercedes Martin, who should have been paid sixty-seven thousand pounds in lost earnings before being thrust into this situation.

"Take the money, please," she said in the empty, pleasant tone she had perfected over the years.

Farmer Greencock's eyes twitched. His mouth creased like he was about to burst into tears.

"However much you take, the police will come for you," said Justin, trying to sound brave and superior, but twisting on the spot as though he was about to pee himself.

Bruce's face hardened. "The vault."

Mercedes wanted to scream in rage, wanted to sigh in despair, but she held it all in, this weird horrid pressure, this fury.

"It's back there," she said, pointing to the security door at the end of the little corridor of meeting rooms.

Bruce waved his gun at the entrance. "Shut the door."

"We don't have to do that."

"Shut the door!"

Mercedes stumbled to the entrance. Mid-morning. It looked like it was going to be a sunny day. The grey pavement outside shone light gold in the sunshine. She stood at the entrance. She could fling herself through it, run down the road, screaming for help. He wouldn't be able to stop her.

Probably.

She closed the double doors.

"Bolt it," he said. "Lock it."

The woman with the bag of marbles whimpered. The mother drew her children to her, into a corner, enfolding them with the bags of shopping still on her arms, like giant single-use plastic wings.

"We're all going," said Bruce. "Come round," he said to Stevie. "Leave the cash there."

Stevie looked to Mercedes for confirmation. To Mercedes, not Justin. In a crisis, no one looked to Justin for leadership. Mercedes gave the smallest of nods to Stevie.

She wondered if she could remember any of the bank's training on how to deal with armed robbers. Stevie had done the right thing, had offered small denomination notes from the counter. Mercedes assumed she'd pressed the silent alarm. Tez was still down the back with a customer. If he'd heard anything he should have pressed an alarm too, or dialled out.

Comply with the robber, the training had said. Comply slowly, offer them as little as possible, stall for time, wait for help, protect customers. The money in the branch was insured, customers weren't. And dead customers were bad for business.

"We can let these people go," said Mercedes. "The children, please."

The woman with the kids was on her phone. She was actually on her bloody phone, surreptitiously tapping and swiping. Their lives were on a knife-edge here and, in possibly their final moments, her life was still mediated through a mobile phone screen. Why did it not surprise Mercedes at all?

"We're all going to go get the money. Up. Move," said Bruce, adding, "I'm really sorry. This isn't what I had intended at all."

The eight of them shuffled down the corridor. Justin and Stevie led the way, then the woman and her children, the marble lady, and then Mercedes herself nearest to the gunman. At each door, Bruce tried the handle and flung the door wide to inspect the room. At the third one, the door wouldn't open.

"Keys," said Bruce.

"It's ... it's locked," said Mercedes dumbly before actually engaging her brain. "Site maintenance have locked it," she lied. "There's been water damage and—"

"Water damage?" said Justin.

She couldn't remember the name of the film, but Mercedes had a sudden image of an old horror movie in which a man could make other people's heads explode just by thinking about it. Mercedes willed Justin's stupid head to pop. Sadly, it didn't.

"It's empty," she said, as matter-of-factly as she could. "There's nothing in there."

MARVIN AND TEZ crouched beside the meeting room door. Tez's knuckles were white as he gripped the door handle and held it shut.

The voices outside moved on.

Tez opened his mouth to speak. Marvin put a finger to his lips.

Tez clamped his mouth shut and held onto the door handle.

The voices faded completely.

"I think they've gone," said Marvin and groaned.

"Don't worry." Tez put a comforting hand on Marvin's shoulder.

Marvin shook his head. "This is playing havoc with my knees." He awkwardly rolled away and tried getting to his feet.

"We shouldn't have done this," said Tez. "Hidden, I mean. If he finds us now, he'll be angry."

"If you want my opinion, he sounded angry as it was."

Marvin realised he still had Sam on the line. He put the phone to his ear. There was the sound of rushing wind and juddering breaths.

"You still there?" he asked.

The harsh breaths grew louder. *"I'm coming to you now,"* Sam panted. *"Just on South Parade."*

Tez tapped Marvin's knee and pointed across to the wall, and a white push button under a plastic cover. "I've pressed the silent alarm."

"Good man," said Marvin. "Tez and I have everything under control," he said to Sam.

"God help us if you're in charge," she replied. *"Stay hidden. Don't go all John McClane on us."*

"Who?"

"Die Hard," said Tez helpfully.

Marvin looked up. "Do you have any air vents we can crawl through?"

Tez held up his hands in a circle. "Big enough for a rat."

"I've got one of those at home. Should have brought it."

"Marvin?"

Marvin shook his head. "Sorry. Blind terror makes me talk nonsense. Most things do."

14

Justin punched the code to let them all into the back offices of the bank. He didn't hesitate, he didn't play for time, he didn't try to plead with Bruce Greencock to change his mind and let them all go. Bruce asked and Justin complied. Mercedes wasn't sure what she would have done differently, but she was convinced she wouldn't have rolled over like a cowardly dog in this way.

"I tell you this food is defrosting," said the mother with all the shopping. She said it to no one in particular; just a soft tone, a personal commentary, like she was narrating her life story or rehearsing lines. "I'd bought the Taste Japan crispy katsu curry for when the Whitstables come over on Tuesday, and it's not the kind of thing you can refreeze."

"You can't refreeze chicken, mummy," concurred the little girl.

The gunman prodded the marble lady roughly.

"They said it, not me," said Marbles.

"In here," said Bruce, and they turned in through an open door.

It was an office space they had barely used since the last round of staff cuts, three years back. In it were four desks and a couple of cupboards. An old computer router cabinet stood in the corner, its high front covered in loops of coloured network cables, the whole thing doing nothing but gathering dust. Bruce did a cursory sweep of the room, as though searching for secret exits or hidden weapons. There was a single phone in the room. Bruce placed it in the middle of the desk nearest to himself. There were two windows glazed with frosted glass, but they were high in the wall.

"Right," he said, stepping back so he could see the people around him. "Who else works here?"

Before Justin could leap in with a stupidly honest answer, Mercedes said, "Just us three. Saturday crew. Justin, Stevie and me."

Stevie gave her a scrutinising look. For a moment, Mercedes feared she had two moronic colleagues on her team. Then Stevie's face brightened and she nodded vigorously in agreement. "Yes. Just us three." The woman might as well have given a big comedy wink.

"My name's Delia," said the marbles woman.

"I didn't ask for names," Bruce snapped. "You?" he said, swinging his weapon towards Justin. "How much money is in the vault?"

Justin stammered. "It varies."

"Guess!"

"Four, five hundred thousand. It ... it could be less."

"It's enough. I only need two to get Tigerheart off the ground."

"Tigerheart?" asked Mercedes.

"It's his new cabbage," said Justin.

Mercedes opened her mouth to say something, but for a few seconds she could only puff out her cheeks in confusion. "You're robbing a bank to fund a cabbage farm?"

"I—" Bruce hesitated and a terrible change washed over his face. It was like witnessing a full blown existential crisis, with all the accompanying angst, the sleepless nights and dread-filled days compressed into a couple of seconds. He looked at his weapon as though he didn't understand why he was even holding it. He held his lips firm, as if trying to prevent himself from throwing up. He looked like a man waking from a sickening dream.

"I … I'm doing it for my kids. I'll do anything for my kids. I … just need the money, then I'll go."

He looked up. There were silent blue flashing lights reflected in the frosted glass.

SAM REACHED the clock tower island where the esplanade leading down to the sea met the promenade. She parked the Piaggio on one of the nearby residential streets, as she had a strong suspicion she'd be blocked in once the police got themselves organised. She jogged round to the left and up Lumley Road.

"Heading up to the bank now," she said for her dad's

benefit, assuming he was still on the call and could hear what she was doing.

Lumley Road was the town's main shopping street. It ran from the clock tower roundabout up to Lumley Hotel at the other end. At the furthest end were the more conventional shops – clothing, high street lenders, charity shops – but nearer the seafront they were given over to tourist places. Sam ran past open-fronted sweet stalls, a fudge and rock shop, fish and chip shops, the Tower Cinema and shops selling beachwear, with inflated floats and cartoon characters hanging from the arcade awnings.

As she squeezed past spinning racks of postcards and foot-level boxes of buckets and spades, Sam saw there were already three police cars and one police van outside the Eastshires Bank. They had positioned themselves so that traffic could not drive past on either the main road or the quieter road from the park. Officers were already out of their vehicles. Three of them were waving their arms high and driving the pedestrians back.

Herding pedestrians was worse than herding cats. At least cats had the decency to pretend they weren't complying. Pedestrians operated on the contradictory basis that a) yes, they very much needed to get back from the 'dangerous thing' that was going on and b) they really ought to hang about as close as possible just so they could work out what the 'dangerous thing' might actually be. People jostled for position in that sweet spot of close enough but not too close.

An officer pulled cones and tape out of the back of one of the cars and started to work on some rudimentary boundaries. The officer was remonstrating with the shop owner on the corner of Rutland Road, opposite the bank.

"But how long for?" said the shopkeeper. "People aren't going to be able to get into the shop."

"No, they're not, sir," said the copper and then turned to Sam. "Madam. Get back. This area's off limits."

Sam held up her phone. "I need to speak to whoever's in charge."

"You get back. You can talk to someone in a bit."

"But I'm on the line with someone inside the bank," she said.

That stopped the officer. He frowned in momentary thought and then lifted the tape. "With me, ma'am."

Sam ducked under. The police officer pointed a gloved finger at the shopkeeper. "Don't you start messing with my tape."

"I'm not," said the man, defensively.

"I saw you. You were touching it."

The shopkeeper stepped back behind the cordon into the growing crowd. Dozens of people held back by the magic power of blue and white tape, thought Sam. There was something odd in the British psyche. Give them a wall of police with riot shields and the British would fight them off with bricks and bottles like any other nation. Give them a length of flimsy tape, a polite notice or an obvious queue, and the British felt compelled to comply.

15

Mercedes thought it was patently clear this bank robber didn't know what he was doing. His eyes flicked between the lights in the small frosted window and his hostages. When there was a thump at the front door to the bank and a muffled shout, he almost jumped in alarm.

If it had been her robbing the bank, she'd have done things very differently. She supposed she wouldn't have bothered robbing a bank, for starters. The chances of getting in, getting out and getting away without being caught were vanishingly slim, and banks just didn't hold the kind of cash that made those risks worthwhile. Add to that the exploding dye packs in the bank wads, the smart water defences over the door, and the amount of CCTV both inside and out, and escape was nigh on impossible.

This guy, Bruce, had already lost. The only questions yet to be answered were how long it would take from him to be captured, and how many casualties there would be during that time.

But if Mercedes had decided to rob a bank—

"Phones!" Bruce snapped.

People looked at him blankly.

"All of you. Your phones. On this table. In fact, empty your pockets."

With a succession of clatters, smartphones and keys were produced. Stevie's keys had a photograph fob embossed with the words *I LOVE MY PUP*.

"Bit phallocentric of you to assume everyone has pockets, *Bruce*," said Delia, emphasising his name, trying to claw back from her earlier fear, seizing control of what she could. "Got me a big pouch here." From the front pouch of her dungarees, she took a scratched phone with a colourful homemade cover and put it on the table.

Bruce looked at the woman with the M&S bags and the children. She was still swiping on her phone.

"Put it on the table."

"But it's *my* phone. How can I be expected to post to Insta if I've not got it?"

Bruce reached out and snatched it from her. The woman gasped silently as if her throat had just been slashed. Bruce glared at the screen.

"You've been tweeting about this? With photos?"

"Insta," said the woman, weakly. "I didn't say anything bad about you."

"Jesus!" he growled and slammed it down on the table.

"That's an iPhone 13!" she said. Then, as Bruce swung round at her again, squeaked, "Please don't shoot me."

The children clung to their mother. Mercedes found herself disgusted rather than moved by this. If they imagined this self-absorbed creature had their best interests at heart, then they were sorely mistaken. Mothers' Day gifts, a hundred variants of mugs with WORLD'S BEST MUM written on them, all fed into those lies that irritated Mercedes: the notion that your parents were things to be treasured, that they were irreplaceable, that they always knew best. Parenthood was a matter of luck and no one had to pass a test to be allowed to breed. There were some godawful parents out there. Mercedes knew this for a fact, and she could see a prime example in front of her.

Bruce's reaction was far less cold. He recoiled at sight of the children cowering in alarm. He stepped back and raised his weapon.

"I won't hurt you," he said.

He pulled the gun barrels from the cloth and bag wrapping, revealing them to be just lengths of pipe, taped together. "These are from my own children's climbing frame."

"Not even armed," said Delia, a smile of disbelief on her face.

"Going to get them rewotsited, or something," said Justin.

"Rebrazed," said Bruce.

Mercedes spun on the bank manager. "You knew?"

"What?"

"You knew he didn't have a real gun?"

Justin's mouth flapped. "I ... I ... yes."

"You knew! And yet you let him hold up the bank!"

Justin flung out an arm in protest. "He was very convincing!"

"But you actually knew, you utter pillock!"

"I got carried away! Swept along with it and that! And he's got a machete!"

"The gun's not real?" asked Stevie, apparently ten seconds behind everyone else.

"I think I'll be having my iPhone back, then!" said the mother, lifting her son aside bodily to free herself.

The iron rods dropped to the floor with a clang and Bruce had the machete in his hand once more. "I'm still armed," he said. "Now, is that your pockets empty or do I have to search you all?"

There were dumb looks and head shakes all round.

"Bags on the table, too. What's in them?" he said, nodding at the mother's shopping.

"A couple of meals. Something special for when the Whitstables come over. A raspberry and mascarpone meringue roulade that I'm sure is ruined. A pair of Chicken Pie-evs for tonight. It's a tortured pun, but really quite delicious. Oh, and some organic hand-reared Devonshire lamb cutlets drizzled in a mint and rosemary roux."

"Everything is ruined, isn't it, mummy?" said the girl.

Delia plonked her bulging bag onto the table. "Marbles."

"Marbles?" said Bruce.

"Sorry. Hand-blown glass marbles served in a canvas bag with organic, locally sourced dust."

"Are you trying to be funny?"

"Trying not to wet myself, actually," she said, staring pointedly at his blade.

He looked at the pile on the table. "Phones. Bags. Phones!" He turned to Mercedes. "How do I cut off all the phone lines to the outside?"

Yes, she thought. If she was holed up in here with hostages, she'd want to cut off the phone lines too. If she was going to rob a bank. Say, if she was going to try to recoup the wages she'd been denied over the years, she'd want to disable the phones. She'd want to kill the CCTV camera feed as well. She wondered if she might suggest that to him.

16

The police officer escorted Sam round the cleared street to where the police van was parked up beside an octagonal fish shambles outside the Hildreds shopping centre. He led Sam into the back of the fishmonger's large wooden hut where, among the fridges, damp crates and an overpowering stench, a pair of officers were in conversation. A stubble-chinned man with hair trimmed so short he was only one barbering accident away from complete baldness had the three pips of a Chief Inspector on his shoulder epaulettes. In her work with DefCon4, Sam had been in contact with a number of local police officers, but knew some of them only by reputation. The name of the Skegness Chief Inspector momentarily eluded her. Her mind was saying 'Fuzz-something', but that couldn't be right.

"Did you check the front door to the bank?" the Chief Inspector asked the officer with Sam.

"Andy did."

"And it was locked?"

"It was locked."

"Hmmm." He realised Sam was there.

"This woman says she's on the phone to someone inside," offered the officer.

"The bank robber?" asked the Chief Inspector.

"It's my dad. Who is not the bank robber," she added quickly. She held up the phone and put it on speaker. "Dad, I'm outside with the police."

"We're still here," Marvin whispered.

The Chief Inspector inclined his head towards the phone. "Sir, this is Chief Inspector Dave Peach. Can you tell me where you are and your situation?"

"Fuzzy Peach," Sam nodded softly to herself, remembering what the other officers called their guv.

Chief Inspector Dave 'Fuzzy' Peach gave her a sharp look, but said nothing.

"I'm in one of the little meeting rooms with Tez Malik. He's one of the bank people."

"I'm the mortgage and business advisor," added Tez. *"As Mr Applewhite said, we're in one of the meeting rooms on the ... is it the south side of the building? The bit facing towards the beach."*

"East side then, surely," said Marvin.

"I thought Skegness was more sort of angled to the south," said Tez. *"If you look on a map..."*

"No. I got taught this method by Brian Blessed. Are you too young to remember Brian Blessed? He climbed Everest, but also, and perhaps more significantly, he and I found our way across the Brecon Beacons without map or compass—"

"And the robbers?" Peach cut in.

"Um, we think there might only be one," said Tez. *"It sounded like the farmer who came in for a loan earlier."*

"One?" said Peach. "Are you sure?"

"We think he took them into the back rooms."

"Where's Delia, dad?" Sam asked. "Is she still there?"

"I think she's with the other hostages?" said Marvin. *"Sorry."*

Sam felt a sudden heaviness on her chest and immediately thought of Delia's family, at home, who had no idea what was going on.

Peach cupped his hand over the phone and turned to one of his officers. "Only one. This is good news."

"You think you can talk him out of there?" asked Sam. The man ignored her.

"A criminal gang, we'd need the firearms, helicopters, TAPT from Nottinghamshire. Big budget expenditure, and budgets are so tight. Sure, things look fine at the moment, but all we need is a bunch of mods showing up again and our local policing budget is blown. If it's just one man..."

"This is a somewhat bigger issue than the mods," the other officer pointed out, reasonably enough as far as Sam was concerned.

"You kidding me?" said Peach. "A hundred hooligans on mopeds who don't realise that Quadrophenia was decades ago, coming down the seafront in search of trouble."

"What's Quadrophenia?"

"Exactly. You'd think the fact most of these mods are old age pensioners should make them easier to deal with but, let me tell you—" He realised Sam was standing there, watching him. He cleared his throat. "Yes. Thank you for bringing this to us." He spoke into the phone "Sir, if I give you a number would you be able to phone us on it?"

"I have a pen," said Tez.

"Good." As Peach began to reel off a number, Sam saw a familiar face emerge from a car which had just drawn up beyond the open front of the fish hut.

Detective Constable Lucas Camara was a distinctive figure: a tall, angular man. Although Sam didn't want to think of him as awkward or gangly or slightly robotic in his movements, there were shades of those things in his attitude and movement. A better comparison, she thought, and a more charitable one, would be a long-legged wading bird that had taken on human form and decided to devote its time to solving crime. She liked thinking charitable thoughts about Camara, and hadn't yet decided if it was because he was a sane man in a world gone mad, or because she fancied the dark-haired detective just a wee bit.

Sam gave him a wave, felt it was too jaunty given the seriousness of the situation and tried to correct it mid-action, which made it look clumsy and weird. She gave up on the wave. Camara hurried over. He never hunched but he always acted like he was mildly embarrassed for being so offensively tall.

He raised his eyebrows in greeting to Sam and gave a nod to Peach. "Sir. What's the sitrep? Anything I can do?"

"Lone suspect, we think. I'm waiting on a call from a person inside." He passed Sam's phone back to her. "Thank you for your help, miss. If you'd move over there, behind the tape."

"My dad's inside the bank," Sam told Camara. "He's hiding and he's got a phone."

Camara's eyes widened. "Marvin's in there?"

Sam nodded. "So's Delia. She's with the other hostages, but Marvin's hiding in a side office with Tez."

"And there's images from inside," said Camara, holding his own phone.

"From the bank's CCTV?" asked Peach.

"Instagram. Someone called @bexcanboogie. She posted a video right at the start and she's sent like a dozen posts already."

Camara held the phone out for all to see the social media posts. The first one of the day was pedestrian enough.

SORT OUT YOUR *ATM* MACHINE *EASTSHIRES BANK!* SOME OF US HAVE BUSY LIVES. *WHY IS IT MY JOB TO REPORT THE FAULT IN YOUR MACHINES??*

"It wasn't more than ten minutes later that she'd posted this video," said Camara. "Along with the comment *THIS JUST HAPPENED. SOMEONE CALL POLICE.*"

The sound quality was poor, but it clearly showed a big man wielding a large knife at the bank manager.

"And we're going to let all these nice people go, aren't we?" said a woman's voice.

"What?" This was the robber's gruff voice. He juggled the big knife with something in his other hand that looked like a wrapped up shotgun.

"Oh God! Delia!" said Sam as she saw Delia on the screen, briefly but very clearly cowering against the counter.

"Don't you go anywhere!" said the robber. *"Everyone get down on the ground! This is a robbery!"*

The video became jumpy, then ended abruptly.

"This is terrible," said Sam.

"Behind the tape now, miss," said Peach.

"But I know that man," she said. "The robber. I know him. He's a local farmer. Bruce Greencock."

"You sure?" said Peach.

"He's a client." She saw the chief inspector's blank look. "DefCon4. We do security. I. I do security."

"Then it seems you know half the people in the bank right now."

A phone outside started ringing and was immediately answered. Peach stepped outside and called for someone to bring him a megaphone.

Sam's phone buzzed. She pulled it out eagerly in case it was her dad.

YOUR GEOLOCATION IS NOT COMPATIBLE WITH YOUR DAY'S SCHEDULED ACTIVITIES. PLEASE RETURN TO THE OFFICE.

Sam stared. DefCon4's automated systems attempted to run her life, that was a given. This tech-enabled snooping on her whereabouts was nothing short of creepy. How was it possible that the system was smart enough to know she wasn't where she was supposed to be, and still somehow unaware that the office in question had burned down? She pocketed the phone and decided she had bigger things to worry about right now, and a bleating phone app was not going to change her mind.

～

BRUCE LOOKED ROUND at the group in the back office. The bank people, Justin, Mercedes and Stevie stood to his side, watching him carefully. The members of the public hovered, distracted a little by the unfamiliar surroundings. Delia in the dungarees looked like either a hippy or a mum on the verge of a nervous breakdown. The Instagrammer – what was it? Bexcanboogie? – seemed more put out by the loss of her phone than by any threat to her children. He didn't know the names of the horrible little tykes, deciding to think of them as Falafel and Hummus. The children were opening desk drawers to see what was inside. One of them pulled out a hole punch and squeezed it open and shut. It squeaked slightly and made them both laugh.

He had to find a way through this. He needed to keep control of the situation, but he had no real idea of how to do that.

"Listen!" he barked. There was silence at that. It was a flat, scared silence. "I didn't plan to do this thing here, but it's done now. I'm going to need you to help me by sitting here quietly while I try to work things out." He gave a pointed look at the children.

There was a squawk from outside, and then a voice. It was muffled, coming through thick walls and reinforced windows, but amplified to the point of distortion.

"This is Chief Inspector Dave Peach of the Lincolnshire Police! Come outside with your hands high above your head!"

"Well, that's it then," said Justin. "Game's up."

Delia put her hand up.

"What part of sitting quietly wasn't clear?" snapped Bruce.

"Yes, I heard you, but I have a suggestion."

He glared stonily at her. "What?"

"You say you need to work things out, right? Well, you've got all these people here. I reckon we could all get our thinking caps on and help you." She looked round the room. "Am I right?"

"What the hell?" said Justin.

Mercedes spoke up. "No. That's a very good idea. For one reason or another, we're all keen for this to be over. We should discuss the best way to do that."

"We have a whiteboard over there," said Stevie, pointing. "I'll find some pens."

"Wait! Stop!" Bruce said. "I don't know why you think this is some sort of team exercise. It's not a group activity. It's for me to decide what happens here." He stabbed a finger onto the desk in emphasis.

"The decisions are yours Bruce, that's definitely the case," said Delia. "But we can help with some practical stuff, help you focus."

"Do I looking like I fucking need help?" he roared.

There was a stunned silence. Bruce felt it was a silence in which anything could happen and he realised that, for a second or two, he had completely lost control over himself. If the mood had taken him, he might have resorted to terrible acts of violence.

"When we use bad language we've already lost the argument, haven't we, mummy?" said the little boy. Falafel.

"Aunt Judith swears," said the little girl. Hummus.

"Aunt Judith has a drinking problem. It's a proper illness, isn't it, mummy?"

"Look, I know you're all trying to be helpful," said Bruce with deliberate calmness. "And I ... I don't really know what I'm doing."

"Okay," said Mercedes, taking one of the offered board markers from Stevie. "So, let's get some suggestions down, shall we?"

17

Camara and Sam stepped outside the fishmonger's hut so he could take notes from her while Peach and his officers spoke to Marvin and Tez inside. It should have felt good to step away from the fishy stench, but Sam wasn't sure she was even breathing. It felt like she had taken a sharp gasp of breath when she heard her dad and friend had been taken hostage, and she wouldn't let go of it again until they were safe once more. She felt dizzy, waiting to exhale.

"You okay?" asked Camara, putting a supportive hand under her elbow.

"Should I be?" she said.

"It's possible to feel all manner of things when our loved ones are in danger."

"I don't think I've ever had a scare like this before," she said and then, despite herself, chuckled. "I mean there was the lumberjack trick."

"Lumberjack trick?"

"He'd devised it for the International Federation of Magic Societies competition in ... I must have been about six or seven. It was in Holland. The trick involved him being inside a fake tree trunk when it was sawn in half with a chainsaw."

"Fake chainsaw?"

"No. Very real. That's why I was terrified. The success of the trick relied on his being able to drop down and squish into the base of this tree trunk. This was a man in his fifties at the time, and you've heard him complain about his knees. I was on the fourth row and terrified. This—" She waved her hand at the bank on the far side of the fish stall and police van. "I wouldn't be surprised if he does something foolish."

"Your dad will do everything in his power to get safely back to you," said Camara.

Sam felt a sudden jolt of anger. "You do not know him, Lucas. My dad is many things. He's funny and he's fun and wants to laugh and have the whole world laughing with him, but do not, for one single instant, pretend that he thinks about the needs of other people or himself."

"I'm sure he loves you."

"Of course he loves me! But that's not enough. He's only in there because he's so damned careless that he's in danger of losing the house we both live in. He's like ... he's like the pied piper of Hamelin. He'll play his tune and wiggle his curly-toed shoes and we'll all go merrily dancing off with him into a dark cave beneath the world."

Camara nodded slowly. "Curly-toed shoes?"

Sam snorted with further unexpected mirth. "I'm sorry.

Fear makes me bitter and angry. Of course he loves me. Of course he cares. But he's a fool."

"A lucky one though. He survived the lumberjack trick."

"Of course he did. Got an honourable mention, only losing out to Norbert Ferré." She looked at Camara, trying to read something in his long chiselled face. "What's going to happen now?"

Camara thought. "First up, despite what Peach says, the Tactical Armed Policing Team will be on their way here from Nottinghamshire. That's like the SWAT team. They train for this stuff all the time. Very good at their job. A trained negotiator will be called for too."

"It's going to come to that? A siege?"

He shook his head. "Not necessarily. This guy Bruce could come to his senses at any moment and come walking out of there, hands held high. He's just one man. He's got no back up, no one in his corner. He's alone, and loneliness will probably break him."

18

"Okay, everyone, let's work on this together," said Delia, turning to the whiteboard in the back office. "Now Bruce, I did some business development with the Skegness and District Local Business Guild a while back, won an award in fact, and they taught me the importance of having a clear vision. Shall we work through what your vision for this could be?"

Bruce shook his head. "This is stupid. I don't have a vision. Not unless it's to undo what led me here."

Mercedes stepped forward, her face earnest. "Bruce, we can do exactly that. You haven't done anything yet that can't be reversed. We can just go outside and talk to the police and all explain it's been a terrible mistake."

"That's ridiculous!" spluttered Justin. "He threatened me with a deadly weapon. He's going down."

Delia held up her hand. "Only constructive thoughts please, Justin. Now, how should we capture these ideas?

Shall we call vision one 'Bruce lets us all go and hands himself over to the police'? That means vision two is some version of 'Bruce robs the bank and gets away with it', yes?" Delia wrote them down on the board.

Bruce could see that Justin was angry and scared, but he had a point about Bruce going down. "Get rid of the first one," he said to Delia. "It's not realistic."

"Great." Delia rubbed option one away with the heel of her hand. "Perhaps there are other options. Anyone? What else should we think about?"

One of the children raised a hand.

"Er, yes?" said Delia. "What's your name?"

"Edith. I'm seven."

Bruce found himself oddly disappointed with the normality of the name. He decided to stick with 'Hummus'; in his own mind, at least.

"You have an idea for something else we should think about, Edith?" asked Delia.

"Yes," said Edith solemnly. "We should think about people starving in Africa, and eat up our couscous."

Delia's hand was poised to write, but she paused and turned to Edith. "An important point, Edith. Thank you."

"Write it down, then."

Delia wrote *couscous* at the top of the board and turned with a sigh. "Well Bruce, it looks as though we should focus on ideas to help you rob the bank and get away with it."

"What about cameras?" said the woman with the shopping bags. She pointed at the ceiling. "I guess there are cameras in here?"

Delia added it to the list. "So, what options does Bruce

have to deal with the cameras? Can someone from the bank tell us?"

The cashier, Stevie, spoke up. "We can access the camera feeds. Well, someone can."

Mercedes nodded. "We can turn them off, or we can make it so that they only feed a particular computer."

"That one," said Bruce. "I want it so that I can see the cameras but people outside can't."

"You're helping him," Justin hissed. "Why are you helping him? Have you lost your minds?" Justin paced the floor, his skin shiny with sweat.

"It's very simple," said Delia. "Everyone in this room wants to make sure that nobody comes to any harm. That includes Bruce, I believe. If we all keep our heads and sort this situation out, then that's a good thing, isn't it?"

"Gah!" Justin looked as if he was going to explode. "What kind of people would this great nation be if we just negotiated with every Tom, Dick and Harry that threatened us, eh?"

"You're not helping," said Mercedes.

"Yeah," said Stevie. "Just chill."

"Oh well, that's rich!" bellowed Justin. "You just help him as much as you can. You have clearly misunderstood the customer-centricity course, Mercedes. It's only supposed to apply to *actual* customers, not bank robbers!"

"I have an idea," said the woman with the shopping, her hand in the air. "I think you should tie that man up. Gag him, too."

Delia wrote it down on the board. "Actually, let's elaborate on this theme of managing hostages," said Delia, adding a box on the board and making a fresh set of bullet points. "You're going to need to sort out drinks and toilet breaks. The more hostages you have, the harder that will be."

The comment hung in the air for a few moments.

Mercedes nodded. "Delia has a good point. Is there an option to let some of these nice people go, Bruce? What about the children?"

Bruce turned to look at Edith and her brother. Hummus and Falafel. Their mother was fiddling with the watch on her wrist, not even paying attention.

"I don't want to go," said Edith. "I want to stay here with mummy and Evan."

At that, the little boy next to her burst into tears. Bruce, who had found his own children confusing enough, couldn't see what had triggered this reaction. Evan sobbed loudly, and then his sister joined in as well. The two of them wailed louder and louder, seemingly in competition with each other.

"Can you stop them doing that?" Bruce said to their mother.

She looked up from her watch. "Stop them?"

Bruce waved his machete in the general direction of the blonde noise machines.

"What kind of parent would I be if I did that?" asked the mother.

Bruce didn't know how to answer that. It sounded like a trick question. "I want them to be quiet."

"And stifle their emotions? Crush their spirits? You can't just do that, especially if you're going to break the sacred bond of trust."

"What?"

"They've been patiently waiting for you to tie Justin up and gag him. It's all about carrying through with the things that you've said you'll do."

"No one's tying me up," said Justin. "I am the manager of this branch! That position comes with a degree of concomitant respect."

Bruce wanted to think, and these people were conspiring to stop him from having any clarity of thought. He hadn't actually agreed to tie up Justin, had he? Perhaps he had. He couldn't remember. There were too many things happening, too many voices, too many ideas.

"Right, everyone shut up," he barked. "And that includes you two too," he said to the children, who immediately closed their howling traps and looked at him through red-rimmed eyes.

"Perhaps we should get back to the board?" asked Delia, tapping the pen in the MANAGING HOSTAGES box. "What do you think about the idea of letting some people go, Bruce?"

"I'm not doing anything hasty." In truth, he was worried that anyone stepping out of this room would take too much knowledge of his situation with them.

"Moving on then, I imagine you'll want to get access to money?" asked Delia.

"If we need to access the main vault, it needs two of us," said Mercedes.

"This collaboration will not factor well into your next performance appraisal, Mercedes," growled Justin.

Delia made a note on the board. "What about carrying the money?" she asked. "Bruce will need some bags."

They all looked at the woman with the shopping bags. She gave a heavy sigh. "I only came in to report the faulty ATM," she said. "Fine, you can have these. They're proper M&S bags for life, very strong."

She began unpacking items from her bags onto a desk. "Everything from the chiller cabinet and freezer is going to be ruined."

Mercedes gently took the second bag and began to help remove the contents. There were more chilled ready meals, plus a number of dry goods. Bruce noted a rectangular tin of mustard powder, a tube of chilli flakes, a bag of flour and a bag of sugar.

"Planning some spicy cooking?" he asked.

"Hairy Bikers' chicken schnitzel, if you must know," said the mother. "And be careful with that champagne."

"I will," said Mercedes. "What's your name?"

"It's Becky. Becky Mitten. Two t's, with an 'e' not an 'o'."

"Sorry about your groceries, Becky. These bags should work well for Bruce, thank you."

Delia was paying careful attention to the shopping. "Do I spy Cornish pasties?"

"They're chicken and chorizo empanadas with a honey glaze," said Becky.

"We've cooked Gordon Ramsay's beef empanadas, haven't we, mummy?" said the boy, Evan, his tears completely forgotten.

"Shame we can't cook these," said Delia.

"Who can think of food at a time like this?" Justin muttered.

"Actually, the microwave in the break room is a combi

oven," remarked Stevie. "Although I'm not sure how it works."

"Yes, I suspect I'm the only one who ever bothered to read the instructions," said Mercedes.

"You won't need food," said Justin. "The police are outside. We won't be in here that long."

Bruce stood tall, suddenly alert to the possibility that the police were trying to gain entry to the building right now.

"The front door is secured with an iron bolt security lock," Mercedes told him. "It will resist most attempts to pick the lock and you certainly couldn't crowbar it open. But of course, they might barge their way in with a battering ram thing. It's very unlikely they could get in quietly that way, though. You'd definitely hear them."

"Righty-ho," said Delia, heading back to the board. "So, perhaps there's an important thing we haven't talked about yet, Bruce. How can you escape from this? I guess if you're going to get away with it, then you have to escape from here, and you don't go home."

"I can't go home," mused Bruce. He wasn't going to dwell on the irony of this situation. In an attempt to save his farm, he'd created a situation where he could never go back there. The climbing frame would never get fixed. His children would never climb on it again.

"You could go to Poland," said Stevie.

"Pardon?" said Delia.

"I had a Polish boyfriend once and—"

"You had a boyfriend?" asked Mercedes in tactless surprise.

"I did," said Stevie firmly. "And the Polish definitely grow and eat a lot of cabbage over there."

Delia jotted ESCAPE TO POLAND on the board.

Stevie scowled at Mercedes. "You think I'm some sort of sexless nun or something?"

"Well, not a nun," said Mercedes.

The little girl, Hummus – no, *Edith* – had her hand raised.

"Edith?" said Delia.

"If we write down the man's secret escape plans, won't the police know where to find him?"

"Point," said Delia. "I'll put some other options down to throw them off the scent." She amended the list to include Peru, Penzance and Peterborough.

19

Camara had his notepad in his hand. "This guy in there. Bruce Greencock? Tell me about him."

"Owns a farm out on Marsh House Road," said Sam. "It runs all the way down to the coast. Cabbages. He's got a thing for cabbages."

"A thing?"

"I mean he's passionate about them."

"Family?"

"I think he lives alone. Divorced I guess, but I never asked him."

"And his state of mind? Would you say he was of a fit state of mind?"

"Apart from having a thing for cabbages?"

"Apart from that."

"Absolutely. I was over there this morning. We were talking about business plans and insurance premiums. Very ordinary stuff. He was definitely making plans for the future, you know? We were trying to get his premiums down by putting these security dot things on all the valuable gear. You know, the tractor and harvester and—"

Realisation socked Sam in the chest and she fumbled for her phone.

"What is it?" said Camara.

"We put tracking devices on all his shotguns."

"What?"

"Tiny Bluetooth-enabled tracking devices. Any phone with the app in range..." She unlocked her phone, found the security widget app.

Camara looked back at the bank. "You're not going to be close enough for Bluetooth."

"But if Bruce installed it on his phone... Besides my dad has it on his. If they're both on, we can triangulate on any widgets in the building."

The app screen awoke, Sam tapped her PIN in and a local map appeared. She zoomed in with two fingers so she could see the local streets.

"There!" A pulsing blue dot in the location of the bank was marked as MARVIN'S PHONE.

"And these?" said Camara.

There was a cluster of other pulsing dots next to Marvin – seven, eight, nine – too close together to tell. They were marked with hashtags and number strings.

"Bruce won't have had time to register each of the widgets on the database. He's got a lot there. One should be the shotgun. The others..." She frowned. "Did he bring all the shotguns?"

"They're heavy items," said Camara.

She clicked her fingers. "He put the spare widgets in his pocket this morning. Maybe he's got more than one gun, but the others could just be spare widgets."

"So, regardless, that's him." Camara tilted his head.

"It's not GPS, and it's working through walls," she conceded. "I can't guarantee the location accuracy."

"Oh, no. But this is good. And TAPT are here."

A big square bloke, wearing police black camos but conspicuously lacking any of the usual hi-vis garb, came through the automatic doors of the Hildred's shopping centre in the company of a police officer who was struggling to keep pace.

"Come on," said Camara to Sam. They followed the men into the back of the fishmonger's stall.

"Sergeant Kemenes Kovács. Call me Kenny," the big bloke was saying to Peach.

"Chief Inspector Peach," replied Peach and shook his hand.

"Sir. We've got five three-man teams setting up out of sight in the shopping centre behind. Women's clothing shop. Plenty of room. They've been very accommodating. I've taken the liberty of getting PC Lightfoot to scout out observer positions on the shopping centre roof but want to co-ordinate with you before deployment." The lantern-jawed sergeant made a show of looking round the small area, and the stacked crates they were using as seats. "Is this ... shack your critical incident command base?"

"It is."

"Doesn't the Lincolnshire police have—"

"Budgetary issues," said Peach curtly.

"They're expecting a big influx of mods," said Sam helpfully.

"Mods?"

"Geriatrics looking for equally geriatric rockers with whom to start a very slow ruckus."

"The complexities of local policing—" began Peach, but Sergeant Kenny cut him off.

"—Means we're operating out of a fish stall," he said. He pulled down a tray of cooked prawns in a clingfilm covered tray and ate one. "Some of the lads and I haven't had breakfast."

Camara tried to step into a more prominent position in the cramped room. "Sam here put some security trackers on the suspect's shotgun only this morning. We've got a potential location fix."

"And you are?" asked Sergeant Kenny.

"DefCon4. Security company," she said. "I've really got nothing to do with all this." She paused to correct herself. "My dad's in there. And my friend. And I met Bruce this morning. The, er, suspect. Prior to all this, of course. We were putting security trackers on his valuables. He's got a bunch of them on him right now." She held out her phone so all could see the blinking dots on the screen map.

"And have your company got access to the CCTV in there?" asked Peach.

"I don't know if that's anything to do with us," said Sam.

Kenny made a distasteful grimace. "Most banks only have cameras for show. They'll have gone to the cheapest third-rate provider they could find."

"Ah," said Sam, heavy with the knowledge of who the cheapest third-rate security provider usually was.

20

Marvin had been eyeing up the drinks trolley in the corner of the side office for some time.

He and Tez sat on the floor behind the desk, ensuring they were out of sight of the little office window in case anyone walked past. They hadn't seen or heard anyone for a while, though.

They had a wad of printer paper and a pen sitting between them, to be used as a silent communication tool. They had agreed talking out loud was to be kept to a minimum. The phone call to the police was still there if they needed it, but they had made it clear they would not be chatting for the sake of it, and the policeman on the line had told them keep still, stay hidden, and pass on any information they came upon.

Marvin jotted a note and passed it to Tez.

My phone's got plenty of charge, we can move around, maybe find out more info for the police?

He looked at Tez's face, eyebrows raised to ask the question.

Tez took the pen and wrote a response in a blocky, almost childish script that Marvin wouldn't have expected of the man.

Risky. What if we get spotted?

Marvin tapped the side of his nose.

I'm an old hand at being sneaky! I have an idea.

Tez pulled a doubtful face, but Marvin ignored him. He stood up from their temporary hiding place, walked to the front of the office, and took a few moments to stretch himself. Tez followed suit and popped up from behind the desk, wide-eyed like a cartoon meerkat. Marvin struck a magician's pose and raised a finger in the air, indicating that he was about to show Tez some magic. He went to the coat stand in the corner of the room and took a wooden coat hanger from it, dropping the jacket draped around it to the floor. Tez made a muted growling sound, from which Marvin gathered it was his jacket.

Marvin then went over to the drinks trolley and hauled the sleek black coffee machine off the top, leaving the little caddy of bottled waters next to it. The machine was heavier than it looked, possibly because it also carried a full tank of water. He shoved the machine against the wall. Then he opened the sliding side door, quickly removed the cups, saucers, tea bags and replacement coffee pods stored there, and lifted out the middle shelf.

He made a small *ta-da* motion to indicate the capacious inner space. He dropped to his hands and knees and began to climb in.

"You'll never fit!" Tez hissed.

"I've fitted into smaller spaces," Marvin whispered back. "There was this lumberjack and chainsaw trick I did in Holland once—" He grunted and huffed as he dragged his feet into place with his hands. There was a moment of panic when he feared he would end up wedged with his foot out of the door and his knee trapped under his chin, but with a bit of wiggling and the odd twinge, he squeezed himself into the space.

Although he was twisted into a shape unimaginable for most people of a similar age, his left hand was still free. He reached around himself and slid the door shut. He could close it fully, which was good, but he would need to get around, so he opened it enough to get a decent view and stuck his arm back out.

"Phone!" he hissed to Tez.

Tez passed him the phone, looking quite dubious. "What are you doing?"

By way of demonstration, Marvin put his hand outside the half-open door again and used the coat hanger to punt himself along the floor. He could only move a tiny distance with each movement, but that was also good, because he needed his exploration to go unnoticed.

"This is madness," Tez whispered.

"We have friends who need our help," Marvin whispered back.

"You're going to get us killed."

"You're repossessing my house," Marvin reminded him. "I am filled with a nothing-to-lose attitude at the moment."

After a couple of minutes of intricate manoeuvring, he

realised it might have been wiser to start by placing the tea trolley in a more convenient location for his exit.

Tez must have noticed his growing frustration, because he grabbed the handle of the tea trolley, turned him around and slid him outside the door. "Bon voyage!" he whispered, withdrawing back into the office and closing the door silently but firmly.

THE WHITEBOARD in the back office of the bank was a mass of notes, scribbles, arrows and doodles. There was a helicopter with a rope ladder hanging from it, from when Stevie had discussed the possibility of the police SWAT teams arriving by chopper. There were rows of flowers along the bottom left hand edge, drawn by the little girl, Edith 'Hummus' Mitten. Along the bottom right hand edge was an oval surrounded by squares and names, which apparently represented Evan 'Falafel' Mitten's fantasy dinner party. He'd put Craig Revel Horwood off *Strictly Come Dancing* next to the American president.

"It's a plan," said Bruce doubtfully.

"Yes," said Mercedes, slowly. What it had been was a time-killer, and in that respect, at least, it had worked.

It should also have been a clear demonstration to Bruce that any plans he had to seize the money and escape were utterly doomed. If he loaded up a bag with cash and ran out the front door, the police would have him in seconds. If he was lucky, they would wrestle him to the ground. If he was unlucky, they would fill him with bullets first. Mercedes wasn't sure if there were such things as SWAT teams in the UK, but she knew the police had access to guns when they needed them. And even if Bruce somehow made it past the police and avoided getting marked by the smart water system's forensic code, hidden dye packs would explode in his bag, marking the loot and him. If, by some miracle, he circumvented all these measures, then there was the brutally inescapable fact that his name and appearance were publicly known. There would be no ground for him to go to. In such a situation, any sane human being would hand themselves in.

"Right, let's do this," he said.

"We're doing it?" asked Mercedes.

Bruce's broad shoulders shrugged. "It's like Justin says. I'm going down for this anyway. Best go down trying."

Mercedes gave Justin a withering glare, but the power of the stare just bounced off the buffoon.

Bruce stabbed a finger at a portion of the board. "Secure front door." His finger moved to another. "Cut communications." Another portion. "Kill security cameras. Go to vault. Collect small denomination bank notes to the value of two hundred thousand pounds. Make escape."

Make escape. Two small words to encompass the impossible, thought Mercedes.

And make chicken and chorizo empanada!" said Evan.

"We can definitely cook them when we return."

"And bring bowls and spoons for the roulade. If it's salvageable."

Salvageable. Such a long word out of a precocious child's mouth sounded worrying rather than impressive.

"Why not take all the money in the vault?" asked the mother, Becky Mitten. "Don't limit yourself."

"You're giving him ideas!" Justin spat.

Bruce threw him an irritated look. "I'm not a thief, Becky. I mean ... I mean I'm obviously a thief – although I am going to pay it back. With interest. Two hundred thousand is what I need. I worked it out."

"Very noble," said Delia, judiciously.

"You've all gone mad," Justin sighed.

"Now will someone please tie Justin up," said Becky. "I think that will probably suit us all very well."

"Not really, it—" Justin began, but Becky had already selected a wheely chair for him to be tied to.

"Come on!" he whined.

"This is happening," said Bruce, weighing his machete meaningfully in his hand.

Becky unfastened the leather shoulder strap from her handbag and used it to tie Justin's wrists behind him. She stepped back to regard her work and Delia nodded in approval.

Bruce stepped forward. "Now, do you want a gag, or can you be quiet?" he asked Justin.

Justin made small grumblings of protest, but then clamped his lips firmly shut.

"Good." Bruce looked at Mercedes. "You. You know how the security systems and vault and that work."

Mercedes didn't particularly want to be singled out, but honesty overcame her. "Not a hundred percent, but better than anyone else here."

Stevie began to look offended, but immediately relented. "Yeah, she's right."

"Good," said Bruce. "The rest of you, sit down. We're going to have to tie you up too."

"You can't!" said Becky.

"We helped you," said Delia.

Bruce didn't look comfortable with this new phase. "Yes. You did. And now you're going to help me by sitting here, tied up, while—" He paused.

"Mercedes."

"—Mercedes and I go sort things out."

"You can't tie up the children," said Stevie. Mercedes couldn't help noticing Becky hadn't bothered to raise the same point.

Bruce massaged his chin in thought. "They'll come with us."

"And leave mummy here?" asked Evan. He didn't quite say it like it was a terrible thing.

"You'll get to see the bank vault," said Bruce.

"It'll be like going to visit Gringott's Bank in Harry Potter," said Mercedes.

"We're not allowed to have Harry Potter books in the house," said Evan.

"JK Rowling is a problematic author," said Edith.

"Oh," said Mercedes.

Bruce went to the router cabinet and tore out several lengthy network cables. He instructed Stevie, Delia and Becky to sit down and proceeded to tie each of them, hands behind their backs, to chair uprights. Stevie and Becky were tied to the two remaining wheeled chairs in the room, Delia to a wooden chair that looked like it belonged in a kitchen rather than an office. Mercedes moved to help, thinking to hurry things along and possibly leave some loose knots in the process, but Bruce double-checked them and added extra cables of his own. By the time they were done, Edith and Evan were helping fetch cables from the cabinet, colour sorting them before handing them over.

Bruce stood. "Done. Now to check the doors and prepare some defences."

From the foodstuffs on the table he gathered together the flour, sugar, chilli flakes, mustard powder and the bottle of champagne.

"What are you doing with my shopping?" asked Becky.

"Planning some spicy cooking of my own," said Bruce. "Going to take your marbles as well, Delia, if you don't mind."

"Feel free," said Delia.

21

Marvin was making very slow progress in his coffee cabinet canoe. He'd steered himself out the door and was slowing punting across the lobby to the main front doors. They were stout things of dark old wood, perhaps original from when the bank building was built several decades ago. Through the gap in the trolley door he could see there were huge wrought iron bolts securing the door, but no means of determining if the door was properly locked.

With little grunts of efforts, he propelled himself to the door.

"I'm going for the door," he whispered to the phone resting on his scrunched up knees.

There was a tinny reply from the police inspector, but in the position he was in, Marvin couldn't make it out.

"This reminds me of the time Lionel Blair and I tried sea-canoeing in Canada. You know, Lionel Blair? Consummate entertainer, *Give Us A Clue*, all that. He was Canadian originally, did you know that? Anyway, Lionel needed the loo and we drew up to the shore, but there was this bear waiting for us on the shore." Marvin paused to get his breath and think. "For the life of me now I can't remember what sort of bear it was. You'd think I'd remember the colour. Anyway..."

Marvin realised he was as close to the front door as he was going to get without running onto the thick entrance carpet, which might possibly prove impassable for the trolley's little wheels.

"Hang on," he said and slid the door wider so he could climb out. This was a slow process for old knees. It took a full ten seconds to co-ordinate one leg, and Marvin just got a foot out of the door when he heard a door bang open and voices approaching.

"Bugger!" As rapidly as he could, he pulled the leg inside and slid the door closed.

"See?" said a man's voice. The bank robber, Bruce, Marvin imagined. "Now, come along you two. I want you to be quiet, understand?"

There was a pause.

"Understand?" repeated the man.

"You're sending very mixed messages," came a child's voice. "How can we tell you we understand if we're supposed to be silent?"

"Come on, we're wasting time." A woman's voice. Mercedes. "They understand."

"No, not really," said the child. "Children need clear boundaries, so please explain whether it's silence you really want."

"I really want silence. Now, hold Mercedes' hand." Bruce gave a sudden bark of laughter.

"What?" said Mercedes.

"Edith Mitten. Evan Mitten. You have a pair of Mittens. One on each hand."

In the confines of the dark cabinet, Marvin tilted his head in appreciation.

"But mittens are identical," said the girl, Edith. "We're not."

"Your pun is contrived and doesn't work," said the boy, Evan.

Bruce harrumphed.

"I thought it was funny," said Mercedes. There was the clunking sound of a heavy key turning in a lock.

Marvin could have sworn in irritation. There was the long, irritating scraping sound of heavy furniture being dragged across the floor and in front of the door. He was grateful his hiding place didn't become part of the barricade.

"There," said Bruce. "Now to secure the back door and the upstairs in case SWAT decide to come in that way."

"Are you going to use the champagne to do that?" asked a child.

"I certainly am," said Bruce. "Using a trick I learned off Brainiac."

"Brainiac?" said Mercedes.

"Remember Brainiac? Think it was on Channel 5. With John Tickle."

"You're making this up," she said as they moved away again.

"What kind of name is Mercedes anyway?" asked Bruce.

"Are we going to go there?" said Mercedes.

"It's unusual. Your dad a big car fan?"

"That's right. Bring out the jokes. And you know absolutely nothing about my parents." The voices were moving away again. "For your information," said Mercedes, "Mercedes is a perfectly common name in Spanish-speaking countries."

"You Spanish?"

"My heritage is not a subject for discussion."

There was the sound of a door.

"I'm not mocking," said Bruce. "You're talking to a man whose surname is Green*cock*—"

The door clicked shut and there was silence.

Marvin swore at the bad timing of it all. If he'd been a minute faster to the door, he'd have had it open and been able to let the police in. He opened the door a crack to let in a modicum of light and put his phone to his ear.

"Did you hear all that, inspector?" he said.

"You should be staying hidden, Mr Applewhite."

"Bruce brought Mercedes out, and the children, something and something Mittens."

Inspector Peach spoke to someone else nearby.

"Don't do anything stupid, dad," called Sam from a distance.

"Of course. You know me," he said and put the phone back on his lap and punted the tea trolley back towards the office where Tez remained hidden. He rapped gently on the door of the office. Tez peered round the door, his face anguished.

"Jesus Christ, Marvin! You'll be the death of me."

"Interesting. Do Muslims say 'Jesus Christ'?"

"That's what you knocked to ask?"

"I need to know what the code for the key pad is, Tez. I need to get in the back."

"I can't tell you that," said Tez. "It would be a major breach of security."

Marvin tried hard to pull a quizzical face, but in his current position – scrunched up on the lower shelf of a tea trolley – he wasn't certain he'd manage it. "Tez, your bank is being robbed. I'd say that ship has sailed, wouldn't you?"

"I'll open it," said Tez.

It was only a few feet away, so Tez crept out, like a cartoon burglar, and typed the code into the keypad. He pushed the tea trolley through the doorway and retreated back into his sanctuary.

22

Mercedes thought Bruce's attempts to create defences against armed police were methodically laid out, if somewhat bizarre.

Without her assistance Bruce determined the main weak points on the bank were the fire exit door leading out into the back alley and the stairs leading down from the unused first floor. From the corridor there was a security door which led into a tiny, almost square section of corridor, then the fire exit door. Both could be opened instantly from inside, but not the outside. In the square of corridor was a heavy fire extinguisher on the wall.

"Perfect," said Bruce and took it off the wall.

"We shouldn't play with fire extinguishers," said Evan Mitten.

"I'm not playing," said Bruce. "I'm adapting." He looked at the glass panel in the security door and nodded. The fire extinguisher was taken back into the corridor.

"This way," he said. He led them to the kitchen. "Two microwaves?"

"Microwave – and that's the combi oven," said Mercedes, pointing at the two devices.

Bruce unplugged the microwave and hoisted it off the counter.

Out in the corridor, Mercedes watched in bemusement as Bruce first of all kicked out the lower glass panel of the security door to the fire exit area, then threaded the microwave power cable through it. He wedged the bottle of champagne in the microwave, closed the door, and turned the timer all the way round. It was only when he placed the now opened bags of flour and sugar on the top of the microwave that Evan asked, "What is he doing?"

"I actually have no idea," said Mercedes.

Bruce closed the door and pulled the power cable through, plugging it into the nearest power socket. The socket switch was off.

There was now a microwave loaded with fizz, with cooking ingredients on top, in the square of corridor.

"Flour and sugar are explosive," said Bruce.

"Right," said Mercedes. "And the champagne?"

"Brainiac," said Bruce. "Trust me."

"If I knew what you were doing..."

Bruce had her open up the security door to the upstairs.

"No one uses it at all," she said. "It's just open office space."

There was a steep flight of wooden steps, dotted with the remnants of carpet grippers. Bruce ascended slowly, cautiously. Mercedes saw he didn't let his head go any higher than the top step. Was he afraid a police sniper would shoot him through a window?

"Okay," he said, in the measured tones of someone who had assessed things. "Where are the marbles?"

"We've got them here," said Edith.

Bruce collected them from her and took them upstairs, where Mercedes heard him pour them carefully across one of the upper steps. There was a loud *tick-tick-tick* as one marble rolled away and bounced down the stairs. Grinning, Evan picked it up.

"Should work," said Bruce, coming down. He paused to unscrew the light bulb in the ceiling light halfway down the stairs. "Dark is better. Now, fire extinguisher?"

Edith pointed to the CO_2 extinguisher he'd brought through. Bruce pulled the funnel nozzle upwards, cast about a moment, found the mustard powder and chilli flakes, then proceeded to pour them into the funnel. He thumped the extinguisher on the ground to make them settle.

"Good," he said.

"Is it?" said Mercedes, none the wiser.

He now held two empty spice containers and a lightbulb. He fussed a moment, wondering where to put them. He went to put them in his coat pocket and realised there was something else already there. He reached in and came out with a handful of shotgun shells and some sheets of plastic squares.

"You always walk around with ammo in your pocket?" asked Mercedes.

"No," he said, frowning. He brushed one of the plastic

squares with his thumb. "These are security widgets. We were putting them on my guns earlier and..."

He trailed off, bored with his own sentence. He put the shotgun shells neatly in the mustard tin, then pointed at the red flashing light on a camera in the corner of the corridor.

"Let's sort out that CCTV."

23

There were things that were inevitable in life. As sure as the tide coming in and out, as sure as the cold east wind sweeping in from the North Sea, there were events that were unavoidable. A child begging in the fairground for the money to go on 'one last ride' would be sure to be begging for 'one last ride' five minutes later. If there was a half-price OAP special on at the seafront cafes, there would still be some tight bugger counting the number of chips on his plate and demanding more. And if there was a security job tendered out to the cheapest corner-cutting security firm, that job would go to DefCon4.

"Our company is the installer of CCTV in Eastshires Bank," admitted Sam after consulting her phone. A few moments later she had the imagery of interior cameras on her phone. Two minutes more and she had the same images up on the laptop placed on the fish-stall counter, between jars of tartare sauce and Styrofoam trays of crab sticks.

"Thank you very much, Sam," said Kenny, the firearms commander. "Let's take a look."

With keyboard clicks, he scrolled through. Lobby, corridors, offices, doorways—

"Hell, that's Delia," said Sam softly.

The screen showed an image of an office space. There were four occupants, all strapped to chairs. Two were clearly bank staff. A man was wearing a suit and a woman the sort of frill-fronted blouse no woman in the last two decades would have worn freely. It had to be uniform. The woman tied up next to Delia must have been another customer. The quality of the image was poor. Facial features and expressions were very hard to make out.

"What's that on the board?" said Kenny.

The five people in the fish stall tried to squint at the image.

"Can you enhance the image?" said Peach, stroking his bristly chin.

"That's not really a thing," said Sam.

"*Bruce robs the bank and gets away with it,*" read Camara slowly.

"That's what it says?"

"And there's a picture of a helicopter," said Kenny. "He plans an escape by helicopter?" He cocked his ear suddenly, as though expecting to hear the sound of an approaching chopper.

"That word's Penzance," said Peach. "And it says Craig something at the bottom."

"Craig Revel Horwood," said Sam.

"Who's that?" said Kenny.

"The judge off *Strictly*."

"Off what?"

"*Strictly Come Dancing*," said Peach. "You know, the dancing show on telly. To be honest, I don't know who half the celebrities are this year. I think they're scraping the barrel."

While Sam scrutinised the image, a part of her mind suggested they'd know when *Strictly* was scraping the bottom of the barrel when her dad got a call from the production team.

"Does Bruce know this Horwood character?" said Kenny.

"Or anyone in Penzance?" said Peach.

Sam was fairly confident the answer to both those questions was 'no'.

Kenny stepped away. "Can I get the access details for this so my spotters can log in?"

"Shouldn't be a problem," said Sam.

There was a woman at the doorway to the octagonal fish stall.

"Excuse me, I'm Zahra Bi," she said. "You're Chief Inspector David Peach."

Peach looked at her blankly. The woman was tall and bony, with large dark eyes, a snub nose, and a primly pursed mouth. She carried a heavy, old-fashioned carpet bag in one hand and a set of keys attached to a soft toy parrot which was a little too large to be a practical key fob.

"You are Chief Inspector David Peach, are you not?" she repeated.

"Well, yes, of course," said Peach.

"I am the hostage negotiator."

"Zahra Bi?"

"Lincolnshire Police outsources its hostage negotiations to a third party. I was notified when TAPT were summoned."

Peach stood. "Your ID?"

The Asian woman stepped inside.

"I make a point to never carry ID. Paper-based identification is a very old-fashioned idea, to my mind. You might as well ask me to provide a utility bill as proof of address."

In the small space, Peach tried to puff himself up. It was an embarrassing gesture to watch. "Is that so? Well, we'll have to see about that, won't we?"

"Noted. Now before this goes any further, you should know that I get paid whether the negotiations succeed or not. We must be very clear on that point, mustn't we?"

"Yes, we must," said Peach.

"I shall require a space to work in," said Zahra Bi, looking for somewhere on the wet floor to put her bag, saw there was none and held onto it. "Excuse me, but this appears to be a fish-seller's hut. Is this your base of operations?

"It is. For now."

"That's not normal, is it? I sometimes don't pick up on the idiosyncrasies of individual behaviour, but really, this doesn't seem normal."

"It's not," said Sam. "Inspector Peach is trying to cut costs. He's worried about a costly invasion of geriatric mods and doesn't want to blow his budget."

"I'm not sure I understand," said Zahra stiffly. "If some of that was slang, then I'm unfamiliar with it. Now, a place where I can work...?"

"Hmmm?" said Peach, still flummoxed by the woman's arrival.

"You *are* in charge of this incident?"

"I'm Chief Inspector Peach, yes."

"Very well then. A place to work and a drink if you could stretch to it."

Sam reached to the shelf behind her. "Tub of whelks?"

Zahra's little nose twitched distastefully. "Maybe a glass of water. Tap water will be fine. What's the situation?"

"We have a lone gunman with seven to nine hostages," said Firearms Kenny.

"That's an imprecise number," said Zahra.

"Two people in the bank were hiding, but they may not stay hidden for long," said Peach. "One already appears to have gone walkabouts."

"My dad," said Sam. "Sorry. He's prone to wandering. He used to be a magician."

Zahra made an alarmed face. "Like Gandalf?"

"Stage tricks."

"I see. Has the bank robber made any demands?"

"We've not established a line of communication with him yet," said Peach.

"He was going to the bank to get a loan for his cabbage farm," said Sam. "The man is big into his cabbages. Crazy."

"It's a rich source of vitamins C, K, B6 and folate," said Zahra.

"No one likes cabbage," said Peach.

"Have you conducted a survey?"

"No."

"Well, then. Family? The suspect, not the cabbage."

"He lives alone," said Sam. "His wife left him, taking the children."

"What age?"

"They'd be teenagers now."

As they spoke, Zahra was rapidly writing notes of coloured post-its and sticking them on a sheet. She pointed her pink biro pen at Sam. "You. You know him?"

"Me? I've met him. Once."

"Describe his character."

"He's ... he's a bit boring."

"Not itself a character trait."

"He's a middle-aged farmer. He works from dawn till dusk. He likes Dolly Parton."

"For her music or personally?"

"You think he's into...?" Peach mimed large breasts.

"The Dollywood Foundation has given millions of dollars to children's literacy, welfare and medical charities."

"I really don't know," said Sam.

"Oh, she has," said Zahra.

"I meant, I don't know what he likes about her. The music, I think. He's very keen to see his children again. I think he sees the revitalisation of his farm as key to that. That's what the Tigerheart thing is all about."

"Tigerheart?"

"A cabbage he's developing. It's got stripes."

The man's delusional," said Peach.

"Stripes are fun," said Zahra.

"I'm not sure if I could actually see any stripes in the sample he showed me," said Sam.

"Very well. Possibly delusional."

"We're just looking at CCTV from the interior of the bank," said Kenny.

Zahra looked at an image on the laptop resting on a food box featuring a jaunty cartoon lobster. She pointed at the image. "These video feeds are live from inside the bank?"

Sam nodded. "The foyer of the bank and all of the corridors are covered, as you can see."

"How can I see that all of the corridors are covered?" asked Zahra.

Sam smiled. "I can tell you that they are. This view and this view show the same corridor from opposite ends. And it's the same story here and here." Sam tapped the screen as she spoke.

Zahra reached out with a spotless white cloth and wiped the laptop screen where Sam had touched it. "Good surveillance is vital. I don't want a fingerprint to compromise our work."

At that moment, every view went dark.

"My fingerprint did not do *that*," said Sam.

24

Mercedes stepped back from the panel on the DefCon4 cabinet. "Done," she said.

"Done?" said Bruce. "You just turned it off."

Mercedes tilted her head. "If the bank wanted to invest in genuinely secure security cameras then I'm sure they'd have it linked to some physical cable buried in concrete that couldn't be accessed inside the bank. But yes, this is what we've got and now it's turned off."

Bruce looked up at the camera in the corner, waved at it and shrugged. "Phone lines cut?"

"Well, unplugged," said Mercedes.

"CCTV disconnected."

She waved a hand over the cabinet before them. "And now the money," she said.

"Exactly." He looked at the two little Mittens. "Would you like to see inside the bank vault?"

"Yes, please," said Edith. Evan nodded.

"Lead on," Bruce said to Mercedes.

She took them out into the corridor and to the keypad door leading to the basement level. She headed down.

"It's quite rare for banks to have walk-in vaults in basements these days," she said conversationally, thinking she might as well give them the tour while she was here. "All high street banks have a secure vault or strongbox of course, and most are still walk-ins. Although many high street banks don't even bother to use them. Cash is effectively dead, as you know."

At the bottom she turned to the left, tapped another keypad, and led the way into the safety deposit box room.

"Even fewer offer safety deposit boxes for customers," she continued. "They're expensive to hire, awkward to maintain, and people don't feel the need to keep vital documents or the family jewels in the bank's care anymore. This one was installed when the bank was built in the 1930s."

The safety deposit box room was lit by stark strip lights set into a relatively low ceiling, and it gleamed like silver. Three of its four walls were taken up by safety deposit boxes. The smallest were the size of postcards, the largest the dimensions of an oven door. Each had a small hoop handle and a keyhole. Mercedes' eyes immediately went to her own safety deposit box. Her own box of secrets. She had the letter from her dad inside her jacket, which she would soon enough be putting in there.

"This isn't the vault," said Bruce, astute as always.

"No, it isn't," she said. "The bank vault is operated with a key which breaks into two parts. In the olden days, these two parts would be taken home by two members of staff – the bank manager and one other. Both were needed to open the vault, so no one person could open it by themselves."

"Really?"

"Yeah. Which was fine if you could rely on staff to remember to bring the key in, or not lose it, or not quit and disappear with it. So in the Eighties we went for something simpler."

She went to a black safe set into the wall by the door, entered the six digit code and opened it. Inside was the heavy ring of keys for the safety deposit boxes and the long vault key. She took it out with both hands.

Bruce coughed in surprise. The children made appropriate *ooh*s of wonder. "It's massive," he said.

The key, fashioned from heavy steel, was eighteen inches long, with a complex array of teeth and notches.

"Back then they didn't mess about," she said. "This key is over thirty years old. Never been a need to change the system."

She passed the key to Bruce and he hefted it weightily in one hand.

"And now to the vault."

"Mrs Ogilby let us watch Harry Potter in class once, at Christmas," said Edith, immediately putting a hand over her mouth as though sharing the most shameful secret.

"I put my hands over my eyes," said Evan. "For a bit. You don't have little trains and goblins in *your* bank vault."

"Sadly not," said Mercedes. "This way."

Out of the safety deposit room there was another keypad-controlled door, and a small antechamber in front of a large vault door. It was a circle of steel six feet across, set into a square wall. There was a wheel and a keyhole and supporting struts. It looked like a bank vault out of a movie or a cartoon, and people often seemed surprised this was so, even though they could not articulate what else it should look like. This was Skegness, they'd be thinking. How could such a symbol of financial power exist here?

Mercedes waved Bruce forward.

He lifted the key. "I just...?"

"Put it in, turn it. Two full turns. It's a lock."

Bruce did as guided, and with the satisfying clunk of bolts sequentially falling away, it unlocked. The children rushed forward to help Bruce turn the vault wheel and haul the door open. He pushed them away from between the door and the wall in case they might be crushed, even though such a thing wasn't possible.

The vault was lit from within. It was small chamber, still larger than either the kitchen or bathroom in Mercedes' flat on Braceby Road. There were shelves and wire cages around the walls. Many of them were partly filled with locked boxes, or tied folders of letters, contracts and other documents. The cash was stored in plastic bank bags and paper wraps on the nearest shelves.

Bruce Greencock stepped inside and put his hands on the packs of money. There were several stacks of cash, each the size of a cereal box. The entire cash supply of the bank could have fitted into a large suitcase.

"This is it?" he said.

"Nearly half a million pounds," said Mercedes. "Never looks as big as you think it should, does it?"

He picked up a bundle and weighed it in his hand as

though that might make it more real.

At that point it occurred to Mercedes that, if she was quick about it, she could shut the vault door while Bruce was preoccupied and lock him in there before he had chance to stop her.

She didn't.

Instead, she said, "There are some dummy packs in there with explosive dye. We will need to check for them."

Bruce looked at her. "You're being very helpful." The way he said it, it wasn't an accusation or suspicion but a compliment. An attempt at making a human connection.

"I'm in a helpful mood today," she said.

"I mean, you're meant to be protecting the bank's money."

She shrugged. "They don't always have my best interests at heart. Have you, by any chance, heard of the gender pay gap?"

Bruce's lips quivered in an uncomfortable expression as though all matters female were a source of embarrassment. She might as well have said, "What do you know about tampons?" or "What's your opinion on proper-fitting bras?"

"I've heard it mentioned," he said stiffly.

She made a hum of acknowledgement. "I've recently discovered that I have been ... left behind by colleagues – male colleagues – who were certainly no more deserving of pay rises than me."

Bruce tutted. "But you seem the most competent person here. Definitely more so than that blithering idiot, Tubby Johnson."

"Why, thank you, Bruce," she said.

25

"**Y**ou broke it," Chief Inspector Peach said. He couldn't take his eyes off the now blank feed on the laptop.

"I don't think so," said Sam. "It's the same on my phone. The feed has been turned off."

"Is it possible this has been done from inside the bank?" asked Zahra the negotiator.

"But Bruce Greencock...?" She shook her head.

"What is it?" said Zahra.

"Nothing."

"You shook your head. Like this." And she mimicked Sam's motion.

"I'm not saying he's not particularly technologically-minded—" Sam said.

"But..."

"He's more of a nuts-and-bolts, hands-on kind of man."

"So he got someone else to do it."

A uniformed officer entered the fish stall. "Got your desk and chair as requested." He wheeled in a trolley. It appeared to have come from a shop or a library, as it was made from wood and shaped more like a bookshelf than a desk.

"This place is crowded enough," said Peach.

"Get the mobile critical incident command base," said Kenny the firearms sergeant. "You can't operate out of a fish stall, sir."

"I have to think about all possible operation needs," said Peach. "And the budget."

"If you're counting pennies in a place that stinks of dead fish, you're doing something wrong, sir."

"Cones," said Zahra.

"What?" said Peach.

"I see some orange traffic cones on the street out there. We're going to need to move them well away from the bank."

"What? Why?"

"Are you familiar with Jung's work on colour psychology."

"Um, no."

"And you want us to open up a meaningful dialogue with the suspect?"

Peach wavered as though his command was being undermined.

"It will *cost* you nothing to move them," she said.

Peach nodded slowly.

"Check the shop displays facing that way too. Remove all of the orange coloured goods. Keep checking the line of sight. We can have reds and yellows in sight of the bank, but no orange. Understood?"

"But I don't see—" he began.

"That's quite clear." She turned to Kenny. "Your officers are ready to make a forced entry into the bank?"

"We've got options," he said.

"Then check on them and we'll co-ordinate an approach."

Dismissed, Kenny stepped outside. Peach had directed an officer to oversee orange elimination.

The stiff thin woman sat down on the garish floral deck chair with which she'd been provided. She grunted with minor approval as she saw there was a lower level to the trolley where she could place her heavy bag. She began transferring the post-it notes she had written to various spots on the top shelf of her new desk.

"Now, chief inspector, I have something I need you to look into. We need bicycles."

Peach gave a nervous laugh. "We can use the squad cars if we need to go—"

"—Not for transport, you understand. We need at least five bicycles placed on the street. It should be an odd number, and some should have wicker baskets on the front."

"Bicycles? Really?"

"Bicycles on the street promote calmness of thought, as they suggest a slower, more wholesome pace of life. These are all results of research into situations quite germane to this one. I will leave the placement to you, but it's important you arrange them in a way which supports that view."

Peach was momentarily lost for words. "Bicycles. Right." He left the fish booth, making an exasperated huffing sound.

Satisfied with herself, Zahra delved into her bag. She

brought out a turned wooden object and held it thoughtfully. It might have been an old-fashioned pepper pot, or an ornament. She placed it carefully on the desk and reached into her bag once again. Zahra produced more objects and arranged them on the shelf in front of her. They appeared to be a random selection of things. There was a small giraffe, which might have been one of those toys which was held upright on unseen elastic and went all wobbly when you pressed upwards on its base. There was a pebble with a stripe of quartz through it, a poker chip, and a bottle opener. She peered at them with great concentration, rearranging them a couple of times, and then finally sat back, satisfied.

"You're still here," she said to Sam "Miss Applewhite, isn't it?"

Sam had been standing in the shadows, holding her breath, uncertain what was happening, but aware some sort of process was taking place.

"I am," she said.

"Why?"

Sam shrugged. "Fascinated observer, I guess. That thing with the colour orange and bicycles..."

"Yes?"

"That was just for clearing out the police officers, right?"

Zahra shifted in her seat to look at Sam. The woman had a closed face, taut and unyielding, like it had been carved from a piece of wood. "I don't lie to people. Unless it's strictly necessary."

"You said you had done research into it and were familiar with Jung's theory of colour or something."

Zahra made a little noise. "I wasn't too rude to the police, was I?"

"Not that I noticed."

"I think I have it now," she said. "This situation will need Bridey MacDougal."

Sam was about to question the wisdom of bringing in someone else to a time-critical situation, when she registered the change in accent. Whatever Zahra's accent had been previously, it was now Scottish.

"Bridey MacDougal?" Sam asked.

Zahra nodded and reached into her bag again. She pulled out a colourful agate brooch, roughly shaped in a Celtic cross.

"Bridey's persona is wonderful for working with those who are a little agitated," said Zahra, in those same smooth, clear tones. "I expect Mr Greencock to instinctively trust the Edinburgh Morningside accent, as so many of us do. Bridey also speaks quite slowly, which might be helpful for extending the timeline of a conversation."

"Great!" said Sam. It was heartening to see someone actually working to a solid plan.

Zahra pulled a phone handset towards her from the metal trolley. "Is this hooked up for recording?"

Sam nodded.

"Real hostage situations are rare, so I need to think of the future training opportunities this situation can offer."

Sam realised the truth of this. "How did you get trained, then?"

"Mostly self-taught," said Zahra. "It's not an easy field to get established in when you live in this country. My employer wouldn't foot the bill for sending me to Quantico, but I absorb everything ever published on the subject, and I practise my skills regularly."

Sam burned to know how one practised hostage negotiation skills.

"And now you must leave while I prepare," said Zahra.

"Um, ah, okay," Sam nodded.

"Three things," Zahra said as Sam was about to step out onto the street.

"Yes?"

"First, the colour orange and bicycles. True or not, the suspect, if he is looking out the bank window, will see police officers busy doing something he cannot comprehend. That means the police are evidently up to something and know things he doesn't know. Suddenly, he is no longer in charge."

"Ah."

"Secondly, I said had conducted research germane to the situation. I didn't say what research I had conducted. Nor did I say I was familiar with Jung's work on the psychology of colour. I merely asked if Chief Inspector Peach was familiar with it."

"Sneaky."

"Thirdly, these items," she said, gesturing to her strange array of totems on her trolley. "Even the use of a superfluous word such as 'germane'. All things have an impact and may even have a specific purpose. Fourthly, and quite importantly, if someone says to you they never lie to people, do remember that a liar can say that and stay true to their nature."

Sam nodded. "That was four things."

"Then may I re-refer you to point four," said Zahra in her softly posh Scottish accent.

SAM STEPPED out to find Camara waiting there. She looked back at the fishmonger's stall. "You ever get the impression everything is a crazy circus and not even the monkeys are in charge?"

"There's a solid chain of command," Camara said. "The superintendent in the control room at Lincoln has total oversight. The guys know what they're doing."

"Are you trying to placate me?"

He produced a wry smile. "Oh, I've long given up on trying to steer you in any way, Miss Applewhite."

She frowned. "The tracker widgets I put on Bruce's guns..."

"They'll help us keep tabs on him inside the bank."

"...I'm wondering how many weapons he brought today. I saw them all this morning."

Camara narrowed his eyes. "You want to go check out the farm."

"It could be useful."

"We've sent a squad car out there already. This is a police matter now..."

"And I'm understandably terrified for the life of my dad. And my friend. And the other hostages. Well, maybe not terrified for them. It's a sliding scale of compassion, I guess. Point is, I need to do something and I was the last person to be at Bruce's farm. If there's some vital clue, a minor change that gives us an insight..."

Camara shook his head but it was in defeat. "Curse you for making actual logical sense. I'll go tell the chief I'm taking you to the farm. I'll meet you by that rock and candyfloss stall over there."

As Camara went back into the fishy command centre, Sam walked swiftly towards the blue and white tape. There was a growing crowd at the edge of the police cordon around the bank now. The tape notionally kept people out of the bank's eyeline, and thus, Sam supposed, the sights of any would-be shooter inside.

At a guess, the crowd was made up of a few locals and a large quantity of holidaymakers. Shorts, sandals and sunglasses were much in evidence. A few bared shoulders showed pink sunburn, which demonstrated considerable dedication in a seaside resort where the number of genuinely sunny days was limited. Given the size of the crowd, it seemed the tense inaction of a bank siege situation was as big a draw for the Skegness visitor as the beach, the amusement halls or the fairground. Ice-creams and take-out hot drinks were the snacks of choice for the dedicated onlooker, although many of them also had phones in their hands.

"Are you police? What's happening?" asked a young woman with ash-blonde streaks and hoop earrings.

"I'm not police," said Sam and ducked under the barrier.

"You been following *bexcanboogie* though, yeah?"

Sam hadn't even looked at the Instagram account of the

woman inside. She had the app on her phone, had an account too, but never used it.

"He's doing it for love, isn't he?" said another woman, holding an iced coffee and phone, resting her elbows on the handles of child's buggy in which sat a decidedly bored-looking and food-smeared tot.

"What?" said Sam, automatically.

"I've got a lot of time for Bruce," said buggy woman.

"Is he a friend of yours?" asked Sam.

"No, I only just saw this. I'm definitely *#teamBruce* though."

Sam looked around the crowd and saw there were some nods. Somehow, the situation had already created tribes and factions. She opened her phone's Instagram app, ignored the junk shop images and beach views making up her latest feed, and searched for this *@Bexcanboogie* account. The woman had eight thousand followers and Sam wondered how many of those had appeared in the last hour or so.

She dug into the social media commentary which had sprung up around the woman's posts. She found the latest video, wobbly images taken in a back office. Bruce waving his gun around. She thumbed up the volume in time to hear him say "—doing it for my kids. I'll do anything for my kids."

There were hundreds of comments. The hashtag *#teamBruce* had gained a serious foothold.

"What would you be if you're not *#teamBruce*?" asked pushchair woman.

The lass with hoop earrings laughed. "Someone said they were *#teamJustin* but I think it was a joke. There are a bunch of wanker banker types who started *#teamEastshires*, but the other main group is *#teamHostages* who are wringing their hands about the kiddies being in there. It's like they weren't listening or something! There's no way Bruce is hurting any children.'"

Sam turned away, dismayed. She'd often wondered about the people who sent marriage proposals to murderers in prison, and what motivated them. She could see these women had imagined Bruce's entire personality based on the smallest fragments of evidence.

Camara joined her at the agreed point while she was still trawling through the posts.

"You okay?" said the detective.

"How come he's letting this woman tweet?" said Sam.

"He's confiscated the phones," said Camara. "But what we think is that woman has got a smart watch she can use for sending messages. He'll spot it sooner or later. It's why we've not had any more video, though."

Sam gazed at the feed.

PHONES CONFISCATED AND CAMERAS BEING DISABLED

JUSTIN'S GETTING ON EVERYONE'S NERVES. GONNA SUGGEST THAT BRUCE TIES HIM UP

OMFG, YOU GUYS! BRUCE HAS AGREED THAT JUSTIN NEEDS TYING UP. RESULT!

Sam couldn't quite understand the casual tone. Bruce had a gun, yet *@Bexcanboogie* was doubling down on exploiting the opportunity for social media fame.

Around them in the crowd, there was constant discussion.

"Will he get away with it?" someone said.

"I wonder how much money they've got in there? What would you spend it on?" said another.

It was bizarre. A heady mix of local drama coupled with daydreams about a lottery win. And all because of Bruce. The man she'd met that morning had been ready for a business meeting. Perhaps he'd been a little over-confident about the charms of cabbage, but he was preparing for a discussion, not a robbery. Why would he even have taken a gun with him?

"Which team, mate?" a teenage boy stepped in front of them, brandishing a pair of T-shirts, one over each arm.

"Sorry?"

"Which team? *#teamBruce* or *#teamHostages*? Tenner apiece." The lad raised a T-shirt bearing an image, taken from a video. It depicted Bruce with shotgun pointed. The image had a grainy, rough-print look which, to Sam's eyes, made it look like an art print. Iconic even. The Che Guevara of the cabbage fields. Beneath it was the slogan *I'M DOING IT FOR MY KIDS*.

"Jesus," Sam sighed.

"I can do 'em for eight. Two for fifteen quid."

Camara held up his police ID. "Why don't you shove off, eh?" he said, which was the rudest she'd ever heard him.

Sam's phone was ringing. It was Rich.

"No news on dad or Delia yet," she said.

"I can seeee you," he sang.

"Huh?"

"Look up. Look round. To the left. Too far."

Sam turned and looked. She had no time for games but impatience urged her on. She peered between rooftops, just making out a tiny silhouette figure and glint of sunlight off something.

"Great. I can see you too," she said unenthusiastically.

"Good. Now, get back up here. I've got something to show you."

"I haven't got time, Rich."

"It could literally bring the whole thing to a peaceful end."

"Really?"

"Really."

She turned to Camara. "We need to make a detour. Rich says he's got a plan."

"I know that man's plans and schemes," said Camara. He had indeed been witness to a dummy animal escape drill for Rich's proposed ice age theme park. He'd also, on more than one occasion, had to tell Rich he'd illegally parked his helicopter.

Sam turned to press on back towards the City Lights rooftop office where Rich was still clearly stationed. Sam's phone buzzed with an alert.

The DefCon4 app pointed out that one of the security motion sensors at Greencock Farm had been set off. This seemed an unlikely coincidence, and it occurred to her that the police were almost certainly on the site and would have triggered some of the sensor equipment in the yard.

The second notification was more vexing:

Your continued absence from your expected locations has triggered a workflow to address your safeguarding needs. A message has been sent to your supervisor, Doug, so that he can ascertain your whereabouts. Doug will then either approve the deviation or initiate a disciplinary

ACTION. IF YOU NEED TO SELF-CERTIFY AN ILLNESS, YOU CAN DO SO IN THE MYATTENDANCE SECTION OF THE APP.

Ah, there was an idea! Sam tapped through the screens of the app. If she declared that she was ill, then DefCon4 would stop distracting her. It was all well and good sending messages to Doug, but head office and its systems had not grasped the fact that Doug was a cactus, and that no human apart from Sam herself was ever seen in the Skegness office of DefCon4.

Sam paused. She wasn't sick, so it didn't seem right to declare that she was. The thing she really needed at this point was compassionate leave, based on the extreme situation her father (and her friend) was in. Was that an option that she could choose? She searched on the app and found that it was! She located a screen where she could request one or more days of compassionate leave. It had a calendar to select the time period. The thought that this might go on for more than one day was horrifying, but Sam decided she had better play it safe, so she selected two days, so she had some leeway.

YOUR REQUEST FOR COMPASSIONATE LEAVE HAS BEEN RECEIVED. THIS WILL NEED TO BE AUTHORISED BY YOUR SUPERVISOR, DOUG. YOU MAY NOT TAKE ANY LEAVE UNTIL YOU RECEIVE AUTHORISATION. THIS WILL NORMALLY BE GRANTED WITHIN 5 (FIVE) WORKING DAYS.

Sam stared at the screen. Doug was in no position to authorise the leave. If she cancelled this request and declared a sick day instead, would it raise an immediate red flag? She tried to cancel the request for compassionate leave.

THIS WORKFLOW HAS PASSED TO A STAGE WHERE YOU ARE NOT

PERMITTED TO VIEW OR EDIT. PLEASE WAIT FOR ITS STATUS TO RETURN TO ONE WHERE YOU ARE PERMITTED TO VIEW OR EDIT.

She grunted with frustration and tried to self-certify a sick day instead.

THERE IS A CONFLICT ON YOUR CALENDAR. OUR RECORDS SHOW THERE IS A PENDING REQUEST FOR COMPASSIONATE LEAVE. THIS REQUEST MUST BE ADDRESSED BEFORE ANY FURTHER STATUS CHANGES CAN BE LOGGED. PLEASE ALLOW 5 (FIVE) WORKING DAYS FOR THE STATUS TO BE UPDATED.

26

In the back office, it was Delia's turn. "I went to the shops and I bought an apple, a BMW, a coat by Balenciaga, a doggy chew toy for Petey aaaand ... an Everyman multitool."

"What's one of those?" said Stevie.

Delia tried to explain, which was hard when she couldn't use her hands to outline the shape of thing.

"It's a metal tool. Like a wallpaper scraper, except it's also a good for filling holes and hoiking out nails, and you can use it to scrape off paint and clean rollers."

"Sounds like you made it up," said Justin.

"I've got one in my workshop. Use it all the time."

"Workshop?" said Becky.

"Mmmm. I run a shop down near the pier. Upcycled goods, objets d'art, crapestry. *Back to Life.*"

Becky made a peculiar noise: part surprise, part

recognition, part a clear statement that she would never go inside such a shop. "I've seen it."

"You should come in," said Delia. "We've got some lovely pieces. Some jewellery that would go really well with that jacket of yours. And a nice range of rings."

"Oh. No. I don't really do second hand. You just don't know where they've been."

"In the case of rings, on fingers usually," said Delia.

Becky shook her head in polite distaste. "I obviously adore antique jewellery but…"

"That's just a word meaning really, *really* second hand."

"It's Justin's turn," said Stevie.

Justin huffed a sigh. Slouched uncomfortably in his seat, his shirt tails had come untucked. There was an unhappy and strained look on his face. "I don't want to play. I'm just concentrating on getting out of here."

"Ah, think yourself free," said Delia.

"Can you do that?" said Stevie.

"And I need a wee," said Justin.

"And playing games will take your mind off that," said Delia.

Justin huffed as though the previous huff hadn't done the trick. "Fine! I went to the shops and bought an apple, a BMW, a coat, a dog toy—"

"A coat by Balenciaga," said Becky.

"I said a coat."

"But a Balenciaga."

"A coat's a coat."

"And it was doggy chew toy for Petey," put in Stevie.

"A Balenciaga coat and a toy for Petey then," said Justin. "And a – what was it? – Everyman multitool and ... free access to the toilet next door."

"Can you buy access to a toilet?" asked Delia, keen to pursue a line of fairness and sensibility.

"It begins with 'f' so it counts," said Justin.

"It's not a great shopping list, is it?" said Stevie. "I mean, I would love to get Petey a toy but..."

"It's all just *stuff*, isn't it?" said Delia. She looked about herself. "Makes you think, doesn't it? Here we are, surrounded by money, figuratively speaking, and it's all a bit nonsensical, isn't it?"

"We should just cherish the simple things in life, shouldn't we?" said Becky nobly.

"I just want to be home," said Stevie.

There were noises of general agreement. Delia found herself thinking about her own kids, Milly and Alfie. It was true she loved them most when they were fast asleep and silent, and for ninety percent of the rest of the time she felt a low-level background urge to asphyxiate them for being so bloody untidy and annoying. But right now she wanted nothing more than to be with them, her arms wrapped round them, asphyxiating them with love rather than irritation. And, yes, that intermittently absent, frequently thoughtless and consistently useless husband of hers, she missed him too.

"I just wish that man would get his money and go," said Becky. "Try his chances against the cops."

"Ah, let him take it," Delia sighed. "Good luck to him."

"Let him go?" said Justin. "Are you serious?"

Delia shrugged. "It's the bank's money. What do I care?"

"The bank's money means that it's your money," said Justin. "He's stealing from you."

"Well, I'm deep into my overdraft. He's welcome to steal that."

Justin seemed to find that funny, although Delia felt he wasn't laughing with her.

"It's just a drop in the ocean, isn't it?" said Stevie. "You see so much money. It's like ... do you ever think about words?"

"Eh?"

"Like 'sausages'. You say the word 'sausages'. Sausages. Saus-ages. Sausa-ges. Sau-sag-es." She worked through a nonsensical series of pronunciations. "Eventually, you say it so often it seems to lose all meaning."

"You say 'sausages' to yourself a lot, do you, Stevie?" said Justin.

"Got to fill those long winter nights somehow," muttered Becky.

"But money's like that," said Stevie. "Eventually you've seen so much of it that it loses its meaning."

"My point exactly," said Delia. "It's just paper and numbers."

"You are an employee of Eastshires Bank, Stevie Lingard," said Justin. "That kind of attitude to money is unprofessional. Dangerous even."

"What do you care?" said Delia. "It's not your money either."

"Is it my money he's stealing?" Becky asked earnestly.

"It's all just money," said Delia. "It's money that's insured in some way, and if Bruce wants to steal half a million or whatever, it's not going to make Eastshires' stocks go up or down one jot."

"But it's not *his*," Justin insisted. "He's stealing it."

"Meanwhile massive corporations refuse to pay billions in tax, but we don't bat an eyelid about that."

"Oh, you're one of them," said Justin as if suddenly understanding. "Always punching upwards."

"That's sort of the direction you're meant to punch," said Delia.

"It's an aspect of the British character I've never liked," said Justin wearily. "Building up our heroes and then knocking them down. They did it to Churchill, didn't they? As soon as the war was over, booted him out and let that whoever-it-was take over. I suppose you think Bruce Greencock is some sort of plucky underdog."

"I've never understood why it's an underdog," said Stevie. "Is it because we love dogs?"

"It's a dogfighting term, you cretin," said Justin.

"As in fighting with dogs? Ooh, no, I don't approve of that," Stevie said, firmly.

"There's the underdog which is beaten by the top dog in the fight. That's the underdog."

"Shouldn't it be bottom dog then? Or overdog for the other one?"

"Bruce..." Delia paused to gather her thoughts before speaking. "There's no doubt the man has made some bad decisions today."

"Bad decisions?" said Becky disdainfully.

"Stupid, stupid decisions," Delia agreed. "But that doesn't make him evil. No one wakes up in the morning and goes 'I'm going to do something horrible and evil and unpleasant today.'"

"We are literally living through proof that some people do that," said Justin.

"He waved a bloody sword in front of my children," said Becky.

"And ... and that's bad," Delia conceded.

"Are you sure?" said Becky. "You seem to be on his side."

Delia growled. "I'm not on anyone's side. I'm just saying ... shit happens."

"Amazing," said Justin, deadpan. "Five minutes of waffle and your blistering insight is that shit happens."

Delia tried to contain her thoughts and her temper. Meanwhile, Becky twisted in her seat. Either because she had itchy pants or thought she could wriggle out of her bonds.

"Okay, okay," said Delia. "Bleeding heart liberal cards on the table. Bruce is only in this situation because he needs the money to keep his cabbage farm afloat. There are people with money and there are people without money. I don't even know what category I'm in. I seem to have to work all the hours God gives just to stay stationary, but I've got a house and there's food on the table, so I don't know. But I do know that if the richest people in the world – and I don't even mean people, I mean the banks and the companies and the governments and whatever. If they just gave everyone their fair share then you wouldn't have desperate people killing themselves and each other to get what's theirs. If the bank's petty algorithms hadn't denied Bruce his loan, then none of this would have happened."

"What a load of commie bollocks," said Justin with slow disbelief.

"I think I already give enough to the needy," said Becky. "I did a MacMillan coffee morning, and a fun run for Children in Need. Gary Barlow liked my post. Or at least someone who said he was Gary Barlow."

"I give money to blind dogs," said Stevie.

"You mean guide dogs for the blind," said Becky.

"No, no. Blind dogs. They bring them over here from Romania and Serbia and find them new homes."

"Bloody immigrants," Justin laughed bitterly. "Watch out. Between Miss Snowflake and dog-mad Stevie, we'll be giving everything away."

There was a long, unfriendly silence.

"However, I do sometimes think," said Becky as she wriggled, "that those rich Americans, you know the ones, might spend less of their money sending rockets into space and actually do something about fixing the world's problems."

"There you go," said Delia softly.

Becky gave a final twist, there was a tiny trilling beep, and she gasped. "I've done it!"

Delia craned forward to look at her bonds. "You got free?"

Becky shook her head. "No, I've turned on my watch's speech command function. I can now literally post to Instagram with my hands tied behind my back."

"Christ," Justin muttered.

"Of course," said Stevie, two minutes later, "technically it wasn't the bank's algorithms that turned down Mr Greencock's loan."

Delia looked at her. "Say what?"

There was suddenly a deeply troubled look on Justin's face.

27

Mercedes took a bound wad of notes off the shelf, riffled through it, and passed it to Bruce to put in a carrier bag. She found an ink explosive in the next one and set it aside. Superficially there was no way to tell a dummy pack from a real one. They were made from genuine stacks of banknotes, hollowed out, then gummed together around the explosive charge.

"I thought they only had them in movies," said Bruce.

"Nope. We've had them for years," said Mercedes. She took the pack, tore it apart and removed the explosive device. It was not much bigger than an old-fashioned zippo lighter, composed of various components in a soft plastic shell. She tossed it to Bruce for him to scrutinise. "They're activated by a radio signal when they leave the bank premises. Ours are on a one minute timer, I believe. The explosive burns hot and loud. You wouldn't want to be holding one when it goes off."

Bruce gave her a calculating look.

"They arm automatically when they leave the bank. Perfectly safe until then. But it would probably take your hand off."

Edith and Evan Mitten were by the vault door, playing some sort of guards and passwords game in which one of them was refusing to let the other through without the proper documentation.

"You do know you're not going to get away with this," Mercedes said to Bruce.

"You sound like Justin," he said grimly. "I thought you were all for keeping things calm and compliant."

"I'm trying to do the best for my customers," she said. "And myself. And I'm telling you, as things go, you don't stand any chance of getting away with this."

His face contorted sourly. "Going to tell me to give myself up?"

Mercedes didn't respond to that directly. "We laid it out on the board upstairs clear enough. You step out the door with a bag of cash, you're either going to be shot or arrested."

"I'll make a deal. I'll get away."

"And spend the rest of your life on the run?"

"It's not about me," he said.

"No. It's about the cabbages and your children."

"Exactly."

"So, you'd be happy with a plan that provides for the farm and your children, but in which you are captured by the police?"

He heard the tone in her voice and gave her a searching look. "You have such a plan?"

Mercedes was about to tell him when Edith shouted, "No! No! You can't come in! Get back in the sea!"

Evan's shoulders slouched and he stepped away from the door.

"It's okay," said Edith, looking at the adults. "We're just playing illegal immigrants."

"I'm a paediatric nurse fleeing war-torn Sudan," said Evan.

"That's what *he* says," said Edith.

A phone began to ring. Mercedes found herself momentarily perplexed. Bruce had confiscated all the phones and she was fairly certain she had successfully disconnected the landlines. It took an second or two to realise the ringing was coming from Bruce's coat pocket.

He put down the money bag and reached into his pocket. It came out with a whole handful of things: a plastic bag with flat rectangular lozenges in it, a couple of shotgun cartridges, and his phone. He stared at the lozenges, perplexed, then put them and the cartridges on a side shelf before looking at the phone.

"Unknown number," he said.

"Could be the police," said Mercedes. "Or some newspaper reporter."

"Should I answer it?"

It was funny really. Here was the bank robber, with a machete tucked into his leather belt, shotgun cartridges in his pocket and bags full of loot, and he was asking her if he should answer the phone. Even in a bank siege she automatically assumed a position of competent authority, but all the power and prestige still belonged to the man next to her.

And she'd been about to tell him a possible plan, her plan. That would have been the point where she would have crossed the line. There was being a compliant, non-confrontational hostage, and there was being a full-blown accomplice. She had disabled the CCTV. There was no evidence she was doing anything other than acting according to bank policy. Everything up until this moment could be pinned on stupid, short-sighted Bruce Greencock.

If she took the next step and told him the plan, she'd finally get her hands on the sixty-seven thousand pounds of hard-earned back pay she deserved. On the other hand, a careless word from the robber himself, and she would be in as much trouble as he was.

That line was in front of her as clear as if it had been drawn on the floor of the vault. The phone continued to ring.

28

B ruce tapped the answer button on his phone and put it to his ear.

"Hello, am I speaking with Bruce Greencock?" It was a Scottish lady.

"Bruce? No, sorry. I don't know who that is." Bruce wanted time to think. How did they know who he was? Obviously they did, because they'd called him on his personal mobile phone. Why had he said he wasn't Bruce?

"This is Bridey MacDougal for Bruce Greencock. I can wait, if it's not convenient for him right now." She had a light voice, nice and clear.

"I'm kind of busy right now," he said.

"I won't take up much of your time, sir."

"What is it?"

"I was just after a chat. I could perhaps talk to you for a while."

"Who are you?"

"Bridey MacDougal."

"I mean who ... *what* are you?"

"I'm outside the bank right now. I've been asked to give you a call."

"You work for the police then?" Bruce asked.

"I sometimes help the police, but I don't work directly for them, no. I'm not a reporter or anything. I'm not a phone hacker from the News of the World *or anything. This is Bruce himself, isn't it?"*

Bruce knew he could carry on pretending to be someone else. She hadn't even asked his name. He liked to be straightforward though, and there was an overhead in maintaining a pointless lie that he didn't want to waste his energy on.

"Yes, this is Bruce."

"Good."

"I just wanted to make sure it wasn't a scam call."

Mercedes was exaggeratedly miming '*Who is it?*' in front of him, with big hand gestures and everything, but Bruce ignored her and stepped back.

"Well hello, Bruce," said the woman, Bridey. *"I don't blame you for being cautious. Scam calls are such a nuisance."*

"Nuisance. Waste of money. Waste of effort."

"Oh, I know what you mean."

"It's the fact that someone thinks they can sit on a phone and take money from those of us who've earned it with hard graft. The world needs to be better than that."

"The world should *be better than that, Bruce. You're right. It's my job to help us all get a better understanding of the situation we're in. That means I'm here to help you as well, if you'd like."*

"Oh yes? You think you can help me? Seems to me that I'm holding all the cards."

"You are in a powerful position, Bruce, that's true. The possession of great power necessarily implies great responsibility."

"Is that a Spiderman quote?"

"William Lamb. He was prime minister to the young Queen Victoria. The queen was but a teenager."

Bruce looked at Edith and Evan Mitten. They were still playing some nonsense game.

"Everyone's fine here, by the way." said Bruce.

"Oh, I am glad to hear that."

Mercedes was still mouthing at Bruce, her lips so wide they almost made a sound through sheer force alone. 'Who is it?'

'Police negotiator,' he mouthed back.

'Who?'

'Negotiator!'

'Put the phone down,' she told him.

"And who do you have with you now?" Bridey said on the line.

"No one," he said automatically, not sure why and immediately corrected himself. "I mean, everyone. We're all here, together."

"That is good to know." There was the click of a retractable pen on the line. *"For my records, can you tell me who you have there? Don't want to miss anyone out, do we? We have an important job to do and the great responsibility."*

"I'm sure it is a Spiderman quote," said Bruce.

"Aye, perhaps you're right."

Mercedes stepped forward to grab the phone from him. Bruce pushed her aside but ended the call anyway.

"What is your problem?" he demanded fiercely.

"You're just blabbering on to her," said Mercedes. "Were you going to tell her everything?"

"No," he said firmly and then added, "Why do you care?"

"Because we need to work out what you're going to do. We need to work it out together. You think we can trust the police to not make a mess of it?"

"Actually, she sounded quite nice," said Bruce, but he knew Mercedes was right on this point. He needed to work it all out. He needed a plan, and he was sure that, before they were interrupted, Mercedes was going to give some suggestions.

He looked at the bags of money on the floor. They weren't going anywhere. "Okay. Everyone back upstairs. Best check on the others."

29

Camara followed Sam up the metal staircase round the back of the arcade on South Parade and onto the roof.

"Rich?" she called as she walked across the roof. "What the hell is this?"

Rich stood up from a folding chair and gave a cheery wave. In Sam's absence, the rooftop had been transformed. The patchwork of tarred roof and tile remained, as did the mouldy portacabin. But around it, Rich had created something that was half beachfront bar and half military command tent.

"It's a Crisis Management Centre," said Rich.

More like a mid-life crisis in physical form, Sam thought. There were deckchairs and a parasol and something that looked like a small palm-covered tiki bar. Then there was a marquee tent where trestle tables of electronics equipment crowded together. Sam recognised the symptoms. This was classic Rich. There was no situation which he thought was beyond his control. Obviously, his enormous wealth couldn't fix everything, but it could pave the way for any attempt he cared to make.

"I can see it's chaos down there," said Rich, "so I've taken advantage of this space. Let me give you the tour. You too, detective." He gestured for them to step inside his wind-tugged tent.

"Here are the communications links and computer resources. If we need to do a press conference, or create a video bridge with subject matter experts, here is where we'll do it. Over here we have monitoring equipment. We have video coverage of every part of the bank, and a boom microphone that might come in handy. All footage is being recorded. We have a drone coming later so we can get greater coverage."

"The police have this situation under control," said Camara.

Rich ignored him. Sam couldn't believe how much equipment was in place in such a short space of time. "What's this?" she said, pointing to a large cabinet which Rich hadn't yet explained.

He opened its door. "Snacks. You'll be burning a lot of calories with the stress of the situation, so there's plenty of picnic food here. Happy to pour you a glass of calming fizz if you think it will—"

"No." Sam shook her head. "This is not a jolly holiday, Rich."

Rich looked wounded. "That's harsh, Sam. You know I care about Marvin. I'm doing what I can."

"Hello, sir. Miss Applewhite. Detective Constable Camara."

Jurang Peninsula approached from deeper within the tent. Rich's butler was clearly the one setting up all the equipment. The suited, well-spoken gentleman was Rich's incredibly capable right hand man, although more often than not, Sam guessed he was Rich's enabler. Peninsula rarely seemed to offer Rich words of caution when they were very much in need.

Peninsula placed a case on the table. "This will allow you to monitor air traffic transmissions. Your own helicopter is on standby." He turned to Sam. "Miss Applewhite, I must thank you for the opportunity of providing Motikiti with some enrichment activities."

"Motikiti?" said Camara.

"A cat," said Sam.

"Yes," said Peninsula. "He enjoyed it very much. The plaster will be dry in seven days, and I will return to paint it."

Sam didn't dare ask what he was talking about.

"Show her the video," said Rich.

"What video?"

"It's part of the plan. I've been monitoring the social media feed, taking into account what you mentioned this morning, and acquired this."

Peninsula was already holding it up so that Sam and Camara could watch.

· · ·

"WELL, HOWDY, BRUCE," began the blonde woman on the screen. Her lined face was carefully made up and she wore a white rancher's jacket with roses embroidered on the sleeves. *"I heard about what's going on in England—"* her American pronunciation made it 'En-ger-land' *"—and I know you are a big fan. I encourage folks to dream big and you sure are doing that, ain't ya? But I'm also a big believer in working hard and playing fair. In this stormy world of fear and hate we can sometimes lose sight of what's right and wrong. Ain't that the truth, Bruce? We need to dig deep, find our way, and do the right thing to make that brighter tomorrow for everyone. Love and kindness spreads from heart to heart, and I hope you know that, when you choose to do the right thing, loving folks everywhere will be there to support."*

THERE WAS A PAUSE FOR A BRIGHT, reassuring smile.

"Oh, my God," said Camara, incredulous. "Is that Dolly Parton?"

"Very nearly," said Sam, looking closely. She tapped the screen as the video continued. "She's nailed the voice, and she has some of the mannerisms down pat, but she's a lookalike, yeah?"

Rich conceded the point with a small shrug. "Dolly wasn't available. Well, I mean it's still night-time over there, and no contacts of mine could be persuaded to disturb her. I had to go to an agency, yeah. The very best though. Maybe if we had a few more hours to wait until they're all awake I'm sure we could probably sort out—"

"This is, um, a really interesting idea," said Camara. "But I'm struggling to see how we could show it to Mr Greencock."

"Ah, well I got that covered," said Rich, gesturing to Peninsula.

The butler gave a brief, apologetic bow. "To my shame, when I was tidying up at your father's residence this morning, I saw some of the documentation in the filing cabinets. This included the computer logon details for Mr Doug Fredericks on a yellow post-it note."

Sam was about to point out that Doug was definitely a potted cactus and should not have had logon details of any sort, before recalling the cactus had taken its name from the desk nameplate of a former DefCon4 employee Sam had never met.

"He left ages ago," she said. "The logon can't still be valid."

"But it is, and I was able to access certain files in the DefCon4 system."

Peninsula looked suitably contrite, but Rich was grinning like a schoolboy with a bag full of gobstoppers.

"We've got Bruce's number!" he said. "We can WhatsApp it to him."

"No," said Camara, softly in dismay.

"Really, no," said Sam. "I forbid it."

"But it's Dolly!" said Rich.

"A fake Dolly."

"Who can do a passable rendition of *Islands in the Stream* – assuming we can find a lookalike Kenny Rogers for her to duet with. Bruce is a fan, you said. This will work."

"No, no, no," said Camara. "We have no idea what psychological impact this might have on the man."

"Can't beat a bit of Dolly," Rich countered.

"It's not Dolly!" said Sam.

Rich looked crestfallen, the schoolboy's gobstoppers had turned into Brussel sprouts.

"This," she said, waving her arms to indicate his base of operations. "This is well-meant. Yes, keep an eye on things – but you absolutely do not have my permission to go sending Dolly-a-gram messages to bank robbers. You hear me?"

Rich pursed his lips and kicked at imaginary pebbles on the ground.

"We've got a farm to check out," Sam said to Camara.

Rich shrugged in sad and desultory fashion. "Can't I tempt you to a piña colada before you go?" he said, gesturing to his tiki bar. Sam was already heading for the stairs.

Although before she got there, her exit was blocked by a parade of two dozen people in platinum blonde wigs, and a variety of outfits ranging from country-style tassels and denim to gem-spangled yellow dresses. They sashayed and strutted onto the roof. One young woman had made artful use of clothing and defining make up to turn herself into a passable Dolly, but most were just women (and a couple of men) in wigs and outfits.

"Oh, God," Sam quailed. "What is this?"

"Plan B!" said Rich swiftly. "Definitely Plan B. It's my whole troupe of stand-by Dollys."

"We're not look-alikes," said the lead Dolly, who Sam clearly recognised as Cat, owner of the café next to the now fire-damaged DefCon4 offices and leading light of the Skegness Operatic and Dramatic Society. "We're very much doing an artistic interpretation."

"Yes, yes, of course," said Rich.

"And no amount of makeup and push-up bras is going to be a replacement for actual acting talent, is it, Rhianna?" said Cat sourly, glowering at the passable young Dolly next to her.

30

Marvin punted his trolley with glacial speed into an area that was unfamiliar. This part of the bank was for staff only. So far it was a blank corridor, with a door to the right and a corner turning left. He opted to go around the corner. As soon as he had made it round, he could hear voices. It wasn't possible to make out the conversation, but he must be getting closer to where everybody was. He made sure his tiny movements along the corridor kept him close to the wall and headed towards the sounds.

Marvin was almost close enough to make out individual voices from the room up the corridor. His progress was slow, but that was fine. He was getting some serious complaints from his knee joints and his lower back about being scrunched up in this tiny space for so long, but he ignored them.

The sound of a door handle turning made him withdraw

the arm holding the coat hanger and slide the trolley door closed. He left the smallest gap so that he could see.

There was some movement and a pause. Marvin could see a woman's legs directly in front of the trolley.

"I'm not sure why this is here," came Mercedes voice, slightly confused. Marvin stayed very still, hardly breathing.

"Is that Harrogate water?" murmured a child. "It's a good brand. Can I have a drink please?"

There was a brief clunking above Marvin's head as something was moved on the trolley.

"I'm going to pop this in the kitchen," the woman said. Marvin felt himself being wheeled along.

He gave a small sigh of frustration.

31

Mercedes opened the combi oven door. Fragrant steam rolled out, a meaty aroma with a blast of umami. Quite mouth-watering.

"Empanadas!" declared Edith, clapping her hands.

"In my day, kids'd be happy with burger and chips," said Bruce.

"That's kids nowadays too," said Mercedes. But what did she know? When she'd been a child, she'd have been bowled over in amazement if her mum had managed to produce either burgers or chips. Every childhood was different.

Mercedes opened a cupboard and took out half a dozen plates and several bowls. She gathered cutlery from the drawer and gave them to the children. "Carry these carefully through to the room where your mum is." She picked up the tray of empanadas.

"What can I carry?" said Bruce.

"You're the bank robber," Mercedes reminded him. "You get to tell us what to carry."

He nodded awkwardly and tried out a smile. There was a submissiveness in those gestures, an acceptance of her tenderness and kindness. The man who 'held all the cards' was so bloody lonely and out of his depth, he was seeing her as something between saviour and confidante. A sort of daft reverse Stockholm Syndrome.

The four of them made their way down the corridor.

Becky Mitten, Stevie Lingard, Justin Johnson and the marble woman, Delia, were still tied to their chairs as they should be. Mercedes would not have been surprised if they had managed to escape, somehow. Peculiarly, she realised she would have been disappointed if they had.

"Oh, my babies!" said Becky and leaned towards her children.

The blonde kids put down their cutlery and crockery and gave their mum polite, restrained hugs.

"They smell nice," said Stevie.

"They're mine," said Becky and looked round challengingly. "I will need reimbursing."

"Okay, food time," said Bruce. He moved forward to untie Stevie, then seemed to remember himself. "Mercedes, untie them. But everyone stays in their seat."

"Some of us are going to need the toilet soon," said Justin.

"And it'll be over soon," said Bruce, which Mercedes thought was an ambiguous statement and frightening to anyone who thought about it long enough.

With hands freed and wrists rubbed to bring life back into them, plates were dished out and food distributed.

Cooked empanadas were accompanied by trays of prawns and sushi, miniature pork pies, gooey desserts in ramekins, and rapidly collapsing raspberry and mascarpone meringue roulade.

"I have no idea what we'll be feeding the Whitstables when they come over," said Becky, snootily.

"But you'll have some exciting dinner party conversation for them, mummy!" said Evan enthusiastically.

Mercedes found something awful, cloying, and just plain wrong in the relationship between the children and their mother. She wanted to drag the two of them away, shove them into a sand pit with buckets and spades and not let them out until they had discovered what childhood was truly meant to be.

"And will it be over by dinnertime, huh?" said Justin around a crumbling mouthful of pork pie.

"I spoke to the police negotiator woman," said Bruce. He sat apart from the rest of them on the edge of a desk. The machete rested across his lap. He wasn't eating.

"And what did she say?"

"Opening dialogue. Right?" said Mercedes with a look at Bruce. "Bruce hasn't given her his list of demands yet."

Delia found a small smear of mascarpone inside the packaging and scooped it up with a finger. These were high quality snacks and it would be a shame to waste any. "Oh, you do need to come up with some demands," she said.

Bruce's face creased in a frown. "I just need enough money to make sure I can develop Tigerheart so that my children have a decent future."

"Yes," said Delia, throwing her hands in the air. "You just

want to have some money, same as Mariah Carey just wants to come on stage and sing songs."

"I don't follow," said Bruce.

"Mariah Carey is a legend! Why is that? Because she makes sure people take her seriously! She has tour riders where she specifies which champagne, plants and candles should be in her dressing room."

"I don't think we need anything like that," said Bruce, glancing around the room, possibly judging whether it needed a potted plant or two.

"No, but the point is you need to say you do. Give them something concrete to do for you."

Mercedes nodded, encouragingly.

"We can help you come up with ideas," said Stevie. "But I don't think candles are quite right for you."

Delia picked up a pen. The whiteboard was full, so she crossed the room to a flip chart and found a blank page. She wrote BRUCE'S DEMANDS at the top of the page. "Is there something cabbage-related that you'd like, Bruce?"

There was a pause. Mercedes glanced at the others. She could see everyone (including Bruce) wondering what that might be.

"I've already got a cabbage," said Bruce.

"If you had a portable stove you could cook it and we could all try some," said Mercedes.

"Steaming would retain more of the nutrients," said Edith. "Boiling cabbage is very old-fashioned."

"We could steam it lightly, toss it in olive oil and add some caraway seeds, couldn't we, mummy?" added Evan.

Mercedes raised her eyebrows. Shoving these kids in a

sand pit would not be enough. They needed taking to a theme park and abandoning until they learned to be proper children

Delia jotted ideas on the board. STEAMER, OLIVE OIL, CARAWAY SEEDS. "I know we're just getting warmed up, but we need to think bigger."

"Big like a pony?" asked Evan, his eyes wide.

"Well, yes. That is definitely quite big." Delia added PONY. "Maybe we will need a scented candle after we introduce boiled cabbage and livestock."

"Something to brighten up the room would be nice," said Bruce.

Justin, Mercedes and Stevie all spoke at the same time.

"A motivational poster!"

"A vase of colourful flowers!"

"A lava lamp!"

Delia added them all to the list. "We should be more detailed, more specific! Should we say that only freesias will do, or it must be a vintage seventies lava lamp? This is a list of demands, so it should be demanding. Bruce – this is your list!"

Bruce nodded. "Freesias are nice, but I prefer lilies."

"Bit funereal, Bruce."

"I like lilies," he repeated. "And lava lamps should be as big as possible. Those little novelty ones are pointless."

"Good." Delia looked at Bruce's outstretched hands, indicating the size of lava lamp he wanted. "Shall we say the bulb should be greater than forty centimetres?"

"Yes. And it should be copper-coloured, with classic red wax. None of this purple glittery nonsense."

"Great work Bruce, we'll get you the lava lamp of your dreams, don't worry."

"We could ask for some comfortable furniture," said Justin. "Those of us who are tied up risk lower back problems on these typists chairs."

Bruce laughed. "A sofa for Justin."

"A chaise longue!" said Becky.

"Let's add that to the list. Some fluffy cushions as well."

Justin scowled as Delia added it to the flip chart. "This is ridiculous."

"The pony will need something to eat," said Stevie.

"And a coat in case it gets cold," said Edith.

Delia's hand moved at speed across the paper PONY FOOD, PONY COAT.

"And where will the money come from for all of this?" asked Justin, sitting up straight. "Hmmm?"

"*That's* what you're concerned with right now?" asked Becky. "The police will get what they need."

"I realise that. I play golf with Chief Inspector Peach. He's got a limited budget, you know!"

Bruce stared at Justin. "I see. In that case, we'd better add some champagne." He pointed at Becky. "You. What champagne is expensive?"

"Um. Perrier-Jouët Belle Epoque is very nice. Lovely design on the bottle too."

"Six bottles of that."

"But—"

Bruce silenced Justin with a raised hand.

Delia made a humming sound as her pen was poised to

write down the champagne order. "How are we spelling that Perrier stuff?"

"I'll write it for you," said Edith. She took the pen and wrote it down in beautiful handwriting, accompanied by the correct French accents on the letters. "I've been thinking." Edith looked up at her mum. "This is like a superpower isn't it? We can ask for anything?"

"Yes," said Becky. "I suppose it is like a superpower."

"We always say if we had a superpower we would use it for good, don't we?"

"Um, yes darling, we do say that." Becky glanced around the room, clearly not realising where her daughter was taking this.

"So why don't we ask for something that does good in the world?"

"Oh, I see! Were you thinking the champagne should be organic?" Becky smiled. "Might have to go to Waitrose for that."

"No, I mean maybe we should make them go to Calais and take some of the refugees out of that horrible camp? Give them a nice house on our road?"

"Interesting idea, sweetheart. Maybe not on our *actual* road." Becky addressed the rest of the room. "Sorry, she saw a documentary the other day."

"It's a great idea," said Delia. She added HOUSE REFUGEES to the board. "How many Edith? Twenty, fifty?"

"Fifty," said Edith.

Delia stood back and looked at the flip chart. "So we're asking for the means to cook Bruce's cabbage, which is a steamer, olive oil and caraway seeds. We want a pony, and also something to feed it and something for it to wear. We want a motivational poster, a vase of lilies, and a copper-coloured lava lamp with red wax and a bulb height of not less than forty centimetres. We want a chaise longue for Justin, six bottles of Perrier-Jouët Belle Epoque, and fifty refugees from Calais to be housed near to Becky." Delia smiled at the woman before looking at Bruce. "Can you get behind these ideas, Bruce?"

"Yes, I reckon so. I'll phone the negotiator woman."

There were approving nods from everyone, except Justin. Bruce waved the machete at Mercedes. "Now, tie them up again."

"What?" said Becky. "But we're helping you."

"And some of us definitely need the toilet," said Justin.

32

Marvin slid the tea trolley door open and looked around.

"I'm now in a kitchen area," he said into the phone for the benefit of anyone listening. "My previous hiding place has been compromised. Can't take the trolley out again or they'll think the bank has poltergeists."

"I'm switching disguises," he whispered into the phone. The kitchen offered few options.

"Disguises?" the policeman on the line said. *"You need to stay safe and hidden, sir."*

Marvin couldn't recall if the man had said his name was Beech or Peach, or even possibly Leach. He didn't want to insult him by getting it wrong, and having been on the phone for quite some time now, it had passed beyond the polite time to ask. Marvin had gotten round it by employing a non-specific mumble when uttering the name.

"Inspector *Mng*each, I need to get closer. My daughter's

friend, Delia, is in here somewhere, and I doubt my daughter would forgive me if I let her come to harm. She only came here to cash some cheques. Who writes cheques these days? I'm no spring chicken and even I've gone contactless."

"Sir, it's chief inspector and you need to do as you're told."

"Chief inspector—?" Marvin left it hanging to encourage the man to repeat himself, and maybe even tuck in the relevant surname.

"Yes." Which was of no use. *"Your daughter would like to see you safe. Think what would happen if you came to any harm."*

Marvin thought about that. For one, his debts would vanish and his creditors could chase each other round until Kingdom Come. True, Sam would lose the house, but it looked like they were going to lose that anyway. Sam would certainly be free of her self-imposed duty to care for him; free to get on with her life. He wasn't so naïve or so deluded to think that his death wouldn't have a negative impact on her, but there was definitely a sense that her own life was on hold; that she was tethered to him in some way.

"Where is Sam?" Marvin asked.

"She's assisting the detective with our enquiries,"

"Detective Camara?"

"Detective Constable *Camara,"* the chief inspector said. He was clearly obsessed with rank.

"Nice lad, he is," Marvin said with feeling, and put the phone in his pocket while he tried to extricate himself from the trolley. It was not easy. Marvin had many things to be thankful for as the years had advanced. He was still supple enough to get into all manner of positions, and he doubted many of his contemporaries could do the same. But unusual exercise and staying in one position for prolonged periods always came with a price. If he survived the day, Marvin would need to invest in a cartload of painkillers and sessions with a chiropractor.

The kitchen was a small room. The air was filled with the tang of just-cooked food. It smelled like chip shop chicken pies, but there was a spicy tang to it as well. If his mind was not otherwise occupied, he might have realised he was hungry. But he was a man on a mission. Disguise options were few in number. Fridges and cupboards offered no suggestions. His eyes settled on the bins in the corner.

Ah, bins. Here, Marvin was glad to be living in the current age. If this had been a kitchen from more than twenty years ago there would have been a single swing-lid bin with a bin bag into which everything went, and he would have been out of luck. But – oh, blessed modern age! – there were three bins in the kitchen, of different sizes and, naturally, different coloured lids. Yes, there was a swing bin for actual rubbish, into which staff probably threw their old tea bags and waste food, and there were two recycling bins – one for paper and one for glass and plastics. And – fortune be praised – they both were of that modern design which demanded recycling bins be huge boxy things of moulded plastic, with curves and corners and an overall presence that seemed to say, 'Look at me. I'm stylish and sexy and big enough to accommodate all your recycling needs.' Normally, Marvin looked upon such bins as too damn big, cluttering up spaces. But right now he eyed up the paper recycling bin and thought it would quite possibly house a crouching gentleman of a certain age.

He carefully emptied the five inches of discarded paper in the bottom of the bin, scowling at the yoghurt pot lid someone had put in there, either accidentally or in the mistaken belief that tin foil was a sort of paper. Marvin found a bread knife in a cutlery drawer. He was surprised and delighted to find it sawed through the plastic bottom of the bin with very little effort. He also cut a small spy hole in the front of the bin, so he could see where he was going. He found it easier to get in by lowering the bin over himself and squeezing through the hole he had cut, leaving his feet poking out to shuffle upon. He checked he could crouch and conceal himself completely. It was possible, although his head would be pressing against the lid's large slot for the posting of recycled paper.

"On the move again," he murmured for the benefit of the phone. "I feel like Dusty Bin. Do you remember Dusty Bin, chief inspector? What about Ted Rogers? Great comedian. Great singer too. Worked with Bing Crosby and Perry Como. And me, it goes without saying. But everyone remembers Ted best for a partnership with a robot bin off that quiz show." Marvin shuffled to the door. "Going in search of the hostages," he said, shuffling through and into the corridor.

Soon, Marvin was opposite the door to the room with the hostages. He settled his bin into what he hoped was a normal, casual bin placement, and cautiously raised the lid by an inch to get a better view. The corridor was empty. He listened carefully, but could hear nothing. Not even the voices of the hostages. He lifted the lid fully off and stood erect, failing to keep completely silent as his joints cracked loudly. He needed to move quickly now. If he went into the room and untied the hostages, did he have a plan for getting them out of there? Maybe the sort of plan where you threw a chair through a window wouldn't work, but he could do something. He lifted the bin over his head and placed it on the floor. Just as his hand touched the door handle, a man's loud voice shouted from within the room.

"I need to use the toilet! Let me take a pee! It's getting quite urgent now!"

Marvin cursed softly. This was terrible timing. He scrambled underneath his bin disguise and settled the base onto the floor. He heard footsteps approaching and realised he hadn't swung the lid back in place. He reached a hand underneath the bottom edge, grabbed the lid and scooted further along the corridor, away from the voice of Bruce who was now shouting back.

"Wait a minute! We can sort something out!"

Marvin was very exposed without his lid, even though he was a good six feet away from the door. Marvin took his chance. He flipped the lid up, over, and into place just in time.

Bruce poked his head from the room and looked up and down the corridor, a confused look on his face. Marvin held his breath and made sure he didn't move at all.

"Come on! I need the loo!" The man was complaining again.

Bruce turned his attention back to the room and Marvin let his breath go.

"There's a bin out here. If I bring it in you can use it as a toilet," said Bruce.

Marvin froze. This was a rather revolting development.

"I beg your pardon?" came the man's voice haughtily. "Do you seriously expect me to urinate in front of these women?"

"Fine. You can come out here and do it in the corridor," said Bruce. "I don't care about seeing your penis, but I'm not letting you out of my sight."

Marvin could do nothing. He heard movement from inside the room and knew he was about to be showered in urine.

"You're making me very nervous. I might actually need a number two."

Marvin very nearly moaned out loud.

"Hang on. Just wait a second, Bruce."

Was that Delia? It sounded like her voice. Marvin was elated to hear her sounding fit and well. It momentarily distracted him from the prospect of being shit upon by Eastshires Bank twice in one day. He made a note to himself to remember that line for Sam. It was good enough to make her roll her eyes, a proper dad joke.

"What?"

Delia again. "The rest of us need the loo too. Why don't we all go along and take turns, then you can make sure we don't do anything rash? We're just trying to help you end this in the easiest way possible."

Marvin raised a small silent thank you to Delia as Bruce agreed. A few minutes later, the group trailed off down the corridor.

33

Camara drove Sam to Greencock Farm.

She had offered to take him in the Piaggio Ape, but arguments regarding its energy efficiency and superior manoeuvrability on narrow roads held little sway for a man who would have had to fold himself up like a deckchair in order to squeeze into the tiny cab.

Sam felt a peculiar and unshakeable sense of guilt as they sped away from the town, as though she were abandoning her dad and going off on a frivolous drive in the country. South of Skegness, low hedgerows, scattered trees and miles and miles of unremarkable fields filled the landscape. A combine harvester was out in a field, working through acres of dry and brittle rapeseed crop and sending clouds of brown, husky dust into the air. The sun was high, the clouds of the morning had burned away. It was turning into the kind of summer's day that picture postcards and the

Skegness tourist board hoped people thought occurred most of the time in this corner of England.

Camara turned off the main road and down Marsh House Road. The road was gated but, as always, it was left open. There was a police car parked by the entrance to the farmyard, with an on duty police officer who had clearly mastered the art of standing still and looking officious, legs slightly spread, hands together behind his waist. He approached Camara's car, recognised the detective and waved him through.

Camara parked his car and they both got out. As he approached the other officer on the scene, who was poking around the sheds, Sam opened her DefCon4 app and clicked to 'resolve' the Greencock Farm motion detector alarm alert which had popped up earlier. Her phone buzzed immediately. To her annoyance the DefCon4 app was berating her for not sticking to her schedule. She had been hopeful its nagging might be suspended while the request for compassionate leave was in the system, but apparently not.

PLEASE RETURN TO AN EXPECTED LOCATION FOR YOUR DAY'S TASKS OR IMMEDIATELY CONTACT YOUR SUPERVISOR. YOU ARE IN BREACH OF CONTRACT IF YOU CANNOT JUSTIFY THIS DEVIANCE.

Sam was in breach of contract. It sounded alarming, until she reflected on the fact she had never actually seen a contract, and certainly never signed one. It was something hinted at via the app, and the Employee Handbook that the app often referenced, but never offered links to.

She would catch up with her missed tasks when this was all over. She was adept at juggling the varied demands of her job, so she reckoned she could smooth over much of it after the fact. At some point she might need to make a phone call to head office, but that particular horror was an absolute last resort, as it rarely resulted in anybody doing anything helpful.

"Any sign of the family?" Camara asked the officer by the sheds.

"I think he lives alone," Sam called over.

"Neighbour half a mile up the road says the wife moved out a few years ago," said the officer.

Camara passed Sam a pair of latex gloves and some shoe covers before they went into the unlocked house. "In case this place becomes evidentially important," he said. "Touch nothing, yes?"

Sam nodded and Camara led the way in.

"So, you knew he lived alone?" Camara asked as they stepped into the kitchen.

"Just an impression," said Sam. "Smell that?"

Camara sniffed. "Furniture polish?"

Sam nodded.

"And fresh paint," said Camara.

Sam hadn't noticed that on her first visit, but he was right. Somewhere in the house, decorating had recently occurred.

"The man keeps a clean and tidy house," she said. "Maybe he always did. Maybe he's on the rebound."

"Rebound?"

"You know, that thing when a relationship's on the rocks or beyond saving and you – by this, I pretty much mean the bloke – tries to do all the little things they should have done when the relationship was still alive."

"Overcompensating."

"Exactly. That. The gun cabinet's this way."

"Is that what Rich did?" said Camara. "Towards the end."

"Oh, we're discussing my tattered love life now, are we?"

Camara made a polite and silent gesture, a sort of passive un-shrug.

"No," she said. "That would require some degree of awareness on his part. He just went into total denial, refusing to believe I could possibly want to leave him."

"So when he did realise you had left him...?"

"What do you mean?" She gave him a funny look. "The denial phase is still going strong. You?"

"I'm not in denial."

She tutted. "What about your exes?"

He made a dismissive noise. "All came to an end by mutual agreement. No corpses littering the battlefield. No major psychological trauma."

"Sounds a little like denial," Sam said. She stopped at the gun cabinet under the stairs and pointed to the fuse box. "He kept the key up there."

Camara felt along the top of the fuse box, retrieved the key and unlocked the cabinet. Sam looked at the array of guns.

"Well?" said Camara.

"Six shotguns and a rifle," said Sam. "They're all here."

"What? Are you sure?"

She moved her hand along the rack, not touching. She recalled them taking out the guns one by gun, she misplacing a tracking widget, Bruce correcting her. She looked at the split box of shotgun shells, remembered the steps by which they had worked through the cabinet.

"Six shotguns and a rifle," she repeated. "All here."

"But that's not possible."

"He might have had another shotgun elsewhere," she said, but the words felt wrong even as it came out of her mouth. If there was another cabinet he would have shown her. And he didn't strike her as the kind of man who would keep an illegal shotgun just lying around.

"I need to call this in," said Camara and took out his phone.

Sam stepped away to give him room and went into the living room.

"Touch nothing," Camara reminded her.

"I know."

She had been in this room earlier. There was the dated television, and there the almost antique music system. She inspected the CD collection on the shelf above it. Yes, there was some Dolly Parton, plus some Linda Ronstadt, Woody Guthrie, Shania Twain, Bob Dylan, Joni Mitchell and Elvis. An American country vibe ran through the man's tastes. There was an acoustic guitar propped up in the corner of the room. Sam ran her fingers over the strings. It was horribly out of tune.

"Touch nothing!" Camara called.

"Okay!" she retorted.

She went to the mantelpiece. The porcelain poodles had painted-on faces. One of them looked a bit cross-eyed and dopey. Delia would have loved them. There was a section in her shop pretty much devoted to ugly pottery animals. The more imbecilic the expressions on their faces, the better.

When she had been in the house that morning, Sam had noticed the photographs on the mantelpiece were peculiarly aligned, arranged at an angle so they all faced one corner of the room. She looked to the corner to see if it was where a favourite chair was positioned, but no. It then occurred to her, looking at the window, they had been placed so that the sun, sweeping round the south of the house, never fell directly on them. Bruce was so fastidious he even arranged photos to stop them fading in sunlight.

The pictures covered a range of decades. The most recent photo was a badly staged image of what Sam took to be Bruce's absent family. A family meal featuring two girls and a boy, probably none older than twelve: a triptych of sullen, disinterested and bored faces, and a woman with an unfortunate fringe raising a glass of white wine to the camera. Two more photos showed more willing subjects. There was a family holiday with three scampering youngsters, crowded round their mum on a beach. Blurred rocks and grass in the background suggested somewhere more dynamic and rugged than the Lincolnshire coast. Another photo was taken from a log flume ride at a theme park: gasping startled faces and eyes screwed shut in fear. Three children and their mum. Bruce was not in it, and it wasn't because he was behind the camera.

There was a photograph of the Greencock's wedding. *Christine and Bruce, 12th October 2002.* The wife, Christine, had not yet adopted the unfortunate fringe. Bruce still had a modicum of youthful vitality in his cheeks.

Sam took the final photograph to be a copy of a Polaroid camera image. The colours were fading to whites and browns. It was clearly several decades old and showed a teenage girl in front of a five bar gate, with a man in a checked shirt and a woman in a floral dress. All three of them in wellington boots. The name of the farm on a post was half in shot. The teenager was unmistakeably a young Christine. A glance at the buildings in the background told Sam it was a photograph of this farm, the gate the one they had just come through.

"Wait. Hang on," She stared at it, almost forgetting Camara's directive and touching it, then screwed up her face as she tried to puzzle it through. It was this farm, but it was Bruce's future wife with the family by the gate. And the farm name, although half cut off, ended in 'ghby'. It was not yet Greencock Farm.

"This isn't his farm," she said.

She went out into the hallway.

"That's what I'm telling you," Camara was saying on the phone. "If he has one, it's not one of the ones from the farm. Our witness is certain."

"It's not his farm," Sam said to him.

34

Toilet visits done, hostages tied to their chairs once more (with Delia insisting on the wooden kitchen chair once more because it was 'good for her posture), Bruce prepared to phone the hostage negotiator.

"Remember, you're in charge," said Delia.

"I am," he said.

"If you want to walk out of here with the money, you need to stay strong," said Mercedes.

"I will," he said.

Bruce put a call through to the number that had previously called him.

"Put it on speaker," Mercedes whispered as it began to ring. Bruce immediately complied.

"Bruce, what an absolute pleasure to hear from you again!" said the firm but warm Scottish tones of Bridey MacDougal. *"How are things?"*

Bruce could hear the smile in her voice. Strange how that

worked. How was it possible to know someone's expression from just their voice? "I've got a list of demands."

"Oh, have you now? Someone's a well-prepared young man."

"It's stuff I'm going to need."

"As you know, I am very much here to help, Bruce. I'll get a pen and paper so that I can note these down carefully. I am very interested to know what it is you'd like. Go ahead and tell me when you're ready."

"First things are so we can eat the cabbage."

"The cabbage, yes."

"I'll need a steamer, some olive oil, and some caraway seeds."

"Got that. Your cabbage is called Tigerheart as I understand it. You must be very proud."

"I am. It's got stripes. That's the USP." Bruce waited to see if Bridey was confused by the acronym, as Justin had been.

"A unique selling point is so very important. It could make a really solid brand."

"Yes! Thank you!" he gushed, so pleased someone understood. He swallowed the brief surge of excitement, remembering his situation had moved on from pitching his cabbage. "Anyway, next on the list is a pony."

"Mmm-hmm. Pony."

He hesitated, wrong-footed by Bridey's calm acceptance. "A real pony," he added.

"Yes."

"You know, with fur and hooves and... You know, a pony."

"I understand," said Bridey smoothly.

"And we'll need something for it to eat, and a coat for it to wear as well."

"*Pony, got it. We'll need to talk logistics at some point, but we can come back to that.*"

"Then there's a motivational poster, a vase of lilies, and a copper-coloured lava lamp with red wax and a bulb height of not less than forty centimetres."

Bridey murmured gently as she copied them down. "*So, can I just check Bruce, what do you mean by a motivational poster?*"

Bruce realised he had no firm idea. "Those things with animals? Like wallpaper with cheesy slogans?"

"Get a dog one!" shouted Stevie. "I've got one at home that says 'Home is where the cute puppy is.'"

"A dog one," repeated Bruce.

"*I heard. You have someone there who has strong opinions on the subject! Can I ask who that was?*"

"No."

"*No problem, Bruce. Just trying to build a picture of how things are for you in there. It sounds like you've got a great group of people with you. Well done for making a connection. Not everyone has that skill. Do you have more things on your list?*"

"Yes. There's a chaise longue, and six bottles of Perrier-Jouët Belle Epoque."

"*Is that a kind of champagne?*"

"Yes. Fancy bottle."

"*Fancy bottle. Got it. I'm not one for fancy things myself. I like things that are decent, honest, straightforward.*"

"It's a very nice champagne," Becky called out.

"*Someone else with strong opinions.*" There was just a hint of laughter.

"The last thing on the list is the re-homing of fifty

refugees from that camp in Calais," said Bruce. "They need to be given a nice place to live round here."

"But not too near," Becky put in again.

"Well Bruce, what an intriguing list. That last one especially. Is the refugee situation something that is close to your heart?"

Bruce saw a trap opening. He obviously needed to say it was important to him, or he'd be undermining the whole effort to make them take him seriously. In truth though, he knew very little about refugees in Calais, or anywhere else for that matter. "I don't really want to talk about it."

Mercedes nodded approvingly.

"That's perfectly fine, Bruce. The refugee request is a tricky one, of course, but I'll make sure we get onto the Home Office and explore that right away. What kind of a deadline are we talking about here?"

"Deadline." Of course there would need to be a deadline. No point in all of these things happening after he'd escaped. Bruce was in a quandary. If he told them they had until the end of the day he would be giving the impression he planned to remain here all day. At least. Maybe he should give them a deadline of just one hour, but that felt very unrealistic.

Mercedes caught his eye. She mimed pressing a button on a phone and mouthed *mute*. He muted the phone.

"Tell them they have an hour to get hold of the basic items, and gain a commitment to the refugee re-homing. That is your starting position. They will want to negotiate, but you stay strong."

"I have a suggestion," said Delia. "Tell them to ask Hilde Odinson about the lava lamp. In fact, if they gave her most of the list she would probably be able to find them. She is a resourceful young woman."

Bruce turned away from the others before returning to the call. "The deadline is one hour. You can certainly find the minor items in that time and get a commitment to the refugee demand."

"We're going to need more time than that, Bruce. You realise how difficult some of these things will be to track down?"

"I'm reliably informed you can get some of the items using the services of a young woman called Hilde Odinson."

"I shall look into it, but she won't be able to help with an international political situation, will she?"

"Not my problem, just make it happen!" said Bruce and ended the call.

35

Bruce's office was in a greenhouse attached to one of the poly-tunnels in which he grew the fruit and vegetables not cultivated large-scale in the fields. Sam supposed it was in here that Bruce Greencock had cultivated the Tigerheart cabbage and either bent the cabbage's genes to produce stripes or, more likely, bent his mind until he could see stripes where none existed.

There was a display board made from a large remnant of plywood, with plans pinned to it. The display held maps of the farm, with dates stretching fifty years into the future and marked out with areas with names like *Frostwarden*, *Goldenball* and *Nutri-Leaf*. It seemed like Tigerheart cabbage was only the start of a long-term vegetable empire.

Camara had insisted on taking photographs of everything in situ on the desk, in the warm muggy space, before letting Sam go anywhere near it, even with latex-covered hands. Bruce operated his business in a manner that

would have impressed anyone before the advent of the
personal computer. He kept rows of lever arch folders, fat
piles of receipts, invoices, letters, and bills that strained the
folder hoops to breaking point. Pencil annotations dotted the
margins of many documents: items ticked off, totals
calculated and re-calculated.

Bruce was a businessman who had yet to embrace the
digital world.

Sam sorted through the papers, searching.

"What are you looking for?" asked Camara. "Does it
matter if the farm is his or not? We came to check the
shotguns."

"Crime is all about three things," she said absently,
pulling down another folder. An unsecured envelope slid out
onto the desk. She ignored it and looked at the date at the
top of the first document in the folder. Sam was proficient
with files and filing. She wished she wasn't, but her job with
DefCon4 had instilled in her an unwanted affinity for
documentation, policies, and all things paper based. Her job
to date, varied and peculiar as it was, had included doing
lengthy health and safety paperwork for local businesses,
navigating the local courts' prisoner management systems
and, perhaps the most Herculean task so far, cataloguing the
monstrous and varied collection of antiques at the nearby
Candlebroke Hall. The fastidious filing system of a tidy-
minded farmer was child's play in comparison.

"Three things?" prompted Camara.

"Huh? Yeah. Criminals need means, motive and ... the
other one."

"Opportunity."

"Right. If Bruce is trying to rob the bank to bankroll his cabbage obsession, it would be bloody peculiar if the farm he was trying to prop up was never his in the first place."

"This personal theory being based on an old photo of a teenage girl and a farm with a different name?"

"Willoughby Farm!" Sam firmly pushed the boards of the folder wide as she uncovered the found page. Something within the lever arch mechanism went *toing!* in protest. The document in front of her was a contract, laid out in some long-winded legalese.

Sam scanned through. The document, whilst long, was unambiguous.

"Christine Willoughby's dad sold the farm to Bruce Greencock in two thousand and one." She closed her eyes momentarily. "That was before the wedding."

"So, no mystery. Farm sold to his future son-in-law. Maybe for a knock down price as some sort of dowry."

Sam laughed. "What century are you from?"

"Or tax dodge. Maybe I'm trying to see into the mind of the local farming community. Time runs slower round here. Old country ways. Harvest festivals, corn dollies, Lammas Day bread."

"Burning nosy coppers in a giant wicker man and giving farms away as dowries, sure. Still, you wouldn't give it to the son-in-law when you could just give it to your daughter."

"Maybe she didn't have the passion for farming," he suggested. "If I know anything about farmers—"

"And you so clearly do."

"—I know they want their farms to be tended by someone with respect for the land."

"Oh, that's Bruce all right."

Sam thought of the photos on the mantelpiece, recalling that, apart from the wedding photo, Bruce didn't appear in any of them, even when there was no excuse not to. She had a sudden vision of a family of four – a mother and her children – and a man on the periphery who was notionally their father.

"He was a man married to his job," she said.

"And so his actual marriage fell apart."

Sam began to close the folder then saw the envelope which had fallen off the shelf. She might have ignored it but for the company logo printed on it.

Bonner-Sanchez.

It was unusual to see the name of a commercial oil and energy company on the home office desk of a Lincolnshire farmer. It was as incongruous as seeing post from an arms dealer or NASA.

It had already been opened and Sam didn't even consider moral qualms before taking out the letter. It was short, succinct, and there was a little table with numbers in it at the bottom. One of those numbers was seven point six million pounds.

"Why the hell's he robbing banks?" Camara whispered.

"The man's loaded," Sam nodded in agreement.

36

"Can we go somewhere where there's a window?" said Edith. "I want to see the pony when it comes up the steps."

"No windows," said Bruce. It got him thinking though. How would the delivery of these things take place? There was a good chance it would make him vulnerable.

"New activity," he announced. "We need to figure out how they can get these things to us without me being captured or killed.

"Bruce, I'm very happy to see you're getting such value from our collaboration," said Delia.

"Let me draw!" asked Evan, holding out his hand for a pen. He turned the flipchart onto a new page and started to create a picture. He began with sticky-up ears and a long face with goggle eyes. He then gave it legs.

"That's lovely darling, you're emulating Picasso!" said Becky proudly.

"Or is it Escher?" said Delia. "I'm getting a bit dizzy trying to count the legs!"

"So that's the pony, mummy," declared Evan. "And this is how all the stuff gets delivered." He drew a bag hanging from the pony's back. It was helpfully labelled *Bag*. "In there goes all the other stuff."

"Sweetheart, I don't know if you've ever seen a chaise longue, it's what the John Lewis catalogue would call a day bed."

"Oh, I would love us to have a day bed for the guest bedroom, mummy."

"Yes, well, it's a bit big for that bag."

Evan stared at his picture, his chin in his hand. "Well then, here's what we must do." There was only a small gap at the back of the pony, but he squashed a rectangle into the space.

"A wheelie bin?" said Justin.

"How dare you mock the artistic creations of a child!" roared Becky. "Apologise right now!"

"But—"

"NOW!"

"Mummy, it is actually a wheelie bin," said Evan.

"Would that be big enough for a chaise longue?" said Edith.

Justin started to puff himself up a self-righteous manner, so Mercedes stepped forward and took the pen from Evan.

"Enough yelling, all of you. You're onto something here, Evan. Re-do the picture on another page and make this thing bigger than a wheelie bin. Bruce can text it to Bridey so that she knows how we expect the handover to take place."

"Yes," said Bruce. "I will."

"Oh, oh, oh! I have an idea!" said Delia.

"Yes?"

"If they put some carrots through the letterbox then we can use them to make sure the pony doesn't wander off. One of us opens the door and lets it in, yeah?"

"As long as the police SWAT team don't try to sneak in at the same time," said Mercedes.

Bruce gave her a nervous glance. Mercedes shrugged.

37

Marvin remained immobile in the bin while the hostages had taken a toilet break, under close supervision. His knees were locked in a quite excruciating position, but he couldn't afford to budge until the coast was clear.

The muttering, murmuring posse returned and re-entered the room. Marvin could not hear all that was said inside. There was some general grumbling about being tied up and harsh warnings giving. Then there had been some protracted conversation in which the only bit he heard clearly was someone loudly demanding an apology for mocking a child's artistic efforts.

Several minutes later, he heard the door open, and the woman Mercedes telling the children to stay together. Bruce didn't speak, but Marvin heard heavier footsteps and guessed that Bruce had at least taken Mercedes and the children with him.

He didn't hurry to move. For one thing, his joints needed a bit of advanced warning, and secondly, he didn't want to pop out at the wrong moment. He recalled that one time he and Linda had performed for a corporate awards evening aboard a cruiser on the Thames. The company was paying, and Marvin and his assistant had made the mistake of partaking of the free bar before the show. The end result was Linda popping out from the wings of the tiny stage with a drunken 'Ta-dah!' before Marvin had finished filling the cabinet where she was meant to be with sharp blades. Doing the reveal before the trick was generally a no-no, akin to washing up the pots before the meal was eaten, but the corporate guests had been so drunk none of them noticed, bursting into stunned applause at the sudden appearance of the woman in a spangled bikini. Marvin had never been sure if the moral of the story was that great entertainers could finesse their way through any on-stage calamity, or that, on some occasions, his magic played second billing to a slender young woman who was not wearing much.

Cautiously, Marvin edged nearer the door.

"—don't know what you're complaining about," a woman was saying. "He let you go to the toilet, didn't he?"

"So we should be grateful for that?" a man spat. "You don't have to be so pally with him. He's a criminal."

Marvin recognised his voice. The man very much in need of a number one, possibly a number two. That made him Justin.

"If you'd given him that loan..." said another woman.

"Would you leave it, Stevie?"

"If it was for less than ten percent of the value of the

collateral, which I'm guessing it was, Eastshires branch managers can make a discretionary loan—"

"A loan to that idiot yokel? A man who'd lose the money in a week? He can't be trusted with it."

"Really?"

"Hell's bells, woman! His big idea is a stripey cabbage. It hasn't even got any stripes in it! He put a dent in my Vebjörn with his machete! He's a nutter!"

"And now we're in this situation because you didn't give him the loan. My poor Petey is probably worried sick—"

"Oh, fuck your dog, Stevie!"

There was a gasp and a muffled sob, then the other woman said in coldly cruel tones. "I think we should tell Bruce what Justin has done."

"Now, come on, Becky," said Delia reasonably. "Things are bad enough…"

Marvin had been listening so intently, it belatedly occurred to him that, yes, Bruce was clearly not about and it was probably safe for him to move. He rose gently, knees creaking, lifting the lid above his head. He walked the bin over to the room and opened the door.

He entered and found four people tied to office chairs. Three women and a man.

"Who are you?" said Justin.

"Marvin!" whispered Delia in surprised delight. "Oh, Marvin!"

"And why are you wearing a bin?" said the woman in the frilly mauve blouse of a bank employee. Stevie.

"That's pretty rich coming from people tied to chairs," said Marvin.

Delia smiled. "Are you all right?"

"It's been a varied day," he said, reflectively. "Where's the bank robber?"

"Bruce has gone back down to the vault with Mercedes," said the bank cashier.

"*And* my children," said the other woman emphatically. Becky. Marvin vaguely recalled the woman, and two blonde tots, coming into the bank after him, earlier.

Justin spun his chair and propelled himself towards Marvin. "Untie us then. We don't know how long they'll be."

Justin's hands were tied against the metal upright of the chair with lengths of what looked like telephone cord. Marvin picked at it with nimble fingers.

Delia pushed herself forward.

"Marvin, it's wonderful to see you. But you shouldn't put yourself in danger like this." Delia appeared to be in good spirits. She looked somewhat bedraggled, and her hair was a mess – but that was sort of Delia's brand.

"I've got the police on the line here," he said, pausing momentarily to try to retrieve his phone from wherever it had got lodged. "They've been with me all the way."

There was a tinny, inaudible response from the phone, probably Chief Inspector *Mng*each trying to say the police might have communicatively been with Marvin but definitely not morally or philosophically.

"Why don't you take the bin off?" said Delia.

"My knees are pretty well locked in place now," said Marvin. "Nothing that a day or two's bed rest wouldn't fix. I have new respect for Kenny Baker."

"Who?"

"Small actor. He was the one inside that robot in Star Wars. R5-D4 or whatever it was called. We did *Snow White* together at the Blackpool Grand some years back."

"My children are being held elsewhere in the building," said Becky. "Is this wise?"

"Wise? Define wise," said Marvin waving an arm at his bin situation. "At my age it's pretty unwise to climb into a bin on collection day."

"Trying to escape could put them in danger."

Justin's hands were freed. He chuckled and leapt to his feet, rubbing his wrists. He climbed onto a table to gain access to a small, frosted window.

"I'm talking to you!" hissed Becky. "Don't you *dare* do anything before we talk about the consequences!"

Marvin toddled over to the cashier, Stevie, and encouraged her to rotate and present her knotted hands to him.

"Shush now everyone," said Justin, teetering slightly as he leaned over to see if he could reach the window.

"Don't shush us, you jerk!" Becky was close to Justin's desk and she lunged forward. She grunted with the exertion, but managed a limited cantering movement with her feet, chair clattering across the floor. She surprised them all with her turn of speed, and before anyone could react she had lunged forward and had Justin's ankle caught in the crook of her neck.

"Aargh! Get off!" Justin kicked his leg to try and free it from her grip. He slipped and crashed down onto the table, on his backside. The woman released his ankle, but she wasn't done with him.

"You were going to leave us all behind and put my kids at risk!"

"It's a tiny window!" he retorted. "It doesn't open and we can't fit through it. I was just *looking!*"

"Don't try mansplaining windows to me, you arse!"

She bit his hand as he struggled to get up.

Marvin stared in horror at the weird fight scene unfolding in front of him.

"Please!" Delia hissed. "Could we all just keep the noise down. You should be ashamed of yourselves. Marvin here has risked everything to come in here and help us."

"And I'm still stuck in this bin disguise," Marvin pointed out.

Justin rolled off the table, walked over to Marvin, grabbed the top of the bin and hauled it over Marvin's head. "There you go."

Marvin grunted and rubbed his knees. "Thanks."

"Take a seat, mate."

What Marvin hadn't expected was that Justin would then propel him backwards into a chair. Justin shrugged the bin and lid into place over his head.

"What the hell—?" said Delia.

"He's running out on us," said Becky.

"You were going to grass on me to Bruce!" Justin snapped back. He gave the bin suit a test, walking at a shuffle.

"Ooh, tight fit," he said from inside. "Right, I'm going to head to the front door, open it and let the police in. Save all your ungrateful, commie backsides!"

"Now, wait a minute—" said Marvin, making conciliatory motions from his seat.

"Coward!" Delia shouted after him and then, realising she was being too loud, lowered the volume. "Coward!" she whispered.

Moments later he was gone from the room.

"That's what I thought," said Sam.

"What do you know about hydrogen production plants?" he said.

"Imagine we know very little," said Camara.

"Hydrogen is the fuel of the future," Rich said. "Well, that's also what they said about nuclear energy. Used in fuel cells it's super-efficient and entirely carbon neutral. Important stuff. The problem is creating it. You can do it through biological processes or by refining fossil fuels, but they aren't perfect."

"Since when did you become the scientist?" said Sam.

"I'm an inventor and therefore a scientist," said Rich.

"You happened upon a crazy idea for picking up dog poo," said Sam

"Build a better mouse trap – or in this case, a dog poo collector – and the world will beat a path to your door. Fact is, my recent endeavours have meant I needed to read up on the competition."

"Competition?"

He nodded. "By far the best and cleanest way to get hydrogen fuel is to use electrolysis on water. Using pure energy to separate hydrogen and oxygen molecules."

"Use energy to make energy?"

"I know, right."

Rich snuck between them, wrapped an arm around each, and turned them all to face the sea. "And where can we find abundant quantities of energy and water?"

Sam's eyes focused on the gleaming white towers miles out to sea. "The wind farms?"

Rich nodded sadly. "Doggerland, to be precise. I told you

the Germans and the Dutch were looking to build an artificial island out there in the same spot as my safari park. Well, Bonner-Sanchez have taken the lead and are already beginning construction of their own. A hydrogen plant."

"But they're an oil company, aren't they?" said Camara. "You know, Bonner-Sanchez, oil spills, dead fish, unhappy seagulls. I've seen the news."

"And they can see the way the wind's blowing. Oil is dead. Long live hydrogen. Point is – and here's where your buddy Bruce comes in – hydrogen has to be brought ashore at some point. There need to be pipelines." Rich consulted the letter again. "Bruce's land runs right up to the coast. Much of it is marsh and fen, quite unusable for anything except drowning lost travellers. And he owns it."

"They're offering seven million pounds to buy him out."

"Nearly eight," said Rich. "It's a lot of money, but it's technically a lot of land. If you believe the rumours, Bonner-Sanchez have got some dodgy oligarch financiers behind the scenes so they've got money to spare. Anyway, if the sea levels rise like they say, then in fifty years it will be underwater. Just like this place. It's only the dykes and drainage systems keeping it above water now. If this offer's on the table, I'd advise him to take it."

Sam stepped away to give her brain space to think. "This is madness."

"Oh, the hydrogen thing is a really good idea if they can get it up and running," Rich assured her.

"Not that." She looked over at the bank two streets over. Silent police lights reflected off shop fronts. She absently took a flute of Buck's Fizz from a silver tray and downed it while she thought. "He works all hours to make something special of his farm," she said, mostly to herself. "His father in law sold it to him so it's passed on to a new generation of farmers. Bruce is so focused on the farming that he loses his wife and family in the process. He's all about the money. And, yet, when Bonner-Sanchez offer him millions for his land— How old is that letter, Rich?"

"Over two years old."

"They literally write him the cheque, but instead of taking them up on it, he tries to get a loan for a fraction of the amount. Even turns to robbery to get his hands on it. That's the definition of insanity."

"If you expect criminals to have sane motives, you're going to be disappointed," said Camara.

Mystified, Sam's eye was drawn to movement in the streets. She stepped up to the binoculars and looked down.

"Someone's brought a portable toilet along and put it by the cordon," she said. She tried to read the signage. "Charging a pound a go."

Rich shrugged. "That's capitalism for you."

"Makes more sense than Bruce's plan," she said, miserably.

39

"It just seems there's no way of making this work," said Bruce.

"Mummy says only losers think like losers," said Evan.

Edith gave him a sharp look. "Mummy says Dion only won the talent contest for 'political reasons'."

"Look," said Mercedes, "why don't you two go over there and count the money, huh?" With a wave of her hand, she sent them to the other side of the vault.

"Let's play *Escape to the Country*," said Edith. "You'll tell me what kind of luxury second home you're looking for, and I'll tell you how much it will cost."

The two settled down with the piles of cash.

Mercedes looked at Bruce. "You're going to prison. *That's* going to happen."

"We've established that," he said. There was a taut

weariness on the man's sweaty face. The inevitability of it all was sinking in.

"But you'd be happy to go to prison if your kids got the money."

"It's not just the money. They need the land. They need the farm."

"Where are they now?"

Bruce drew in an unhappy breath. "With their mum. I don't know where. I thought they might have gone to stay with some friends in Thetford but..." He shook his head. "The only thing I know is they're still in this country. All of their passports are still in the hallway drawer."

"Right. But you've got a son or something you want to inherit the farm." She pursed her lips. 'Inherit' sounded too much like she was expecting Bruce to die. Bruce didn't seem to notice.

"Riley is a great lad," he said. "A bit indoorsy, though. You know that *Fortnite* game all the kids are playing."

Mercedes didn't.

"No, it's Lola who's got the farmer's gene," he said. "Always one for playing in the muck as a kid. Got her own little section of the greenhouse to grow things in. I was teaching her to drive the tractor. Started her when she was eight years old. Couldn't reach the pedals but she wanted to learn. You got a place? To live, I mean."

"I have a flat," said Mercedes and wished she didn't sound defensive.

"You see, I don't know how people can cope with that."

"It's all right."

"You've got no land, Mercedes. You've got nothing to produce food from."

She was prepared to point out she had a fridge, a Tesco club card, and several takeaway apps on her phone, but decided that would be facetious.

"You've got to have land," said Bruce. "Every one of us needs land to produce the food we eat and the clothes we wear. Without land, we're nothing. There are dark days ahead." It was a weighty and pompous statement to come out with, and it sounded silly coming from his lips.

"Dark days," she said. "Right."

"Too many people, not enough land, not enough food. Sea levels rising. Planet heating up. You seen that *Mad Max*?"

"Um."

"Imagine that, except it's not biker gangs in leather. It's people starving and struggling. Dark days. We need to start future-proofing and planning long-term. We have to protect the ones we love. That's what it means to be a parent."

Mercedes did laugh at that.

"You don't think so?" said Bruce.

"You haven't met my mum."

"No?"

"The most useless excuse for a mother you could ever find."

"I'm sure she's not all that bad."

"You have not met her, Mr Greencock." Mercedes turned around, as though trying to locate her flat from here, even though they were underground. "She's there right now, in that flat of mine. It's my flat, but she's living with me."

"Well, as you get older—"

"She's fifty-four years old, Bruce. She's not old. She's not ill. And yet she's living with me. Nothing wrong with her."

"She works?"

"A few hours a week down at the bargain store on the retail park. Tills, I think."

"Your dad?"

"Single parent family," she said. "At least, I thought we were. My mum got pregnant on holiday." A mocking smile pulled at her rigid expression. She knew it was an ugly look. "Literally got off with a Spanish waiter on the Costa del Sol. Cliché! A teenage mum, and the only thing I even remotely got from him was my first name. My mum said he liked it. How they got round to discussing baby names in the few hours they knew each other is still beyond me."

"I'm sorry," said Bruce.

"I don't need your sympathy."

She calmed herself. The two children were happily playing their game. Evan wanted to buy 'house number three' with the 'converted stable annex', but Edith said it was way over his budget. Children and parents. Cabbage-obsessed dads like Bruce. Social media junkies like Becky Mitten. Precocious kids without a clue like Edith and Evan. Everyone was messed up. The dark days weren't coming: they were already here.

"You want Lola to get the money for the farm?"

"All of them really, but, aye, that's the long and the short of it," said Bruce.

"Kids, stay here," she said, and led Bruce back through to the safety deposit room. She opened the wall safe to take out the keys. "I have a box here."

"Right?" said Bruce.

She made a dismissive shrug-shake. "They're not all being used. I get it at a vastly reduced rate." She went to her safety deposit box and used the bank keys to open its outer door. She paused before taking the actual box out.

"Do you know what it's like to be an only child with a mum who can barely take care of herself?"

Perhaps Bruce thought it was a rhetorical question and said nothing.

"There's lots of children with only a mum or only a dad," she said. "Less common back then, but there were some. I think I could have coped if my mum had just tried to support me."

"She neglected you," said Bruce.

"Not how you think. There was food on the table. Mostly beans on toast. A lot of beans on toast. She thought a fish finger sandwich was a treat. No – I mean support when it counted. When I was being bullied at school. When I got kicked out of the school choir for no reason."

"School choir? It's hardly ChildLine stuff, is it?" he said.

"You don't understand, you ridiculous man. It's not the school choir. It's not the bullying. It's not the beans on toast. It's all of it. It's—" She fixed him with a glare, making sure she met his gaze. "If you had a broken window in your house, you'd repair it. If the table was wonky, you'd stick a bit of ... something under it."

"Folded card."

"Folded card. That. If your bedsheets were too thin in winter, you'd put another blanket on. You'd do something. You'd care. You'd make sure clothes were washed. You'd talk to your children. You'd give them the talk, when it was necessary."

"Er, what talk?"

"Any talk! Opening a bank account. Applying to college. Getting a driving licence. Any talk! Things a child shouldn't have to work out for themselves. No, it's not ChildLine stuff. Social Services were never going to swoop in and tell my mum to cook better dinners or actually give a shit when I was struggling with my GCSEs. None of that. It doesn't mean I deserve a mum with tiny dreams, who couldn't see beyond the next weekend. A stupid woman who never did anything more exciting in her life than go on holiday to Spain once and get pregnant. It doesn't mean I deserved a life … half-lit."

She hauled the box out. It was a cube of steel the size of a hat box, with a single lock for which she had the key. She placed it on the table in the centre of the room.

"She never even tried to track down my dad," she said as she produced her key. "My father was 'the one that got away'. A momentary Prince Charming, a fly-by knight. Never even tried."

She unlocked the box. There was a stack of envelopes in the bottom of the box, held together with an elastic band.

"But I did," she said. "And it was easy, too."

She removed the letter she'd received that very morning from her jacket and placed it with the others.

"I got in touch with him six years ago. He's not a waiter anymore. That was just a summer job. He's a businessman. Makes parts for lifts, elevators. He owns a big house in Murcia, olive groves. Got a place by the beach in Los Narejos. I've got pictures somewhere."

She placed a hand on the pile, as though about to go through it for pictures and postcards to show him. Then remembered she had brought him here for quite a different reason.

She pointed through the door to the vault. "We get the money you want and we put it in here."

"In the box?"

"In the box. Then you surrender to the police."

Bruce frowned. "I'll go to prison."

"You will go to prison," Mercedes agreed. "But your money will be here. Then in six months, two years, however long, I will take the money and find a way of giving it to your children. Or put it in an account or something."

Bruce's frown remained. "They'll know the money is missing."

"So we make sure they don't know. We burn the rest."

"Burn it?"

She nodded. "Money doesn't burn well, especially the new polymer notes, but if we find something to help it along — Just a pile of melted plastic and ash. They won't be able to tell how much. You'll tell the police you did it as ... a protest against capitalism or something."

The frown was still there. "I'll be in prison and you'll have my money. How can I trust you?"

"How can I trust *you*?" she said. "Yes, at any moment, I could run off with the cash; but equally, at any moment, you could tell the authorities what we've done. There's no way I can explain away hundreds of thousands of pounds in my safety deposit box. It only works if neither of us breaks the deal."

"But if the bank decides to look in the boxes...?"

"They don't. And I'm in charge of the next round of deposit box audits."

The frown was easing. "Why would you do this?"

"You're a good man," she said. "You care for your family. I owe the bank nothing. I mean, you've met Justin, right?"

There was a small wry smile on his Neanderthal face. "You are a kind woman. You remind me of my wife, back when things were different."

She recoiled before she could do otherwise.

Bruce saw it and laughed. "I didn't mean it in a ... creepy way. You actually look a lot like her. Hang on..." He got out his phone and laboriously swiped through his apps. "Hang on. Hang on. Here."

He thrust the phone in her face. Once Mercedes had stepped back so she could focus on it, she realised he was actually right. Nose, eyes and jawline, they were not dissimilar. The former Mrs Greencock had a complexion that was redder and more uneven than Mercedes' but the similarity was there.

"Huh," she said, nodding in agreement.

Bruce looked at the safety deposit box, soon to be filled with cash. "Maybe you should put a little something in the box for yourself too," he suggested.

"Maybe I should," she said, like it had only just occurred to her.

Muffled talk from the rooms above came to a sudden crescendo with a shout of "Coward!"

"The natives are restless," said Bruce and headed out.

"We heard shouting," said Edith at the foot of the stairs.

"A real brouhaha," said Evan.

Mercedes followed Bruce up the stairs. He moved swiftly but carefully, not wanting to walk into an unexpected situation. He stepped around a big recycling bin that nearly blocked the corridor.

Bruce entered the room, Mercedes heard an exclamation of, "Who the hell are you?"

She got to the doorway in time to see an old man getting up from his seat and offering a hand to Bruce. "Marvin Applewhite," he said. "You may have heard of me."

It was the man who had been at the counter earlier, with Delia and her bag of marbles.

Bruce whirled.

There was a scuffle behind Mercedes. She turned in time to see the bin in the corridor lift itself up a few inches and move awkwardly along the carpet.

"Justin has gone!" Bruce said, bursting from the room.

Mercedes stepped aside and pointed silently at the bin.

Bruce goggled at it for a moment, then gave it a savage sideways kick.

"Ow!" came Justin's voice from inside. The lid wheeled down the corridor and Justin was left lying on his side, hanging out of the bin like a failed hermit crab.

"What are you doing?" Bruce asked.

The two children at the end of the corridor looked on with mild interest, as though watching a poor stage performance.

"I've seen worse fancy dress," said Edith.

"Like when mum went to the Whitstables' anniversary party as Brexit," said Evan.

"It's not what it looks like, Bruce!" said Justin. "You need to let me explain."

Mercedes shook her head and pointed wordlessly to a door adjacent to the hostages' room.

Bruce pushed Justin into the office – a somewhat grander room with a single desk, a sturdy chair, and a water cooler and printer on a table by the barred window – propelling him towards the chair while looking for something to tie him down with.

40

On the way down the stairs from the rooftop, Camara said, "Have you ever heard of survivorship bias?"

"Would you be shocked if I said no?" said Sam.

"It's the gateway to the Lucas Camara Theory of Criminal Intelligence."

Sam wanted to give him a curious look, but it was hard when the other person was three steps behind and two feet above you.

"Go on," she said.

"Survivorship bias. Back in World War Two—"

"Oh, it's a history lesson!"

"Shush! Back in World War Two, our planes were flying out from here, over the sea to do battle with the Luftwaffe. Took quite a toll on them. Planes shot down, others limping back with bullet holes. And some bright spark took a look at the returning aircraft, saw where all the holes were and thought 'Cripes!' —"

"Cripes?"

"It was the war. Swearing was rationed back then. They said 'Cripes!' and made plans to add extra armour to those bits of the planes where they were all shot up."

"Makes sense."

"Doesn't it. But it was wrong. There was this clever Hungarian mathematician, based in America, who realised that kind of thinking was all shades of wrong. Those planes which came back had taken hits in those areas and *still* managed to limp home. It was the Spitfires and Hurricanes hit in other places that had exploded or crashed over the battlefield. The bullet marks they saw were in areas that could take the punishment. The data was based only on the survivors and thus gave a false picture."

Sam reached the bottom step and turned to look at him. "Interesting. Clever. You even used the word 'thus'. Now, is this about criminals, or did you just want to talk about planes?"

"Criminals, it's the inverse. We only ever get to study the ones who leave a trace behind. The ones who get caught. We only have evidence on those kinds of criminals: the lazy, the unlucky, and the just plain stupid. There's this prevailing attitude among coppers that criminals are mostly idiots. It warms our cockles when things look grim."

They walked down the alley towards the sunny promenade.

"We don't really know how intelligent the average criminal

is," said Camara, "because the clever ones – the really clever ones – we never catch, except by dumb luck. So, if all the intelligent ones are getting away with it, the crooks we do encounter must be statistically stupider than the average."

"Says the man who just used the word 'stupider'."

"For effect."

"Hmmm. I think the 'thus' and the 'stupider' cancel each other out. So, the Lucas Camara Theory of Criminal Intelligence is … crims are idiots?"

"The ones we meet. Idiots. Morons. Crazy. Deluded."

"What you're really saying is I shouldn't try to understand Bruce's motivation. Because he's an idiot."

Camara chewed on that a little while. "Don't ascribe rational motives to any criminal, Sam. Don't put yourself in their shoes. It doesn't work."

It was enough to give Sam pause for thought as they walked up to the thick crowd by the cordon. "I think it does make sense," she said slowly.

"Oh?"

"Bruce doesn't want the money."

"Um, he's literally robbing a bank."

She shook her head. "My dad's in there. You know why? Because the bank is threatening to take his home from him. From us."

Camara looked suitably downcast. "Sam. That's … a terrible thing to have to go through."

"Our homes are important to us. Bricks and mortar and the land." She sniffed in suppressed amusement. "You said it yourself. Bruce probably had the passion for farming his wife did not. He felt an attachment to the land. For some people, land is everything."

"Enough to turn down millions of pounds?" said Camara, not disagreeing but contemplating. "I wonder if his wife saw it that way."

"She did leave him after all," said Sam.

Sam pushed her way through the crowd. Was everyone in Lincolnshire now here? Surely nobody was left to run any of the businesses in the town.

"Hard hats for sale. Fifteen pounds each. Don't be caught out when the bank blows, get your hard hats here."

Sam caught the arm of the vendor. "What on earth are you doing?"

"Fulfilling a need, miss. Supply and demand, yeah?" The vendor was a small skinny man who carried an enormous net bag filled with hard hats. They looked used, as if he'd taken them from a building site.

"No!" Sam shook her head emphatically. "There will only be a demand for these if you go round scaring people. Nobody's said that the bank's going to blow."

He stood tall and put a hand to his mouth. "Bank's gonna blow! This lady just said it! Get your hard hats here!"

Sam was about call Camara to move over and arrest the dangerous agitator when the vendor ducked into a gap and disappeared into the crowd. It was getting difficult to move around now.

"Genuine commemorative mead!" shouted a voice. Sam recognised it. She pushed through the crowd and saw a woman with a large microphone. She was being filmed by a camera on a tripod. Were these television people? Sam thought television cameras looked bigger than this thing, but maybe they didn't need to be massive any more.

"So you're local?" said the TV woman. Sam saw she was talking to Ragnar Odinson. It was his voice she'd heard shouting about mead.

Ragnar Odinson: Hilde's granddad and patriarchal leader of the clan of grubby would-be Vikings camped out at the Elysian fields caravan park. The man was a genial one-man crime wave, although he also had a stunning eye for a business opportunity.

"Aye," said Ragnar. "Local family, the Odinsons." He looked directly at the camera and held up a bottle of mead with the label in frame.

The woman saw what he was doing and without missing a beat, or losing her smile, pushed the bottle out of shot with her free hand. The other hand continued to hold the microphone to Ragnar's face.

"Mr Odinson, why don't you tell our viewers on DailyLincs what you think about the events we've all seen here at the Eastshires Bank today."

"Our family's not much into banks," said Ragnar to the camera. "We're more traditional."

"More traditional than banks?"

"Aye. If we have money we keep it or we spend it." The bottle rose back into frame and Ragnar pointed at it for the viewers. "If we invest, it'll be in a fine product like Odinsons' mead. You can taste Skegness in every bottle."

"Thank you, Mr Odinson."

Sam, near to him now, had to ask. "What on earth does that mean? You can taste Skegness in every bottle?"

"It's a tagline. Tha's got to have a tagline. Our Hilde said so. She gev me a load to have a look at, so I made one that sounded a bit like some o' the others. You don't like it?"

Sam wasn't sure how to respond. "Well it's gone out on television now."

"Aye. I'm right pleased wi' that! Now, let's get to these customers."

Sam turned and saw Ragnar had a queue. It was thirsty work standing around in a crowd. She hoped Ragnar didn't have too much stock with him: she knew how alcoholic Odinsons' mead was. Things could get ugly if the whole crowd got steaming drunk on the stuff.

There was a toot from up the road and Ragnar waved. Sam groaned as she saw Ragnar's nephews, Gunnolf and Hermod, waving back from the windows of their huge cherry red truck. It looked very much as if it was piled high with more supplies of Odinsons' mead.

B ruce emerged from the office and closed the door behind him.

"Justin tied up?" said Mercedes.

Bruce nodded. "You should check the others are properly secured."

Mercedes gave him a disbelieving look.

"We're in this together now, right?" he said.

Mercedes rolled her eyes. "We are not yet 'in it together', Bruce. If and when we decide we are indeed 'in it together' our plan will only succeed if no one realises we *are* 'in it together'."

She could tell from his expression that he didn't comprehend.

"Our plan depends on you taking the fall for the bank robbery and me being above suspicion. I must be able to come into the bank at a later date and remove the concealed money. In front of the people you've got tied up next door –

in front of the police, in front of the media – you must be the criminal and I must be the victim."

Bruce's expression had shifted. He seemed to understand, although it looked like he thought the situation was somewhat unfair. That he had to shoulder a specific burden she had given him.

"In fact," she whispered, "we need to ham it up a bit."

"Ham it up how?"

"Make me the victim. Hit me."

"What?"

"Hit me. So it leaves a mark."

"I'm not hitting you," he said. "I don't want to hurt you."

"I don't want you to hurt me either. I want to leave a mark."

Bruce was shaking his head, disgusted.

Mercedes looked at the machete in his hand. He saw her looking, but before he could pull away she grabbed the fat knife, the fleshy cushions of her palm against the blade.

"No!" he whispered.

"We must."

He tried pulling, she gripped harder. She could feel the sharpness against the skin, picture the flesh under pressure whitening but not yet parting.

"Don't," he said.

"Please don't do this!" she said louder.

"Let go!"

"You're hurting me!"

She gave a final squeeze and with a conscious act of will pulled away from him. For a moment the pain was just a cold sensation. Then she looked at her hand. There was a wonderfully convincing flow of blood coming from her palm.

She hissed in real pain, put the hand to her blouse to staunch the flow – and make sure she got blood on her. She retreated from the back room corridor and into the front lobby space.

Here, she thought. Here was her biggest problem.

Mercedes had kept Tez and Marvin Applewhite safe with the off-the-cuff lie. But things had changed. She had to find a way to let Bruce know about Tez, but she also had to ensure no one ever found it was her who had squealed. She was surprised Justin hadn't already given Tez up. Perhaps he'd just forgotten. So, the balancing act. She would have to play the hostage and victim while in potential earshot of Tez. Simultaneously, she would have to maintain the relationship with Bruce without disclosing there was bank employee out here. A balancing act.

She slid dramatically along the wall just up from where Tez was still hiding, leaving a bloody smear there.

"You cut me!" she said. "I said I'd do what you want and you cut me!"

"You made me do it," said Bruce, coming through after her. "You should have let go."

"It really hurts!"

Bruce looked bewildered. "And whose fault is that?"

"I'm sorry," she whimpered, looked at her hand and hissing at the sight of it. It was actually a fairly deep cut. Not life-threatening, not tendon severing, but it would definitely need stitches. "There's a first aid kit in the kitchen," she said.

"Right, let's get that then," said Bruce.

She followed him back through the keypad door. She couldn't avoid glancing back, beyond the bloody smear on the wall, to the door behind which Tez was still hiding. As performances went, she was quite pleased with it.

"Then *you* check the others are properly tied up," she told Bruce.

42

Closer to the cordon, the morbidly curious onlookers were jammed solidly together, with everyone trying to gain the best spot and hang onto it. The social niceties which kept people from barging each other out of the way on a day-to-day basis had given way to something more primitive and tribal.

The sale of *#teamBruce* and *#teamCops* T-shirts definitely hadn't helped. Some people were facing off against each other, using tiny aggressive moves. Cups of tea were being knocked from people's hands. There were insincere mutterings of "sorry" and sly smiles.

She caught sight of a familiar figure moving through the crowd and followed. It was Rich's butler, and he had an armful of T-shirts. He leaned towards a man who was waving a *#teamBruce* placard.

"Can I offer you a free *#teamBruce* T-shirt?" Peninsula said softly.

"Thanks," said the man and pulled it over his clothes. It showed an enormous image of a bright green cabbage, cut in two to show its inner layers. Sam stared, trying to work out if it was a picture of Bruce's Tigerheart. *Was* it striped? Maybe.

Peninsula had moved on. "Can I offer you a free T-shirt?" he asked someone else.

As Peninsula moved through the crowd, everyone was gradually being dressed in cabbage T-shirts. So this was Rich's latest move? To show Bruce the street was teeming with people who were excited by his Tigerheart.

"Absolutely nuts," she muttered.

Sam lost Peninsula in the press of bodies. She stayed close to Camara as he got them through the cordon and back into the fishmonger's stand, the nerve centre of police operations. The heavy scent of cold wet fish still filled the air, but it smelled like someone had tried to combat it with a floral perfume. The negotiator, Zahra Bi, was poring over a written list in front of her.

Chief Inspector Peach and the firearms sergeant, Kenny, were crammed in the corner. They had two laptops and a phone propped up on the shelf. One screen had the tracking widget app up. Dots pulsed in different sections of the bank. The other screen showed body-cam footage from street level. Sam identified Rutland Road, the side road by the bank. Armed police in SAS black were crammed against red brick walls.

"You're going in?" she said.

"TAPT may be called on," Kenny said simply. "We're exploring possible access to the first floor windows."

"This is an operational matter," said Peach. "No civilians."

"That's my tracking software," she pointed out.

"Sam is confident Greencock does not have one of the guns from the farm on him," said Camara.

Irritated, Peach ran his hand over his close-cropped bonce. "Then where did he get it from?"

"You sure he's armed?"

"The Mitten woman tweeted images. Out on the street, they're selling bloody T-shirts with him holding a gun!"

Sam didn't mean to read the sheet of paper over Zahra's shoulder but she did and her eyes glanced upon the words: *lava lamp, red wax, bulb – 40cm height.*

"What's this?" she said.

"The suspect's demands," said Zahra. She tutted to herself, took off the Celtic brooch she'd been wearing, dropping both it and the Scottish accent. "This is not a normal list of demands. We might usually get asked for pizza or a priest or a bus. Not ponies."

"Ponies?"

"Ponies. Quite illogical."

Sam pointed at the lava lamp request. "That's Delia. That's absolutely Delia."

Zahra nodded. "We could hear voices in the room while Mr Greencock read out his list. It would appear the hostages have been providing him with suggestions."

She pointed at the wall behind Sam, and the sheets fixed to it with colourful transparent headed drawing pins. There were nine sheets: Justin, Stevie, Mercedes, Tez, Becky, Edith, Evan, Delia, Marvin. There were photos stapled to some of them, mostly of what Sam assumed were the people themselves. Although she was mildly mystified by the picture of a black-faced French bulldog stapled to the Stevie sheet.

Sam realised she had rested her arm on a damp box. She now had a slightly fishy smelling sleeve.

"One can almost pinpoint which people came up with which demand," said Zahra. "But this is good news."

"Is it?" said Sam. Peach scoffed in agreement.

"It suggests they are all in good spirits. Terrified people do not write wish lists. Also, they are all in one place."

"Including your father," said Peach tersely. "Just got himself captured."

Sam's throat tightened sickeningly.

"As best we can work out, he snuck into the room with the hostages disguised as a paper recycling bin and was caught untying the hostages' bonds," said Peach.

"That's very him," she said.

"Really?"

"Hiding in unusual spaces. Good with knots. Not doing what anyone expected."

Peach frowned.

"Stage magician and professional fool," said Sam. "How is he now?"

"The phone line went dead, but we couldn't hear anything specifically untoward."

"As I said," said Zahra, "there's a surprising level of bonhomie among the hostages."

"They're helping him?" said Camara.

"Hard to say," said Zahra.

"Oh, they bloody are," said Peach.

"Stockholm Syndrome?" suggested Sam.

"It's a phrase that gets bandied about a lot," said Zahra smoothly, "but there's almost no research data to suggest Stockholm Syndrome really exists. The case which gave name to the syndrome involved a bank robbery. In that instance, the hostages' behaviour could just as easily be attributed to the callousness of the police on site as to some mystical bonding between perpetrators and victims."

"We've been nothing but scrupulous and fair throughout," said Peach. "You've offered to get them a pony, for Christ's sake!"

"The list might be a little difficult to fulfil," Zahra agreed. "However, we can probably outsource the acquisition of these items."

"If Bruce was refused a loan, perhaps the hostages share his disdain for the banking system," said Camara.

"That thought had crossed my mind," said Zahra.

"Bruce is not a bad man," Sam said, immediately feeling silly, given the situation they were currently in. "He's a regular guy."

"Beware the fury of a patient man."

"The man's not furious, though," said Camara. "His house is full of photos of his family. He's keeping it neat and tidy, ready for when he supposes his family's coming back."

Sam was about to counter him and point out there was something to be read into the state of the house. The photos of the family spoke of love, but also of love with great chunks missing from it. The house itself practically shouted out the cracks in the man's sanity. The neatness was not in itself obsessive, but the overall image was of a place trapped in amber, constantly in preparation for the family's return. Sam had not seen them, but she imagined the children's bedrooms were being kept exactly as they were on the day Christine and the children left. For children who were already growing up and wouldn't recognise the place if they did return. Bruce's normality could be concealing a boiling sea of rage.

"We've set aside a café in the Hildred Centre for the families of the hostages, Miss Applewhite," Peach said. "There's family support liaison officers there. You must be worried about your dad."

Sam wasn't listening. An idea, an image, had seized her. She ran from the fish stall.

"In the Hildred Centre!" Peach called after her.

She ran along the road to the cordon by the nearest corner. People were thronging against the tape barrier. Sam scanned the crowd. "You!" she said, pointing at a teenager.

"I ain't done nothing, mate!" the lad said automatically.

"You still got T-shirts for sale?"

"*#teamBruce* or *#teamHostages*?"

"Bruce."

"Of course, of course."

He held one out to her. The picture was not one of Peninsula's cabbage images but of Bruce brandishing a weapon above the tagline I'M DOING IT FOR MY KIDS.

"Bloody hell," she said and ran off with it, back to the fish stall.

"Oi! That T-shirt's a tenner!" the teenager shouted, adding, "Two for fifteen quid to you!"

Sam, puffing, bounced off the door frame of the fishmonger's and back into the room.

"Do you always make dramatic entrances?" said Zahra.

Sam held up the T-shirt for all to see, took a moment to catch her breath, and said, "That's not a shotgun at all. It's the rungs, the poles, from a climbing frame outside the front of the farmhouse."

The police officers looked at one another.

"There was a climbing frame in the yard," Camara said.

Sam nodded. "He told me this morning he was bringing the rods into town to be re-something-or-othered. I'm not up on metalwork."

"It *looks* like a double-barrelled shotgun," said Peach.

"An easy mistake to make," said Kenny.

"A fake shotgun?" said Camara.

"An accidentally fake shotgun," Zahra suggested.

"How can you accidentally rob a bank?" said Peach.

43

In the Hildred Shopping Centre, among the card shops and pharmacies and clothing outlets, there was Berkin's Bakery, a café which had gone for a rustic look with pine chairs and soft lighting. The walls, the floors, the furniture, and ninety percent of the food, were differing shades of brown. The café had been set up for family members of those held inside the bank: a place to support them as well as, Sam recognised, somewhere to corral them. Keep them from wandering off or doing something stupid, like talking to the media.

The police family liaison officer met Sam at the door. Sam felt a weird compulsion to explain who she was and how she was linked to her dad. As though the officer was a nightclub bouncer and would kick her out if her name wasn't on the list.

"I'm just looking for somewhere to sit out of the way," Sam said.

"And that's fine," said the officer.

She stepped cautiously inside. There were three other occupants, four if you included the dog. A hunched woman sat alone, shredding a croissant with her fingers and posting stamp-sized flakes of it into her mouth. A young round woman in an angora sweater entirely unsuitable for the season, sat with a little black dog in a baby stroller. The dog's mouth lolled open and it panted asthmatically as it looked at Sam. The round woman tickled its ears sadly.

A man in a polo shirt and beach trousers which stopped four inches above his ankles, watched the phone on the table in front of him. "My wife's still posting messages from inside the bank," he said to Sam, as though she might naturally be interested.

Sam nodded, distracted. "That's um *@Bexcanboogie*."

"Yes. She has lots of followers." He gave a sad little smile. "I thought it was nonsense, but it's very brave of her really." He angled the screen to show her the Instagram page. The latest posts only had a speech-to-text app logo as an accompanying image and said things like YOU GO, THANKS. THE HELL HE'S RUNNING OUT and GRASS ON ME TO SPRUCE TIGHT. FIT RIGHT.

With silent permission, Sam scrolled to the latest one.

"LET THE POLICE SAVE ALL YOUR UNGRATEFUL, CORNY BACKSIDES. NO, WAIT A MINUTE COWARD!" she read. "Does that mean something?"

@Bexcanboogie's husband nodded sagely. "I'm sure there's a coded message within it. Even now, she's fighting for what she believes in."

Sam wasn't sure what fight this was, but thought it better

not to ask. Mr Bexcanboogie was keen to tell anyway.

"We've got freedom of speech, haven't we?" he said. "No one can silence us. It's like the first thing on the bill of rights, right?"

Sam didn't want to burst his bubble and tell him he was about five thousand miles and one whole country away from being with that.

"She only went into town to get some shopping. We were going to have chicken katsu curry when the Whitstables came over. I really don't know what we're going to serve them now."

"No. It's a worry," Sam said.

"Can we get you a cuppa?" said the police liaison.

Over at the counter, a woman in a beige apron stood to attention by the till. It seemed that, against all odds, her café had been called up to do its national service, and by golly, it was going to do it right. "I can stretch to a cappuccino," she said.

"Tea would be fine," said Sam.

It was late lunch and Sam had neither eaten nor drunk since Marmite eggs benedict this morning. She couldn't face food, but a quenching cup of tea would be a good idea.

She stepped away from Mr Bex. Focused on the screen, he barely noticed. She sat equidistant between the woman with the French bulldog and the older woman shredding pastry.

"Nice dog," she said to the woman in angora.

"Petey's worried sick," she said.

"Understandable."

The older woman seemed to see her for the first time.

Her fingers continued to twitch. Sam wondered if she was smoker.

"You've got someone in there?" the woman said.

Sam swivelled on the polished chair to face her. "My dad. And my friend, Delia. You?"

"My daughter, Mercedes. She works at the bank."

"I'm sure they're all fine," said Sam.

"Are you?"

"I've just spoken to the police inspector. They know how it's sort of going. Everyone's in good spirits, I think."

"You never expect thing like this to happen, do you?"

A genial farmer estranged from his family, with a peculiar passion for stripey brassicas, holding up a bank with two lengths of pipe and a machete? thought Sam. "No, you don't," she said.

"It's just the two of us, you know. Mercedes and me. We share a flat. Two best buddies. Like something out of a sitcom." She had reduced her croissant to little more than flaky dust. When the café woman brought over Sam's tea, she swapped the plate of crumbs for a fresh croissant.

"Who was in that one, the *Liver Birds*?" said Mercedes' mum. "Nerys Hughes and—"

"Polly James," said Sam automatically.

There was a faint smile. "You're too young to remember that," said Mercedes' mum.

"So are you," said Sam.

"Oh, I watch the old ones on repeat channels. ITV4. Forces TV. When I get home, I want nothing more than a quiet night in with my girl."

Mercedes' mum had a certain type of face. Lined and

cowed, with a faint edge of constant bewilderment. It was a face belonging to someone who had been weathered by life without learning anything from it. It was an anonymous face, invisible almost.

"My dad cut Polly James in half once," said Sam.

"Did he now?" said Mercedes' mum.

Sam's phone buzzed in her pocket. It was surely the DefCon4 app complaining at her again, but she checked anyway. It was the DefCon4 app, but this time it was flagging a top priority task. She very nearly put her phone back in her pocket, but she clicked through to take a look, just in case. It turned out to be an urgent procurement task from the Lincolnshire Police. As Sam read the details, she realised she was looking at Bruce's list of demands. Her stomach roiled with horror at the idea she had almost ignored a task relating directly to the situation in the bank.

Sam clicked on the app to indicate she was working on it, and for the first time in many hours it gave her a big green tick to show she was doing the right thing. According to the system.

She approached the cordon and waved to Camara. "I need to check something."

"Yeah?"

"It seems DefCon4 has been commissioned to procure Bruce's demands – and within the hour, as well."

"Well, they couldn't have asked a better company," he said.

Sam blinked. "You really don't know anything about DefCon4, do you?" She looked at the instructions again. "I'm probably going to need Hilde Odinson."

44

A few minutes later, Sam and Hilde Odinson were standing in the street and staring at a screen while Camara looked on. Hilde was Delia's backroom workshop assistant, a part-time thief of unregarded things and a full-time Viking. The Viking preoccupation was more her grandad's thing, but this young woman had a tenacious loyalty to her grandfather's eccentricities.

There was a diagram on the screen.

"So I need to make that thing in the diagram there?" asked Hilde.

"Yes you do," said Zahra, appearing at the doorway of Ewan King's fish stall. "Are there going to be any difficulties in getting that done in an hour?"

Hilde shrugged. "The work itself is easy enough. I can use my welder round at Delia's. Does it really want one of the wheels to be bigger than the other three?"

Zahra peered at the screen but held back from touching it. "I think we can confidently say this is not to scale. In fact, I suspect it might be the work of one of the Mitten children rather than an avant-garde. Let's assume it is a cart intended to make transportation easier."

"So, we should make something like this, but not this," said Sam.

"Precisely. Make the wheels all the same size. It will need to be strong as well."

"Aye," said Hilde, eyeing Camara. "About the materials I'll need. I've not always seen eye to eye with the police on such matters."

"Hilde, we've spoken about this before," said Camara flatly. "You're a smart young woman. Just because something is 'just lying there', to use your words, it doesn't mean you can help yourself."

"Aye. I know that now. So where can I get wheels from?" She pointed at the diagram. "They want big uns 'n' all."

"Surely you can think of something," said Zahra.

"She's very resourceful," said Sam supportively.

"Down our way, when we say someone is 'resourceful' it's like code for 'a bit dodgy'," said Hilde. "I sometimes think people like me need to be resourceful because they know that being a bit dodgy gets results faster. You want this in an hour, yeah?"

"That is correct," said Zahra.

"I'm going to tek them bikes that's lying around in the street then," said Hilde. "And I don't expect to get any stick fer it, neither."

"That will be perfectly fine," said Zahra. "Isn't that right, Chief Inspector Peach?"

Peach didn't look very happy, but nodded nonetheless. "If it's distracting Greencock then I don't care."

As Hilde dashed off to collect the decoratively abandoned bicycles, Sam called Rich. "I need some help getting some things really quickly," she said without preamble.

"*Cool!*" said Rich, in the voice of someone who was itching to use the words 'scramble the helicopter' in a sentence.

"Can I give you a couple of things? One is expensive and one is difficult. Meet me by King's fish stall with them in forty five minutes."

"*Yep. What do you need?*"

"The expensive one is a case of Perrier-Jouët Belle Epoque."

"*Peninsula can pop and get that.*"

"I'm sure I saw him out and about, distributing cabbage themed T-shirts."

"*The man can multitask. No, shouldn't be a problem. What's the other thing?*"

"I need a pony," said Sam. "I'd come and help, but I need to go and get some other stuff."

"*A pony. I see.*" The cogs were churning in Rich's head. Sam could almost hear them. "*Any leads you can give me?*"

Sam thought for a few seconds. "I've never considered myself a horsey person. To be honest, I'm not even sure I know the difference between a horse and a pony."

"*I imagine it's all about the size.*"

"But, what about when you get a really small horse?"

"Well then, it's a pony."

"Is it though?" asked Sam. "I have no idea. Just get something that looks a bit like a pony within the hour. A lot depends on this."

"On it!"

45

Mercedes entered the manager's office, inspecting the edges of the dressing she had put over her injured palm. Justin looked at the blood on her blouse and her face.

"What has he done to you?"

"A misunderstanding," she said, in a deliberate tone of shameful confusion. It was important everyone saw the injury and the frightened subservience Bruce had forced upon her.

Justin jiggled in his seat and craned to look past her. "He's let you wander off?"

"He's just counting his loot."

The jiggling intensified. "Then untie me. Quick!"

She didn't move. "I don't want to cause any more trouble. He's getting his money, he's talking to the police. He'll be out of here soon."

"You're working with him?"

She gave him a wounded look. "He just wants to rob the bank, Justin."

"Just?" he said, his voice strangling as it shot up. "He's robbing *our* bank. We have a duty of care." He saw there was no budging her and he huffed, face red, tie askew. "This is the difference, right here."

"What difference?"

"Between a branch manager and—" He tried gesturing at her with his head. "Duty of care."

"To the cash in the vault?"

"See, you don't understand."

"I'm not sure there's any difference between me and..." She mimicked his head-pointing gesture back at him. "Except you get to go to the shareholder's banquet. Is it true the bottles of water cost ten pounds each?"

"What?"

"Something Tez said."

"I don't know what you're talking about."

"The water at the banquet. It— Did you know that you and I have been with the bank for the same length of time?"

"You want to go to the banquet? It's just a dinner. Hundred and fifty quid a head but it's just a dinner. I suppose there's the hotel on top, but it's still no more than five hundred total per person."

"I don't care about the dinner."

"Good. I never thought it was that special. Limp vegetables, miserly portions of dessert." A smile crossed his face. "You think you deserve what I have? They don't give out promotions like long service medals. You have to earn it."

"I put in the hours and the effort," she said.

"Your annual appraisal isn't for another eight months, Mercedes."

She felt a bitter taste in her mouth and realised she was in danger of saying things she shouldn't. "I'll go see what Bruce is up to. It'll be over soon."

As she turned away from him, he spoke. "If you took that chip off your shoulder, you might actually get on better."

She half turned back to him, tried to resist the bait.

"You want to blame this on the gender pay gap or something?" he said. "Some sexist bias? Conveniently forgetting the Equal Pay Act of 1970?"

She couldn't resist. She turned back to him fully. "I don't get what I deserve."

He tilted his head. "It's got nothing to do with what's between your legs. Or mine. You get paid what you get paid because it's what you deserve." A laugh blurted out of him. "Don't be surprised. It's the way it is. You're one of life's followers, not a leader."

"Really?" she said.

"It's the hand life dealt you. Heck, you could probably trace it back to when we were babies."

"You didn't know me—"

"Oh, we know your story. Single mum, holiday fling, gets herself up the duff. It's sad but true. I'm sure I've seen statistics. Life opportunities for kids from broken families. And then she saddles you with that name, like it's some kind of joke."

"Mercedes? It's a perfectly decent name."

"For a little Spanish kid." He shrugged. "I suppose you are. Half dago or whatever. It's not your fault, but there's that posh phrase, um, what is it? Nominative determinism. The names we are given dictate what happens to us in life. When Mr and Mrs Johnson gave their little boy the name Justin – Justin, just, justice, kingly, proud – they were putting metaphorical coins in the bank for my future. Your mum gives you that name, she might as well have put a sign above your head with your whole future life story on it."

"You're saying I haven't been promoted because of my name, that if my mum had called me—"

"Ah, ah, ah!" he interrupted. "No, that would be silly. The reason you have that name is because you have the kind of mother *who would give that kind of name* to her daughter. The name dictates nothing. It's just a symptom of the background you come from." He looked smug. "If she hadn't given you that name she'd had given you something equally ghastly. When I was a kid, all the thick kids in my class were called Wayne and Kevin and Darren. It wasn't the name. It was the parents. It's like Bruce. I knew him as a lad too. Not thick, not particularly, but one look at those homemade jumpers his mum put him in, one look at the state of his lunchbox, and you could see there was a man destined to toil in the earth with his hands until the day he died. We're all products of our backgrounds."

"Wow," she said, because the only alternative words that came to mind were foul expletives and might be accompanied by violence.

"You," he said. "You and the whole picture you paint. The girl who tries too hard. The girl with the chip on her shoulder. The girl who overcompensates. You can't hide your personal baggage. We all know you've got your mum living with you at home, clinging on like a chain-smoking parasite. We can smell it on you. We've all seen the letters you get delivered to the bank from ... is it daddy? Is it half-brother Pedro? The tatters of your other family you've got in touch with. It's a mess. It's not professional. Compare with—" He tried to gesture at himself with no hands. "Three bedroomed house, golfing at the weekends. I have an actual white picket fence. I sometimes listen to Classic FM. I have my groceries delivered by Ocado. Those are hallmarks of quality."

Mercedes momentarily wondered if she could just go to the kitchen, get the breadknife and stick it in his stupid fat-clogged heart. Even momentarily, she wondered about it too much.

"Truly an insight," she said. "I suppose you've had this pep talk with our colleagues too."

"Not exactly. I mean, Tez, he's excellent."

"Yeah?"

"I mean the Asians are canny with money anyway. They know the true value of education and they do well in business. The blokes scrub up well too. I hear Tez even waxes."

"Right."

"Not my thing, obviously. I reckon God made men hairy for a reason, but shows he puts in some effort with his appearance."

"I see."

"And Stevie." He laughed again. "I'd probably have to use very small words to explain half of what I've just said. Be thankful you're not Stevie, eh?" He laughed again, inviting her to join in.

"I should be thankful I'm not Stevie," she said quietly.

"Oh, come on. I'm just joking," he said. "I love you all like a family. I'm the daddy and this bank is our family. Better than that embarrassment of a family you've got in Benidorm or wherever."

"He's a businessman, for you information."

"Who? Your dad? Owns an olive tree, you mean," said Justin. "I'm joking. I'm sure he tries." Perhaps Justin recognised he had stepped too far; that his 'joking' had unlocked something nasty within her. He shuffled uncomfortably.

"Look, it's like you say. It will soon be over. The police are out there. There's me in here. I bet the bank people are doing great work behind the scenes. Let the big boys sort this out and we'll all be home in time for tea."

"That would be nice," she said. "I'll leave you to it."

She shut the door firmly on her way out.

46

After collecting her van from where she'd parked it on South Parade, Sam drove round to Delia's shop on Scarborough Avenue. As she entered the junk shop, she could already hear Hilde in the back room with some sort of heavy machinery running. She popped a head around the door to see Hilde wearing eye goggles and grinding the end of a piece of metal. Sam raised a hand in greeting and went back through into the shop. The list she'd been given called for a motivational poster, a lava lamp, and some lilies. She phoned through to the florist while she scanned the shelves.

"Can I order some lilies please? I'll pick them up in a few minutes. It's pretty urgent."

A lava lamp should be easy to spot, but would it be with glassware or electricals?

There were questions from the florist. "No, just lilies. No

greenery or whatever that other thing you mentioned. Only lilies."

There were no lava lamps anywhere here. What about a motivational poster? It needed a dog, apparently.

More questions. "Sorry? No, I don't need a card. Just lilies, and I'll be in a hurry."

Sam stopped at the crapestry collection and stared. Delia's crapestry was a source of both pride and amusement when she welcomed people to her shop. Sam was sceptical about people collecting the worst examples of pictures rendered in tiny stitches, but Delia insisted there was a small but enthusiastic group of crapestry fans. She did seem to have quite a turnover of them. It was normally not so much the fault of the workmanship as the limited range of colours which were used to make them. They often looked like old masters rendered in the style of a Minecraft world. Sam spotted a dog-based crapestry and wondered if it could work as a motivational poster. It had a dog which might have been barking, or possibly mouthing the words of a caption: the ambiguous phrase IF YOUR BALL IS TOO BIG FOR YOUR MOUTH, IT'S NOT YOUR BALL. Did that count as motivational? Sam wasn't even sure what it was supposed to mean. She grabbed it off the wall anyway. Nobody had specified that the motivational advice needed to be good.

She tucked it under her arm and sprinted down the street, because she had suddenly remembered where there was a lava lamp.

47

Rich Raynor was on the beach.

Rich had been on many beaches. He'd snorkelled on the coral beaches of Rapa Nui in the Pacific. He had partied through the night at the Playa d'En Bossa on Ibiza. He'd waded through the warm jade waters of Patong beach in Thailand.

Rich knew beaches and accepted there were no two beaches alike. Skegness beach's charms were of a different order. Skegness had lovely yellow sandcastle building sand. It had plenty of space for dog walkers and kite flyers to roam. It also, critically, had donkeys.

Peninsula was off getting champagne, so Rich had been left with the pony problem. He had phoned every concierge service he had. There were a great many expensive problem solvers on his speed dial, but none of them were able to get a pony to the centre of Skegness within the hour. He was mildly annoyed at how Londoncentric many of them appeared to be. Ponies within the M25 were plentiful, but the horsey set of Lincolnshire was outside their reach and experience.

This was the backup plan. In reality it was more like the backup plan's desperate last ditch effort. He had urged his best people to think laterally, and attempt to get hold of a pony or a smallish horse. One of them was even exploring the possibility of spray-painting a zebra. Here he was though, left with his own, substandard contribution.

"What about a donkey?" he'd said on a conference call.

There was a light cough. "Sir, a donkey has those big ears. It will be very obvious it's not a pony."

And so the donkey idea had been abandoned.

Even so, as time ticked on, Rich had realised the donkey idea had one key advantage: there were donkeys within walking distance of the bank. Right there on Skegness beach.

He strolled over to the donkey man. He was fairly elderly and had the sort of face which most likely doubled up as a department store Santa out of season.

"How are things with the donkeys today? Seems quiet," said Rich.

"Yes. Some sort of excitement in the town there. Nobody wants rides today."

"Well, I might have an idea that could interest you. I'd like to hire one of the donkeys for the rest of the day. I'll need to take it into the town, but I will make sure it gets back safely."

"You have no idea how many times I've heard nonsense like that. Not a chance."

"What? Really?"

"Damn fools roll out of a pub and they say to their mates, 'You know what would make this pub crawl better? A donkey'. I'm a responsible owner, there's no way I'm letting someone take one of these fine beasts round the town for pub selfies."

"No. No, I can see that," said Rich, not expecting an outright refusal. "I can assure you it's not drunken stupidity talking here. I am very much the respected businessman, trying to fulfil an urgent need."

"Oh aye, and what's that then?"

Rich hesitated. Perhaps it would wise not to mention he planned to send a donkey for a tête-à-tête with an armed gunman in a siege situation. It would probably make the pub scenario sound preferable. "It's one of those things where we want to grant a wish to someone in a very precarious situation." Rich didn't like to lie, but he had no problem with occasionally using weasel-words. He hoped there were no follow up questions about who the someone might be, or the nature of their precarious situation.

A donkey absently nudged Rich in the small of the back.

The man nodded. "Maybe we can reach an accommodation then?"

Rich nodded enthusiastically.

"I could do with a couple of hours to myself as it happens. You can take these with you and meet me back here in two hours."

"Excellent. How much?"

The man sucked his teeth. "A hundred apiece."

Rich counted. "Ten donkeys? I only wanted one."

"One's not on offer. If you take one, you take them all."

"A thousand pounds then?"

The man gave him a hopeful look. "I'll give you eight hundred pound back if you return them in good working order."

Rich had his wallet out before the man had even offered the refund. "Sounds like a bargain, sir."

The man held out his hand and Rich, a man who carried a thousand pounds in his wallet just in case, gladly paid him.

48

Twenty five minutes after the initial list of demands was given, Sam arrived back home in her Piaggio van. She was trying hard not to get panicked by the lack of time, but she could not afford any delays now. She reckoned she had just about time to locate the lava lamp she was certain was up in the loft, get back into town and grab the lilies before the hour was up. She opened the door and rushed through – almost immediately stopping dead in her tracks, as though she had run into a wall of jelly.

It took her a good few seconds to figure out what had stalled her. For one thing she'd forgotten about the filing cabinet and its nest of rats. There were rat bodies laid out on a sheet of newspaper on the floor. They were piled into a rough pyramid so she couldn't tell exactly how many there were, but there had to be at least ten. Presumably this was Peninsula's doing. Had he left the corpses so she would be impressed by the number? Then there was the freshly-plastered wall. What on earth had happened here? Rich had definitely been talking about a cat, hadn't he? Was this the work of a regular domestic moggie? It didn't look it.

But mainly it occurred to her this was the home she shared with her dad. Their special place, their own nest. And the fact he was holed up in a bank with an unstable hostage-taker abruptly struck her like a blow. Intellectually, she knew all this already. But like a one-armed woman reaching out with the limb she had lost years before, reality was a step or two behind. The scent of Marmite eggs benedict fractionally clung to the air. In the corner, dust gathered on a box of close up magic tricks. There was a crumpled tea towel where Marvin had absent-mindedly flung it. Moments and fragments of Marvin Applewhite lay all around, reminding her of the slim but real possibility of him never coming home again.

Sam could feel her throat tighten and tears coming. She decided she just didn't have time for all that. She needed to get up into the loft and find the lava lamp. She grabbed a torch, went to the hatch and pulled down the ladder. A piece of paper fluttered to the floor as the ladder descended.

Do not enter the loft.

Sam stared at it. She wasn't at all sure whose writing it was, except it wasn't hers, or how old the note might be. It hadn't been there the last time she went up. She hesitated for a moment before climbing the ladder. Once up in the loft space she tried to picture where she had seen the lava lamp. It was a properly big old one from the Seventies, stored with some other decorative items from the same era. Like bar paraphernalia and a massive stand for displaying plants.

There! Sam stepped over to where the plant stand was and started opening the nearby boxes. She found the lava lamp on the sixth attempt.

"Yes!" She grabbed it, turning to go back over to the hatch, stopping dead when she heard a low growling noise. It came from the dark space under the eaves. She took a step, wondering if the sound had just been a groaning timber. The growling came again.

Was that a pair of amber eyes looking at her? She had once been in a cage with a tiger, and she tried to remember advice she'd been given at the time – even though she was pretty certain this wasn't a tiger. The only thing that came to mind was don't urinate. Generally good advice in most life situations, now it unhelpfully made her realise she needed the loo. She continued to edge towards the hatch, around eight feet away, not looking away from the amber eyes.

"Nice kitty, nice kitty," she said.

The eyes swayed in the dark. Definitely too big to be a house moggy.

She found the hatch with her feet and stepped onto the ladder. She tried to make every movement smooth and unhurried, even though she was in a hurry for multiple reasons.

She stepped off the ladder, pushed it up into the loft and closed the hatch, hardly daring to breathe, expecting something to leap down on top of her. A sigh escaped her as she fastened it closed.

There was a text on her phone. It was from Rich.

WILL DONKEYS DO? INSTEAD OF PONY?

She replied: *Donkeys? Plural? I'll check with the police.*

She scanned her mental to-do list as she trotted to the bathroom:

Empty bladder

Message Camara about donkeys

Get all the items to the police asap

Have a word with Peninsula about the beast in the loft.

49

Bridey MacDougal called Bruce as he was righting the recycling bin Justin had so spectacularly failed to escape in.

"Hello?" he said.

Mercedes, next to him in the corridor, tapped an imaginary watch on her wrist.

"Your hour is nearly up," he said.

"We are working very hard to meet your demands, Bruce. That is quite an eclectic list you provided us with."

"I wanted you to know I was serious."

"Oh, yes. Nothing says serious like a lava lamp and a donkey."

"Pony," he said. "We – I – I asked for a pony."

"Yes, about that. We might have to make some substitutions, some exchanges. It's like when Sainsbury's deliver your shopping, they try to swap like for like if they haven't got the thing you asked for."

"I don't get my shopping delivered."

"No, me neither. I don't see the point. I want to see the shine on the apples for myself. I want to pick the chicken I'm going to eat. People these days don't even seem to care where their food comes from. Some children today, you tell them where milk comes from and they're horrified."

"Some of them have never even seen a cow," he agreed.

Cow? Mercedes mouthed silently.

Bruce stepped aside. He couldn't concentrate on two conversations at once.

"If you order on-line, live in your little bubble, then you're divorced from what's really real," Bridey was saying. "People need to get out there and live real lives. I saw a review for Skegness beach the other day on TripAdvisor."

"Who reviews beaches?"

"Well, exactly, Bruce. Well, exactly. And this reviewer had given it one star for being 'too sandy'. I mean, if you're going to a company and getting poor service, if you've been mistreated in some way, then of course you should complain, give it a bad review if you wish. But calling a beach 'too sandy' is ridiculous."

"The modern world..."

"Oh, aye. I'm with you there. The police went to your farm."

Bruce was surprised, although wasn't sure why he would be. "And?"

"And they were impressed."

"Impressed?"

"You run a tight ship, Bruce. You're a man who takes his work seriously. I spoke to the constable and he was keen to impress how orderly things were. Says it's a lovely place. I'd like to see it myself sometime."

"I see," he said, neutrally, not wanting to agree to

anything. He felt that if he agreed she could visit it then he'd be somehow morally obliged to step outside the bank to take her there. It was strange and daft, but he felt it nonetheless. "You mentioned substitution, exchanges."

"Yes," she said with slow regret. *"The pony is the tough one."*

"Are there no ponies in the local area?"

"Yes, but not for sale. People get quite attached to their equine friends. Not keen to let them trot into a hostage situation."

"But you've got a donkey."

"I know it's not the same..."

Bruce had met both ponies and donkeys and knew full well they were not the same, but he'd not added it to the list. Whatever value the children expected to get from a pony, they could equally get from a donkey. Children loved donkeys, didn't they?

"I'm sure Edith and Evan will be delighted to see a donkey," said Bridey, as though reading his mind.

"Yes."

"But as long as you're okay with that."

"I like donkeys," Bruce said.

"Some people think they're stubborn, obstinate."

"Hard-working creatures, donkeys. And they don't suffer fools gladly."

"Admirable traits. There's an old saying. Lebanese, I think. 'He who took the donkey up on the roof should bring it down'. I assume donkeys don't like stairs."

"More fool the person who took it up there."

"I suppose that's like us right now, isn't it?"

"How so?"

"Here we are. Police. Roads closed. A number of tired and

scared people inside the bank. And some outside too. We're like a donkey on the roof."

"You calling me the fool?" There was no antagonism in his voice. He realised he was seeking confirmation as much as anything else.

"Oh, don't blame it all on yourself, Bruce. You've been nothing but a gentleman as far as I'm concerned. You've been polite to me. You've treated the bank staff and customers with dignity. I've not heard any threats of violence."

"I robbed a bank."

"You went in unarmed. True, you had the machete with you, but that was to give a bit of razzamatazz to your cabbage pitch."

"That's exactly the word I used."

"You see. You didn't go in in a disguise, so we can hardly say you went in with a premeditated plan of stealing the money and getting away with it. You went in there as an honest man, seeking money you believed you were rightly owed."

"A loan," he said.

"A loan you felt you should have been awarded."

"It doesn't change what I've done."

"Intentions count for a lot. Theft, under law, means you dishonestly appropriated someone else's property with the intent of permanently depriving them of it. You have been honest, intending to take it as a loan..."

"But..."

"No, hear me out, Bruce. There's legal precedent. I looked it up. Back in the Sixties, this bloke called Skivington threatened his boss with a knife in order to get the week's wages he and his wife were owed. He was convicted, but it was overturned on the grounds he believed he was owed the money. He had behaved

inappropriately, but he was no robber. You can look it up if you've got the internet."

Bruce suddenly felt like a donkey on a roof. She was dangling a carrot in front of him, a blameless way out; but he was also conscious of the drop before him, the dangerous stairway into darkness. He was cautious.

"You've not committed a robbery. Not before and not now."

"But I'm here…"

"And why are you there? Could we not make a compelling case that the bank has failed to treat you fairly? You're angry."

"Justin was rude to me."

"This isn't about Mr Johnson, Bruce," she put in quickly. *"Do not blame the man for the failures of the system. Do not latch onto the little details and accuse the beach of being too sandy."*

"I'm not saying the beach is too sandy."

"No, you're better than that, aren't you?" There was a warm burr of assurance in Bridey's cultured Scottish accent. *"You are a good man with a fine business idea and the bank's blinkered computerised systems said no."*

"They did."

"You have been poorly treated and you have done nothing wrong."

"But I have—"

"Well, let me see what we actually have here," she said, in the exact tone of someone exploring a basket of shopping. Bruce could even picture the kind of basket Bridey MacDougal might have. It would be a wicker one with a stiff handle, a Red Riding Hood basket. Bridey MacDougal sounded like everyone's favourite grandma whom he had come to visit at her rustic cottage. *"Now, armed robbery can*

potentially come with a life sentence, that would be twelve to twenty-five years of your life, Bruce."

"Oh, God..."

"But we know you're not a bank robber, don't we? What we have here is the undoubtedly serious offence of threatening behaviour."

"Yes?"

"You produced a weapon with an intent to cause fear. That's high culpability."

"Yes?"

"Also, you have several bank employees in genuine fear for their lives. That's Category One Harm."

"That's bad."

"You'd receive a custodial sentence."

"Prison."

"But given that this is your first criminal offence, the magistrate's court would not be able to sentence you to more than two years. Chances are the sentence would most likely be twenty-six weeks to a year, and that would be suspended."

"I wouldn't actually go to prison? Really? You could promise that?"

"Now, Bruce. If I told you I could promise that, I would be lying. I am not the magistrate. But I do know the sentencing guidelines. You can look them up for yourself. If I were a betting woman, I would be putting money on a year's suspended sentence."

He moved toward a window. He didn't look out, didn't want to present himself as a target to any police snipers. But he imagined the scene out there. The crowds, the chaos, the sheer inconvenience his actions had caused. "But all the fuss I've caused."

"*Oh, plenty of fuss to be sure, Bruce. You have got yourself into a pretty pickle. But you come out of there, come straight over to me on the other side of the road, and we'll whisk you away from all this and, in all probability, have you back home again by Tuesday at the latest.*"

50

Sam parked the Piaggio on the promenade and raced to the florist, the lava lamp hanging from her elbow by its long handle, the dog crapestry tucked firmly under her arm. The old-fashioned bell on a coiled spring above the door nearly burst free as she hurried through.

"Lilies!" she gasped. "I phoned. Quickly please!"

"Certainly madam," said the florist, plucking lilies from a bucket. "How many would you like?"

Sam was annoyed they weren't ready. "What? I don't know! Four."

"Very good. We do have a three for two offer at the moment. I can do six for the same price."

"Fine, six then. Please hurry."

The florist placed them onto a sheet of paper. "Would you like some greenery or Baby's Breath to complement them?"

"You asked me this on the phone! No! Just lilies, quickly."

The florist opened his mouth with another question.

"No gift card!" yelled Sam. "Lilies only! Now!"

He looked affronted by her rudeness, but Sam was past caring. She slammed a twenty pound note onto the counter, and grabbed the lilies. As she sprinted for the door she thought about the admin she'd need to tackle. She turned. "I'll be back later for the receipt."

Sam pushed through the crowd to the police cordon and demanded to be let through. The police seemed familiar enough with her comings and goings by now. She made her way to the fish stall and heard a shout from behind.

She turned to look, taking a moment to process the bizarre sight at the cordon. She went inside the fish stall to find the police. "You'd better come out here."

Peach, deep in conversation with Sergeant Kenny from the firearms group, started to bluster and complain, but Camara immediately followed Sam. Peach sighed and also stepped out.

"Ah, I see you've roped in your friend," said Camara, glancing wryly at Rich over by the cordon.

"Friends," said Sam, as she spotted Hilde wheeling a contraption through the crowd, shouting at people to get out of her way.

"What the hell are all those donkeys doing there?" asked Peach. "Get them away right now!"

"Pony substitute," said Sam as they walked over.

Hilde demanded to be let through the tape. "This is blooming heavy – come on!"

The police officer moved the tape aside, and Hilde

wheeled her cart through. She was immediately followed by a surge of donkeys.

"Hey!" Rich shouted. Sam realised he was holding straps which restrained some of the donkeys, but he had no control at all over the group when they decided they were on the move. One by one, the straps snatched from his grip and the donkeys nosed forward into the space inside the cordon.

"Couldn't get a pony," shouted Rich as he chased the donkeys. "It was a case of getting the whole herd if I wanted a donkey. Is herd the right term for a group of donkeys?"

Hilde was getting irritated at the distraction. "Oi! Come on, I need some help with this cart."

"Great work, Hilde," said Sam, admiring the bizarre contraption. "Talk us through it. We can help take the weight." Sam waved Camara into place. They took hold of the rope at the front of the cart.

"Right," said Hilde. "We've got these two bicycles." She glanced at Camara. "The ones you said I could have. I've welded them side-by-side with some scaffold tubing. Nobody was using that either. There's this tube joining the front handlebar pillars, another underneath the saddles, and the last one is further down here. They are solidly locked together."

"They must be, there's a sofa on top," said Camara in admiration.

"Chaise longue," said Hilde. "Got the steamer as well." She pointed to an appliance which was strapped in place.

"Great stuff," said Sam. She hung the lava lamp onto one of the handlebars, slotted the dog crapestry in place on top and popped the lilies into one of the wicker baskets that remained on one of the bikes. Peninsula appeared from nowhere with a case of champagne, which Hilde fastened down next to the steamer.

Sam looked up when she had stowed all of her things. She wanted a word with Peninsula, but he'd gone already, striding through the crowd. Was he in a hurry because he needed to do something, or just avoiding difficult questions?

"I reckon that's everything," said Sam.

"Apart from an actual pony," said Hilde. "I'm sure you said there was supposed to be a pony, not a dozen scabby donkeys."

"They are not scabby!" said Rich. "They are very well cared for. Probably."

"I think we need to go with what you've got," said Sam to Camara and Peach. "We've got everything else."

Peach gave a weary nod. "Select the most reliable of these donkeys. The others will need to be removed."

"How do we know which one is the most reliable?" Sam looked at Rich, who shrugged.

"You can look at the names," said Hilde. Each one had their name emblazoned across their bridle. "I mean, this one here is called Ditsy. I'm gonna say you don't want to send in a donkey called Ditsy."

"Good plan!" said Rich. "What do we think about Donovan?"

Sam wrinkled her nose. "Hm, not sure."

"Daisy?"

"Duke?"

"Determinella?"

"What?" Everyone turned to look at Hilde who had said

the name. Sam thought she saw Hilde quickly hiding something.

Sam joined Rich, Camara and Peach as they all examined the donkey's bridle.

"It's a funny name," said Camara. "I'm not sure it's a real name."

"I'm not sure it's even a word," said Peach.

"It's definitely the winner though," said Rich, leading it towards the cart. As they passed by, Sam reached out a discreet finger and dabbed the name. Wet paint. She glanced at Hilde and smiled.

51

Mercedes watched Bruce. He was rocking on his feet, balls to heels, heels to tiptoes. It was like he was trying to move but had forgotten how to walk.

"What is it?" she said.

Her voice seemed to wake him. He blinked. "I'm going to give myself up."

"What? You can't."

He laughed, a pop of laughter, bursting from him like bubbles from tar. "I thought you'd be pleased."

The man actually believed that. He couldn't see she was now invested in his enterprise, that she had chips in the game. She'd told him how they might successfully steal thousands of pounds. She'd agreed to help him steal it. She'd made herself vulnerable to him, stepped over the line to become a criminal like him and now — he thought she'd be *pleased*.

"You cannot give yourself up," she said, firmly.

"I spoke to the lady, the negotiator. We talked about it. She told me what prison sentence I might get if I turned myself in now."

"She can't possibly know what sentence you'll get."

"That's what she said, but she also said there are sentencing guidelines. I can look them up myself. I'll probably only get a suspended sentence. It's only been threats of violence, no actual harm."

Mercedes held up her bandaged hand. Around the dressing the palm of her hand was coloured a pinky-brown with dried blood.

"Well, I'll explain that to them," he said. "I'll say what happened."

And that was it: Mercedes' true fear. Bruce – poor, stupid, guileless Bruce – would explain it all to the police. And her role would be revealed, proved, and she would go to prison for what she had already done.

Mercedes realised that she had decided, quite some time ago, and quite unconsciously, that if her plan to steal her owed back pay from the bank was to succeed, Bruce would need to die during its execution. The man couldn't be trusted to keep his mouth shut. He was too damned straight. His own thought processes were so transparent, he might as well have them come up on a screen on his forehead.

"You can't give yourself up, Bruce. It's not even worth thinking about."

"A suspended sentence. That's like being let off," he said.

"Really?" She let her voice drip with cruel sarcasm. "You

came here this morning for a reason. Do you remember what it was?"

Bruce hesitated, not because he didn't know, but because he didn't want to be side-tracked. "I came to get the money for Tigerheart."

"Money for Tigerheart, for your farm, so Lola could make something of it, build a future. That's what you want, right?"

"I can get the money another way."

"People lend money to convicted criminals, do they? And what will Christine and the kids think?"

He stared dumbly at her.

Mercedes held out two hands, holding invisible objects. She waved one hand. "Here is what happens if you give yourself up. You go to court, you get a criminal conviction. If you're lucky you avoid prison. And then you go back to your farm, with no money, the bank carries on as normal, and Justin in there laughs about stupid old Bruce Greencock, who tried and failed to rob his bank."

"Now, wait—"

Mercedes waggled the other hand. "Now, here, you do indeed go to prison. For a year or two. You've burned a pile of bank notes. Not theft, but some sort of criminal destruction. And you do it in the knowledge that Lola is going to get the money she needs to secure the future of the farm, and you've got one over on Justin bloody Johnson, who got you in this mess in the first place."

Bruce looked from hand to hand, even though they were actually empty. He was clearly tempted, weighing things up.

"I mean, it's not specifically Justin's fault," he said, as

though to himself. "He's just part of the system, a little detail. I'm not going to blame the beach for being sandy."

"What?"

"Something Bridey said."

"Sure, blame the bank if you want to. They make the big decisions. Like inviting Justin and the other employees on the stock-sharing scheme to an annual party at a posh hotel which costs five hundred pounds a head and ten pounds for a bottle of water."

"Really?"

"Really. God knows how many people get invited to that. Yes, the system is unfair and biased and punishes the little guy while rewarding the rich. But don't forget that Justin could have given you the money."

"He said my projections were wrong. A computer makes decisions like this."

She shook her head. "A discretionary loan. It's his decision if there's sufficient collateral. But he turned you down. Well ... he knows you and you're not the type he wants the bank to lend money to."

"What?"

"He said, and I'm quoting, he took one look at your packed lunches at school and knew you'd never amount to nothing."

Bruce was apoplectic with energetic fury. "My packed lunch?"

Mercedes shrugged. "He was never going to give you the money. You're not the right type. You and me. We don't get to go to the posh banquets. Your destiny is to get arrested and put on trial, while he paints himself as the hero and sits in the gallery as you get sent down."

"Like hell he will!" Bruce growled and wheeled towards the office where Justin was held.

CAMARA WAS TRYING to organise the donkeys, but they capered free, delighted to be in the open space within the police cordon. He waved forward several police officers and, with a very expressive gesture, directed them to collect the donkeys.

"I'm sure they'll be fine," said Sam.

"Don't want them in the line of fire," said Camara.

Sam was aware that the uniformed officers in the open street were not just wearing stab vests, but thicker, bulkier armour. She couldn't be sure why, but her eyes immediately went to the roof tops. On both sides of the street she saw heads along the rooftop parapets.

Camara saw her looking and nodded. "TAPT are going to go in while the suspect is distracted."

"Going in? As in 'all guns blazing'?" she said.

"Let's hope it doesn't come to that, eh." He shouted to his colleagues. "Donkeys this side of the line, people that side of the line!" He took hold of Sam's elbow. "And let's get all of you behind cover."

52

As Bruce opened the door to where Justin was tied up, he realised his hands were shaking. His fist could barely grip the doorhandle. Emotions – fear, fury and a wild ignorance of what he was doing – pulsed through his body, his arms, his fingers. In the office he forced himself to go to the water cooler and press the button to fill a plastic cup with chilled water. He gulped it down, realising he'd not had a drink for some time.

"Okay there, Bruce?" said Justin cheerily from his tied up position behind the big desk. "Er, thirsty work this bank robbing thing, right?"

Bruce could have spun round on his heel there and then, sliced his machete through the top of the damned man's skull, like cutting the stalks off cabbage. He held himself still, focused on breathing. When he thought he had control of himself he found a chair and sat opposite Justin. He stared at the branch manager for a long moment.

"Something I can do for you?" said Justin.

"These banquets you have—" Bruce started, then had to stop and cough clear the tight nervous energy from his throat. "These stakeholder banquets the bank has."

"Oh, Mercedes been bending your ear too?"

"How many people go to it?"

"Three hundred. Maybe four. Why do you ask?"

Bruce stared at the ceiling while he made a calculation in his head. "Mercedes said you all went to one of these posh banquets, at an approximate cost of five hundred pounds per person."

"Well, that just shows her grasp of numbers," said Justin. "I said it couldn't have cost *more* than five hundred per person. Why are you asking me this?"

"I think you know the answer to that, Justin. It means your little party cost more money than I need to make my business work. Imagine that."

"Why would you compare those two things? They are not related."

Bruce pulled his chair forward so he could stare into Justin's face. He wanted to see the man within, but for some reason couldn't see a human being there at all. "I *am* relating them. They are now related. One is a completely frivolous and unnecessary expense, the other is my actual livelihood."

Justin gave a smile. It was a patronising, rigid thing. "There are certain expectations, Bruce. Those working dinners for shareholders serve an important function. If a valued member of the banking team works hard all year and isn't shown any appreciation, they might go and work for a competitor. And the bank doesn't want that, do they?"

"You mean you might do that."

"Me. Someone else. I wouldn't hold the bank to ransom like that. But events like that are an expected part of the business. It might seem odd to someone in your position."

"In my position?"

"Right now Bruce, you're in a temporary position of power. There's no mistake. You've got me trussed up like a Sunday joint. You're robbing the bank and people will do what you say because they are worried about what you might do. But that's not how true authority works."

"Do tell, Justin."

Justin shrugged. "This has all got to come to an end at some point. The police have us surrounded and you're going to jail. Surely you can see that."

"Maybe."

"You've made a right hash of things. You'll lose everything you haven't already lost. And it will be up to me to restore order and equilibrium to this place. That's what true leadership is about. And that's a commodity which has to be nurtured."

Bruce's machete weighed heavily in his hand. He laid it across his knees. "You really do think you're better than me."

"Oh, Bruce. You can sulk all you like, but I'm on the side of the law here. You've caused a scene today, because when you came here cap in hand—"

"Cap in hand?" asked Bruce. "Is that how you see me? Is that how you see the bank's customers?"

"An archaic phrase, perhaps."

"I didn't come for your charity, Justin."

Justin was affronted by Bruce's perspective. "You did.

You came here, asking for something you didn't have. You looked at what the big boys have on their plate and, like the thief you've shown yourself to be, you said, 'I fancy a bit of that' without thinking about whether you'd earned it."

Dinners. Big boys. Banquets. Bruce frowned. "Packed lunches," he said.

"What about them?"

"You said something to Mercedes."

"Did I? And she just repeated it all to you? Gosh, she really is under your spell, isn't she? Probably enjoys a submissive role."

"Packed lunches. You said something. You said it to her."

Justin shook his head. "I remember you from school. Do you remember? Sitting in the dining hall. You used to bring sandwiches for lunch, folded up in the wrapper from the loaf."

Bruce stared at him, waiting for the punchline. "Yes?"

"I mean we all used to snigger at – what was her name? – girl in our class, stank like she didn't wash. I want to say Theresa Green but that's not a real name. She had free school dinners, sandwiches on a paper plate wrapped in cellophane and we all knew what that meant. We always knew she wasn't our type. Very keen sense of class and social status, us Brits. Social strata, very important." Justin wore an expression of mild disgust mixed with fond reverie. "Everything about you was always so *rustic*."

"Sandwiches wrapped in bread bags?"

"Absolutely. Honestly, I could have predicted our futures at the age of ten."

Bruce stood up. He had too much energy to stay still. He nodded. "You're right," he said.

"I am," Justin concurred.

"At that age I could tell that Tubby Johnson was a stuck-up idiot with pushy parents who filled his tiny mind with the mistaken idea that he was born into greatness."

"Oh, jealousy is unbecoming, Bruce."

"Your uncle got you started in the bank. He worked here and got you the job."

"Personal contacts are very important."

"As is how our mums packed our lunches, apparently. Popped yours in the ancestral Tupperware with a silver spoon, did she?"

Justin smiled. Bruce thought it was a smile of pity, not an acknowledgement of his joke.

Bruce paced. "You genuinely think you are important, that you're valuable. It's obvious, even to me, that Mercedes runs this bank."

"Oh, that's what she told you."

"And you're just some sort of fat bloated figurehead with delusions of grandeur."

"Well, at least my wife didn't leave me for being a failure at the one job I had in life," spat Justin.

"What did you say?"

"You heard me. Did she leave you because cabbages don't make money, or was it because she couldn't stand to live with such a pathetic specimen of manhood?"

Bruce had no words. He was breathing hard. He raised the machete above his head. Justin's eyes went wide with sudden alarm. The fear in his eyes was a shock of savage delight to Bruce. It was beyond delicious. It was a raw shiver of pleasure.

"No! Don't!" Justin whispered.

"No, I have a better idea," said Bruce.

Bruce went back to the water cooler and tapped the top of it thoughtfully. "At the farm, our water comes out of the tap. I suppose that's too rustic for you."

Justin tried to gather himself. "I think you understand very well that those things are simply there for convenience."

"Ten pound a bottle for water at your parties?"

"I really don't know where Mercedes got that figure from. I can't be held accountable."

Bruce grabbed the massive clear blue reservoir which fed the water cooler and pulled it up and off. Water gushed out before he turned it over and set it down on the carpet.

"How much water would you say is in there, Justin? Is that ten pounds worth? A hundred?"

"This water thing... It's really not anything. Nonsense words."

Bruce gave the bottle a kick, sending ripples through the liquid. He squatted, peering at it. "It's not far off full, even after I spilled some. Want a drink?"

Justin did not reply.

Bruce raised the machete above his right shoulder, ignoring Justin's shouts of protest. He made a lunge forward with the right knee, at the same time bringing the blade round horizontally.

"There!"

Justin stared. Bruce admired his handiwork. The neck of the reservoir was completely gone. It wobbled on the carpet a few inches away. The water bottle sat like a brimming mug, in a large damp patch of carpet.

"You maniac," breathed Justin. There was a new smell in the room. Bruce realised it was urine. Justin had wet himself. "Put the knife down, man!"

"I think I will," said Bruce. He rested the machete against the wall and thought carefully about the mechanics of what he intended to do. "I'm a very practical man, Justin," he said as he busied himself. "Comes of that physical life I lead. Destined to work the soil or whatever. It gave me a good appreciation of spatial awareness and problem solving. But I don't expect you to understand that."

"I really don't know what you're saying." Justin's voice had dropped to something not much more than a whisper, as though he was burrowing deeper inside himself, trying to escape the fear he had every right to be feeling.

"Let me talk you through the process," said Bruce. "I'm moving the water container over here on the other side of the desk. Got to line it up carefully. Now, I need to think carefully about manual handling. We do a lot of it in the manual labour business. It's all about using your knees and protecting your back."

Bruce went to the swivel chair Justin was tied to and examined its back. He twisted a couple of the handles that allowed adjustments, grunting with satisfaction. Justin's head swivelled this way and that as he tried to see what Bruce was doing.

"Just sort out the connector," Bruce grunted.

He turned the knob that loosened the chair back, freeing it completely. He removed the knob and pulled

Justin upwards, taking the chair back with him. Justin now stood in front of the desk, tied to the back of the chair, the separated seat and wheels strapped awkwardly to the back of his legs. If he'd been able to move his bound ankles, he'd be able to walk around upright and sit wherever he liked.

"Here we go!"

"Go where?" said Justin.

Bruce pushed him onto the desk. Justin flopped forward, unable to avoid banging his face on the desk top. Bruce assisted him into a prone position by lifting up the bottom of the chair and sliding it up and over onto the polished surface.

Bruce huffed with a face full of desk, and a chair tied to his back. "Mnf! You nearly broke my teeth! Be careful!"

"I need you to appreciate how I'm thinking on my feet here Justin," said Bruce, panting. "Moving live people about isn't easy. You might be trussed up like a Sunday joint, but you're still a lump."

The chair seat, tied to Justin's backside, pointed straight up. Bruce came round the desk and pulled it forward, hauling Justin face first to the edge. "Now I need to apply some precision here. Bit of aiming. But I can use your own weight against you."

Bruce pulled further. Justin's head slid over the edge of the desk. He saw the upturned, cut down watercooler bottle directly below him and maybe had an inkling of what Bruce intended.

"Okay, you've had your fun, Bruce. Enough of this."

"Enough?" Bruce was disgusted. "There's never *enough*

for your lot. And there's *never* enough left over for the rest of us."

Justin started to thrash and holler. Yes, he'd realised what was coming. Bruce should have been appalled by his actions, but he was overcome with a giddy thrill instead. A knowledge that this was a defining point in both their lives, a road taken only once.

"Ten quid a bottle," said Bruce.

"It was nothing like that!" Justin gasped, his chest constricted by his own bulk and the weight of the chair. "You don't understand!"

"How could we?" said Bruce. "With packed lunches like mine. Let's get this done, eh?"

Bruce hauled, aware there was a danger of pulling too far. He didn't want Justin to slide straight off the table and onto the floor. He need to get him just right.

He edged Justin forward. The man made pained, toddler-like grunts of protest as his chest scraped over the sharp desk edge and his head descended. Justin tried to move his head and shoulders about to avoid the water bottle, but he was a big man and out of shape.

He managed a final "Nnh!", the beginnings of a shout, then his head went into the opened up bottle. It had space for a big fat head with room to spare. There was a froth of water and a scream of bubbles. Justin's legs tried to buck him off the desk, but Bruce leaned in and pinned them to the desk with ease. Bruce's feet were wet with displaced water, but that was fine.

Bruce watched Justin's face turning this way and that. The water and the shaped plastic distorted the image, but the man's face was clear. His eyes were open, staring at Bruce. His mouth worked frantically, like a man trying to shout. To plead.

"You'll never know this feeling, Justin," Bruce said. "The sense of a job well done. Of a problem solved."

Justin couldn't hear him, or acted like he couldn't. Still he thrashed, impotent. A beached fish bent over the desk, out of his element. And still he stared at Bruce, even when his face turned red and his movements slowed.

Bruce kept the man's gaze throughout. He could have watched him all day.

53

Constable Regan Lightfoot adjusted his position on his mat on the roof of the Hildred shopping centre and looked through his spotter's scope again. It had been anything other than a regular morning, but he wasn't complaining.

A role with the Tactical Armed Policing Team was usually a humdrum rota of training, training, training, interspersed with moments where that training meant life or death for some poor fool. More often than not, the TAPT lads got called out to deal with some idiot with a knife or a gun. That idiot might be an angry drunk, or a deluded would-be terrorist, or a pathetically lovelorn bloke with murder-suicide on his mind. In the East Midlands, armed bank robbers were a rarity.

Before TAPT, before the police, Lightfoot had served for ten years in Her Majesty's Army, deployed in Cyprus, Germany and South Sudan. Ten years in which he'd barely fired a dozen shots in live situations. In the six years since, he'd not fired one.

For a man of action, boredom and routine were his bread and butter.

Today's operation was warming up to be the most interesting one of his entire career. Fireteam A was still positioned by the police vehicles directly below them. Fireteams B and C were across the road, having made the long route round via a public park behind the row of shops. He could see someone from Fireteam C climbing the drainpipe to the first floor window of the bank.

Lightfoot checked the thermal imaging scope. It was of limited use in daylight at this distance, particularly through the reinforced bank windows. Nonetheless, he called in his finding.

"TAPT Lead, TAPT Lead receiving Spotter, over."

"Spotter, go ahead, over," came Sergeant Kenny's voice.

"Still no apparent movement inside, out."

"That is all received, out."

Lightfoot heard music. He automatically tapped his earpiece, thinking it might be coming through there, but no, the music, growing in volume, was coming from somewhere down in the street. There was fast twiddly guitar, and the beginnings of a tune that was both familiar and elusive.

He looked along the street. While several regular plods were still arguing with the donkeys which had somehow got loose on the scene, a veritable throng of blonde wigs bobbed through crowded onlookers, straight towards the cordon.

Lightfoot thumbed his call button. "TAPT Lead, TAPT Lead receiving Spotter, over."

"*Spotter, go ahead, over.*"

"There's a group approaching the cordon, over. Correction, they're through the cordon, over."

"*What group, over?*"

Lightfoot hummed along with the tune and tried to place it.

"*What group, over?*" demanded Kenny.

"Dolly Partons, sir," said Lightfoot. "About twenty to thirty of them, over."

"*Can you repeat that, over?*"

Lightfoot swallowed. "About twenty to thirty Dolly Parton impersonators coming through the cordon. Officers unable to stop them. Singing *Jolene*, over."

The cleared street was now busy with multiple Dolly Partons who had slipped through the gap intended for the donkeys. The quality of the wigs and outfits varied wildly. Lightfoot swung his spotter scope towards them.

Down on the ground, the tall and lean local detective was shouting and waving his hands, struggling to be heard above the music. He gestured for a colleague to bring him something or other, but a Dolly came and fondled his chin while singing about him not stealing her man.

54

S am looked round for Rich. "You did this?" she shouted over the music coming from a loud PA somewhere.

"What?" said Rich innocently, but with a guileless grin on his face.

"You think this is helping?"

"I gave the Skegness Operatic and Dramatic Society a broad remit on how to bring some Dolly-based cheer to the situation. This isn't specifically my doing."

A Dolly thrust a leaflet into Sam's hand. "Y'all come down to Nails by Tracey later, y'hear."

Sam looked at the salon brochure in her hand.

"I don't think I even hired this many Dollys," Rich said.

Sam would have remonstrated with him further, but was distracted by an argument brewing in the crowd behind her.

"What the hell are you doing wearing our T-shirt?"

"How stupid are you?" a voice shouted back. "This is a

#teamBruce T-shirt. Any idiot can see that. It's got a cabbage on it."

"Well duh, of course it has. Anyone who's in *#teamCops* can see it's spelling out how ridiculous the whole thing is. Who robs a bank over cabbages?"

In a fight as pointless as any war, it was transpiring both *#teamBruce* and *#teamCops* had adopted the cabbage as their emblem of choice. Peninsula's distribution of cabbage-themed T-shirts among the crowd had not had the desired effect of creating a pro-cabbage sentiment among the onlookers. Antagonistic team allegiances now pivoted on whether cabbages were mildly ridiculous and *just a vegetable* or whether they actually stood for the hard-working traditions of the Lincolnshire farmer. Sam wanted to shake them and say a cabbage could be both of those things, but matters had escalated way out of hand before she could do or say anything.

Sam had no way of knowing who threw the first punch, but she had to move swiftly to get away from the combustible heart of the conflict.

TIED to a chair in a back office, Marvin strained an ear to hear and swayed along with the music coming from outside.

"What is going on?" said Becky, in the manner of one who feared she was missing out on something important.

"The hits of Dolly Parton," said Marvin. "I met her once."

"You mentioned earlier," said Delia. "Met her and thingy, the woman with Larry the Lamb."

"No, not Larry the Lamb. Entirely different lamb character," said Marvin. "I met Lamb Chop."

Delia's brow furrowed. "So, who's Larry Lamb then?" She tried to blow hair out of her eyes, not having free hands to push it aside.

"Ah, now there's a fine actor," said Marvin. "I did Aladdin with him at the Ashcroft Theatre in Croydon. I was the genie to his Abanazar."

"You did panto with a lamb?" said Stevie.

"Larry Lamb."

"Shush, I'm trying to listen," said Becky, irritably.

"You've heard Dolly before, surely," said Marvin.

"Except they're singing something different."

Marvin tried listening again. The woman was right. There was a swelling chant, like from a football terrace. And instead of 'Jolene', the singers were calling out for 'Bruc-ie!'.

"The man has fans," said Marvin.

A VOICE SPOKE in Constable Lightfoot's ear.

"TAPT Lead, TAPT Lead receiving Zulu One-Five, over."

It was Constable Bryant, leading Fireteam C.

"Zulu One-Five, go ahead, over," said Sergeant Kenny.

"Have breached first floor window, entering, over."

Lightfoot checked the thermal imaging. There were heat movements in the bank's upper storey. Faint shadows of warmth through the opaque glass. If Fireteam C were inside, then it was only before they'd be heading downstairs. Shotgun or no shotgun, old Farmer Hoggett or whatever his name was wouldn't have a chance against a three-man fireteam with MP5 carbines set to three-round bursts. The men were also carrying shotguns loaded with technically non-lethal beanbag rounds.

Down in the street, Chief Inspector Peach shouted commands to the coppers who had been thrust forward to control the donkeys. Lightfoot felt a little sorry for them, as donkey control was not something the police were regularly schooled in, and these donkeys seemed to be infected by the music and the whirling Dollys.

"TAPT Lead, TAPT Lead receiving Zulu Two-Seven, over."

It was Constable Jim Clay, leading Fireteam B.

"Zulu Two-Seven, go ahead, over," said Sergeant Kenny.

"At rear door. Ready to enter on your signal, over."

Fireteam B were in position too. With three men coming from above and three bursting in from the rear door, the gunman was going to be caught unawares and in a pincer movement.

And the chaos in the street should mask any other noise and have the suspect's attention focused fully elsewhere.

55

Eventually, Bruce decided he would have to move the body.

It had taken Justin maybe a minute to die. It had felt longer, and Bruce's anger had luxuriated in every moment. In the silence that followed the excitement faded. Bruce waited for the shame and the horror to sweep over him. He was surprised when it never came. He had killed a man. He'd never killed a person before. He'd barely killed any animals before, bar the occasional rabbit he'd found dying on the roadside and put out of its misery. He was an arable farmer after all. He expected to be filled with horror at this turn of events, but the sense of a job well done still clung to him, wrapping itself around him.

But now, as Justin's body lay cooling, slumped forward over the desk, he felt it was only right to put the dead man in a more dignified pose.

"Okay, mate," he said. "Time to get up."

He crouched, grabbed Justin's wet shoulders and shoved up, sliding him back up onto the desk. There was some weight to that torso, but it was a moments' work. With a satisfying motion, the dead man's legs and chair base tied to them flopped back to the floor on the far side of the desk. Justin slumped into a seated position. Bruce shuffled round the desk, still holding onto his soaked shirt, and carefully pulled the upper body back to a point where he could re-engage the chair back's positioning knob.

Throughout this manoeuvring the watercooler bottle stayed on Justin's head. The man's dying gasps and wriggles had created some form of vacuum, and the plastic cylinder was wedged on his head, his face mushed against the clear surface. Now upright, water slurped out from around the head and neck with a sudden, shocking noise. It sounded as if Justin was reanimated as a gargling monster.

At that moment Mercedes walked in.

She stared. Her hand went to her throat. She bucked like she was about to throw up and, for a long moment, seemed unable to draw breath.

"What did you do?" she whispered.

Bruce thought it was obvious, but Mercedes just kept staring.

"I killed him," he said and added, "He was annoying," as a justification.

"I didn't tell you to kill him," she said. Bruce momentarily thought there was something odd in that statement, but he couldn't work out what.

Slowly, she got her calm back. "Well, it's done now, isn't it?"

"It is," Bruce agreed.

"And now we need to show them," she said.

"Show who?"

"The police. Show them that we are serious. That *you* are serious. Once they see him, they will do whatever you say, in case you hurt the others."

"Yeah, but I thought the plan was—"

Mercedes held up a hand. "It's all about getting them to do what we want. Trust me."

Bruce frowned. His head was buzzing with what had happened, and he couldn't think straight with the noise coming from outside.

"What do we do?" he asked.

"We wheel the body into lobby for now."

"Shall I take that off?" Bruce pointed at the water bottle still squashed onto Justin's head.

"Definitely not. It adds a certain *je ne sais quoi* to the whole thing. Your phone is ringing."

She was right. It was.

"Bruce, we've got the items you requested," said Bridey. *"They're bringing them to the front door now."*

SAM HAD NEVER THOUGHT of donkeys as being highly strung. Mostly the Skegness ones plodded placidly up and down the beach, but watching the animals from behind the fishmonger's stall, she thought these particular donkeys looked giddy and playful. Sam knew it was wrong to project human thoughts and emotions onto animals, but she felt certain the donkeys were enjoying the songs of Dolly Parton. They cantered happily among the dancing, miming, blonde-wigged performers.

When *Islands in the Stream* started to play, the Dolly performers all seemed to have the same idea, or were very quick to copy each other. Each of them hugged a donkey around its neck and coerced it into being the Kenny Rogers side of the duet. Some of the donkeys had a Dolly on each side, all mugging wildly for the cameras recording the bizarre spectacle. The donkeys didn't seem to mind; in fact they looked as if they were enjoying the attention. The longer Sam looked, the more sense it made. The donkeys were grizzled and beardy, and looked as if they were singing along.

The police sent out to round up the donkeys looked like they'd had little training in dealing with Country and Western impersonators. Sam glanced at Peach: he was mesmerised in the same way she was. He had briefly stopped trying to have the donkeys brought under control while they performed their starring roles.

When the song was replaced by another, the donkeys were released from their duets.

Something sailed out from beyond the cordon and exploded leafily in the road. It was big and round and green. Someone had been to the supermarket and bought actual cabbages. The *#teamBruce* and *#teamCop* ruckus which had started in the crowds had developed into physical vegetable warfare. Another off-course missile arced into the scene. Lucas Camara dodged the twirling Savoy. These were no Tigerhearts (Sam's cabbage-spotting skills were obviously improving), but they made solid projectiles.

"Oi, that's not fair," came a distant cry from the crowd as a teenager started gleefully pelting people with Brussels sprouts.

Camara and the uniformed copper with him were attempting to get Determinella and the cart of goodies over to bank. Camara was pulling on the strap, but the donkey refused to move, its eyes darting at the mayhem around it. Camara leaned over to the officer and said something. The man looked very unhappy and replied, his face plaintive. Camara gave him a stern look. The officer removed his hat and hi-visibility vest. He draped the vest over the donkey's head and put the hat on top in an effort to calm the animal by blanking its view to the side. No doubt someone would soon be posting a social media image of a donkey in police uniform.

But the odd plan seemed to work. The donkey moved forward as Camara urged it on with kind words and a gentle hand on the animal's nose as it walked forward.

MERCEDES COULD SEE a glint of mania in Bruce's eyes. The man would need careful managing now. With murder, he had stepped from one world into another. What he had done with Justin, brutally and theatrically, would play to Mercedes' plan perfectly if handled correctly.

Justin's face was pressed against the inside of the bottle, his eyes tilted sightlessly upwards, his mouth open as if he was about to start patronising her. Mercedes had to hold back a smile.

Bruce, still on the phone to Bridey, helped wheel the dead man out into the corridor and round to the lobby.

"Yes, we're ready to receive," said Bruce. "We're coming to the front door now."

In the lobby, Mercedes remembered they'd rolled several desks in front of the door.

"Aye, we'll have it open in a minute," said Bruce and ended the call. He looked at Mercedes. "Will they shoot me if I open the door?"

"I don't think so," she said.

"You'll have to be the one who does it."

"I'm a hostage," she reminded him.

"Under my control."

She contemplated the blood she'd smeared on herself and her bandaged hand.

"Yes," she said, wondering how best to convey the look of exhausted terror she'd want the world to see.

56

"Put your vegetables down! I repeat, put your vegetables down!" called a uniformed officer armed with a megaphone. "Anyone found to be in possession of brassicas will be arrested. I need you to put down your cabbages!"

Whether it was the intention or not, there was such an outbreak of laughter that hostilities stuttered and slowed.

Near the bank, Camara looked across to Chief Inspector Peach for guidance. The uniformed constable next to him spoke on the radio, too far away for Sam to hear. Camara did not look pleased that he had somehow fallen into the role of lead donkey-wrangler. Peach shouted at his officers to remove the Dolly Partons and loose donkeys from the scene.

Camara stepped slowly towards the bank with Determinella. Sam wondered how this was supposed to work. Nobody from outside was going to be allowed into the bank, and surely nobody from inside would come out.

Camara spoke soothing words to the donkey, stroking its head as he edged slowly, slowly forward. No, he wasn't speaking: Sam could hear him singing to the donkey. The Dolly tunes kept coming. Camara had obviously decided he might as well placate the donkey with a little gentle crooning about how it was all taking and no giving. The donkey remained in place at the top of the steps, and Sam could see the relief in Camara's stance.

As Camara neared the bank, he left the singers and donkeys behind. Several of the other beasts had wandered off to enjoy the cabbages now littering the street.

The Country music cut off. Clearly the police had located Peninsula, or his equipment, and shut him down. A strangely eerie quality descended on the deserted street outside the bank. Camara and the uniformed officer were the only people inside the cordon, and he was moving slowly towards the building. Sam could feel the tension. This was Clint Eastwood walking down a Wild West street at high noon. Camara wasn't wearing spurs, but Sam could mentally hear them jangling nonetheless.

Sam saw Camara reach into the pannier basket of one of the bicycles and pull out a carrot. He looked from side to side, stepped away from the donkey, and walked towards the night safe in the wall of the bank, next to the ATM. Camara pulled it open and dropped the carrots inside. Then he returned to the donkey and patted its nose to reassure it. He led it to the side of the steps and up the wheelchair ramp, towards the bank's front door.

All eyes were now on the door. Was there a plan for Bruce to emerge? Sam wondered whether he would bring a hostage if he did, as the police would surely shoot him. Or was that the kind of thing which only happened in America?

The front door cracked open, and a hand holding a carrot emerged. There was a sharp noise, loud in the silence.

"*Pspsps!*"

Another voice could be heard. "That's what you do for cats!"

"Yes, but I don't know a pony noise!"

The hand became a forearm. It was wearing the mauve blouse of a bank employee.

There was another noise, a clicking of teeth. The door opened a little more and a woman stepped out. Her hands held high, a carrot in each one. Based on what Sam understood of events, and Zahra's display in the fish stall, this was Mercedes. Mercedes Martin. Lived with that pathetic, hunched woman who was possibly still shredding pastry after pastry in the café.

"That's not a pony," said Mercedes. Sam saw a blood stain on her blouse. She'd been hurt in some way.

"It was the best we could do in the time given," said Camara.

OBSERVING FROM ON HIGH, Constable Lightfoot watched the scenes at the front of the bank. His handheld parabolic microphone picked up the dialogue clearly.

The hostage in the doorway looked back over her shoulder. "I'm bringing it in. It's a donkey, but there's not a lot I can do about that."

She was talking to someone, but Lightfoot couldn't see the suspect, couldn't radio it in.

The hostage held the carrots in front of the donkey's nose. "Come on then, good donkey."

The donkey stood unmoving at the top of the steps. Lightfoot willed it to move. He wasn't certain what a good result for this kind of handover would be, but he was fairly certain a donkey-based impasse was far from ideal.

"Come on, here we go!" The hostage made more of the clicking noises and wafted carrots in front of the donkey. It glanced at her but remained in place.

"I think I know what it wants!" DC Camara shouted to the fish stall. "Put the music back on!"

"It's a donkey!" Peach yelled back.

"Put the music back on!" He turned to the hostage. "You'll probably need to sing along."

The look of horror on the woman's face deepened.

"Do we have any special requests?" Peach shouted to Camara.

"*TAPT lead to Zulu One-Five,*" said Kenny in Lightfoot's ear. "*Move in.*"

IN THE LOBBY, six feet behind Mercedes, Bruce shifted uneasily. He'd just killed a man, but the bank's front door being open filled him with more anxiety than murder had. He wanted the door closed. He wanted to shut out the world. Bruce realised he never wanted to face the outside world again.

"Come on, come on!" he hissed.

The music of Dolly Parton issued forth once more from speakers somewhere down the street. Mercedes cleared her throat nervously and sang along, in a reedy voice. The donkey looked up with interest. Oddly, it seemed to enjoy the energy of the song and finally raised a hoof in movement. It walked forwards as Mercedes moved backwards. The weird makeshift cart behind it came up the final part of the ramp.

There was a thump and a clattering from above. A rattling shower, and the sounds of a man falling down stairs after slipping on marbles on a top step. Each impact had a different resonance, a different quality. There were pauses, fractions of seconds, an accidental syncopation of gravity, heightening the auditory landscape of fleshy thumps, bony crunches, painful rolls, and equipment clatters of a man making his way from one floor to another with unpleasant speed.

"Bastards!" Bruce turned and ran towards the back rooms. "Get that door shut!" he yelled at Mercedes.

He swung past the children in the corridor.

"Is the pony here?" said Edith, jiggling expectantly. Evan looked ready to wet himself with excitement.

Bruce ignored them. He crouched to flick the power socket linked to the microwave beyond the door to the rear exit, then grabbed the doctored fire extinguisher off the floor. He barged through the security door to the stairs, already squeezing the extinguisher handle before he saw the man on the floor.

Carbon dioxide, mixed with mustard powder and chilli flakes, sprayed out in a yellow mist. The armed copper had fallen on his back with his legs pointing up the stairs. In the narrow space, he was struggling like an overturned tortoise. And now he had a mouth and nose full of choking mustard powder.

Bruce realised he had made a mistake and was going to be shot at any moment. With that realisation and fear came the knowledge there would be more men. He angled the spray up the stairs. But there was no one there, only surprised faces peering round the doorway on the next floor.

"I'll kill him! I'll kill him!" Bruce shouted as mist obscured the stairway, hoping they understood his words meant he would kill the man if they tried to come down to get him. Not that he intended to kill him regardless.

57

Constable Lightfoot tried to make sense of what he was hearing over the radio. Someone in Fireteam C was garbling incoherently over the comms, making it hard for anyone to hear Jim Clay of Fireteam B.

"*Say again, Zulu Two-Seven,*" said Kenny.

In the street, the bank door opened as wide as it could go. The donkey went through into the foyer and a moment later the door was drawn shut.

"*—microwave with bags of flour on top,*" Jim Clay called over the radio. "*Not sure what's inside it, over. A bottle of something.*"

"*Can you get inside, over?*" Kenny shouted over the Fireteam C jabber.

"*It's a suspicious device, sir,*" said Clay. "*We're stepping back until I—*"

Either the radio was cut off or just drowned by the explosion erupting at the rear of the bank. From his high position Lightfoot saw a pillar of yellow flame bloom upwards and over the roof, burning out almost instantly. Lightfoot had seen flour explosions before, dust particles igniting in the air, the explosion created by rapid gas expansion. More impressive than destructive, it would still be a bad thing to be near its centre.

Sound returned.

"Device exploded, over!" Clay shouted over the radio. By the tone of his voice, the man was okay, although there was a chance he'd been deafened in the blast.

"All teams withdraw, over," said Kenny.

DUST DRIFTED from the ceiling onto the four tied up hostages. A constant alarm was ringing somewhere in the building.

"Are they trying to blow the bank up?" said Stevie.

"I need to see what's going on," said Becky, hopping impotently on her chair.

"As long as no one's set the bank on fire," said Marvin.

As he had grown older, Marvin had thought more and more on the nature of death, and, as he supposed many did, hoped he would die peacefully in his sleep. He didn't want a prolonged and painful death from some gut-rotting cancer or some such. Until now, he had not considered the even less preferable method of being burned or buried alive while tied to cheap office furniture.

The door opened and the Mitten children ran in. There was horrified alarm on their faces, but also a crazed glee.

"The pony's here!"

"Except it's a donkey!"

"Then Bruce did a thing in the man's face!"

"And the door went bang!"

Stevie was agog. Becky looked stunned.

"Bet you wish you had photos of that," Delia said to her.

THE DONKEY HAD NOT TAKEN KINDLY to the noise and commotion. It was bucking and bouncing around the lobby area in alarm. If asked, Mercedes would have said she was trying to do her best to calm and slow the creature. In truth, she knew she was doing little more than turning on the spot and pointing at it, trying to work out what calming noises she could make.

Bruce lumbered through, sweating and dragging a man by the scruff of his neck. He was wearing the kind of black camo gear and body armour one only ever saw in the movies. He was clawing feebly at Bruce with gloved hands while simultaneously retching and coughing.

When Bruce saw the capering donkey he froze. The armed officer wriggled and turned, blindly pushing himself to his feet. Only to immediately knocked down again by a donkey he had completely failed to see through his dust-covered goggles.

The collision also knocked some of the energy from the donkey and it slowed, apparently happy it had made its point.

"Bastards!" Bruce snarled, turning the policeman. He

found the plastic cable ties the man was carrying on the back of his belt. "Bastards tried to break in."

The policeman tried to speak, but just coughed and wheezed. Bruce bound his wrists behind his back, took another tie to reinforce the first, then worked on binding his feet together.

"What was that sound?" said Mercedes.

"Champagne, microwave, flour and sugar," said Bruce. "It was on Brainiac, like I said."

"You'll never get away with it," the cop managed to whisper. A stupid thing to say and probably just a concussed reflex action.

The donkey, whose noseband declared her to have the unlikely name of Determinella, nudged at Justin's corpse in the wheelie chair, perhaps hopeful that the dead man might have a sugar lump or some other treat.

"They didn't take you seriously," said Mercedes.

"They didn't," Bruce agreed, furious.

The police officer was laid out on the floor, angled away from Mercedes. With his mustard-powder covered goggles, he couldn't see her going to Justin's body and wheeling the corpse away from the donkey and towards the front door.

"What are you going to do?" she said to Bruce and nodding at Justin's body. "Are you going to send them a message?"

Bruce either didn't notice her carefully chosen turn of phrase or maybe he didn't care. "Yes," he said.

Mercedes gave Justin a quick check as she parked him in front of the door. Well-strapped to the chair? Yes. Evenly balanced weight, so he wouldn't tip sideways when he was pushed out? Yes. Utterly fucking horrendous death mask trapped inside that bottle? Yes.

"I'll unlock the door for you," she said.

Bruce trotted over, as obedient as a sheepdog.

Mercedes hoped there were people out there with cameras and phones. She slid open the bolts, putting one hand on the key in the lock and the other on the handle.

"One," she said, nodding to begin the count.

Bruce nodded with her.

THE EXPLOSION at the rear of the bank had snuffed out the carnival atmosphere gripping Skegness town centre. Donkeys scattered to the fringes. The music quietened. Vegetable-based warfare stopped dead. Onlookers, phones still raised or cupped in hands, were now silent. This was no longer a weird spectacle. Something *big* was happening here today.

Sam propelled herself from the shelter of the fishmonger's and nearly collided with Camara.

"That did not go well," he said, in a remarkable piece of understatement.

Someone shouted. The front door to the bank was opened and something rolled out. There was only the briefest view of the shoving hands before the door was shut again.

The man on the wheeled chair rolled down the disabled access ramp. He appeared to be wearing something clear on his head. A helmet, thought Sam, instantly dismissing the thought. The chair tipped and tottered off the low curb, and pitched over into the road.

From the way the man's body hit the tarmac, the abrupt halt and the stillness, Sam knew he was dead.

Her insides flipped as she craned to look. She could only think of her dad as she saw a stranger.

"We need to stay back," said Camara.

Firearms officers were making towards the body, crouched but moving swiftly. Sam looked at the inhuman face squashed against the glass.

larms still rang.

Stevie jumped and squealed as Bruce booted in the office door, or at least jumped as much as a woman tied to a chair could do.

Bruce was hauling a man in behind him. The man, covered in dust and powder, wore some sort of police special forces gear. Marvin liked a war movie or cheesy cop show as much as the next man, but had never been able to muster the enthusiasm to learn anything about the military or weaponry. He had no idea what any of the man's tactical gear might be for, or what the insignia on his shoulder might represent, but it was a fair guess the police's attempt to bring the siege to a violent end had failed.

"We haven't got room in here for more," said Becky, as though the man was being invited into an exclusive VIP hostage area.

Bruce ignored her. With fierce, forceful motions he tied

the man up further with some of the spare networking cables and positioned him against a wall. As he did so Bruce muttered furiously to himself, too low and guttural for Marvin to make out.

Mercedes appeared nervously in the doorway. "Where do you want the donkey?"

"In here."

Mercedes' nod was small, timid. She brought forward a seaside donkey which bore a stoically philosophical expression, as seaside donkeys so often did.

"Oh, really!" said Becky. "This is too much."

"You wanted a donkey," said Bruce.

"We wanted a pony. Well, someone wanted a pony." Her head snapped round to look at Delia. "It was you, wasn't it?"

"I don't think this is the time to make donkey-related accusations," said Delia.

"Bring the children," Bruce growled.

The donkey stepped cautiously around the room. The police officer, conscious but dazed, shifted his legs to get out from under its hooves. The donkey nudged the networking cabinet in the corner, then stared at the hostages. Marvin felt judged.

The children, Edith and Evan, were herded into the room.

"We got a pony!" the boy said and pointed, in case anyone hadn't noticed.

"There was an explosion but no one died," the girl added.

Bruce stood in the doorway. Marvin saw he now had a gun in his hand, a nasty looking submachinegun thing. And he had a pistol tucked into his belt, creased against his untucked shirt. Confiscated from the copper, Marvin guessed.

Marvin didn't know if Bruce liked war movies and cheesy cop shows as much as the next man, but he suspected the farmer was of a sufficiently practical bent to know how to use the weapons. And Marvin did not like the look on the man's face. There was a darkness about it. It was the face of a man who had run out of options.

A phone was ringing in Bruce's pocket, but he seemed too far away to hear it any longer.

The door was shut and something heavy placed against it.

MERCEDES DID NOT like the way Bruce was swaying. She especially did not like it as he was swaying with the policeman's gun gripped tightly in both hands.

"Wasn't supposed to happen like this. Wasn't supposed to happen," he said, for the fifth time. His eyes were staring, distantly, at nothing.

"You've done great so far," said Mercedes, not sure how much of an encouraging spin she should put on her words.

"I shouldn't have killed him. I shouldn't. You shouldn't have pushed him out the door."

"You pushed him out the door," she reminded him. "You wanted to send them a message."

"I was angry. I was so angry. But I shouldn't have done it."

"Spur of the moment decision," she said. "You did it. It happened. You move on and do the next thing."

He shook his head. "But it's all gone wrong."

"Not at all. The money's still there in the vault. The plan can work."

"But I'm going to prison!"

She put a hand on his arm, prepared to withdraw it if he responded badly. He barely seemed to notice it. "You were always going to go to prison, Bruce. It's the money that counts. It's the farm and the land and giving Lola and the others a future."

His brows twitched. It seemed as though his conscious mind was attempting to navigate a path back to the here and now, sidestepping horrors and picking its way through the moral doubts and self-loathing.

"You're right," he said eventually. "It's about the children and the land."

"Yes," she said and squeezed his forearm tenderly.

Bruce saw her hand now. His face folded into something she supposed was meant to be tender gratitude. She felt only disgust at his response. She was playing a role, manipulating him to fulfil her own goals, but did he really think she could feel any genuine warmth for a man who had endangered her life. She held her feelings in check.

"Then let's do it," she said and led him towards the vault.

CAMARA TRIED to steer Sam towards the shopping centre. All she could picture was that dead empty place where the hostages' families were corralled and resisted.

"I want to know what's going on!" she said.

"Everything's under control," Camara said.

It was the reassuring tone of voice he'd often deployed, coupled with large, caring, guiding hands. But everything was so evidently not under control. Explosions. Bodies in the street. More than subtle clues that the police had no control. Now that reassuring voice and those caring hands seemed patronisingly dismissive of her very real need to find out what the hell was happening to her dad and her friend, and all those other poor buggers still stuck in the bank.

She shrugged him away and stepped swiftly towards King's fish stall. The negotiator, Zahra, had a phone on the desk before her and was attempting to make an outgoing call. Bruce was not picking up.

"What's going on?" said Sam.

"That's a rather unfocused question," said Zahra without looking round. "I'm not sure what you want me to say."

"What's Bruce going to do next?"

"I am many things, but I am not a mind-reader." The young woman's precise manner was wearing thin on Sam. She wondered if shaking her might elicit a straight answer. "However, I would imagine he's in quite an agitated state of mind right now."

"Dangerous, then," said Sam.

"Yet he's been a very rational individual so far."

"Really? Donkeys and flowers and motivational posters?"

Zahra turned away from the phone to look at Sam at last. "Demands as distractions. Calculated behaviour. There is something about the man I do not understand."

"What?" said Sam.

"It is, as you and I have postulated, possible the bank

robbery began 'accidentally'. Pipework mistaken for a gun. A seemingly honest request for loan money. And yet, over the last few hours, he's maintained control over the bank interior with surprising efficiency. Just now he managed to orchestrate the collection of the pony et cetera at the front of the building, while engaging with armed police officers at the rear. He's taken one of them hostage by the way. And apart from some missing eyebrows, it seems the rest have avoided injury but have been forced to withdraw."

"He cut the CCTV too," said Sam.

"An astute act. For a simple farmer, as some might call him, he's showing surprising levels of competence."

"You admire him."

Zahra pursed her lips thoughtfully. On her tight face, such an act made her lips into a tiny cherry. "We are missing something," she said.

Sam pursed her lips too. "I know what you mean."

59

Mercedes moved quickly and spoke economically, as though time was suddenly not on their side. This was fine with Bruce, as he was struggling enough and needed the day to be done before he spun completely out of control, or collapsed in horrified exhaustion. He wanted it all to be over, yet simultaneously he wanted it to never end. If the vault door shut now and sealed him inside forever, that would not be the worst outcome.

There were bundles of money in the carrier bags they'd left on the floor.

"Two hundred thousand, right?" said Mercedes.

"Right," he agreed. He slung the policeman's gun over his shoulder by the strap and crouched, patting the bags. "Have we got enough here already?"

"I'll count." She did so, lips moving silently as she went through one bag, then the next.

"How can you be so calm?" he said, amazed.

"Terrified on the inside, Bruce."

"I'm sorry," he said.

"It's fine," she said. "There's a hundred and twenty thousand in that one. Seventy-five thousand in that one. Just another five thousand needed."

"You're a quick counter."

"A good head for numbers." She took an extra five thousand from the stacks in the vault, double-checked for ink explosives, and put it in the carrier.

"And a little something for yourself, remember?" said Bruce.

"Oh, of course." She said like it hadn't occurred to her and added an additional pack to the pile.

A tiny, unpleasant suspicion crossed Bruce's mind. In the white noise rush that was his present thoughts, he almost let it go. But he thought on it, and on the two hundred grand he was about to put into Mercedes' care. As he stood he covertly reached for the pile of security tracker widgets the DefCon4 woman had given him earlier that morning and dropped one of them in a carrier bag with the cash. He couldn't wholly say why he had done it, but it was like putting a fraction of himself with the money. A means, of sorts, of keeping tabs on her when he was finally arrested. A threat in case she decided to turn against him.

"Let's put it in the security box then." He followed her through to the safety deposit box room and to her box, still open on the counter. She took her bundle of letters out and gestured for Bruce to put the cash inside.

He folded the plastic bags tightly around the bundles. He

wasn't sure why, perhaps just an instinctive neatness. Two hundred thousand didn't even fill the box. He felt life-changing amounts of money should be huge, and the size of these bundles was somehow unfair.

"Shame we can't steal it all," he said.

"Getting greedy?" she said.

"No, not that." He didn't want to explain any further.

"We have to leave most for us to burn. Got to leave a convincing amount of evidence." She shut the box without putting her letters from Spain back inside and carried it back to the wall space, sliding it back into place.

He looked at the letters on the table. Hand-written letters were such an old-fashioned medium. "Your dad, when you got in touch with him again..." he said.

"Yes?"

"You had his letters sent here."

"It was the address I gave him."

"But why here?"

Mercedes locked the safety deposit box door and faced him. "My mum never tried to find him. She deprived me of my own *papá*. Through her own laziness and pathetic lack of imagination. Right through to adulthood." She picked up the letters, a fat brick of correspondence, and squeezed it. "Why should I, when I've finally found him, share him with her?"

"She doesn't know?"

Mercedes' head shake was firm. "Never going to tell her."

"Seems a bit ... cruel, doesn't it?"

"Nothing she doesn't deserve." She snatched the letters up and marched out of the room.

"If we're going to burn the money, we'll need some sort of accelerant," he said, hurrying to follow.

"Already on it," she said.

60

Mercedes came back downstairs to the vault holding a cloudy bottle with a pink feminine label. Bruce was staring at the ringing phone in his hand and put it away, unanswered.

Mercedes held the bottle up for Bruce to see. "Stevie's nail polish remover. It's got acetone in it. Highly flammable."

"Will it work?"

She sloshed it. It was a big bottle and mostly full. "We can but try."

She squeezed past him and went to the vault. She looked at the documents on the side shelves and, despite her own criminal intentions, felt a pang of guilt for the inconvenience the destruction of important legal documents might cause. They could remove them from the vault, but that would then raise questions about the sequence of events. It needed to look like Bruce had independently decided to burn the cash as some sort of protest. Careful consideration of bank documents did not fit that narrative.

"We have to create the right scene," she said.

"I know how to start a fire," said Bruce.

"Not just that."

She looked at the vault, thought about where she had stood, what they had done.

There were Bruce's shotgun shells and his little plastic stickers in bags on the side shelf. Mercedes gathered those together, plus the ink explosive charges she'd removed from the cash packs. Shotgun shells and ink explosives would be a volatile combination all by themselves, but probably produce more bang than actual flame.

"Okay," she said. "Let's work out what we're going to do."

"Yes, work it out," he agreed.

"We make the fire here, burn the cash. We need to destroy nearly all of it for this to work."

"We do."

"Don't know if that's going to set off more alarms, but it might trigger some sort of response from the police."

Bruce nodded tersely.

"So, we've got to be ready for the next part," she said. "Your surrender."

He sighed.

"Got to give yourself up," she said, pretending to try to smile like they both had to be brave little soldiers.

"And I tell them nothing about this," he said, gesturing at the vault.

"You tell them you coerced and bullied me into helping you generally. All that stuff with the tying people up and the demands, you tell that straight. Just none of this stuff. Okay, let's take a look at you. You're about to meet your public."

Bruce actually stood up straight, like he was a proud little boy heading out for his first day at school. Responding in kind, Mercedes brushed him down. Bruce remembered himself and began to drop the police gun from his shoulder.

"No, keep it," she said.

"What?"

"You're going out there to meet your public, and to meet the police as equals."

"I'm surrendering."

"So don't put your hands on it."

"Maybe lose this one?" he suggested touching the handgun tucked into his belt.

"Sure."

As he put the pistol on the shelf, she straightened the line of his jacket and slipped three ink explosive packs and the shotgun shells in the square front pocket of his coat. They weighed very little and he didn't even notice. She tugged the pocket flap as though neatening it.

"Every bit the hero of the common man," she said.

His phone rang again.

"You are a very popular man," Mercedes said. "And you'll talk to them all soon enough."

She began arranging the cash fire. The stacks of money would not go up easily. Breaking them apart and creating loose piles of notes would be better. The modern polymer banknotes would still be reluctant to catch fire and would need considerable encouragement. She formed a loose volcano of banknotes, then took out her stash of personal letters and removed the rubber band around them.

"Help me," she told Bruce and began ripping them up – letters, envelopes, postcards – to create a pile of kindling in the volcano crater.

"These are your letters," said Bruce.

"I've been hoarding them too long," she said. "I reckon that when this is all over, I'm going to bite the bullet and go out and see him."

"Your dad?"

She nodded. "And the rest of my family out there."

"That sounds good."

He looked at the back of an envelope. Was he trying to memorise the return address? Did he think she was going to run out on him?

"I have a good feeling about this plan," she said. He nodded slowly.

When the letters were confetti, she upended the nail polish remover and squeezed. The clear liquid came out in a pungent jet. She sprinkled it on the paper, then thoroughly doused the cash. There was even enough to make a trail across the floor and over the lip of the vault door. That's what they did in films, right? Make a trail to light the fire from.

"Lighter?" she said.

Bruce looked at her blankly. "Not me."

"I don't smoke," she said.

"Surely you have the means to make fire somewhere in the building," Bruce said.

"Huh," she said, almost a derisory laugh. "You're looking at the only member of staff who remembers everyone's birthday and knows where we keep the candles and matches."

She hurried off again.

IN THE BACK OFFICE, Marvin leaned forward to speak to the young policeman slumped on the floor. "Are you all right there, lad?"

The policeman coughed weakly. There was dribble on his chin. "I've been better."

"Classic British understatement," said Marvin. It was a good sign. "And what's your name?"

"Bryant. Phil." He shook his head as though he could dislodge his dust cloud visor by shaking alone. "Ow!"

The 'ow' was for the donkey which had just walked past and stumbled on his outstretched legs.

"I'd watch your leg there, Phil," said Marvin.

"Sorry," said Edith, who probably thought she was leading the donkey on a circuit of the room but was definitely the one being led.

Phil struggled to bring his legs round and under him.

All the other adults were tied to chairs, but there was now a narrow donkey ride circuit round the edge of the room. It seemed the two Mitten children planned on spending the rest of the afternoon taking turns with the donkey.

"They can't leave us in here with this big beast," said Stevie.

"I thought you liked animals," said Delia.

"Dogs," said Stevie. "I like dogs."

"Well, it's just a big dog, isn't it? With hoofs."

"Determinella has lifted the children's mood. I, for one, am very pleased she's here with us," said Becky, although her tone suggested she more probably wished the donkey, and maybe even the children, were outside.

SAM'S PHONE RANG.

Over by the fish stall, Chief Inspector Peach and Sergeant Kenny of the firearms team were engaged in a stand-up, nose-to-nose shouting match. One demanding a second crack at an armed infiltration, the other trying to argue that the whole thing was guzzling his operational budget without actually referring to anything as vulgar as money. It was clear something in the last hour – the explosion, the failed raid, the Dolly Parton flashmob, or a combination of all three – had triggered the arrival of yet more police. Officers must have been pulled in from Boston, Lincoln and other surrounding towns to swell the meagre Skegness force.

Sam stood in the sheltered doorway of the shopping centre to take the call. It was Rich.

"What do you think Bruce likes to drink?" he said.

"What?"

"I'm in the off-licence. He a whisky man, do you reckon?"

"I'm not sure introducing alcohol is a wise move," said Sam.

"Might relax him?"

"Jesus, Rich. Or it might make him reckless and trigger happy."

"I thought we could reach out to him after the recent excitement."

"Excitement? He just blew up the back of the bank."

"All the more reason for a bit of calm. Thought I could break out some of my custom made aerosol scents."

"I don't think eau de prehistoric cave is going to bring about any calm."

"I was thinking more of a baking bread smell – or what's that other one estate agents use? Cinnamon? Calming smells, an evocation of home. It's like the time that footballer – um, Gazza, wasn't it? – the police were hunting for that gunman up north and Gazza went to talk him out of hiding with a roast chicken and some cans of lager."

Sam massaged her eyelids. "Okay. First up, Gazza was by his own admission coked up to the eyeballs at the time. Secondly, it ended with the gunman killing himself."

"Sort of a result?" Rich suggested.

"No. Are *you* coked up to the eyeballs, Rich?"

"You know I don't touch that stuff."

"No? Then whatever your drug of choice might be, go home and get Peninsula to rustle some up for you. You are not to buy Bruce Greencock a bottle of whisky and then try to talk him out with the aid of baking bread smells, you hear!"

Sam didn't wait to confirm that he had heard. She ended the call and looked around to check that nobody had been listening. She didn't want to be the one to start wild rumours about a whisky fuelled shoot-out.

MERCEDES TOOK out one of the large cook's matches and was about to strike it when she rethought and passed the box and match to Bruce.

"This fire is your 'blow against capitalism'," she said. "Your last grand act. You should do."

Bruce took them both without question. He crouched over the trail of accelerant on the carpeted floor outside the vault and struck a match. The fire caught before he'd even got the match within an inch of the spilled acetone. The flames leapt, spread the short distance to the vault, over the lip and climbed the mountain of bank notes.

The flare of light as the paper caught was bright; momentarily panic-inducing. Regardless of their plans, the sight of a naked fire indoors awoke an instinctive need to put it out. Mercedes stepped back quickly.

Reflected fire shimmered on Bruce's glistening cheeks. He was just as mesmerised. "Didn't think them new banknotes were meant to burn," he said. "Seem to be taking well enough."

The fire couldn't have been going a minute before the flames extended from vault floor to ceiling, rolling out the door to lick at the tiles above their heads.

They retreated to the stairs. Smoke was stinging Mercedes' eyes. The ceiling tiles outside the vault door were blackening and beginning to melt.

61

"Can anyone else smell smoke?" Asked Delia.

"Someone told me that if you can smell burning toast it means you're having a stroke," said Marvin. "Breakfast time has become quite worrying."

"I think it's donkey farts," murmured Stevie.

Constable Phil Bryant was up on his knees now and, Marvin realised, holding his face out in the hopes of wiping his goggles on the donkey when it next passed by.

"Edith, could you possibly help the policeman off with his goggle things?" said Marvin.

"But it's my turn on Determinella," said the girl.

"Evan then," said Marvin.

"Are you giving my children orders?" said Becky.

Marvin, who had a long career of dealing with hecklers, young and old, didn't miss a beat. "I was asking a helpful young person to do a good deed."

"Then the first thing he can do is get mummy's phone out of that drawer. Evan, that one there."

"I must apologise, Phil," Marvin said. "We've not all yet fully gelled together as a cohesive team."

"I have," said Delia. "I'm working on getting us out of here."

"Oh?"

"I'm thinking about spindles and glue."

"Yes?" said Marvin, hopefully.

Phil managed to get one half of his visors wiped clean on Determinella's passing flank.

Evan opened the drawer containing the confiscated phones. He held up Becky's so the facial recognition unlocked it.

"Now, go to mummy's apps so we can check for new posts on her timeline."

"Or perhaps phone for help!" said Stevie.

"Which was what I was going to do *next*," said Becky.

At that moment a piercing alarm beeped loudly from the corridor outside. Determinella bared her teeth and brayed unhappily, sending out flecks of donkey spittle. Edith clung to the beast's neck in alarm.

"Aagh!" squealed Stevie. "The donkey spit went in my mouth!"

The new alarm was in addition to the ones which had been ringing constantly since the failed police intervention. It sounded different. Marvin assumed, with little justification, that the nature of the new emergency was therefore different.

"I told you I could smell smoke," said Delia.

"Can I get hepatitis from donkey spit?" said Stevie. "Or donkey AIDS or something?"

"We need to do something," said Marvin. He yelled "Fire!" before realising it was pointless if his voice couldn't be heard above the alarm that was already trying to alert people to a fire.

"Shall we use the whiteboard to gather suggestions?" asked Evan, picking up a pen.

"Might take too long," said Delia. "Let's brainstorm ways of getting free from these chairs – but we can miss out the part where we write it down. Suggestions, Marvin?"

"Edith, Evan, could you try to untie some of our knots?"

"Mine first," said Becky. "Just rest mummy's phone on her knees."

"I'm going to break this chair apart," said Delia.

Marvin pulled a face. "Delia, you can't just smash it against the wall like they do on films, you know. You'll hurt yourself."

"No," she said, shuffle-jumping her wooden chair to get to the wall. "Spindles and glue. This chair is not all that different to some of the ones that turn up in my shop. Lovely wooden spindles at the back, but the points where they're glued into the seat and backrest are weak. Often pull apart when the glue shrinks with age."

"Oh, that's good," said Marvin.

"But what about the rest of us on wheelie chairs?" said Stevie. "I need medical attention."

Marvin didn't bother to ask what medical attention she'd want for suspected donkey AIDS.

"We can't undo the knots," said Evan.

"They're too tight," said Edith.

"Only losers think like losers," Becky reminded them.

"Once I'm free I can help," said Delia. She reached the wall and turned around so the chair was against the wall. "I'm going to use the door handle to pull the chair apart."

Delia looked over her shoulder and wriggled the chair across and up so that the round door handle was between the spindles running up the back. She had to stand to get the back high enough to do that, but then she kicked her feet away, so that her weight pulled down on the chair. Something would have to give. Sadly, it was the door handle. It sheared off and bounced across the floor.

"Bugger!" she said. "I guess the glue hasn't shrunk yet."

"And now we're trapped in a room with no doorhandle," said Becky.

"It's my turn on the donkey!" said Evan.

BRUCE COULDN'T TELL if the burning contents of the vault were producing lots of combustible smoke, or if the fixtures and fittings of the bank's basement level were also catching. It would make sense to have flame retardant ceiling tiles, and it seemed oxymoronic for fire doors to be able to burn, but as they shut the door on the stairs leading down to the lower level, there was nothing but thick smoke and flame visible through the narrow glass panel.

"It will burn itself out soon," Mercedes said. She sounded more hopeful than certain.

Bruce nodded. "It's done now, anyway."

"It is. Time to go out and meet the police."

"Right. Yes."

He felt a knot of nervousness in his core, which was silly. He had just set fire to hundreds of thousands of pounds of cash, held hostages in a bank siege for the best part of a day, yet the thought of going out to surrender to the police was making his stomach flip like he was about to go on stage.

"Yes, of course," he said.

"And you remember the plan," said Mercedes. "Go out strong. Show them you've made your point. And keep your story straight."

"I will, I will."

62

"Y ou're in the way!" complained Evan, approaching the door on donkey back.

"Sorry," mumbled Delia.

"Why don't we use the donkey on the chair?" said Edith.

"It's still my turn," said Evan.

"But it's important to share," said Edith.

"But we don't give to beggars, do we, mummy?" Evan said to Becky. "Some people have to help themselves first."

"Possibly not relevant right now, dear," said Becky.

Edith took hold of the long leather trap attached to the donkey's bridle and tied it swiftly if inefficiently under the back of Delia's chair.

"Um, I'm hoping this works," said Delia. "As in, I don't want to be dragged to death by a donkey."

"Never work with children or animals," Marvin said automatically.

"That's not helping," said Delia.

Edith urged Determinella forward. Evan, in the saddle, bounced and gave heel kicks to her flanks. Delia's chair tilted back and was dragged along the floor after the donkey, but showed no signs of pulling apart.

"Go faster!" said Evan.

Marvin could see the boy was taking advantage of the situation to get a more thrilling ride. There was no ride more thrilling than Delia's, as her chair was hauled around the narrow circuit. The chair bounced and lurched dangerously as it tilted around corners. Constable Phil tried to make himself as small as possible, fearing being the victim of a drive-by donkey-and-chair accident.

"*Whee!*" shouted Evan.

Marvin reckoned Delia was on her third lap of the room when the chair finally broke apart. She fell backwards onto the floor and rolled into a corner. Something snapped loudly.

Marvin leaned forwards in concern. "Delia! Are you okay?"

"Urgh!" said Delia, rolling over, coughing. "I think I've broken something."

She got up unsteadily from the wreckage of the chair and reached into the big front pocket of her dungarees. She produced shattered fragments of the marble coaster she'd shown Marvin that morning.

"Never liked it much anyway," she said.

"You're welcome!" shouted Evan as he continued his laps.

Delia's hands were still bound, but now she could get to her feet, and the knots were loosened enough for her to shake free.

She turned to the others. "Right, you'd better all hope I can untie you, or you can all have a go on the donkey wall of death. Four out of ten, would not recommend!"

WITH INITIALLY FALTERING FOOTSTEPS, Bruce walked out into the lobby, past the meeting rooms and the counter. Mercedes got to the door first.

"I open it. You stride out like a man."

"Absolutely."

"Think of the children."

"I am."

"In fact, that's what you should say."

"What?"

Mercedes gave him a serious look, straight in the eye. "You go out there and tell the police, 'I'm doing this for my children.'"

"Really?"

"Speak from the heart. Your wife never let you see the children. This is it. This is for your children."

"I'm not sure..."

"There will be cameras. The world will be watching."

"Yes. Yes, of course."

As Mercedes put the key in the door and prepared to unlock the bolts, Bruce's phone rang. For a panicked moment, Mercedes feared it was in the same pocket as the radio-controlled explosive packs and shotgun shells, but his hand went to the other side.

"*Hello?*"

In the fish stall, Zahra snapped her fingers to get silence from the others in the room.

Sam's eyes turned to the phone on the desk.

"Bruce, I was worried about you," Zahra said in her 'Bridey McDougal' accent. "We heard the alarm—"

"*I'm doing this for my children,*" he said, voice flat, dead. "*Here.*"

There was a rustle on the line, of something being passed over. And then a click, a door opening.

Sam started to turn, to go outside, but Camara was there, shaking his head.

Police cameras were pointed at the door of the bank. It was all there in crisp high definition for them to see on the computer screens. The door opened.

"*I'm coming out,*" said Bruce, his voice coming from the phone, from a laptop speaker, and just on the cusp of hearing, from the bank itself across the street.

Police radios warbled. A police spotter spoke to TAPT lead. Peach was on the radio to someone in a control room. Outside, someone was shouting for Bruce to drop his weapons.

Sam tried to see the screen clearer. As he came out onto the access ramp, something dangled from Bruce's shoulder, but his hands appeared empty.

"He's got a gun!" said a woman's voice on the phone. "He's set fire to the bank! He's got a gun!"

Men were shouting in the street. A camera picked up armed officers moving in, crouched, weapons pointed.

"—*was just doing it for my children,*" Bruce said, turning.

Shouts overlapped. Bruce raised his hands. He yelled suddenly, putting his hand to his pocket.

On the screen, something flared in his pocket. There was the firework crack of a gunshot. The police replied with their own gunfire. Stuffing, or maybe not stuffing, puffed from Bruce's jacket and he stumbled back.

63

Marvin automatically put his now untied hands protectively over his head at the sound of gunfire, even though it was clearly outside.

"Shit!" Becky yelled in fear.

"Mummy swore!" Edith yelled in equal alarm.

"What the hell is going on?" said Delia, holding Determinella in the hope of keeping her calm.

"We need to get you all to a position of safety," said Constable Phil, still struggling to disentangle telephone cord from around his army boots.

"And how are we going to get out of here?" said Marvin, pointing at the broken-off door handle.

"Oh yeah, I forgot that." Delia retrieved the broken part from across the floor in the hope it would slot back in and allow them to operate the door mechanism, but it was sheared off and useless.

There was another gunshot. Marvin twitched.

"I need to get out of here," said Stevie. "I can feel it in my stomach."

Marvin gave her a quizzical look. "Donkey spit?"

"I think it's going to work on my innards."

Evan tugged Marvin's hand. "Did *you* shoot people in the war?"

"What war?"

"The Second World War."

"How old do you think I am?" he said indignantly.

"I'm going to break that," said Delia, gesturing at the long thin window down the side of the door.

"We'd never get through it," said Stevie.

"So we can reach the handle!" Delia seethed.

Delia grabbed one of the wheelie chairs, pushed the spider-web wheeled part off with her foot, and hefted the rest like a battering ram. "Tiny support stalk and a big padded bit. Won't injure myself."

"I'd urge caution, madam," said Phil.

Whether it was adrenaline caused by the firefight outside, general fear at being trapped in a burning building, or being called 'madam' by a man her own age, Delia charged at the door with full fury. She gave a war-cry that Marvin recognised as not all that different to some of the karaoke solos she had occasionally performed in his living room. She lunged at the tiny window at full tilt, bounced off the glass and fell to the floor.

"Ow!" she wheezed.

"You put a crack in it though," said Becky encouragingly.

Delia coughed. "Someone else give it a go."

There was a scraping sound and the door swung open.

Mercedes, bloodied and with soot marks on her face, stood in the doorway.

"Come on!" she said. "Time to leave!"

Delia, quickest on her feet, led the way out the door. "Fire exit?" she said, looking at the wispy but distinct curls of smoke in the corridor.

"It doesn't look so good that way," said Mercedes. "We'll go out the front."

"Come on then," said Delia. "Front door it is then."

Partway down the corridor, Becky gave a shriek of alarm. "Oh my God! Marbles! Who left marbles out here?"

"Think they're mine," said Delia.

"I could sue, you know," said Becky.

"I could have broken my neck," said Constable Phil, supporting her while holding onto Determinella.

"Mummy, try taking your shoes off," said Edith. "Maybe you'll be better."

"Darling, I can't, they're Louboutins!" said Becky, aghast.

The slow procession passed through the keypad door which opened onto the public area.

"Where's Justin?" said Stevie. "He not here?"

"I just need to collect a friend," said Marvin and rapped on the door of the meeting room he'd previously hidden in.

Becky, the little Mittens and the donkey passed him by as a group, huddled close.

"Are donkeys brave?" asked Evan.

"Pig-headed more like," said Becky.

"Are we pig-headed?" asked Edith.

"The Mittens are whatever they need to be," said Becky.

Marvin knocked again. The door opened a crack and Tez

peered out fearfully. He frowned at the Mittens and their support animal.

"Donkey?" he enquired.

"No, I'm Marvin, actually," Marvin said, unable to resist. "Have you really been hiding in here the whole time."

Tez looked out into the hazy corridor. "Is it safe?"

Marvin gave a small shrug. "Safe is a relative term." He extended a hand and Tez took it.

"Donkeys are very sure-footed, aren't they?" Becky informed the children.

"How come a donkey is in the bank?" asked Tez.

"Ah, I can explain," said Marvin and proceeded to do no such thing.

64

All of the survivors of the Eastshires Bank siege were transferred to ambulances and taken to Boston Pilgrim Hospital. Apart from Determinella the donkey. A police officer standing with the donkey looked a little put out and perplexed, until one Rich Raynor was able to get to her and explain he needed the donkey to get his deposit back from a man on the beach. The police officer seemed reluctant to hand the donkey over to a stranger, whilst also keen to be rid of it.

Fire engines were outside the bank seconds after the police had cleared the building. The arrival of the big red trucks was a final hurrah for the day's spectacle, but indicated to the crowds of onlookers that things had come to a close. The bodies of the bank manager and the bank robber had been taken away, and it was all now just a matter of tidying up.

Lucas Camara offered to drive Sam to the hospital. They

walked up to where he had left his car by the old DefCon4 offices. They passed the remnants of the pay-to-play sandpit one of the shop owners had set up for the onlookers. It was now a mess of fine sand, mostly spilt out into the gutter, and littered with rubbish and cracked plastic beach toys. Sam saw a screwed up and trampled *#teamBruce* T-shirt in the middle of the closed road.

"Celebratory bottle of Odinson mead for the heroes?" said Ragnar Odinson, appearing out of nowhere like an unwanted wizard and thrusting bottles of the stuff into Sam and Camara's hands. Sam stared at the bottle, then at Ragnar, and blinked as one of Ragnar's many indistinguishable offspring took a flash photo of them.

"Great publicity for us, this is," said Ragnar. "That'll be ten pounds."

"I'll owe you," said Sam as they walked off.

"Neither a borrower nor a lender be," Ragnar shouted after her. "That's Shakespeare, that is."

"Tell that to the banks!" she shouted back.

On the half hour drive to the hospital, Sam checked her phone. There was yet another complaint message from the all-seeing DefCon4 app.

PLEASE RETURN TO AN EXPECTED LOCATION FOR YOUR DAY'S TASKS OR IMMEDIATELY CONTACT YOUR SUPERVISOR. YOU ARE IN BREACH OF CONTRACT IF YOU CANNOT JUSTIFY THIS DEVIANCE.

She put the phone away. "I'm a deviant, apparently."

"Tell me something I don't know," said Camara.

The Pilgrim Hospital, ten storeys of nineteen-sixties brutalist architecture, was the largest hospital for many miles. Camara parked and radioed police control to find where the former hostages had been taken.

"They're being assessed and treated, and initial statements being taken," he told her. "It'll be a while. We'll have to wait."

Sam held up a bottle of mead. It had a cheeky cartoon Viking on the label. "Mead while we wait."

"I'm driving," he said.

"It's only four percent. You said we'll be here a while."

They sat on the bonnet of his car and drank mead, watching the sun begin its slow descent over the back of the hospital. The mead was sweet and syrupy. It was hardly a summer drink, but it went down well enough.

Together they ambled up to the entrance to wait for Marvin and Delia. Two women emerged, one with a bandaged hand and a plaster on her temple, the other seemingly unhurt. They wore the bedraggled blouses of Eastshires Bank staff. The uninjured one was keeping up the conversation between them single-handedly.

"They said there's no such thing as donkey AIDS and you couldn't catch it from donkey spit if there was and I asked if they'd tried and they had no answer for that."

The woman gave a sudden squeal of delight and hurried across to the car park to throw herself into the arms of woman in an angora sweater. The pair of them nearly crushed the little black French bulldog pinned between them.

"I'll just go in and check the situation," said Camara and went inside.

Sam looked at the other woman and tried to give a

supportive smile. She remembered the sheets pinned around Zahra's temporary desk and knew this was Mercedes Martin.

"Crazy day, huh?" said Sam for want of anything cleverer.

Mercedes nodded. It was a small nod, almost a reflexive action.

"You deserve a holiday after this," Sam suggested and when Mercedes didn't respond, looked round at the car park. "Someone picking you up?"

"Apparently not," said Mercedes.

"We could probably give you a lift if you like."

The entrance door slid open and a gaggle of former hostages came out.

"Now, I wasn't in *that* war," Marvin was saying to the children on either side of him, "but I did a concert tour for the troops after the Falklands War. Me and Jim Davidson and a whole galaxy of stars. Not entirely sure we really needed a war over some sheep farms and penguins, but we did it nonetheless." He looked round and saw Sam. "Oh, fancy meeting you here," he said in mock surprise.

Sam put her arms round him and held him tight. When Delia got into range she snagged her by the strap of her dungarees and hauled her into the hug too.

"You smell of smoke," said Sam.

"You seem to smell of fish," said Delia.

"We're a bunch of kippers," said Marvin.

A polished SUV pulled up in the no parking area before the hospital and the Mitten family climbed inside.

"So, no chicken katsu curry then?" said a man's voice, unimpressed.

"I've no idea what the Whitstables will think. I told the

bank I'd be suing," said the mother. Then the doors closed and the vehicle pulled away.

Sam released one arm from her dad but held on with the other. She wasn't sure she'd ever be letting him go.

"Camara will take us home," she said. She looked round for Mercedes, but the woman had gone, silently slipped away.

65

Life on Skegness's main shopping street was slow to return to normal. The police spent the best part of two days combing the street for evidence before focusing solely on the Eastshires Bank building. Council cleaners and property owners set about cleaning up, so by Tuesday the road was open again to traffic and most of the businesses could re-open.

Eastshires Bank remained closed for ten more days. When the police were done, contractors moved in, to repair, to paint and to clean. Mercedes, who had stayed on her end of the sofa and slowly gone out of her mind while her mum watched daytime telly, desperately waited for the call or e-mail which meant she could return to work. Eventually the call came.

The bank was not open to the public yet, but Mercedes went in for a meeting with the interim branch manager, some guy sent in from Leicester to get the place up and running once more.

The interim guy was tanned with bleached blond hair and went by the name of Fabian Howard. He took Mercedes into one of the meeting rooms and sat looking at her with disconcertingly frank admiration for a solid twenty seconds.

"Everything okay?" she said.

"We're just delighted that you're so keen to—" he made an indecipherable motion "—get back into the saddle. Some staff have made a request for extended leave."

"Stevie, you mean," said Mercedes, who had been paying attention to the chat and rumours on the workplace WhatsApp.

"Yes. She told me if the ball was too big for her mouth, maybe it's not her ball."

"I'm not sure what that means."

"Me neither, but she's spending some quality time with her family," said Fabian. Mercedes could almost hear the substitution of the word 'family' for 'dog', like it was a rushed sound edit.

"I am ready to be back in work," said Mercedes.

"Excellent," said Fabian. "We are also offering counselling to all staff involved." He held up his hands. "I know that's a dirty word to some. Counselling. Therapy. Intervention. Makes it sound like we think you're mad or something. But it's just about us making sure our people are okay. Giving you someone to talk to."

Mercedes was about to gently decline when Fabian added, "We know Justin was a well-loved member of the team. A father figure in branch. We know."

Mercedes nearly barked with laughter but managed to supress it. She held her mouth and turned her head away, as though suddenly overcome with emotion.

"No," she said, when she had herself under control. "I just want to get back to the old routine."

Fabian nodded in sympathetic understanding. "And I'm glad. I hear you've got a good head on your shoulders. We could use you."

They went through to the back offices, in search of a workstation and any tasks Mercedes could assist with in getting the branch ready for re-opening. The place smelled of fresh paint, not a hint of smoke. The bloody handprints she had left on the wall had been eradicated.

Her eyes went to the door to the basement level and she immediately averted them. As though Fabian might be able to somehow discern her conscious thoughts travelling down the stairs, into the safety deposit room and the box containing the two hundred thousand.

"Can I?" said Fabian.

Mercedes blinked at him. "Sorry?"

"Make you a coffee? Would you like one?"

"That's very kind," she said and smiled because it was the right and normal thing to do.

66

It took Sam Applewhite the best part of two weeks to convince her DefCon4 app and invisible employers that she had not abandoned her job, or gone off on either sick or compassionate leave, or was indeed anything other than the perfect and compliant employee she had always tried to be. There was a stream of individual tasks, ranging from alarm checks to health and safety compliance to meals on wheels deliveries that either needed belatedly completing or removing. There were reports to write on the unsuitability of the potential new offices she'd been invited to inspect, and a selection of new spaces she should find the time to visit.

One task she'd been given was a follow-up visit to the customer at Greencock Farm and ask them to complete a satisfaction survey. There was no means on her app of telling DefCon4 that this was not possible as the customer had been gunned down in the street by police firearms officers. She might have to phone up the regional office and explain that in person, but navigating DefCon4's labyrinthine automated phone system was not something she had the emotional strength for at the moment.

Another item on her personal work list was the unfinished business at the florists.

The woman at the counter seemed to fail to grasp Sam's intent.

"I just need the receipt," said Sam.

"But you've not bought anything yet," said the woman.

"For the flowers I bought last Saturday."

"Did I not give you a receipt?"

"I was in a hurry. If you recall, last Saturday was quite an unusual day." She didn't want to remind her there had been a bank robbery, an explosion, a donkey swarm and an impromptu Dolly Parton tribute concert. It felt crass and condescending.

"I mean, if you lost the receipt..." said the woman.

The door entry bell jangled behind Sam.

"I didn't lose it," said Sam patiently. "I didn't take it. And I need to claim the flowers on expenses."

"You should have kept your receipt if you wanted to do that."

"Again..."

There was a polite cough behind Sam. She turned, prepared to tell the customer that she would be out of the way as soon as she had her poxy receipt for six lilies, then saw it was the pinch-faced negotiator woman.

"Oh, er, hi," said Sam.

"Zahra Bi," said Zahra.

"I remember. Fancy bumping into you here."

"In truth, I wanted to speak to you and I saw you come in here. But I didn't know the protocol."

"What protocol?"

"Perhaps there isn't one. I could have waited outside for you, but it seemed I would be waiting in ambush. So I thought to follow you in, but to do so immediately would be to interrupt your current business which I seem to have already done." She leaned round and gave the florist a nod of greeting. "I have not come to buy flowers. While I understand the giving of dead plants is considered traditional, I prefer my plants alive. Unless it's food. I would not be averse to receiving an edible fruit or vegetable arrangement, but then that would make you a green grocer, wouldn't it?"

"Nasturtiums and pansies can make pleasant additions to salads," said the florist.

"Is that so?" said Zahra. "I must make a note of that." She proceeded to do just that, in a flip-over notepad taken from her large bag.

"Um, I really just need to get a receipt," said Sam, not sure how she'd wandered into an edible flowers conversation.

"I'm sure the lady could just write you up a new one," said Zahra.

"I suppose," said the florist.

"It was for six lilies," said Sam. "You had a three for two offer on."

"We don't anymore."

"But you did then."

"Some baby's breath with it?"

"No."

"A card?"

"No."

"Doesn't sound like something we would do," said the florist.

"We had this argument at the time," said Sam. "I must reiterate I don't actually want any of these things now. I just need the receipt."

"I see," said the florist, clearly uncertain.

"This woman was one of the heroes of the bank siege last week," said Zahra, leaning in.

"I don't think that's true at all," said Sam.

Zahra shushed her and stepped up to the counter. "Without her insights, and indeed those flowers, there might have been a far less rosy outcome. You will note I utilised a flower pun there."

"I see," said the florist again.

"In fact," said Zahra, "it's our civic duty to thank this woman."

Five minutes later, Sam and Zahra emerged onto the street. Sam had her receipt and a complimentary bouquet of roses.

"Was that you practising your negotiating skills?" Sam asked.

"Indeed," said Zahra.

"And is negotiating indistinguishable from cheekily asking for things to see if people will give them to you?"

Zahra tilted her head thoughtfully.

"I'm surprised you're still in Skegness," said Sam. "You were flown in for this one job, right?"

"Drove. But yes. I'm just doing some follow-up work."

Sam frowned. "Follow-up? The negotiations are over."

"And the man is dead," Zahra agreed. "I am doing this for my continuous personal development. I may have mentioned that I am self-taught."

"You did."

"And I have questions which remains unresolved."

They had reached the corner of the street where an ice-cream booth was doing a reasonable morning trade.

"Can I treat you to an ice-cream?" said Sam. "In thanks for the roses?"

"In the morning? Surely, ice-cream is a dessert. An afternoon snack at least."

"Not an ice-cream fan?"

"I love ice-cream," said Zahra vehemently. "I just don't know if I can get over the absurdity of the suggestion."

"It's just dairy. And the cone is grain-based I guess. It's cheese on toast in a different format."

"I'm not sure if the analogy holds true, but yes, I shouldn't judge constituent foodstuffs on their final form."

"What I always say," said Sam.

They ate ice-creams and wandered down the promenade towards the lifeboat station and funfair.

"What surprises me most," said Zahra after a long lick, "is that Bruce Greencock was able to control the situation in the bank as effectively as he did."

"You mean having the wherewithal to disconnect the CCTV and secure the doors."

"That, yes," said Zahra, "although there was some helpful compliance on the part of the hostages. But beyond that there are certain moments – notably the matter of the donkey and the TAPT firearms teams—"

"Yes?"

"In the space of two to three minutes he took receipt of the donkey and other goods, repelled the TAPT incursion, captured Constable Phil Bryant, and rolled Justin Johnson's corpse into the street."

"He struck me as a methodical man," said Sam.

"I don't believe that's the same thing as quick-thinking."

"No. You think we don't have the whole picture?"

Zahra put her hands, one holding an ice-cream, together, making a vertical slit in front of her face. "People look at the world through a narrow aperture."

"Good word."

"Thank you. We see a fraction of the world, ignore that which doesn't make sense, and extrapolate as best we can from what we do understand. Our pattern recognition skills enable us to survive, but we tend to be drawn to the simplest explanations, not the correct ones."

"You think the police have the whole story wrong?"

"Some of the story, at least. I am going to the police later, to ask them for some details. Then I'd like to speak to a man who might have a deeper insight. Do you have a contact address for Mr Richard Raynor?"

Sam laughed and nearly dropped her ice-cream. "You want deeper insights and think Rich has them?"

"The man strikes me as a creative solutions maker, a lateral thinker."

"You mean his brain moves sideways like a crab."

"If you will."

"Wow," said Sam, juggling roses and ice-cream to get out her phone. "Here," she said, giving Zahra the roses. "I don't like roses, no matter how sweet they smell."

"Oh."

"It's the thorns. I have a low tolerance for pricks. Ah, here's Rich's number."

"I see what you did there," said Zahra.

CHIEF INSPECTOR PEACH had given Zahra as much time as he thought courteous. This allotted time was a little under seven minutes.

"I have a lot to do," he told her for the second time. "The impact of the Eastshires fiasco. I have a superintendent breathing down my neck regarding operational costs incurred that day. I have an entirely different superintendent breathing down my neck regarding tactical decisions made during the operation. I wish I could just put them in a room together and let them slug it out with one another."

"Have you considered doing that?" said Zahra.

"I don't think either would appreciate it."

"You could perhaps arrange a meeting and 'accidentally' invite both of them."

He gave that genuine consideration. "Regardless, it still doesn't leave much over in this quarter's budget."

"And that mod invasion could be coming any day now," she said.

"Are you being facetious?" he said.

"Not at all. Not even sure I'd know how," she said honestly.

Peach was much happier to give her some of Detective Constable Lucas Camara's time. And, fortuitously, it seemed that DC Camara was also more than happy to give it to Zahra.

"It's either this or spend the afternoon looking through CCTV footage for anti-social cabbage tossers," he told her.

"Curious how less than a fortnight ago, that sentence would have made no sense to me," she said.

Camara wanted a coffee, but told her the stuff at the station was diabolical in nature. So they walked out in search of sustenance. After a walk and an ice-cream with Sam Applewhite, Zahra concluded that some people needed to be moving to generate conversation. Moving or eating. Perhaps both.

"Bruce Greencock's death will be judged a lawful killing," she said.

"That would be up to coroner's inquest," said Camara.

"But it will. The explosives in Bruce's pocket…"

"According to Miss Martin's statement he placed them there after she'd removed them, under his instructions, from the cash bundles. Apparently forgot them. After he left the bank, they activated. He had shotgun shells in his pocket too. TAPT officers mistook the resultant bang for actual gunfire."

"But why remove them if he just intended to destroy the cash as some form of protest?"

"You expect his every act to be rational?" said Camara.

"People are complex creatures," she said. "In the moment, every person acts in a way they believe is rational."

"Ah, well, there we come up against the Lucas Camara Theory of Criminal Intelligence."

"Oh, what is that?" she said.

He seemed momentarily put off by her genuine interest.

"Ah, well, it's like... Have you ever heard of survivorship bias?" he asked.

"I have," she said.

67

Z ahra did not reject the offer of Prosecco, but took it with no intention of drinking it.

Rich Raynor currently resided in the top floors of a former hotel on the sea front. He had either bought or rented the building (she imagined the distinction was entirely meaningless to a man of his wealth) and maintained a luxurious suite of rooms on the top floor. The balcony gave an unrivalled view of the boating lake, the beach and the sea. The view might have been grand, the sun hot and high in the sky, and the flutes of fizz entirely charming, but his attempt to recreate a Mediterranean-style playground for the rich and famous in Skegness seemed to be not entirely successful.

She picked up an aerosol can, giving it an experimental spray and sniff. "And what's this one?"

"Male sabre-tooth tiger," he said.

"You could market it as something to keep stray cats out of your garden."

"The thought had occurred to me."

"You're full of ideas, aren't you, Mr Raynor?" said Zahra, putting the can of offensive smells down.

"My good friend Sam says I'm definitely full of something," he conceded.

"You added an additional element to the proceedings in the town centre the other weekend," she said.

Rich's butler topped up his master's glass and swiftly withdrew.

"Am I in trouble?" said Rich.

"Not that I'm aware of. You arranged the many Dolly Partons."

"The Skegness Operatic and Dramatic Society were only too keen to help."

"What was your thinking there?"

"I heard Bruce was a fan. And who doesn't love a bit of Country music?"

"It strikes me as a simplistic and uncomplicated music style," she said. "Naïve even."

"Part of its charm," he said without hesitation. "Its music may be simple, perhaps harking back to a simpler time, but there's nothing wrong with that. Sad songs, happy songs, each song tells a story."

She nodded, not in agreement but in acknowledgement that she might need to rethink her attitudes. "With your resources, you could have simply given Mr Greencock the money he requested,"

"What?" he said. "Flown in by helicopter? A suitcase of cash dropped onto the roof of the bank?"

"That had occurred to you too?"

"I was advised against it. Besides, it wouldn't have worked."

"Bruce had already committed himself to the robbery by that point," she conceded.

"I don't think he would have taken the money."

"No?"

"He was a proud man, in his way. Simple, naïve perhaps, but proud. He'd turned down the Bonner-Sanchez offer to buy his land. He wanted to build, not to borrow. He wanted to build a cabbage empire."

"It's all about the vegetables, is it?"

Rich shrugged. The act widened the gap in his unbuttoned shirt. He looked to the sea and the sun.

"The land, the crops it produces. They made sense to him. He wanted to give his children solidity and certainty in a crazy, changing world."

"And instead he decided to burn the bank's money as a bitter political act."

Rich's nose wrinkled. "I never knew the man, but he didn't strike me as political in that way."

"No, me neither," she said.

"What's that wise Native American saying?" he said. "Only when every tree has been cut down and every river poisoned will people realise you can't eat money. But it's still a convenient means of exchange."

"Something like that," said Zahra.

ZAHRA SAT with Becky Mitten in the shadow of the substantial tree fort play structure dominating the upper end of the Mittens' back garden. The children, Edith and Evan, sat in the shaded upper fort and played silently on individual tablets.

"Obviously, I have taken on additional responsibilities now," Becky was explaining. "My number of followers has skyrocketed and I need to provide them with fresh content all the time."

"I understand," said Zahra. "There is an imperative to maintain one's status in the digital world."

"Well, quite. I've spent a lot of the time working on my previous posts and offering additional clarification and insight. There were a number of voice-to-text posts that were less than enlightening at the time. They're like little puzzles."

Zahra had trawled through Becky Mitten's posts and, indeed, the conversion of speech to text had clearly mistranslated much of what was said, and arranged the rest in a way which nearly defied analysis.

"More than one of my followers has compared those posts to Japanese poetry," said Becky which Zahra felt was grossly unfair to Japanese poetry.

"I'm sure your posts are very beautiful," said Zahra, hoping to segue to the questions she wanted to ask the woman.

"Thank you, they are," Becky smiled. "I was thinking there should be a way of collecting them together in a physical way, so people can buy and keep them forever."

"A way of permanently storing words and pictures that can be sold as product."

"Exactly," said Becky. "I think people will be interested in my story told in that format. I'm looking into it. Maybe it will lead to a Netflix movie." She laughed to show she was joking, sort of.

"I wanted to canvas your opinion of Bruce Greencock and his behaviour in the final hours of the bank siege."

"The man was a thug," said Becky automatically. "No respect for one's personal rights or freedoms."

"I see."

"Tied us all to chairs. Took my phone from me."

"And your children too, right?" said Zahra.

"He did. He did."

Zahra pointed up at the treehouse. "Do you mind if I ask Edith and Evan about what happened?"

Becky made a doubtful face, but Edith spoke up. "He took us in the kitchen and we made chicken empanadas."

"Chicken and *chorizo* empanadas," Evan corrected her.

"And we went into the vault."

"And he let us play with the money before he put it in the bags."

"We played *Escape to the Country*."

"I wanted to buy a property with rustic charm," said Evan.

"How do you mean, playing with the money before he put it in the bags?" said Zahra.

"He let us play with the money," said Edith, looking at Zahra from on high with a condescending frown.

"And then he put it in the bags," said Evan, with a frown to match his sister's.

"What bags?" said Zahra.

"The carrier bags."

"That would be my M&S bags for life," said Becky. "I doubt I'll be seeing those again."

"No," agreed Zahra softly.

68

S am sat at the breakfast bar in the kitchen and looked at the latest alert on her phone. Through whatever means the faceless corporation worked, DefCon4 had found two more potential offices for her to go look at. With the search for a new office and the search for a new home for her and her dad, everything was changing.

Delia came in from the front drive with several flatpack boxes sandwiched between her hands.

"The last of the ones from the shop. You can probably get most of the kitchen stuff in these."

The *For Sale* sign was up at the foot of the driveway. A moving out date was marked in the calendar. Her dad's secret and bitter war with his own finances was coming to a painful close, and soon *Duncastin'* would be someone else's sprawling home, and hopefully Marvin's debts would be settled.

Delia swiftly knocked the boxes into shape and passed one to Sam.

"I'll do crockery and pans," said Sam. "You tackle those drawers."

Sam began to stack plates and bowls in the box.

"Where's your dad?" said Delia.

"I told him to check the attic was empty. Couldn't have him doing this job. Every item in here has a story attached. You wouldn't get a box half-filled without hearing fifty anecdotes about who drank from which cup, or who he whisked up an omelette for."

"What's this stain here?" said Delia, scratching one of the placemats featuring famous paintings.

"That's not a stain, that's the Holbein," said Sam.

"Hmmm?"

"*The Ambassadors*. It's a painting of a skull. You have to hold it at a funny angle and only then can you see the full picture."

Delia tilted the placemat and squinted. "You'd have thought, after everything that happened, the bank would let your dad off with his mortgage repayments," she said.

Sam laughed, even though the thought had crossed her mind too. "What? *Mr Applewhite, as compensation for all the trouble we've put you through, we're going to wipe your massive debts from the record*?"

Delia shrugged. "It'd be nice of them."

"Banks aren't known for being nice."

"Maybe."

Rich came in through the open door, a thumb jerked over his shoulder. "There's a removals van out there."

"I'll give you three guesses," said Sam.

"You're moving out?"

She tilted her head. "Putting most things into storage. If we can't find a buyer, the bank's putting it up for auction in the autumn."

Rich looked aghast. Emotions came easy to him. "You should have said. If it's a money problem, I could help."

Sam raised a hand firmly. "We don't need that kind of help."

"A place to stay then," said Rich.

"Delia has already offered us the use of her spare bedroom."

Delia nodded. She wore an expression that was both supportive and a little worried as to what she'd let herself in for.

"Bedroom? Singular?" said Rich.

"We're working it out," said Sam, in what she hoped was a very final tone.

"I still can't get rid of them," said Rich.

"Rid of what?" said Delia.

"Rich is the current proud owner of ten donkeys," Sam explained.

"The man I bought them off won't take them back," said Rich. "Apparently he's happy to be rid of them."

"I think he got the better part of the deal when he sold them to you," said Sam.

"I like donkeys," said Delia brightly.

"They're stubborn things," said Rich.

"And I like that about them," she said. "They can't be led.

You have to work with them. Anything you do, you have to make them think they wanted to do that all along."

"Maybe they can be part of your Doggerland smell-o-vision theme park," said Sam.

"There weren't any donkeys in the Ice Ages," he said. "But I am investigating putting them to another use."

"Dare I ask?"

"Donkey cheese!"

Sam and Delia looked at each other, then looked at him.

"I've done my research," he said. "Turns out the world's most expensive cheeses are made from donkey milk."

Delia pulled a face. "I know it shouldn't sound anymore disgusting that cow cheese or goat cheese, but..."

Sam was nodding. "Donkey cheese just doesn't appeal."

"You need to have vision," said Rich.

"I'm sure you'll turn it all to your own advantage," said Sam.

Marvin came into the kitchen. "Hey, kids. Do we still have mink living wild in this country?"

"Don't know, dad, why?" said Sam.

"There's ... something living in the attic. It's not small and it's definitely got teeth."

Sam looked at Rich. "I think that's Peninsula's pet, isn't it? You should go sort it out."

"Me?" said Rich.

"You said you wanted to help."

Reluctantly, Rich went to investigate.

Delia put a hand on Marvin's arm. "Hey, Marv. How are you coping?"

"I'm not the one who has to wrestle a mink," he said.

"I meant with—" She gestured around at the emptying house.

He forced a laugh. "It's all just stuff, isn't it, dear. There are worse things in life."

There was a high squeal of alarm from Rich, elsewhere in the house.

69

On the Wednesday morning, Mercedes came into the bank to find a woman sitting in one of the chairs in the lobby area. The woman had earbuds in and was swaying her head to the unheard music. Mercedes looked around for a colleague who might be dealing with her but could see no one.

"I'm sorry," she said.

The thin woman took an earbud out.

"Is someone dealing with you?" asked Mercedes.

"Dealing with me?" The woman seemed to taste the phrase.

"The bank isn't open to customers yet. We're closed."

"I'm not a customer," said the woman. "I'm Zahra Bi. I worked with the police on the robbery the other weekend. You're Mercedes Martin."

"I am."

Zahra stood and removed the other earbud. "I'm listening to Dolly Parton."

"I'm not a fan," said Mercedes.

"Nor was I. But I'm treating it as research. She's a prolific singer-songwriter. *Here You Come Again, Love is Like a Butterfly, I Will Always Love You—*"

"The Whitney Houston song?"

"Dolly wrote it and recorded it first."

Mercedes shook her head. "As I say, we're not open to the public."

"I just have some follow-up questions to ask," said Zahra.

"Follow-up?" Mercedes was sure she'd kept her tone normal but she felt a sudden panic.

More than two weeks had passed since the robbery, and the bank was preparing to reopen to the public. Things would be back to normal and Mercedes could shrug off some of her paranoia about the robbery, and the two hundred thousand in her safety deposit box. She itched to go look at it, perhaps even move it to a safer location, but she had already told herself the sensible thing would be to wait for maybe a year – maybe six months, three months at the very least – when all suspicions had completely died down, then remove it, quit her job and go to Spain to be reunited with her long lost family. She'd already done her research. She would drive down to Portsmouth and get a ferry to the north coast of Spain, thus avoiding airports where big bags of cash would draw immediate and unwanted attention. She'd fade into European society, perhaps even apply for Spanish citizenship through her father. It would all be fine if she could just keep her cool.

"Questions about the robbery," said Zahra. "You can imagine the amount of admin, paperwork and follow up the police have after an incident like the one you were involved with. So much admin. It just so happens that I very much enjoy admin. The filing away of information must be done thoughtfully. I don't just put things in a folder and forget them. I like to curate them, and consider the context for every small detail." Zahra's hands fluttered delicately to indicate how she was taking great care of each nugget of information.

Mercedes nodded. "A details person. Of course. A woman after my own heart."

"Tiny things matter a great deal in context," said Zahra. "I strive to improve my skills, so I like to see everything that I can, relating to the context of an incident. Tez Malik said he would spare me ten minutes to talk."

"I'm sure he's around here somewhere," said Mercedes. "Not that he saw much of what happened," she laughed lightly. "He spent most of the robbery hiding in an office."

"How wise." Zahra followed Mercedes through the lobby. "Of course, you were much more up close and personal with Mr Greencock, weren't you?"

"Held at gunpoint, you mean," said Mercedes.

"Ah, but there was no gun, not in the end."

"I've tried to put much of it out of my mind."

Mercedes knocked at an open door. Tez looked up from his computer.

"Miss Bi here to see you," said Mercedes.

Tez looked blankly for a moment.

"She's with the police," Mercedes prompted.

"Worked for the police," said Zahra.

"Ah, yes," said Tez. "I'm sure I've told the police everything a dozen times. Forwards and backwards."

"Possibly," said Zahra. She had produced a notepad and a pink biro pen and was flicking through pages of notes. "In fact, while I've got you both here…" She looked at Mercedes. "Mr Greencock confided in you a lot, didn't he, Mercedes?"

"Did he?" she said, not knowing what else to say.

"Your physical resemblance to his ex-wife might have been a factor. I've seen the photos. After the police unsuccessfully tried to force their way inside, Tez here told the police that you, Miss Martin, said to Bruce—" she put her finger on a page "—*Are you going to send them a message?* This was moments before Mr Johnson's body was dumped on the pavement outside."

Mercedes stared at her, then stared at Tez. He looked like he'd been caught out doing something wrong.

"I … I wanted to know what he was doing?" said Mercedes.

Zahra tilted her head. "*What are you doing?* That's what you'd say if you wanted to know what someone is going to do. Or, *You're going to send them a message*?" she said with a strong rising inflection at the end. "That would be what you'd say if you were unsure, or if you couldn't believe it."

"Yes?" said Mercedes.

"But, *Are you going to send them a message?* That's giving someone a choice, isn't it?"

Mercedes scowled. "Are you asking me about my tone of voice regarding something I don't remember saying and Tez almost certainly misheard?"

"I could have done," said Tez, quick to comply. "I really could have misheard."

"Ah," said Zahra, as though that thought had not occurred to her. She marked a note on the page. "That would explain things." She smiled brightly at Mercedes, with the open guileless happiness of child. "I'd best get on with asking Tez my questions."

Mercedes nodded hesitantly and withdrew. She closed the door behind her.

She put a hand to her chest, wondering if she could feel her heart hammering against her ribcage. She looked at the closed door. She thought about the money in the safety deposit box downstairs. Screw waiting a year, or six months, or even three. It was time to move the money.

THERE WAS a knock at the door of *Duncastin'*. Sam slid off the kitchen bar stool to go answer it.

Much of the contents of the house were now in storage at a place on the Cowbridge Business Park. Another removals lorry was coming for the furniture and final boxes in a week, then Sam and her dad would just be left with their suitcases and most prized possessions, itinerant wanderers of no fixed abode. She wasn't sure if her dad still technically owned the house, or if it was now the bank's possession. Given that the sale of the property would probably do little more than clear Marvin's debts, the distinction was perhaps irrelevant.

Sam no longer feared that any knock at the door might be serious looking men from debt collection agencies. The men had been, the debts were settled one way or another. In a very real but untrue sense, her dad's money worries were over.

Detective Constable Lucas Camara stood on the doorstep with a square cardboard box in his hands.

"Good morning," Sam said. "If that's a house-warming present, it's woefully inappropriate."

He smiled softly and nodded towards the road. "I saw the for sale sign. Is your dad going to a better place?"

"He's not dying, if that's what you mean."

She stepped back to invite him in. He slid the box onto the counter. As he regarded the cleared kitchen surfaces and the empty glass-fronted cabinets his expression was suitably sombre.

"I'm intruding," he said.

"On the car crash of our personal lives?" said Sam lightly. "Think nothing of it."

He tapped the box. "Your belongings – your dad's belongings – recovered from the bank, now the police are done with them."

Sam looked in the box. "Oh, goody. A lava lamp. I'd been wondering where that had got to."

"Perhaps not the most vital thing at this point in time," Camara conceded.

Sam removed the lamp and her dad's jacket and, perhaps the only item of real consequence, her dad's phone.

"I knew you had it at the station," she said. "I was tracking it."

"Tracking it?" said Camara.

Sam pulled her laptop across the counter. There was a

website for properties for rent in Skegness. She quickly tabbed away to another internet window featuring a map of Skegness and a number of pulsating dots.

"Ah – the security tracker widgets," he said.

"It only shows up when they're in range of someone with the app, but someone at the station must have it." She tapped the police station on the map. "That's most of the security widgets Bruce Greencock had on him, that day."

Camara nodded. "We'll be holding onto all of his effects until the coroner's inquest is done." He sniffed. "Most of them you say?"

Sam zoomed out to encompass the local area. "There's the ones at the farm. The ones at the police station. There's at least one not accounted for." She shrugged. "Probably got lost in the confusion. Possibly stuck to a seaside donkey. Who knows? Doesn't really matter, does it?"

70

Tez Malik's account of the robbery was essentially identical to the statements Zahra had convinced DC Camara to show her. She was objective enough in her work to not be disappointed by this turn of events, yet she was left with an uncomfortable niggle that the jigsaw image of the complete event did not fit together properly. Bruce Greencock's motivations throughout had been inconsistent, as had his choice of actions. Methodical predictable choices had been interspersed with momentary genius and momentary madness.

Tez had been helpful and clear in his answers, and thus entirely unhelpful.

"Carrier bags," Zahra said, as the thought struck her.

"Yes?" said Tez, leaning back in his chair.

"In the police inspection of the scene, and your own clean-up afterwards, were any Marks and Spencer bags for life found?"

Tez gave a helpless look.

"A witness said some of the money was put into carrier bags," she prompted.

Tez's helpless look continued. "If it had then I guess those bags would have been destroyed in the fire."

"Yes," she said. "Perhaps I ought to look into the forensic work carried out on the remains of the money burnt in the bank."

"You could."

"I wonder how they'd know if the composition and weight of the remains was consistent or inconsistent with the burning of—" she looked in her notepad "—four hundred and ninety-six thousand pounds. I am suddenly pondering what if some of the money didn't burn."

"You think that happened?" he said.

Zahra smiled. "I am very much the sort of person who, when a theory strikes me, must follow that strand of investigation. Perhaps even build a hypothesis based upon it."

Tez nodded. "I'm afraid I don't know anything about carrier bags. Or burned money."

"I understand." She stood. "I've taken up enough of your time."

"A pleasure," he said and stood to shake her hand.

While shaking, a further thought struck Zahra. "Did you like Justin Johnson?"

Tez seemed genuinely surprised and it took him a moment to find his voice. "Um, he was a much admired member of the team."

"But did you like him?"

She watched him search for a diplomatic answer. "I didn't know him socially. We travelled together to last year's shareholders' banquet. That's probably the most time I ever spent with him."

"Bruce Greencock murdered him," said Zahra. "You have to feel quite passionate to kill someone."

"Justin was capable of rubbing people up the wrong way," Tez admitted.

"Everyone?"

"We all have our flaws."

Zahra left him. Questions were still unanswered. Truth was, she did not need to find the answers. She had been contracted for the hostage negotiations alone, but she had not developed her own professional practice to this level by leaving stones unturned and questions unanswered. She needed to know Bruce Greencock, to understand his motivations, and thus evaluate her impression of him in those final hours. She had asked all her questions. She now needed to take a more holistic approach. She had yet to visit the Greencock farm. She would go there. She would stand among the cabbages. She would listen to more Dolly and try to tune into the mindset of the farmer-turned-murderer.

As she put her earbuds in and put Dolly Parton's playlist on shuffle, she saw Mercedes Martin in reception. Zahra gave her a wave of thanks.

She listened to Dolly's greatest hits as she drove out along the Wainfleet Road towards Bruce's farm. *I Will Always Love You* came on. Zahra, like Mercedes Martin, had been surprised to discover that the Whitney Houston classic was indeed a Dolly original.

If not for her satnav's instructions, she might have missed the narrow turning that was Marsh House Road. The road was a strip of tarmac between a full dyke on one side, possibly even a river channel, and a steep-sided but seemingly empty dyke on the other. She passed through the gate on the road and pulled up outside the farmyard.

She stepped out and surveyed Greencock's land. A rich loamy scent filled the air. She looked across the fields as *It's All Wrong, But It's All Right* played on her earphones. Zahra wondered if Bruce had looked across these lands and seen them as the wide American prairies or somesuch, and he the romantic pioneer farmer.

A seabird turned in the blue sky, cawing. The main road and the town and civilisation in general suddenly felt very far away. Whatever, you said about this flat landscape, it was certainly quiet and peaceful. A person would have time to think out here.

Zahra opened the gate to the farmyard and walked through. She walked past the climbing frame on the grassed area. She paused for a moment to stare at the missing tubular sections. She thought about the tubing and the ongoing relationship he'd manufactured with his estranged family. On some level, he knew he'd messed it all up.

An alert popped up on Sam's phone. Camara was long gone and she had been staring idly at the security tracker dots on her laptop.

She looked at the DefCon4 alert, relieved it wasn't

another false query about her illness/leave of absence/dereliction of duty on the day of the robbery. She was eighty percent confident she'd put that one to bed and could continue with her job as normally as possible, if her job could ever be considered normal.

The alert was for a motion sensor alarm at Greencock Farm. She mentally debated if such an alarm should strike her as suspicious. The police would have long finished there. Bruce was dead. That left ... who? Bruce's ex? A new buyer? A genuine burglar? An extremely lost seal? In truth, it didn't matter. The only people who could dismiss the alert were herself and the account owner. She had a terrible, momentary vision of how DefCon4's automated systems would handle a client who had paid for an ongoing service but had since died. Before she'd joined DefCon4 she'd never encountered the term 'Kafkaesque'. She still didn't fully grasp its meaning, but this situation seemed to absolutely tick those Kafkaesque boxes.

She prepared to head out to the farm so she could be in a geographically appropriate spot to resolve the alert when a new dot flashed on her laptop screen. One of Bruce's missing security widgets had just winked into new life. Either someone with the app had come within range, or the widget was on the move.

Sam zoomed in. The security dot was slap bang on top of the Eastshires Bank.

"Hello," she said.

71

Mercedes knew it was wrong even as she did it. Her plan had been solid. Her accomplice was dead, the money not even thought to be missing. She just had to wait out her time and allow everything to return to normal, then retrieve the cash, take the ferry to Spain, and begin a new life with back pay the bank owed her. It was a perfect plan. It was a moral plan. True, she might have had a hand in Bruce's death; true, she might have had a fingertip, even just a fingernail, in Justin's death. But both of those men had set themselves on courses with inevitable conclusions. It was a perfect, moral and just plan.

Except that police investigator, Zahra, had put the frighteners on her. She simply had to move the cash, and move it now.

And so she went through the keypadded security door to the back office and down the stairs. She hadn't looked up at the CCTV cameras. She knew they were there; she didn't have to check. It would only compound her guilt if she was discovered. Head casually averted, she had gone into the safety deposit box room, taken the key from the wall safe, and retrieved her own box.

The bank was virtually empty. There were only a few colleagues upstairs, working to get the place ready for reopening. The chances of being disturbed were minimal. Mercedes opened the box and looked at the two bundles of cash, each in a carrier bag, handles neatly wrapped round them. She was convinced something had changed, surprised to see them as she'd left them, then realised the change was within herself. The last time she'd been down here was during the noise and adrenaline high of the siege, with alarms ringing, police outside. Those moments, those bags of cash, were something from another world. *This* was real.

She removed the carrier bags, unfurled and shook them so they took on a more natural shape. She closed her box, put it back in the wall, closed and locked the door. She slipped her own key into her pocket and returned the bank's key to the wall safe. She picked up the carrier bags.

This was it. She just needed to take them outside and put them in the boot of her Ford Focus, parked not twenty metres away on Rutland Road. She was just a bank employee popping out to her car with some bags of lunchtime shopping. There was nothing extraordinary in that.

She dithered, temporarily forgetting how *normal people* held carrier bags. Then, feeling anything other than normal, she left the room, went upstairs, and headed straight out through the lobby. No one stopped her. No one even noticed her. Why would they? This was her being normal, wasn't it?

She stepped out onto the pavement and turned to go down the side street and her parked car. In the park across the road the high sun made dappled shadows through the trees. Every footstep was a step away from suspicion. She'd put the cash in her car. Later she would move it to a location which had no link to her. A storage locker, or something. She pressed her key fob to unlock the car's rear door, lifted it up.

"Oh, thought it was you," came a voice.

It was Tez. He had crossed the road and was coming straight to her. She clamped down on asking "What the hell are you doing here?" and just stared.

He held up two paper bags marked with growing patches of grease. "Went out to get donuts. Thought we could do with a snack." He looked at the carrier bags in her hand and grunted.

"What?" she said.

"M&S bags for life," he said.

"Yes. Yes, they are."

He nodded as though this was of great importance.

Mercedes placed the bags casually in the boot and reached to pull the door back down.

"That police woman – or not a police woman. I'm not sure. She was asking about them."

"About carrier bags?"

"M&S carrier bags. I think she thought some of the money might have gone missing. Which is mad, obviously." Tez grinned.

He looked at Mercedes. Mercedes looked at him. Tez

looked at the bags in the boot. Mercedes looked at him looking and then looked back at his face.

"Obviously," she said.

MARVIN WALKED down Drummond Road in the direction of home, the glossy leaflet he'd just picked up in one hand and his jingling set of house keys in the other. At the corner of Albert Avenue, he saw Sam setting off in her work van. He waved at her. She waved back, but when she showed no signs of slowing, he waved more vigorously and stepped into the road in front of her. She braked sharply.

Sam wound down the window. "You know suicide is never the right choice, right?"

"I was trying to get your attention."

"I've just got to check up on something."

Marvin opened the door to get in beside her.

"Oh, and you're coming with me," she said with forced cheer.

"Since you told me to sell the Jag, I don't get to drive many places," he said.

"You sold the Jag before I told you to," she countered.

"But you didn't know that," he countered back. "Don't turn right," he added, as she reached the junction.

"I want to go that way," she said and pulled out before he could argue. "We're going to check out an alarm."

The traffic on Drummond Road, heading right into town, was at a standstill. Up by the junction with Lumley Road there was a police car blocking the road.

"I told you," said Marvin. "There appears to be a mile long procession of mopeds coming through the town. That's why I was waving."

"The mods have finally arrived," said Sam, as though a grim prophecy had come true. "Peach will be pleased." She looked up a side road, considering possible short cuts.

"It's Peach, is it?" said Marvin.

"Chief Inspector Peach. Fuzzy Peach."

"Right. I couldn't be certain. Thought it might have been Leach or something. It had been bugging me."

Sam took a left hand turn speculatively.

72

Mercedes sped along the A52 heading out of town. It had taken fifteen minutes to navigate around the seemingly endless parade of elderly idiots on their little Vespa scooters. She might have wondered why they needed so many wing mirrors on their vehicles if her mind wasn't focused on much weightier matters.

"Can we talk about this?" came a muffled voice from the boot.

"Shut up, Tez," she said.

"Is this about the shareholders' banquet thing? I'm sure we could sort you out, if that's what it is?" He shuffled and thumped. "It's quite cramped in here."

"Shut up. I'm thinking."

Mercedes was thinking. Her brain was spinning at a high rate of revolutions, but the gears in her mind weren't meshing. From the moment she'd forced Tez into the boot of her car her mind had seized upon a Plan B. It came to her complete and whole, and while it was born solely from desperation, it seemed the only option for her right now. She would have loved to reflect on it, interrogate it, take the time to think about this crazy new plan and work out if it was genius or madness, but those mental gears weren't catching and she couldn't focus.

"The Ford Focus isn't renowned for its large boot space," Tez said.

Mercedes braked sharply for the turning to Greencock Farm and swung into the narrow lane.

"And there's no seatbelt back here!" said Tez.

Mercedes rattled down the lane, one eye on the road, one eye scouting for the farm entrance. She had never been this way before. There was no reason. This was the back end of nowhere. There was nothing but miles and miles of flat fields cut into parcels of land by roads and dykes. Despite having not been here before, she had come searching for something small and specific, based solely on two things Bruce had told her. She had no idea if either of them was correct.

A small car parked at the side of the road alerted her to the farm entrance. She braked and came to a halt behind the first car. She looked at the farm. There was the farmhouse and tall sheds, and a greenhouse extending into a series of polytunnels. The whole place was charming after a fashion. It might have been rustically inviting if it had been located in some genuinely picturesque landscape. In the Peak District or the Yorkshire Dales – somewhere where the land actually had shape and form – this farm could have seemed idyllic.

Here, in the bleak two-dimensional fens, in was merely a blip in the tedium.

"You stay here," she said to Tez.

"You're leaving me here?"

"If you get out of that boot, I will have to kill you."

There was a pause, then a meek, "Okay."

Mercedes got out and surveyed the area. The other car suggested someone else might be here, but there was no movement on the farm.

The carrier bags of cash sat on the passenger seat. It made no sense to take them with her, but she wasn't going to leave them unattended. Especially with Tez in the boot. She grabbed the bags and walked through the open gateway.

She moved directly towards the farmhouse, looking around. If there was anyone else here, she needed to be ready with a plausible excuse.

There was police tape along the seams of the front door of the house. The heavily painted wood was puckered and splintered where the door had been forced. She tried the handle. The tape ripped, the door opened.

"Hallway drawer," she told herself as she closed the door behind her. "Hallway drawer."

She moved purposefully through the house. There was always something eerie about silent and empty houses. Her stomach tightened with nervousness. Breaking and entering was certainly a lower grade of crime than kidnapping mortgage advisors, but her stomach didn't seem to agree. The only sound in the house came from a grandfather clock she glimpsed through the living room door.

There was a shotgun cabinet in the space under the stairs

and, next to it, a low telephone table with a single drawer. She opened it. When she didn't immediately spot the passports her squirming innards nearly gave out, but a quick rummage under the neatly placed letters and stationery revealed five burgundy British passports. She flicked through them. Annabel, no. Riley, no. The third one belonged to Christine Greencock.

She looked at the photo. Bruce had said they looked the same, so had the investigator, and the resemblance was pretty close. Mercedes could wear paler makeup and pass for the woman.

This was it. Plan B. Whatever happened today, Mercedes Martin was burned as an identity. But Christine Greencock could travel south, pay for a ferry ticket in cash, and travel from Portsmouth to Santander where she could assume whatever identity she wished.

Her brief moment of victory was interrupted by a faint sound. It came again. Footsteps on gravel. Mercedes scuttled, bent low, and went through to look out the kitchen window.

A woman – no, not just a woman. That investigator, Zahra Bi, was strolling casually around the farmyard. Zahra's gaze swung across the house and paused momentarily on the gate and Mercedes' car.

"Shit," said Mercedes.

Zahra stared at it, looked round again. Mercedes ducked out of sight.

When she slowly raised herself up again, Zahra was walking towards the greenhouses.

This was not good. None of this was good.

Back in the hallway there was a holdall bag under the

table. The cash could go in that. M&S carrier bags were clearly a red flag. Mercedes stuffed the money in the holdall. As she did, she looked up at the gun cabinet. There was a padlock on the door. There was also a small amount of powdery brick dust on the floor next to it, below the fuse box on the wall. Mercedes stood and felt along the top of the dusty box. There was a key.

"So, shall I tell you my great idea?" said Marvin.

"Hmm?" said Sam, who was concentrating on the single-tracked road ahead.

He held out the glossy leaflet he'd had in his hand the entire journey.

"What is it?" said Sam, not really looking.

"Putten's Holiday Park."

"They booked you for some more shows?"

"No, not that. I spoke to Daryl, the owner."

"Yeah?"

"And he says he can do us a deal."

Sam wasn't following. "What deal?"

"On a caravan?"

Sam understood. "You think we should move into a caravan together?"

"It's within our budget," said Marvin.

"So's sleeping under bridges, but we're not doing that either."

"They have some nice caravans."

Sam tried to picture what a 'nice' caravan might look like,

but she was distracted by the sight of two cars parked near to the gates of Greencock Farm. She didn't recognise either.

Sam drew up the Piaggio Ape van behind the cars and turned off the ignition.

"I'm just going to poke around and turn off an alarm," she said.

"Is the poking around part of the service?" asked Marvin.

"Just stay here," she muttered and got out.

73

Mercedes moved stealthily from the farmhouse, shotgun in one hand and holdall in the other. Or at least she would have moved stealthily if the gun hadn't been so flipping heavy. It hadn't taken her long to load both barrels with shotgun shells, although she had nearly sliced off the top of her thumb when closing it. But carrying it was an absolute chore. It felt longer than it actually was, and its weight was oddly distributed so she couldn't stop it swinging round as she carried it. She ended up wedging it under her armpit and trying to move in a stealthy shuffle.

She edged round the rear of the farmhouse, trying to circle round the sheds and reach the road without moving across the central farmyard and being spotted. It didn't matter that the nosy Zahra character was here. Mercedes simply needed to get back to her car and away. The shotgun was only a final desperate back up.

A little dyke running along the back of the farm buildings forced her to take a route through the big shed. She moved past a tall tractor by the door and round the weird escalator-looking trailer it was attached to.

Through the open shed door she could see the gate straight in front of her. There were now three cars parked there. Or rather there were two cars and a little three-wheeled van that looked like it should be delivering bread in an ancient Italian town, driven by a man in a flat cap. And there was a man in the front. Mercedes' eyes widened then narrowed. Was that the former-hostage, Marvin somebody-or-other?

"Afternoon."

Mercedes turned. A younger woman stood in the shadows by the door.

"Careful with that," she said as Mercedes nearly dropped the bulky weight of the shotgun.

"Who are you?" said Mercedes.

"Sam Applewhite. DefCon4," said the woman.

"Who?"

The woman, Sam, pointed in a non-specific direction. "Security alarms. You set them off."

Mercedes looked up and around at the non-specific nothing Sam had pointed at. "Oh. Sorry. I just came by to collect some things."

Sam nodded slowly.

"This was my husband's farm."

Sam nodded slowly again.

Zahra Bi stepped into the wide doorway. "Hello, Mercedes."

SAM SAW SHOCK ON MERCEDES' face, and perhaps anger, but it was soon replaced by a shy, sympathetic smile.

"Ah, I'm afraid you've caught me red-handed." Mercedes gave a large, dramatic sigh. "You see, the events that took place in the bank have left me somewhat disturbed."

"Have they?" said Zahra.

"My therapist suggested it could be PTSD. I was hurt during the siege. Little wonder I've found myself unable to sleep. I am not eating properly. See how much weight I've lost?"

Sam and Zahra waited. Sam's eyes didn't stray far from the shotgun.

"Well," Mercedes continued. "You can imagine how this has been preying on my mind. I stupidly thought that if I came here I might be able to find some closure."

"Closure?" asked Zahra.

Mercedes nodded. She glanced between the two of them. Sam realised she was seeking an ally, looking for any indication that she might be striking a chord with her story. "I wanted a photo of Bruce. Something about knowing my enemy, you know?"

Bruce's face had been plastered across every news channel for days. If anyone wanted Bruce's likeness, then there was no shortage of material.

"Not just that, though," said Mercedes. "It's about taking back control. I wanted to take something from his life, because he took something from me that day." She looked at the gun she was holding. "I know this is unorthodox."

Zahra turned to Sam. "What are you doing here?" To Sam's ears, it sounded like Zahra was accusing her of turning up to a party uninvited.

"Someone tripped the security alarms here. Oh, and a tracker tile has popped up on the app. One I thought Bruce hadn't used. What are you doing here?"

"I was building up a hypothesis about what really happened in the bank. I have assembled some ideas." She looked at Mercedes. "*I Will Always Love You.*"

"Pardon?" said Mercedes.

"The Dolly Parton song. I mentioned it to you. It very nearly become an Elvis Presley number, apparently. Elvis had wanted to record his own version of it and the young Dolly had been quite excited."

"Why are you telling me this?"

"Because Elvis' manager told Dolly that Elvis would demand half the publishing rights to the song. It would become an Elvis song, not a Dolly cover. That was standard Elvis operating procedure."

"Not sure I see the relevance either," said Sam.

"Dolly Parton was a canny businesswoman and refused to let Elvis record it. A solo effort became a potentially fruitful partnership which was then scuppered by greed and cupidity," said Zahra.

Sam looked at the holdall Mercedes was carrying. She thought of Bruce's stroke of genius in cutting the CCTV camera feed in the bank. She thought about the trick of dealing with events at the front and back of the bank at the same time. She thought about the tracker dot that had come back on the radar only today.

"How much money is in there?" she asked, curious more than accusatory.

Mercedes Martin gave a laugh. It was painfully false. "I don't know what you're on about."

"Hey, Sam!" called Marvin from the gate. "You'll never guess who I've just found! Young Tez! From the bank! He was in the boot of this car!"

Sam only glanced at her dad for an instant, but when she looked back Mercedes had slung the holdall into crook of her arm and was aiming the shotgun with both hands. She held it like someone who knew absolutely nothing about guns. That made her more dangerous, not less.

"I'm really not very pleased about this," said Mercedes tersely, which was probably the most British thing a gun-wielding criminal could say. She waved the gun. "Everyone outside."

Mercedes marched them towards the gate.

Marvin didn't see them. He was leaning into the boot of the Ford Focus and helping a wobbly Tez climb out. When he finally peered around and saw them approaching, he smiled. "Oh hello. What's this?"

Sam jerked a thumb at Mercedes then at Zahra. "Bad guy. Good guy."

"You keep telling me that 'guy' is not really gender neutral," said Marvin, "and that it underscores the idea of a default male perspective."

Couldn't he see the woman with the shotgun? Here he was, chattering away when there was a crisis unfolding. Apparently, in his old age, a man who had died a hundred times on stage was unafraid of anything.

"Back up, back up," said Mercedes.

She herded them together on the roadside, moved to her car, paused, and turned back to them. "Phones."

"What?" said Sam, but Zahra was already cautiously removing a phone from her pocket.

Mercedes put the holdall on the floor and unzipped it. Sam could see the edges of dark green carrier bags and, despite the situation, wondered how much cash was actually in there.

"I don't have a phone at the moment," she said, as Zahra and Tez tossed theirs into the bag.

"Don't play games with me." Mercedes Martin, gun raised, was hissing between clenched teeth. Fear and adrenaline had made her fall back on villainous cliches.

"It's true," said Sam, shuffling to place herself marginally in front of her dad. "The police took it as evidence. Only returned it this morning. It's in the kitchen at home."

Mercedes glared at her, then tossed the bag onto the back seat of her car. Sam could feel relief slowly washing over her. Let the woman escape, let her try to run with the cash. Sam guessed Bruce had left a tracker widget with the cash. It was a matter for the police now.

The sense of relief grew as Mercedes got into the driver's seat of the Ford, the shotgun beside her. Almost instantly she and the gun came out again.

"Keys."

"Sorry?" said Zahra.

"Where are they?" she demanded.

Marvin made a show of patting down his pockets like an absent-minded old man. Sam wasn't even sure it was an act.

"Come on!" shouted Mercedes.

Marvin stepped forward and held out his hand with a flourish.

"That is not the right key," said Mercedes.

"No? How about this one?" Marvin held out another.

Sam wanted to curl up inside. The man was making a whole music hall routine out of it.

"What about this one?" he said.

"Stop this nonsense." She backed towards Zahra's car. "I'll just take this car instead."

"Ah, not without this key," said Marvin, holding out yet another set.

"What?"

"It locks the gate that goes across the track up there."

"You locked the gate?" Mercedes asked.

"I believe they call it 'securing the scene'," he said.

Marvin turned and, with a suppleness belying his age, threw the key in a perfect arc. It sailed across their heads and plopped into the muddy dyke by the roadside. The sound it made was gloopy and wet.

"Why would you do that?" Mercedes roared. She looked at the shotgun, considered it. "You will get that key for me!"

"Please, he's old," said Sam, waving.

"Everyone!" Mercedes spat.

Tez made a silent, pleading gesture at his suit. Mercedes pointed the shotgun up into the air and fired. The recoil nearly punched her to the ground and she staggered back. However, the implication was clear. Sam led the way down the thickly grassed slope and into the dyke.

People who fell into dykes drowned. Every kid who grew

up in the fenlands knew this. Dykes were dangerous. They were always deeper than you expected. Mud could hold legs tight and draw you down. Fortunately, the weather had been very dry recently, and although the dyke was at least six feet wide there was only enough muddy water in the bottom to reach up to their knees.

The water was cold and stank of agricultural run-off.

"We should spread out to look," said Zahra.

"Are we actually doing this?" said Tez, prodding the soupy brown surface diffidently.

"Apparently so," said Sam.

In less than a minute, all four of them were covered in mud up their legs and arms. There was no sign of the key.

"I think it was more up this way," said Zahra, moving further along.

"Why didn't you just give her the key?" Sam said to Marvin.

"She's the bad guy, right?" he said.

"I'm not the bad guy here," said Mercedes.

Sam gave her a frank look.

"I'm just taking what I'm owed," the woman insisted.

"Really?"

Mercedes looked at Tez, the gun moving with her. "While the men are getting the pay rises I deserve. Shareholders' banquets. Water at ten quid a bottle."

"Look," said Tez, raising dirty hands in miserable and terrified surrender. "I don't know if it actually cost that much. I mean, it sounds silly now that I think on it."

"And look at you now," said Mercedes. "Crawling in the mud, where you belong. It's almost worth it just for this."

A thought came to Sam. "Did you kill the bank manager?"

"Of course, I didn't," said Mercedes, but her expression changed partway through the sentence, as though there was at least some truth in Sam's accusation. "Hey—!" she yelled and raised the shotgun.

The barrel moved past Sam and up. Sam turned. Zahra Bi, who had been moving slowly down the dyke, away from the gate, was now scrambling up the bank.

"Stop!" Mercedes shouted. "I said stop!"

Lumbering muddily, Zahra ran past the cover of Sam's van. Mercedes fired. The van window smashed. From down in the dyke, Sam heard a soft mewl and saw Zahra's body tumble to the ground, arms outflung.

In the echoing silence, Marvin said something.

"Huh?" said Sam, stunned.

"Double-barrelled shotgun," said Marvin.

"Huh?"

"She's had her two shots!"

As Sam finally grasped what he was saying, she saw Mercedes had also heard him or come to the same realisation. Wide-eyed with alarm, Mercedes ran to her car to retrieve the holdall. Sam clutched at grasses and hauled herself up the nearest bank.

Mercedes' feet thumped on the loose stone of the farmyard. She was fleeing on foot.

Sam crawled with mud-caked legs up to the flat grass.

Zahra lay on the track road, a foot peeking from behind the Piaggio Ape. She needed medical assistance. The main road was a good half mile or more up the track. Mercedes had all their phones.

Sam stood. Mercedes was running towards the big shed. There would be a landline phone in the house, wouldn't there?

She called to Tez. "Tend to Zahra. Put pressure on the wound."

Tez nodded dumbly. Sam ran to the farmhouse.

She barged the door in and staggered into the kitchen. Muddy feet slipped on Bruce's polished clay tiles. Bruce's imprint on the house was already in decline. There was a thin film of dust on all the surfaces. Sam's muddy shoes were only hastening the decline.

She gripped an upright beam, sending horse brasses jangling as she hurried into the hallway. There was the phone. Sam grabbed the receiver and put it to her ear. It was dead. She tapped the button on the cradle repeatedly because that's what people did in films, but to no effect. She looked under the table. The telephone wire hung unconnected. A broadband box was fixed to the wall with no connectors suitable for a phone.

"Why would you even keep it—?" She was complaining to a dead man.

She sprang up and ran back out. She would have to go help Tez and Marvin with Zahra's injuries, maybe run up the road and wave down a passing vehicle. It'd maybe take ten, fifteen minutes...

There came the throat-clearing roar of an engine from the shed. Mercedes was planning to steal an agricultural vehicle to make her escape cross-country. Sam sprinted to the shed as the tractor jerkily, falteringly moved out of the far doors, pulling the big Brassicator harvester behind it.

Sam ran after it, hoping to get to the tractor cab but then Mercedes, clearly finding more confidence, sped up as the tractor rolled out onto the field. Sam fell back, glanced at the cabbage harvester, saw the standing space for the harvester operator and, without giving further thought, stepped on.

74

Marvin crawled on hands and knees up the bank. There would be a price to pay for such exertions, but he ignored his complaining limbs and forced himself to keep going. He found Tez beside the young Asian woman at the side of Sam's van.

He had expected to see her sprawled out, her torso peppered with shot, blood seeping unstoppably through her clothing. Instead she sat leaned against the van, inspecting the minor rips in her jacket sleeve.

"It stings," she said to the fussing Tez, who was trying to get her jacket off without actually physically laying hands on her.

"I saw you go flying," the bank worker said.

"She mostly missed," she said. "In my opinion, if someone tries to shoot you, you should let them think they succeeded."

"Here, let's get this off you," said Marvin and took hold of her jacket lapels to ease the garment off.

"Wait a moment." With her uninjured hand she dipped into her pocket to pull out a phone.

"She took our phones," said Tez.

"Decoy phone," said the woman.

"Why would you be carrying a decoy phone?"

"For situations like this," she said.

"Oh, I like this one," said Marvin.

Together, the men tried to tend to her possible wounds while the clever young woman phoned the emergency services.

THE TRACTOR MOVED at a fair lick across the cabbage field. Mercedes was driving in a diagonal line, angling towards the road in the distance. They rolled through the furrows and over the crop, a rolling ship on a loamy sea.

Sam stood in the trailer operator's working space, a caged square with the harvesting screws and travelator to one side, and the conveyor belt arm that normally fed cabbages into a collection hopper to the other. She saw the crushed cabbages lying wrecked in their wake and briefly wondered if they were Tigerhearts.

She guessed Mercedes was just aiming to get to the road. How she intended to make her escape from criminal justice from there was anyone's guess, but Sam didn't have time to wait and find out. She needed Mercedes to stop, to let her call for an ambulance.

From where she stood Sam looked at a complicated bank of controls. There were buttons and a joystick. She pressed buttons experimentally. One of them started the conveyor system. The whirling prongs of the harvesting screws whirled into life, ready to grab cabbages from the earth.

"Okay," she said and tried the joystick. The hopper feeding arm off to the side swung round. She moved it out and in a couple of times. At its furthest angle, she could make it reach forward and slap the side of the tractor cab.

Mercedes shifted in her seat and looked back. Her eyes widened.

"Consider that fair warning!" shouted Sam, although her voice was possibly lost in the wind. "Now, slow down!"

Mercedes didn't slow down. If anything, she sped up. They were almost at the edge of the field. A wide dyke bordered the field there. Mercedes swung the tractor round to track the field edge, looking for a gap, a bridge, any way through.

If Mercedes wasn't going to slow for her, Sam would have to force her. The harvesting screws were spinning uselessly above the ground. If she could force them down, into the soil, perhaps it would slow the tractor. She slammed buttons at random until something did the trick. The harvesting prongs dug deep into the topsoil. The trailer bucked violently. The tractor's forward motion and the harvester digging in worked against each other, slewing the whole vehicle side to side in a violent fish-tail motion.

Mercedes was shouting but she wasn't slowing. She was trying to combat the dragging trailer with extra revs. Sam grabbed the handrail to avoid being thrown off. She forced the screws deeper into the ground. Mud flew from churning wheels. Thick diesel smoke stung Sam's eyes and made her retch. The segmented conveyor belt chugged and rattled. Trailer and tractor moved like antagonistic ice-skaters, swung round sideways. Then something hit the lip of the dyke and the world pitched over. The vehicle jackknifed and slid down. Sam leapt before she fell, not wanting to be trapped in the dyke with the machinery on top of her.

She landed feet first with a gloopy splat. For the second time in a few short minutes she was immersed in filthy cold mud. The tractor and trailer loomed over her at an unnerving angle. Somewhere under the water, the harvesting screws were still spinning. The surface churned and bubbled, like a volcanic mud pool. It was not the time for Sam to reflect that farming was notorious for its high incidence of industrial accidents. Crushed and drowned by farm vehicles, or churned up by submerged mechanisms was probably not a common farming accident, but she didn't want to become that unlikely statistic.

The tractor cab was sliding deeper into the dyke. The side door swung open and Mercedes dropped down, pulling her bag of loot with her. She was surprised by the depth of the water and nearly disappeared up to her middle. She clung to the bag, which momentarily puffed with air and became a buoyancy aid.

"You bitch," she said. The words were full of venom but Mercedes lacked the energy to inject them with much passion. "Why did you have to do that?"

Sam didn't bother answering, she had her own life to save. The mud was too thick to swim in, too runny to wade through. She flopped towards the roadside bank in a sequence of small leaps and flails. The sound of the creaking machinery and the tractor's slow but certain descent into the dyke spurred her on.

Mercedes was a couple of metres further along and had a greater distance to go. Lugging the cash across the muddy surface was slowing her down.

Sam grabbed the rushes on the bank and pulled herself up a short way. "I need a phone," she panted. "Give one to me."

She looked back. Mercedes was sinking deeper, still struggling forward. The bag was invisible now. Mercedes clutched onto its strap, below the surface. Behind her, the conveyor belt rumbled on, harvesting clod after clod of thick, sticking mud.

Sam hauled herself up into a securer position and turned to offer Mercedes a hand. "Here. Reach for me."

Mercedes coughed. Or perhaps it was a laugh. "I'm not giving you a phone."

"I'm saving your life."

Mercedes struggled forward with vicious independence. The tractor and trailer groaned. Her mind perhaps clarified by the thought of ten tonnes of machinery coming down on top of her, Mercedes lunged forward and reached for Sam's hand with her own.

They slapped fingertips to fingertips, then Sam found Mercedes' hand and began to haul against the sucking mud. "We can do it!"

Mercedes suddenly jerked and spasmed. "It's got me!" she grunted.

The mud bubbled. The harvesting machinery turned. Mercedes eyes were wide and white in a mud-spattered face.

"Kick away from it," said Sam. "Push off your shoes," she added, though she didn't really know what that would achieve if her feet were truly caught.

"It's got the bag," Mercedes groaned.

Sam laughed, though she was far beyond actually finding it funny.

"Let go, you idiot!" She pulled harder. Her shoulder ached savagely. The hand holding onto the bank squeezed tighter until she was digging her nails not only into the grass and soil but into the flesh of her palm.

"I can't..." said Mercedes.

The trailer slid deeper. The tone of the machinery changed.

With a scream, Mercedes came free. Sam pulled her up and over the surface of the mud. Sam thought she could hear a siren somewhere.

The conveyor turned. Fat lumps of wet mud rolled up the belt. Patches of ripped fabric stuck out from them, along with bundles of battered banknotes.

Sam continued to claw her way up the bank to the roadside, pulling the limp and miserable Mercedes with her. A couple of cars had pulled up, motorists who had seen the tractor accident. Sam flopped onto the tarmac, a beached brown seal. A police car and an ambulance were coming down the road towards them.

Mercedes flopped next to her, not sobbing, but gaunt eyed and desolated. "It's not fair. It's not fair..."

"No," Sam agreed.

"I just wanted what I was owed."

Sam realised she was still clutching the woman's hand. She let go and rolled away.

There were running feet, the green trousers of a paramedic in her eye. She waved her hand, flicking mud.

"Greencock farm. Gunshot victim," she panted.

"It's okay," said the paramedic, not understanding.

A police helicopter circled overhead. Sam found herself thinking Chief Inspector Peach would be annoyed at the impact all of this would have on his quarterly budget.

75

By the time the mud on Sam's clothes had dried, she was back at the farmyard, the paramedics had dressed the minor wound on Zahra Bi's arm and had moved onto the lightly traumatised Tez Malik. It was uncertain if he was more traumatised by the kidnapping or his ruined sharp work suit.

Mercedes had been taken away in the back of a police car. When the police officer who remained on site had asked Sam what was going on, Sam had nearly guffawed in his face. She barely knew, and what she did know would have required a diagram with lots of arrows. All she managed to say was, "She shot the windows of my van." There would undoubtedly be questions later.

Marvin, on the other hand, was leaning against the bonnet of the Piaggio Ape van and clearly having lots of fun: giving his account with mimes of thrown keys and shotgun-wielding maniacs.

Zahra Bi was standing inside the open door of her own car. She gave Sam a small wave.

"You okay?" said Sam.

Zahra looked at the dressing around her upper arm and nodded "Very muddy but not really hurt."

Sam realised Zahra had pulled off her caked trousers behind the door and was folding them stiffly. Sam, who didn't generally take to chatting to people who were only wearing their underpants, hesitated, not quite knowing where to look. Zahra's pants had a green and pink floral pattern. Sam wished she didn't know that.

Zahra looked at her looking, and shrugged. "It seemed logical. No point making the car dirty." She wrapped the trousers in the marginally less muddy jacket and bent over to put them in the passenger seat.

Sam looked away. "So was Mercedes orchestrating events during the siege?"

"I think we might never know," said Zahra. "Bruce is dead. She might have set him up for that. However they hid the extra cash, Mercedes did not need him after it was secured."

"How did you know Mercedes had stolen the money?"

"It was only a hypothesis," said Zahra. "Too many inconsistencies, and nothing but a pile of ash where the cash had once been."

"It's a mystery. I got the impression she was a model employee."

"Your close friend, Lucas Camara, is of the opinion criminals are irrational and impenetrable."

"He is? Close friend? Really?"

"Of course. It's plain to see." There was the shutting of a car door. Sam turned back. Zahra was behind the wheel, the window open.

"Is this what you do, as a trained negotiator?" said Sam.

"Jump in mud and get shot at?" Zahra gave her an admonishing look. "I'm not even being paid for this. This is just part of my continuous professional development. Got to keep on top of my skills. My employer regularly throws me in at the deep end without actually providing me with the relevant training." She started the engine.

"I thought you worked for the police," said Sam.

"Outsourced. I work for a security company."

"Really?"

Zahra pulled out past the Piaggio Ape. "Company called DefCon4. You won't have heard of it."

Sam spluttered as Zahra drove away. She raised a hand to wave. "But ... but... I'm one too. I'm DefCon4. I've never met another—"

She faltered. The little car accelerated down the track. Sam felt a peculiar longing, like she was watching a rare species vanishing.

With a sigh, she trudged over to her dad. The windscreen of the van was crazed with cracks, one side window was smashed. The Ape otherwise seemed fine. It was a surprisingly robust vehicle.

"You've got mud on you," said Marvin, pointing.

Sam peeled a fat dried flake off her cheek. It was an oddly satisfying sensation. "And are you okay?"

"A little hurt," he said.

"Really?"

He nodded solemnly. "I quote. '*Please. He's old.*'"

"Really?"

"That stuff cuts deep."

"You are a ridiculous man, dad."

Sam leaned on the van bonnet next to him. There was just about room for them both. She frowned and looked down the rock. "Er, how were the police and ambulance able to get through the gate?" she asked.

"Gate?"

"The locked gate. The key."

He chuckled. "At what point did you think I actually had time to go shut the gate? Or where I got the key from?"

"I saw you throw the key."

"You saw me throw *a* key."

"Yeah?"

"It was the house keys."

"You threw the keys to our house in the dyke."

"Well, it's not our house anymore, is it?"

Sam pressed her lips together. The sky was a picture postcard blue. Sea birds swooped near the horizon. "Do *you* think it's all unfair?" she said.

He breathed in deeply. "What's unfair? The house, keys, money. Like I said, it's all just stuff, isn't it?"

She considered it. "That was a good throw, though."

"For an 'old' man."

"For an old man."

"Magician's hands. It's all in the wrist work you see. Back in the late seventies, I used to train for wrist flexibility by throwing frisbees. They were all the rage. Jasper Carrott and

I both lost our frisbees on top of the Pebble Mill building. Stuck up there for years, they were."

Sam nodded slowly. "Jasper Carrott's frisbee. Not heard that one before."

"I have an inexhaustible supply."

She didn't know whether to laugh or cry. It was time to go home. To go in search of a home. "Don't go changing, dad," she said.

"Not much chance of that, is there?" he replied.

ABOUT THE AUTHORS

Heide lives in North Warwickshire with her husband and a fluctuating mix of offspring and animals.

Iain lives in South Birminghan with his wife and a fluctuating mix of offspring and animals.

They aren't sure how many novels they've written together since 2011, but it's a surprisingly large number

ALSO BY HEIDE GOODY AND IAIN GRANT

Bountyhunter

Life is full of impossible questions.

How did Sam Applewhite end up living in a tiny caravan with her dad?

How does local company Synergenesis survive with no customers and a cast of clueless employees?

And why is everyone desperate to get their hands on a stuffed kangaroo toy called Joey Pockets?

In the height of summer, it's not just holidaymakers who are drawn to the seaside town of Skegness. Desperate thieves and callous killers are searching for a hidden treasure and they don't care who they hurt in their quest to claim it.

The most important question of all is, can Sam get to the bottom of this mystery before those closest to her are put in further danger?

Bountyhunter

Clovenhoof

Getting fired can ruin a day...

...especially when you were the Prince of Hell.

Will Satan survive in English suburbia?

Corporate life can be a soul draining experience, especially when the industry is Hell, and you're Lucifer. It isn't all torture and brimstone, though, for the Prince of Darkness, he's got an unhappy Board of Directors.

The numbers look bad.

They want him out.

Then came the corporate coup.

Banished to mortal earth as Jeremy Clovenhoof, Lucifer is going through a mid-immortality crisis of biblical proportion. Maybe if he just tries to blend in, it won't be so bad.

He's wrong.

If it isn't the murder, cannibalism, and armed robbery of everyday life in Birmingham, it's the fact that his heavy metal band isn't getting the respect it deserves, that's dampening his mood.

And the archangel Michael constantly snooping on him, doesn't help.

If you enjoy clever writing, then you'll adore this satirical tour de force, because a good laugh can make you have sympathy for the devil.

Get it now.

Clovenhoof

Oddjobs

Unstoppable horrors from beyond are poised to invade and literally create Hell on Earth.

It's the end of the world as we know it, but someone still needs to do the paperwork.

Morag Murray works for the secret government organisation responsible for making sure the apocalypse goes as smoothly and as quietly as possible.

Trouble is, Morag's got a temper problem and, after angering the wrong alien god, she's been sent to another city where she won't cause so much trouble.

But Morag's got her work cut out for her. She has to deal with a man-eating starfish, solve a supernatural murder and, if she's got time, prevent her own inevitable death.

If you like The Laundry Files, The Chronicles of St Mary's or Men in Black, you'll love the Oddjobs series."If Jodi Taylor wrote a Laundry Files novel set it in Birmingham... A hilarious dose of bleak existential despair. With added tentacles! And bureaucracy!" – Charles Stross, author of The Laundry Files series.

Oddjobs

Printed in Great Britain
by Amazon

16021254R00255